The crowd parte most adorable anima. maybe four feet in length, with a torpedo-shaped body, short, steel-gray fur, and a white spotted underbelly. A bulbous head, containing intelligent black eyes, smiled back at her, causing her infectious laugh to broadcast over the collective.

A man she hadn't noticed knelt next to the seal and turned his head slowly at the sound of her laugh, seemingly searching for someone or something. He wore dark mirrored sunglasses, but somehow, she knew the power of the gaze behind the glasses would be transfixing. With the descending sun on her back, the pendant she wore grew hot and felt like a kind of pressure pushing her back. Raven couldn't take her gaze off the man as the sun shone on his face, making it awash with light. She could tell his hair was very light and that he had a short beard and muscular body.

The weight of his stare scared her.

The Sea Archer
by

Jeny Heckman

The Heaven & Earth Series

The Sea Archer

Cover Art by *Debbie Taylor*

The Wild Rose Press, Inc.
PO Box 708
Adams Basin, NY 14410-0708
Visit us at www.thewildrosepress.com

Publishing History
First Fantasy Rose Edition, 2018
Print ISBN 978-1-5092-2206-3
Digital ISBN 978-1-5092-2207-0

The Heaven & Earth Series
Published in the United States of America

Dedication

To Jeffrey, for making my heart whole and being my
other wing for flight.

Acknowledgements

I'd like to thank many people for the metamorphosis of this book. First, my editor, Dianne Rich. You took a new author completely and helped me find my way.

The Wild Rose Press for taking a chance on me. Debbie Taylor for the beautiful cover art.

Dr. David S. Owens, UW Cardiovascular Genetics director and surgeon, who specializes in hypertrophic cardiomyopathy. Thanks for giving me the 411 on OHC. Also, Jamie Rosencrans, for guiding me in the right direction.

Suzanne Linda, at the University of Hawai'i, regarding solar energy and the pitfalls of where to place them on island. The Marine Mammal Center and N.O.A.A. for facts regarding the Hawaiian Monk Seal.

The island of Kaua'i and its residents for providing the background information and lending a degree of authenticity this haole wouldn't have otherwise had.

A huge shout out to my beta readers. Beth Trigg, Annelise Christy and Sarah Gregory. Thanks for reading those first drafts and not laughing hysterically.

Sophie Logan, at Sharper Editing, for helping me to understand the craziness of English grammar! Your talent and friendship mean a lot to me.

Love to my family for supporting my dream. My parents and mother-in-law for always remaining positive. Jeff and Debbie for being the greatest friends and release outlets anyone could ask for. Nicole, Jesse, and Natalie for your support and love. Finally, my children, Paisley and Charlie, for being my beating heart and greatest source of joy.

Prologue

The dank of Tartarus was only eclipsed by its supreme blackness. Cronus heard the echoes of water dripping, as one by one his siblings were shackled and sent to their respective purgatories.

Disoriented, the deity tried to call out but was hoarse, as well as temporarily blind, from the murky shadows. He closed his eyes, trusting his instincts rather than the gloom, perfumed with sulfur. Lowering his head, Cronus attempted to think through the events that transpired.

Zeus's crimson, arrogant face, and those of the rest of his children judging him, as he lay vanquished on the steps of Olympus. The destruction of his own kingdom, Othrys, incited an ire deep within him that inflamed the deep recesses of his being. The irony of the events was lost on the immortal, for he too had desired the power of the universe and stolen it from his father. Enraged by his own defeat, Cronus's predecessor created a prophecy that his son's children would too claim his throne, thus reversing the prosperity he'd enjoy. Cronus had dismissed the prediction as a cry of one already defeated.

His stomach roiled and heaved with the emetic, with which Zeus tricked him, leaving the humiliation like black acid. One of Cronus's sisters plummeted into the abyss with a bloodcurdling scream cut short. The god attempted to stop the seconds passing, but his powers were abating. Time moved and tried to gain purchase yet hovered just beyond his reach.

With robes hanging off thin, fragile frames, three ancient looking hags moved through the spaces of light and shadow and passed by his cell. The unseen barrier of his incarceration, as if made of tungsten, held him at bay. Their voices seemed to crack and spark, fingers worrying over the tools of their trade.

"Coeus, tell me of these women," he commanded of his brother who stood nearby.

"They're the Moirai, daughters of Zeus and Themis."

"Themis!" The old god recoiled but couldn't hold back his shock and anger. "Does our divine sister not sit with us then?"

"No, brother—she's part of the new order now."

"And why do her children appear in this form?"

"They produce the fates."

"And what of their purpose?"

"They ally with your son and even now lay out the fabric of time."

"Time!" he bellowed. "He dares try me? I alone am the master of time."

"It's the fate of time, brother. What will be, who will live and die, who will serve what fate in life."

Cronus heard a noise and watched as his brother looked down at his feet, where inky black bonds slithered across the floor like silent serpents. They seemed to sear into his flesh, as they encircled his ankles and wrists. Coeus screamed out, faded, then disappeared. Cronus's gaze darted around the space; if there was an opportunity to be relieved of his own immediate fate, he needed to find it, and soon.

Far above Cronus, Zeus basked in victory, arrogant in his success. Asserting his new authority, he called for his brother.

"You must keep him separated," Zeus counseled Hades. "Father's cunning. If the opportunity of escape presents itself, he will seize it."

"The Titans are now secure, and only our father remains. Place the Cyclopes as guard, for they'll want him here as we do," the dark god replied. "He asks for companionship from some of the Primordials."

"Which ones?"

"I fear his powers have weakened his mind, for he asks for those intent on damping his spirit."

"Misery? Discord?"

"Among others."

"Perhaps he bears the weight of his behavior and chooses this form of self-punishment."

"Perhaps. Or evil deeds are on his mind."

"Allow him the companionship but keep him here, so any mischief he conjures is likewise contained."

Cryptically, Cronus smiled as he continued to listen to his sons speak. A plan formed in his mind, but he'd need help. Who among the gods would be willing to betray Zeus? The great manipulator of time slowed his mind and considered his revenge.

****

The occupation of the Moirai, or Fates, was to control the threads of every life from birth to death. The day had been an arduous ordeal, and the sisters were nearing their nadir in patience, as Zeus was unwilling to heed their advice on important matters. In perfect synchronization, they lay their heads down and stilled their minds for slumber. Almost immediately, the fabric near their heads began to pop and bubble. A shroud of thin ebony threads snaked their way around each neck, carelessly knitting strands, like a spider's web, into a perfect mask of the old hags' faces. The mask glowed, vibrated, then sparked, turning to gold. Nearby, a bag of runes began to pulsate in time with the webbing and the Moirai's collective heartbeat. It was the Spinner who rose first sat at her spindle and began to weave. The essence of Cronus's allies, Misery, and Discord, among others, seeped into her skin like acid and she began to chant out a prophecy in an ancient language.

The Allotter reached for her measuring rod and then turned and rose. White fire shot through mystical veins, threaded under aging brown spots on her leathered hands. She held up the woven strands, containing runes and whispers. The elements within each sister's veil carefully influenced their actions.

There was a pause, and all three of the hags tried to look through their shared, single, unseeing eye. Their movements guided without their control or the knowledge of why was just outside their grasp. As the dreams intensified, distracting them once more, so did the pulsing. It was as if each movement forged more energy, absorbing it from all the living things around them.

The runes and lots chosen, woven, and measured, the last step belonged to the Cutter, for she was Inevitability. And she chose the time and manner of death for the damned. Reaching for her implement, she continued the incantations with her sisters. As the shears started to squeak close, the strands began to sever, with crackles and sparks, startling the silent

4

blackness.

****

Themis, goddess of counsel and prophecy, had no wrath, only divine judgment, with no interpretation or bias. So, when the orb beside her had begun to glow, she moved to it, through it, and above it to understand its purpose. A prophecy, not of her creation, was forming and it was a powerful one.

She watched the light condense—smaller and smaller. When complete, it would be a miniature ball of energy and fire, without encasing. The properties began to take shape, and she saw Cronus's plan to defeat the Gods unfolding.

She vanished into the ether and reappeared at the bedside of her daughters, the Moirai. Themis heard the screams of lesser deities descending into Tartarus as several life strands sheared clean.

"On this day and forevermore, the passage of this prophecy will not endure.
Release the minds and tools of their trade, so that we may live another day. And to the master of this plan, who plots his revenge and takes his stand. His exile remains here in this dark kingdom until power is divided and each enters the Elysium. The architect of this betrayal must come to see, forgiveness in conclusion of same time and space is my proclivity. The modification of this prophecy I expatiate so that hope may preponderate."

The statuesque goddess kept murmuring specific enchantments until the full amended prophecy formed. She brought her hands close to her center and blasted them forward, creating a light so white and compelling that no other color existed. The Moirai blinked into awareness as the veils bubbled, then dissolved. Each looked around, first in confusion, then comprehension of the truth in its entirety. Silently, Themis left to inform Zeus of all that had passed.

****

"Assemble the family," Zeus ordered within seconds of Themis's revelation. His pristine white hair floated around his handsome face, taut with rage. His blue eyes turned to ice, when none of his threats manipulated Themis into revealing the traitorous culprit he so desperately wanted to uncover. For surely Cronus could not have acted on his own.

"We have but a few moments to flee, nephew," Themis informed him. "You must wait for that knowledge, for I know your wrath, and must protect this innocent if we are to survive."

"Innocent." Zeus spat, then called out to the collective. "We have precious little time. One among us has aligned with Cronus and betrayed us. The Moirai were deceived and have measured, woven, and sealed our fates."

The gods and deities spoke over each other, speculating about the Titan ruler's accomplice and what it meant for their future.

"Silence, you fools," Zeus ordered. "The gods will descend to Tartarus for eternity if we do not flee."

Screams of outrage and palpable fear hovered thickly, as each immortal shot accusatory glances at one another.

"Hold, for Themis speaks," Themis commanded. "The prophecy has been made. For now, life as we've known it on Olympus is done but Cronus may not yet rule. We've time, if only for a short while."

"What is the prophecy?" Poseidon asked.

"If the last drop of your blood dies in your heir, we'll descend into darkness and the life Cronus will choose for us there." Zeus's gaze connected with Hades.

"What must they do?" asked the dark god, apprehensively.

"Conquer the fears and failings of you and them both, then the heirs must collect in the same time and place, so says the oracle." He watched the confusion spread. "Each of you must find a place of refuge until you're called to serve. Themis assures me that we'll be able to transfer remaining power one to another, as we fall. My brothers"—he indicated Poseidon and Hades—"and myself, who rule heaven, earth, sea, and underworld, will be able to guide our spawn, but only for a short duration."

"And these creatures will somehow understand our plight?" Apollo queried.

"The children of tomorrow must accept their role, as you must accept yours," Themis replied. "Placing them at the same time and space will be arduous and take generations. We need a strong foundation. Who among you will accept that destiny?"

"I shall go first," announced Poseidon, god of the sea.

"I confess it was my desire. Your power nearly matches my own and will do what is needed to begin," Zeus responded, then gestured to the young musician who also stepped forward. "Apollo, you too will go."

"With guidance from Demeter," Themis interjected, to the dismay of the mighty ruler.

"What of this, Themis?" Zeus demanded.

"Demeter's the goddess of our seasons, our fertility. She brings life and light to dead soil and is relentless in her quest to search for understanding. She must guide the pair in what they seek, and we may give her a gift to help in that guidance."

"What gift?" Demeter asked suspiciously. She questioned the implied burden.

Themis signaled to the giant but lame blacksmith god, who carried a small box of oak wrapped with metal straps and who at her signal opened it. Themis brought her hands to her abdomen, floating one above the other as if holding an imaginary orb. An oblong of energy emerged from within, and she laid the prophecy gently inside the box. She glided her hand over the seam, making it impenetrable, before handing it to Demeter.

"One piece of yourself may go with your blood," she informed the large group. "If they succeed you will dwell in the Elysium until the day we're together once more. Now quickly, find your cover, conserve your power, and we may win the day."

Zeus watched in consternation, as one by one his family disappeared. He looked around his kingdom and the earth below. He'd always feared he would be thwarted by his offspring, but instead had underestimated his father's ability to rise again. Black cords and bindings serpentined their way toward him, and the ruler smiled derisively at them. Collecting energy and anger from the air, he balled it into the center of his chest. Perhaps, he thought, the children wouldn't be his destruction but his salvation. With a primal scream that covered the heavens, he fisted his hands and flung them outward, in an explosion of thunderbolts to carry him away, before the blackness devoured him.

Chapter 1

Raven sat on her plush white couch, knees drawn up to her chin, clad in periwinkle pajamas and fuzzy pink socks. She had turned the couch from the center of the living room so that it faced the large floor-to-ceiling windows overlooking Puget Sound. When she reached for the box of tissues, she discovered it was empty, and her frown deepened. Looking over at the linen squares Donovan insisted should be there, Raven rolled her eyes. She remembered him saying only Philistines would lower themselves to use paper tissues. Rolling her eyes again, she stood up. Who even talks like that, she thought wearily. Deciding maybe wine and chocolate were needed more, she dabbed her watery nose on her sleeve and proceeded farther into the condo.

The kitchen was unblemished, with its frigid white-walled tile and marble countertops. Reaching for the cupboard where she hid her stash of chocolate, Raven's eyes danced across the photo of her goddaughter Abby, taped on the door of her stainless-steel refrigerator. She sniffed and smiled. Abby was caught in mid belly-laugh the summer before when she popped up from the slip 'n slide in her backyard. Donovan would never have allowed the photo to be placed there, let alone taped to such an unforgiving surface. Raven didn't even remember putting it there after he left. She looked into the cupboard and discovered there was no more chocolate either.

"Fuck!" she stated emphatically. Staring into the near empty cupboard, she tried to will her dark-chocolate, salted-caramels into existence but to no avail. Screw it, she thought irritated, all I really need is the wine.

Using one of Donovan's fancy bottle openers, she tried to attach it to an unopened bottle. After two full minutes of trial and error, Raven poured the contents, more than socially acceptable, into a large crystal glass before retreating toward the couch. Gulping greedily, she pulled the glass away and looked at it appreciatively.

"Oh, God damn, that's good."

A tiny stream of sunlight beamed off the faceted surface perfectly, and a small dance of color and fire on the steel gray of the living room wall. First staring at the display in confusion, Raven quickly turned from it and looked around blankly at what had been her home with Donovan.

The sterile environment held no hint of her own personality. There were no colorful family photos on the walls, just black and white stills of her performances and glossy articles of him and his celebrity triumphs. In fact, the only actual photo in the living room was a twenty by twenty-eight close-up of their wedding day. She staggered a little and weaved over to it, not noticing the red wine sluicing over the rim of the glass and onto the floor. A candid one taken in a stolen moment when white rose petals fluttered all around them. He was turned toward the crowd, handsome and confident, laughing and waving but she had looked at the camera, caught in an expression of—what? Revelation? Fear? Uncertainty? She looked at it, blearily trying to identify the emotion. Did some part of her already know it was destined to damnation? She was quite sure he'd chosen the photo because of how he looked in it, which was terrific, and probably hadn't even noticed her expression. How come she, herself, was only really seeing it for the first time now?

Upon their first meeting, Raven, hired to give one of her first performances, played her original music at an art show. The floors and fixtures, glossy and expensive under the lights, featured beautiful glass creations, from a local but world-renowned glass-smith. The beauty in his talent reflected in her music. Donovan, nearly twenty years her senior, stopped to listen appearing mesmerized.

"You play well," he remarked. *"How long have you been performing?"*

"Um, not very long. I guess, maybe, about a year," she admitted, embarrassed to say it was her first major gig.

Fortner seemed to read the story in her starry-eyed look immediately, and the corners of his mouth turned up. He reached into his pocket, withdrawing a small, slim titanium container, and pulled out a business card, extending it to her with an elegant, manicured hand.

"My name is Donovan Fortner. I am the owner of Fortner Talent and Publicity, downtown." He nodded at her to accept the card. *"I want you to call there tomorrow and set up a meeting with my assistant Monica, to discuss some possible options for you."*

"Oh," Raven replied, a little breathless. *"Um, sure…thank you."*

He merely nodded and returned his attention to the stunning young brunette he'd brought as his date. Raven stared after him. He was tall, trim, and resplendent in a charcoal suit, with a blood-red tie, in a perfect Windsor knot. His hair had streaks of silver at the temples, and his dark gray eyes were cool, appraising, and intelligent.

She made an appointment, and he'd signed her to his agency that very day. Tremendously talented in his chosen profession, and highly respected in the industry, Donovan never let her forget who would be in charge, beginning from their initial meeting.

She would stare into the mirror as her golden tresses were saturated the raven color of her name, freckles covered in heavy makeup, and her lush body packaged for show business. He mocked and questioned her tastes and choices. As the performances grew and her name became known, she transformed into the superstar he alone envisioned. Stage presence, costumes and set designs, backup singers, dancers, and of course, the music, all became decisions made exclusively by the older man.

"Raven, I need to talk to you about your sets. The touchy-feely, unplugged music isn't your niche. It's not your brand."

"Brand?"

"Yes," he said, sighing at her ignorance. "A brand. What people associate with you. Your genre of music must captivate the younger audience. That means your look, music, act, attitude, press—everything gears toward selling to that market. Honestly, Raven, we've gone over this several times."

In fact, they hadn't, but she didn't want another

argument she wouldn't win.

"Well, why can't I just write something to fit that brand?"

"Because I don't think your talent extends that far." *Donovan* *hadn't* *attempted* *to* *hide* *his* *condescension.* *"I think we have far more talented and highly motivated writers. You will be playing their offerings."*

"But—"

"Do not argue with me," *he snapped, exasperated.* *"Christ, I've been doing this a very long time. You have not and need to trust my expertise. Do you understand me?"*

Raven had simply nodded. He was probably right. What she liked to listen to and create wasn't necessarily what others wanted to hear. Trusting him to understand far better what was right for her success in the industry, she always acquiesced. He began taking her on lunch dates, quiet dinners, lavish theater productions, and finally, bed. They were married two years later when she turned twenty-one.

Now, thirteen years later, she was amazed that two fat tears could still leak from her eyes, and once more started for the couch. The light hit the facets of her glass again, and the color exploded even more forcefully from the crystal. She stared in fascination that the sun could create that kind of light, color, and power. She didn't have power, color, or light anymore, if she ever had it in the first place. Thinking for a moment and looking at the glass, she decided there was color in her music. From nowhere she turned and violently hurled the glass onto the wedding photo, shattering the crystal and splattering the clean surfaces with claret. She screamed out her frustration and anger until she lay down on the couch and the afternoon turned to night.

****

"*Oh* my Lord," Que sang as she opened Raven's door with her key, then threw it onto the small entry table. Hesitantly, she walked into the living room, glass crunching underneath her feet. Scanning for the source, she noticed the ruined photo and furniture. Drawing back, she nodded, as if to say, *yeah okay, I'm fine with that*. Que walked back to her friend's bedroom, to find Raven lying on the floor.

"Oh *hell* no." She walked over to Raven and brushed her greasy black hair from her face. "What in the hell you doin', girl?" Raven groaned but didn't open her eyes, pissing her friend off even more. "Raven!"

"What?" she croaked.

"What is this? Come on now." Que helped her stand up, saying, "Get your skinny white ass up off this floor." Becoming vertical turned Raven puce. Que jerked back quickly, stating with emphatic attitude, "I know you ain't gonna hurl on me." Then peered at her patient dubiously.

"Ugh…" The room spun wildly, and Raven's mouth turned down in anticipation of throwing up.

Que half-dragged the troubled woman onto her bed, then moved quickly to the bathroom for a cold cloth, water, and some pain reliever. She knelt in front of her and began to wash her face. Raven took in her best friend's natural corkscrew afro, in a stylish puff around her beautiful cocoa-colored face. Big red pouty lips and the kindest, deepest mahogany eyes she'd ever seen, tried to smile back at her.

"I know you're hurtin', honey." Que took a deep breath and clucked, as she wiped away some of the tears streaking Raven's face. "Papers are signed, all official, what're you gonna do now, it's all scary…" She considered Raven's incredibly large, troubled, baby-blue eyes, framed by long, dark, wet lashes. "But there's a reason this happened, baby. There's a reason this man wasn't for you. God has a plan, and we aren't smart enough to know it."

"But what am I supposed to do now, Que?" Raven looked miserably at her friend. "He manages me. He runs it all. He's in charge of everything. I don't know how to do the stuff." She looked out the window. "I know, I should. The whole thing was just so stupid. I should've paid attention. It was just so easy to let him do it. I'm just so…stupid."

"You aren't stupid. A little naïve maybe, but baby you're supposed to be able to trust your husband. Here." Que shook two tablets into her hand and gave Raven the glass of water. "I want you to take these and drink this."

Raven pushed back her hair absently, swallowed the medication, then closed her eyes, waiting for relief.

"You know Rave, you guys have been goin' through this process for a while now. Why're you still doin' this to yourself?" When she didn't answer, Que stood up and walked toward the kitchen. "I'm gonna make you something to eat."

"I'm not hungry."

"Tough shit, you'll eat it. Now go take a shower, cause girl, you stink. And get dressed."

Raven followed her best friend with her gaze, groaned, then walked into the bathroom. Closing the door, she stripped down and tried to focus on her image reflected in the mirror. Mascara from the day before streaked down her tired face, and she had lost weight in the last eight months. Closing her eyes, she mentally berated herself. She didn't love the man anymore, so why was this so hard? Why did she let him have such control over her? Moaning, she stepped into the shower and let the scalding hot water rain down over her. The cold, wet tile of the shower beckoned, and she pressed her forehead to it, remembering what started her on this course.

That night, Amanda, one of Raven's previous backup singers, also managed by Donovan, held a reception to launch her own independent career. Raven, in search of a restroom, mistakenly opened the wrong door, to a darkened room. There she witnessed her husband kissing Amanda, one hand on the woman's face and another under her shirt and on her breast. Both looked up when the sliver of light from the doorway widened. Donovan's brows rose, more impatient than chastened.

"Yes, Raven, may I help you?" When she just stood there with her mouth open, he offered casually, "Oh, of course. Raven, I think you remember Amanda." She looked at the woman.

"Hey Raven," Amanda said, having the decency to look sheepish.

"Ah." Raven let out the breath, she'd been holding. "Good evening, Amanda," she said stupidly, then looked blankly at her husband.

"Yes, well," Donovan said, taking his conquest's hand and approaching his wife. "This is significantly awkward, and we'll discuss it later tonight."

He walked back out into the party without letting go of Amanda's hand, making Raven's humiliation complete. And that had been it. Donovan came home, smelling of the young starlet's perfume, saying he'd given the matter some thought and felt his marriage had run its course. When Raven asked him if he had ever loved her, he laughed.

"Raven, I told you, it's ridiculous. A bored housewife's illusion created by greeting cards and bleeding hearts." He rolled his eyes and chuckled, then noticed her stricken face. "Yes, okay, if you need to hear that to cope with this challenge. Yes, darling, I loved you. I believe we have benefitted each other tremendously and I will, of course, continue to manage you, if you wish. In fact, you'll need my help, at least to transition."

Then he exited the condo and didn't return, leaving her to wonder when he had turned so cruel. Why hadn't she seen that condescension before, that absolute control and equally absolute indifference? It was as if she were no more than a pesky fly he had finally swatted.

After her shower, Raven brushed her teeth and hair, then stood in front of her closet, trying to decide what one wears when they start their life over. She dragged on her most frayed, hole-ridden pair of blue jeans and a threadbare navy-blue hoody, just because she knew he'd hate it. After lacing up a pair of beaten up tennis shoes, she walked back to her kitchen. Que had cleaned up the wine and lain fruit and some cheese on a plate at the kitchen island. The bag she brought it in was neatly folded on the counter.

"Here, start with this. I'm gonna make some lunch,

and then we're all gonna have a talk."

"All?"

"Yeah," Que said, "you, me, and him."

She nodded toward the dining room table, where Raven's twin brother, Wyatt, sat pretending to read the paper. Raven was elated. He stood up and opened his arms to envelop her. Laying her head on his chest, she listened to his steady heartbeat, as he kissed the top of her head.

"What the fuck're you doin'?" he murmured.

"I'm trying to learn how to be a divorced woman whose husband cheated on her in front of the whole damn world."

"How 'bout you become a divorced woman that doesn't give a shit." He tried to look her in the face, but she hugged him harder. "Preferably one that learns how to stand on her own two feet?"

"Because one involves wallowing and one involves hard, painful work."

"You've done that before. I think you're up to it." Wyatt tilted her head up to his and kissed her forehead. "Don't ya think?"

"Lunch is served," Que sang, setting a plate with an enormous sandwich on the counter. She reached for two smaller ones and gestured for the twins to sit. "So," Que said, sitting down herself, "where to go, what to do from here?"

"What d'ya wanna do, Rave?" Wyatt asked, taking a large bite of his lunch.

"I don't know, go on vacation?" she teased. Both her guests looked at one another and grinned in epiphany. She eyed them both. "What?"

"A vacation?" Wyatt asked.

"Oh yes," Que said.

"Vacation? No, I was kidding. Didn't you hear what I said before, Que? I have to figure all this out. He's overseen everything, and the one thing I do know is that I don't want him to be my manager anymore, which means I don't have one. Which means I'm going to have to find one that isn't nasty, greedy, or incompetent. I don't know what gigs he's been promised. He was supposed to…"

"What better way to figure it all out?" Wyatt placated. "Go someplace warm and lay on a beach."

"Or better yet, just get laid," Que suggested, as Wyatt winced.

"Laid!" Raven laughed. "I just got divorced."

"Yeah, but it's been happening over eight months, and I'm bettin' it was a significant amount of time before that since you've been getting' any. Something tells me Cap'n Sugar Britches wasn't that good at it anyway. It'll relax you."

Raven laughed at Que's nickname for Donovan. Where her ex-husband had tolerated Wyatt, he vehemently hated her best friend. The feeling was extremely mutual.

"Um, can we stop talking about this?" Wyatt suggested, looking between the two. "Seriously, I don't want to hear about it." Both women continued to giggle but agreed to let it go.

"I do know it's been damn near a decade since you've had a decent vacation," Que stated.

"That's not true. I've been everywhere."

"To perform, maybe, but not to just hang out," Wyatt interjected.

"Where's the one place you've never been?" her

friend asked, trying to keep her on track. "Someplace you've always wanted to go to?" Enjoying herself, Raven turned pink.

"You'll think it's stupid."

"No, I won't," both said in unison.

"I've never been to Hawai'i."

"Hawai'i?" Que's brow furrowed. "That's here. Don't you wanna go to, like, the Bahamas or something? How have you not been to Hawai'i?"

"Donovan always wanted to play the massive arenas and big cities, and for some unfathomable reason that didn't include the islands."

"You should do it then. Take some time, figure some shit out."

"What about my tour dates?"

"You'll get 'em from dickhead or whoever, then call and cancel them. Hell, you can even interview new people to run the works while you're there. You're in the position to do that now, Rave. People would fall all over themselves to come to you. The point is to go away and figure it all out."

She bit her bottom lip and thought about all the problems this idea would bring until her brother spoke the next words.

"What're you afraid of Rave? What do you have to lose?"

Chapter 2

Finn climaxed hard, hearing the cries of pleasure and seeing the visual feast of the woman's body gyrating vigorously above him. He met his partner, a tourist, laying out on the beach the week before. She came from Tennessee and she hooked him with her southern drawl, but the reel was her deep dimples and ample breasts.

Breathing hard, they looked at each other, and she began to giggle. At least, that was the word that came to mind for the high-pitched sound that emanated from her. Exhaling forcefully, he took in her body, straddled on top of him, slick with sweat and glistening in the moonlight. He extricated himself from her and sat up. First kissing her lips, then breasts, he stealthily maneuvered them to the side of the bed. He ran his hands down her back to cup her bottom, then picked her up and walked them back toward the bathroom.

"Where we goin' sugar?"

"Shower. Wanna join me?"

"Well, yeah darlin'."

While in there, Finn watched her makeup, a woman's shield of honor, melt away in soap and water, revealing fresh alabaster skin. She had the tiniest sunburn on her nose. To Finn's way of thinking, she looked more beautiful natural, than with the war paint now circling the drain. They washed, had sex, and washed again, before exiting to dry off. Pink and fresh, she turned toward the bed, but nuzzling her neck, he walked her backward toward the chair, which held her clothes.

"You're going to think I'm a total shit for doin' this," he murmured, kissing the other side of her neck, "but I can't ask you to stay over tonight." He kissed her temple then settled his gaze to look at her directly. When the panicked look of not measuring up crossed her face, he continued quickly, "It's just I have an extremely early get-up."

"On a Sunday?"

He pulled away and turned to the chair, retrieving the skimpy floral print dress she'd worn earlier that night. Handing it to her and kissing her cheek, he turned and grabbed his jeans.

"I'm meeting my research team out at Hanapepe Bay," he said, sliding the worn denim over his hips and leaving them unbuttoned.

Finn could always tell the ones that had romantic notions of being curled up in bed all morning to giggle over the morning paper and plan the life they'd have together. Those girls tended to hang on and hover, so he determined he was dodging a bullet with this one and needed to move her on her way.

"Oh, okay."

"Fantastic night though." His lips quirked up into a sexy smile as she flushed with warmth. Finn paused a couple of moments more so his next line would ring with some sincerity. "God, you are so incredibly beautiful."

"Aw, thank you," she said in a lowered tone, aimed at seductive. "I like you too."

She dressed, and he watched as she descended the stairs to her car and exited his life. Taking a deep breath that puffed out his cheeks, he exhaled through pursed lips and lowered his head in relief. *You are so incredibly beautiful.* It was all he had to say to make up for leaving and never calling again. You are so incredibly beautiful meant it's not you, it's me. His smile dropped when it tickled on the edge of his consciousness that it was true; it was him.

Finn brushed his teeth, removed the jeans, and slipped into bed once more, laying one hand on his chest and the other on his well-worked johnson. He did have to be to the beach in the morning, maybe not as early as he'd said, but early enough. The issue was he never enjoyed staying over with a woman, not at his place or hers. It was too personal, sharing breath and space. He liked things the way he wanted them. It was more honest to end the night quickly, to his way of thinking. He didn't have to fabricate intimacy or lose all feeling in his arm because some woman had slept on it.

Most men envied his good looks, healthy body, and good charismatic nature, but that nature could also turn on a whim. His alpha type personality didn't tolerate anyone working outside of his plan. Men witnessed his prowess with women often enough. They would have guffawed at his brilliant ability to kick one out of bed after sex without recourse. However, it wasn't like Finn to tell them such things. He wasn't cruel. He just wanted things his way, and intimacy wasn't a part of it.

****

Six hours later, Finn pulled into the small parking lot at SeaHunt Researchers on his 2012 chopper.

"Great day, boss!" announced Jake, one his junior

researchers.

"Absolutely." Finn turned, looking at the sky. "Should be all day. You guys ready down there?"

"Yeah, probably in fifteen."

"A'ight, get it done. I wanna get going in no more than ten."

The smell of sunscreen preceded Holly and Dawson, his two female researchers, walking down from the admin building with coffees and the daily directives. Holly, a petite, girl with a cheerleader's body, gave Finn a sly smile and looked up at him through long dark lashes. He gave her a wink, knowing she'd float on it all day. Generally, he didn't go for his researchers because they were primarily students—over age, but students nonetheless, which tended to create baggage. However, this one was stacked, reasonably intelligent, wanted him, and wasn't shy about letting him know it.

"What do we got?" he asked as they approached and took one of their coffees without asking.

"Ah, Dr. Bowman wants us to go to Waimea and look at…"

"No," Finn said, grabbing the sheets of paper. He walked toward the building to have a word with his boss and called over his shoulder, "Gear up for Honopū Beach."

"Honopū Beach?" Dawson queried, turning to her classmate. "I didn't think we went out that far."

"I don't think Finn gives a shit." Holly retorted, appreciatively watching him walk away.

"Damn, he's got a nice ass."

"I know, right," giggled Dawson, tapping down on the brim of her well-worn baseball hat. "Come on, might as well keep him in a good mood and get our shit done."

They walked down the pier, toward the water. Hearing every word, Finn grinned as he entered the admin building.

"Hey, boss," he yelled.

When he received no response, he walked directly back to Dr. Bowman's office. Five years his elder, Nate sat behind his desk, the picture of a man not able to do what he truly wanted to do for a living. He obtained his position when promoted from within SeaHunt. It was the only facility on Kaua'i explicitly created for the research of the endangered Hawaiian monk seal.

Finn came to the position as a foremost expert on the species. Nate stepped out of the field and became not only the younger man's boss but one of his closest friends.

"What d'ya want, Taylor?"

"What crawled up your ass?"

"Tanner was up all night throwing up. Annie was throwing up this morning, and I wanna throw up just thinking about it," Nate informed him, continuing to write on some forms.

"Shit, stay the fuck away from me."

"Sorry, just wiped out. Whatcha got?"

"I wanna let you know I'm heading to Nā Pali instead of Waimea."

"Fine, I...wait...what?" Nate looked up, exasperated, from his papers. "Why?"

"'Cause today's the day I become a father Nate, and I'm not gonna miss it."

"Alaula's not due for a couple of weeks yet, and she was late last time." Nate nodded at a picture of

Finn's pride and joy.

"She's about forty-two weeks, and it's gonna be today." Finn looked at his watch. "Shit, she's probably in labor right now."

Nate looked blankly at Finn. Exhausted, he extended a thumb and forefinger across both his reddened eyelids, under his small rectangular glasses, before perching them back on his broad nose. He knew his favorite marine biologist had a sixth sense when it came to his animals.

"Fine, whatever, Alaula it is."

"Light of dawn, baby," Finn said, referring to the meaning of the seal's name. He turned his back, giving a hang-loose sign, leather bracelets sliding with the action. "She'll live up to her name plus about six." He pushed open the door and strode outside to the sunshine.

"How the hell does he know that shit?" Nate muttered, then shook his head as he heard the volume on the boat's radio increase and someone belting out they'd been thunderstruck.

Finn rode hard across the water, researchers trying to hold on, while the wind blew riotously through his hair. Mirrored sunglasses reflected the water rocketing past, as he pursed his lips into a smile, then grinned, bouncing his head slightly to the beat of the music.

Chapter 3

"What have I got to lose?" Raven looked derisively around her bedroom.

An explosion of clothes, jewelry, makeup, shoes, guitars, and sheet music decorated every surface. There was nothing more to lose. It lay all around her in plain sight.

She formally requested all papers and contracts pertaining to her professional life from Fortner Talent and Publicity. The one saving grace about her situation was that Wyatt had insisted an independent lawyer draw up their prenuptial agreement. At the time, it caused a major rift between them, and Donovan almost talked her out of it. However, shared blood and experience reminded her that no one, not even her new husband, wanted better for her than her brother.

After two weeks of soul searching and another two to cancel all her tour dates, dissolve the staff Donovan had employed and settle accounts, Raven rented a bungalow and was down to packing for her trip to Kaua'i. From there, she would make decisions regarding all the people she interviewed and whether or not they would join her team. Professionals, like an attorney, an accountant, and a publicist. She would retain her old personal assistant of nine years, Jason Dell, as her new manager.

Raven decided this trip would be a starting point

for change. The over-the-top, highly technical, synthesized sound with pulsating beats and lights that Donovan always demanded would be gone. Raven knew it needed to be something different but what, she'd yet to discern. The only decision she was sure of was that something needed to change.

Now sitting cross-legged in her room, hair once more in her natural, buttery-golden waves, she was surrounded by what seemed to be the entire contents of her condo.

What in the hell was she doing? This kind of thing required bravery. To go to a foreign place, knowing no one, being a shy, nervous introvert, with no direction, no man, and no life. Hot, greasy licks of panic slid around in her belly. She looked out her bedroom doorway onto the common areas of the condo. This space had never felt like her home, but she was still afraid to leave it. And tomorrow she would do just that for three full months.

"Argh, focus," she demanded of herself.

Decisions on which clothes, toiletries, guitars, and projects she wanted to bring, needed to be made. After spending the rest of the night packing and cleaning up her place, she could finally slide into the soft, cool sheets. Luckily, sleep came quickly.

Raven stood, shackled to the stage with lights flashing, and people screaming and cheering her name. Donovan was in one of his bad moods with eyes glowing hot. She tried to yell that she was bound, but he patently ignored her and turned his attention to another black-haired beauty. Suddenly the crowds began to scream and part. Confused, she looked into the distance and saw a great wave hurtling toward her without breaking. Raven turned to Donovan and screamed for him to release her, but he was now running too, running with the new woman, to a new life. Music, reckless and wild, simmered in her blood, moving painfully throughout her body and fire burned in her belly, as hot as the sun. It seemed to liquefy her bonds. Now free, would she cower, run, or stand her ground?

At the moment between deciding and being conscious of it, she jerked awake. For a split second an unknown face and strange, breath-taking eyes, reflected off her own. There were people there she felt she should know in a misty landscape, and then they were gone.

****

Que, her seven-year-old Abby, and Wyatt drove Raven to SeaTac airport around five the next morning. Her brother embraced her hard and kissed the top of her head before grabbing her by both shoulders and squatting to eye level.

"You can do this. Just go and enjoy yourself." He tilted her head up when she lowered it and peered into her eyes. "Meet people. If I can get away and come out there, I will, but I wanna meet some new people, okay? Preferably blondes, with big..." She hit his stomach. "Ow!" He pulled her into a hug and said softly, "Forget him."

"I'll try." Giving a nod of approval, he stepped aside to make way for Que and Abby.

"You're gonna have so much fun." Abby giggled.

"But who am I gonna play with?" Raven whined. Abby pursed her lips and wrinkled her nose, thinking.

"We can read to each other over the phone."

"That will definitely work." She hugged the little

30

girl close and felt her eyes sting as Abby ran over to Wyatt. He swung her onto his shoulders and began singing the newest kids' craze.

"See the light at sea and something with me," Wyatt sang.

"No, no," Abby said, disgusted. "See the light as it shimmers on the sea, as if just for me."

"Oh," the man said, chastened. "Well, excuse me."

Que shook her head, sighed out a laugh, and turned to her best friend.

"A'ight, go have some fun, snap some pictures, swim with a dolphin, have sweaty sex with a smokin'-hot beach dude, that says 'tubular' or 'totally awesome,' a lot."

Rolling his eyes and pretending not to hear, Wyatt turned back to Abby as the two women embraced.

"Call us when you land, okay?"

"Okay. I love you guys," Raven called, trying to hold back tears.

Smiling, she hitched her guitar case higher on her shoulder and started for the door. She turned at the last moment to look at her brother for strength. *Love you,* he mouthed, then patted his chest and grinned. She grinned back and was gone.

****

Six hours and twenty-seven minutes later, Raven stepped off the plane at Lihue Airport after an exhausting flight. She'd been seated in first class, next to a man, who in his words was, 'her biggest fan,' and spoke endlessly of everything she ever did. If that wasn't enough, a teething baby, having a hard time adjusting to the altitude, cried for most of the flight. Sleep, therefore, was impossible.

Relieved to be on solid ground again, Raven smiled at the large photos of graceful hula dancers on the wall. The small open-air baggage claim smelled of exhaust, dirt, and humidity if one could smell such a thing.

She retrieved her rental car and soon was traveling down the Kaumuali'i highway, warm wind blowing through her hair. Glancing up at the heavens, she wondered if she could get to Po'ipū beach without being rained on by the one dark cloud bruising the sky.

Within two hours she had obtained her keys, picked up some groceries, and pulled everything out of her suitcases. However, looking toward the window and the ocean beyond it, she resolved to leave the clothes in favor of sitting on the lanai with a glass of chilled chardonnay.

A beatific smile slid onto Ravens' face as she held her gold pendant. It was mesmerizing as she swung it like a pendulum on its chain around her neck. She'd inherited the pendant, medallion really, from her mother. Wyatt had its twin on a thong around his own neck. Each depicted a kind of harp, not unlike the instrument her mother had played for the Missouri Metropolitan Theater. They were the most treasured possessions the siblings owned, and the one thing they had to tie them to their parents.

Her intention upon arrival had been to unpack and get settled in right away. However, that was before travel, lack of sleep, and the warm wind blowing through her hair came to seduce her. Now, all she needed was the buttery notes of her chardonnay and some quiet. A song about single ladies sang out as her cell phone rang. She rolled her eyes at Que's choice of ringtone and thought about not answering it. However, a rude realization occurred to her that she'd forgotten to check in with her friend or Wyatt. Knowing it would probably be one of them, she extended a leg and hooked a foot around the strap of her purse before dragging it across the floor to retrieve the phone.

"Hello?"

"Hey, thanks for the call to say you're safe."

"I'm safe, Que." Raven lazily smiled. "I'm getting drunk on chardonnay in paradise, and it's only ten-thirty in the morning. How's the weather there?"

"Oh, same goes here." Que looked out the window at the dark gray clouds and the torrential downpour overflowing her gutters. "Flight good?"

"No. I'm gonna take a nap, maybe then I can try to comprehend an original thought. Hey, you got a date tonight. Ya nervous?"

"What? Oh, no, I'm not goin'."

"Why not?"

"Ab isn't feeling too hot."

"Really?" Raven opened her eyes. "Does she have a temperature? Maybe she's low on vitamin D again?"

"I'm not sure that's it."

"I shouldn't have had you guys come out so early this morning."

"No, I don't think it's that either. She's just been so tired lately, kind of short of breath. I'm wondering if it could be asthma or allergies or something. Probably only growing pains. I just made an appointment for her."

"Wait, what time is it there?"

"One-thirty." Her friend looked at the clock. "You're three hours behind, right?"

"Um, yes." Raven quickly calculated the time.

"Yeah, so I left a message and asked for a callback."

"Aw, poor baby. Hug her for me." There was a knock on her door. "Que, someone's here. You wanna hold on a sec?"

"Naw, go on ahead and get settled in. We'll talk tomorrow."

"Okay, love you. If you talk to him, tell Wy I'll call him later okay? Kiss Ab."

Raven ran to the door and a man, already weary from the day, stood there clad in a brown uniform.

"Hello. I've got some boxes for a Ms. Hunter?" He looked up at her. "This the right place?"

"Yep." She looked past him at three large boxes on a trolley and groaned audibly. Ugh, more unpacking.

She resolutely signed for the lot. After dragging each into the bungalow and scanning the battlefield, she tried to develop a strategy for success. However, she only skimmed over the melee until her gaze settled on the upright piano she had secured with the house.

Walking over the top of the clutter, Raven sat down and began playing the ringtone from her cell phone. Frustrated with herself, she stopped midway through and began to play a famous cartoon medley, until the vibrations of the chords mellowed out to supreme silence. Spontaneously, she started to play a rendition of Canon in D, moving her head to the rhythm of how she interpreted the music.

It was hours later when Raven finally opened her eyes again. Energy hummed deep in her blood, leaving her feeling centered in a way she hadn't in a very long time. Glancing at the shadows that had shifted around the house, she turned to the clock and noticed with a jolt that it was late afternoon. She decided if she didn't get organized, she'd have to wake up and spend the next day indoors with the clutter, thereby wasting another day. So, organizing room by room, she found homes for all her things. By the time sunset beckoned, she was ready to see her first on Kaua'i. Grabbing her keys, she slipped lily-white arms into a light lemon cardigan and ran down Po'ipū Road toward the beach. She saw several other people moving in the same direction.

It wasn't far, only a half mile away, but her excitement made the clear, aquamarine water seem miles away. The lengthening streaks of amber from a sun desperate for its rest reflected in her eyes. Raven removed her sandals, stepped onto the cool, smooth sand next to the lifeguard tower, and breathed in the heady aroma of some kind of flower and suntan lotion.

There was a commotion on the east side of the beach, near the rocks, where a large group of people had congregated. Curious, she walked over and tried to see what was happening. The crowd parted just enough for her to behold the most adorable animal she'd ever seen. It was a seal, maybe four feet in length, with a torpedo-shaped body, short, steel-gray fur, and a white spotted underbelly. She was genuinely enamored with the bulbous head, wild, intelligent black eyes, and long whiskers that hung down from a stubby, round snout. He seemed to smile, causing her infectious laugh to broadcast over the collective.

A man she hadn't noticed knelt next to the seal, turned his head slowly at the sound of her laugh, seemingly searching for someone or something. He wore dark mirrored sunglasses, but somehow she knew the power of the gaze behind the glasses would be transfixing. With the descending sun on her back, the pendant she wore grew hot and felt like a kind of pressure pushing her back. Raven couldn't take her gaze off the man as the sun shone on his face, making it awash with light. She could tell his hair was very light and that he had a short beard and muscular body.

The weight of his stare scared her. A ripple in the water and the bark of the seal broke the spell of their gaze. She turned, stumbling further down the beach, breathless. Sitting behind a tree at a picnic table, she gazed back at the group, no longer seeing the man, and decided the heat and fatigue conjured him. His looks, personality, and demeanor, of course, would be perfect. Would he fall madly in love with her and profess it with great fervor? Of course, because the man she made up was flawless.

Raven rolled her eyes at her own stupidity. If she ever did meet a man like the one she'd just conjured, who was so —well, beautiful—she wouldn't have the slightest idea how to speak to him. As the sun finally settled, she watched the colorful performance of nature. Shaking her head, Raven decided it was far and away the most overwhelming and bizarre experience she'd ever had.

Chapter 4

Alaula's massive sides bulged and heaved, stiff with labor. Her grunts could be heard all the way out in the boat floating nearby. Finn had swum downwind of the animal and now sat inconspicuously on some rocks, away from the eye line of the mother seal.

"Damn," Finn muttered, clenching his jaw. "Breech."

He raised the binoculars again, then taking a chance, he stealthily navigated the rocks to some soft sand and a better vantage point. The mother was helpless and concentrating hard. He didn't want her stressed anymore by his presence while trying to deliver her pup.

The mother, he'd be surprised to know, was aware of his presence. She felt a kinship with this particular human and always felt security rather than fear when he was nearby.

Finn could sense her struggle and pain, as anxious as any father would be. He never questioned the quasi-connection he had with sea life, always believing that most marine biologists had a certain level of uncanny ability. To Finn, it was more about being observant of the animals, rather than some kind of telepathy. A talent, of which Nate liked to accuse him, along with being a sea creature himself in another life.

Alaula looked back over what would've been her

shoulder, toward her hind flipper, trying to gain comfort, inching her pup out with every movement. Rolling and gyrating, groaning and turning until there was the explosive expulsion of a small, wriggling black mass, escaping from her womb.

The boat members gave a loud cheer and Finn, who'd been grinning, turned and silenced them with one scathing look.

The pup, encased in its creamy amniotic sac, tried to bark. It flopped and wiggled, then stilled, as if too tired to even breathe. After a last great effort, it was finally able to break through the thin barrier. Finn moved a little closer as the mother began to call to her offspring. The pup looked around in the general direction of the familiar sound and began to inch its way up to her, getting caught in its afterbirth. She called out in encouragement again, flipping sand over the pup and her birth leavings, prompting the seal to move faster.

"Why does she do that?" Dawson asked on the boat. Holly glanced up and watched the seagulls swoop above.

"Maybe to hide everything from the birds." She pointed up at the gluttons circling for food.

"Aw," Dawson replied, "good mama."

"That was so cool," Jake commented, video camera capturing the pup as he finally found nourishment and latched on.

Finn, alone on the beach, beamed with pride. This seal was alive. No one knew if he'd stay that way. However, right now, he was alive, and that was worth a celebration.

"Kaimi," he said, watching the youngster suckle.

"Kaimi, the seeker."

He looked toward the boat and his team documenting the scene with photos and notes. After a time, he lifted a hand into the air and rotated a circle, indicating it was time to leave. Walking into the water, he had a strange feeling, almost a pulling, and turned to take one last look at the pair. He almost swore the new mother looked at him and barked. He smiled and instantly dismissed this notion, before swimming with long, clean strokes to the waiting boat.

Back onboard he moved with purpose to the bridge and took the controls from Jake. As they moved away, the small group watched the duo, valiant in their efforts, bond. Alaula laid her head down, exhausted. She'd earned her rest, and they would leave her to it.

"So, what happens to the mom and pup now?" Finn quizzed the trio, as they motored back to the harbor.

"Mom doesn't eat for five to seven weeks while her baby nurses." Jake immediately answered.

"Pup," Finn corrected. "And how much weight will she lose?"

"A third of her weight," Jake answered again.

"Dawson, how much weight will the pup gain in that time?"

"Like, a hundred pounds."

"More like one fifty to one seventy-five. Holly, how much did that pup weigh?"

"Um, like thirty pounds?"

"Are you asking or telling?"

"No, it's thirty pounds."

He questioned them further, eventually trailing off for everyone to enjoy their own thoughts on what they'd witnessed. As usual, the girls tended to congregate in the cabin when Finn drove, to the chagrin of Jake, who was then relegated to stand or sit alone in the stern.

Finn's gray and white, checked board shorts were slung low on his hips, and his light blue tee played across the muscles in his chest as he steered. He turned briefly to look behind and around the boat for traffic. Noticing the girls eyeing him, he smiled and considered, causing a seductive grin to slide across Holly's face. He faced forward again, working the controls.

"Ah, Finn?" Holly addressed him tentatively.

"Yeah," he said without looking back.

"I was just wondering something."

"Wondering what?"

"What's your tattoo of? The one on your back?" She clarified, just in case he had more than one and pointed to the part of it that was extending beyond his tee shirt, blowing up in the wind.

"Oh," he lifted the tee-shirt up, exposing his back. "It's a trident."

The black and white artwork was shadowed beautifully, almost looking three-dimensional. It was a long, regal trident. The staff began in the small of his back, tracing straight up each vertebra, to between the bottom of his scapulae. The joint connecting the prongs was ornately grooved, and the arms of the trident splayed across the planes of muscle in his back and onto his shoulders. Each prong was capped with a medieval and sinister arrowhead. The center prong rising straight up his neck, also capped by an arrowhead, was so razor sharp that the result was both beautiful and ruthless at the same time.

Holly let one hand rest on his hip and allowed her other fingers to linger on the smooth surface of his skin.

By the time they reached the docks he was wondering if he should indeed get Holly naked and risk the fallout. In any case, he didn't think anything could destroy his mood.

Nate stood on the dock in typical khaki cargo shorts and gray long-sleeve tee, obtained from the brewery across the street. His aviator sunglasses sat hooked on the back of his head. Not exactly the picture of a boss, Finn thought, grinning.

"So, one hard-core bitch today, eh man?" Nate reached out for the lines thrown to him.

"Ya heard?" Finn nimbly jumped off the boat laughing and began to tie it off. "She labored hard, man. The pup was pretty average size but breech, so I'd say hard-core bitch was pretty accurate. She was perfect."

Nate straightened and turned toward the team, telling them to finish docking, then turned to Finn and jerked his chin.

"Come in here a minute. I gotta talk to you about a couple of things." Finn straightened and took an exasperated breath.

"Why doesn't this sound like a good thing?" When his boss didn't answer, he turned to his crew. "I want all that data entered and pics uploaded before you take off." The crew groaned but grudgingly accepted the time-consuming task.

He entered the reception area and walked straight back to Nate's office. Sitting down on a padded reception chair, he crossed an ankle on a knee. Nate threw him a beer from the small mini fridge he kept in his office.

"Still got some work to do out there, boss," Finn said and began to throw it back, but Nate held up a hand.

"Naw, you're probably gonna need it."

Finn inhaled, closed his eyes for a second, then removed his glasses and threw them on the desk. He snapped the beer open, bracing for whatever was coming.

Nate was always caught off guard by Finn's eyes, when confronted with them so abruptly, even after all the years of friendship. The color of blue graphite, with almost sea-green starbursts in the center and dark charcoal rims, they were almost from another realm of the universe.

"A'ight," Finn said cautiously, "what?"

"So, I got a call from Sunderland. He met with that team."

"Which one, solar panels or turbines?"

"Turbines." Nate slid on his reading glasses and looked down at a notepad on his desk. "That outfit from LA."

"Yeah?" Finn stared at him suspiciously. "And?"

"Yeah." Nate hesitated. "He's going through with it."

"Motherfucker!" Finn roared and jumped from his chair, continuing with a colorful stream of expletives that could be heard all the way down to the docks.

The crew looked at each other and began to work faster. They didn't want to hang around any longer than necessary now.

"Finn…" Nate waited him out then said forcefully, "Finn! God damn it, sit down."

He stopped his tirade but didn't sit. Instead, he prowled like a big cat, before walking to the window, crossing his arms over his chest, and looking out to ocean, seething.

"Did nothing I say make a dent at all?" he asked, without turning around.

"Yes, but he's thinking of the larger picture."

"Larger picture?" the younger man repeated. "Did he not see the data I gave him?" Now he turned and raised his hands. "And what about the politics? I can't imagine this'll go over big with anyone. I mean who wants to look at turbines fuckin' up their view?"

"I don't know. Somehow he's worked out something with all the players, and they agreed to a trial run."

"What about the data?"

"He says he ran a cause-and-effect and ultimately decided that he'll get the facility to run more efficiently. It's the only facility on Kaua'i, Finn, and it's a fucking expensive one." He drank his beer.

"There's going to be a fight."

"Oh, hell yeah, there'll be a fight. Everyone's gonna go nuts. All the arguments will be made. That could work in our favor."

"I just can't believe…"

"He's got a foundation to answer to, Finn, and investors. They're excited about being pioneers of the technological research or some such shit. And they need costs down, or they're going to start cutting things."

"And it's good for the environment."

"And it's good to say it's for the environment."

"There's only fourteen hundred of them left, and

they're just gonna pull the plug on 'em?" Finn all but spat.

"No, they'll do what they can, but it all costs money. They sponsor other species too, Finn. Other programs. If they start pulling out because we're unwilling to adapt, then what happens to the seals? To speak nothing of our program. They barely came out here before. We have to be able to stay, or it's going to be that way again."

"It doesn't matter a good God damn at this point. If they pull money, the seals die. If those ridiculous things are built, they're also gonna die."

"You don't know that."

"Oh, don't I? Really Nate?" Finn raised his eyebrows at his boss, then turned and slammed himself back into his chair and reached for his beer. "Where are they gathering their data from, some shitbag computer?" Finn demanded. "Those turbine blades don't give a shit whether animals swim into their path. And the animals sure as hell aren't expecting them, 'cause they don't fucking belong there." He concentrated on his beer. "Can I talk to Sunderland and try to make a dent?"

"I'm sure dentin' his head wouldn't be helpful," Nate consoled, raising a hand when Finn began to speak. "Besides, he's on his way home now. We're meeting again next week in Honolulu. Then don't forget his wife's throwing that fundraiser in a few weeks, and he expects us all to be there."

"I want in on that meeting."

"Like that'll happen." Nate snorted. "Come on, let's go get something to eat. We'll let the grunts finish up."

"Can't. Dee's making dinner."

"Oh yeah, it's Sunday."

"All day, but I'm sure she also heard about the pup before its own mother did. She'll want to celebrate." Finn looked at him scathingly. "I want in on that meeting, Nate, I mean it."

"I'll see if I can't set something up that you can take part in, okay?" Nate held up a hand when his subordinate started to speak. "I know. I'm hurting too, but we have to put out one fire at a time, and it helps no one, least of all the seals, when you go off like this."

Finn just glared at him, grabbed his sunglasses from the desk, and punched out the door into the sunlight.

Approaching his house thirty minutes later, Finn could hear Israel Kamakawiwo'ole singing about rainbows, his grandmother's favorite. Knowing her as he did, he headed straight back to her garden. It always lifted his spirits to walk through the French doors and into the Eden she had created. Hau trees with bright red blossoms, plumeria with their soft, dough-like petals, giant hapu'u tree ferns, orchids of every color, and in the center her pride and joy, a massive fifty-year-old banyan tree planted on the day of her son's birth. The woman could literally grow anything—fruits, vegetables, flowers, life. She had most certainly created his.

"Dee?"

"Ah, *hola ka'u mea i aloha ai, pehea i oe*?"

She peeked around a shrub and stood up, wearing a bright pink muumuu with teal, gold, and blue flowers splashed over it. A wreath of plumeria encircled the brim of her sizeable, trademark floppy hat, which sat somewhat haphazardly on her pinned up, messy, silver hair. Intelligent eyes, the color of bright bluebells, sparkled out at him and there was a long smudge of dirt on her nose and cheekbone. Finn smiled at the being that was his grandmother, as he always did, but this time, it didn't quite reach his eyes.

"I'm fine. So, what're you doing out here?"

"Oh, puttering." She eyed him briefly, then looked again. "Finn, what's happened?"

"What? Oh, nothing," he muttered.

"It's not nothing. I heard about the birth on the squawk-box. I thought we'd be celebrating tonight. Did something happen to the pup?"

"No, nothing like that." Lifting his hands, he smoothed back his hair a little. "Nate just told me they're going ahead with those tidal turbines in the water. Probably about six, seven miles off the PMRF."

"I'm surprised the Navy would let them do that. Why are they putting them way the hell out there?" She placed a hand on top of her hat to straighten it while brushing her other hand off on her dress.

"Admittedly, I don't know for sure if they are. It's just what was floated before, and there's a lot of hands in this pie, so who knows how and why. All the other beaches are pretty picturesque and touristy."

"And they sure as hell aren't gonna set them off Nā Pali."

Sighing, Dee walked over to the outdoor table on the porch, where a pitcher of homemade lemonade perched. She poured out two glasses and handed one to Finn. Slipping out of his flip flops, he paced in the freshly cut, plush grass, sipping the sweet and tangy beverage.

"They're meeting next week. So, I'm hoping Nate will let me try to figure out how to change Sunderland's mind, for all the good that'll do."

"He's not an unreasonable man, Finn," she called out, walking into the kitchen to put the lemonade away. "Just give him facts and numbers. When that doesn't work give him pictures."

She took one from the refrigerator of his Alaula's playful face, then walked back outside and handed it to him. "Now, how can you say no to a little face like that?" She looked deviously at him. Then, only because she wanted to see him smile, purred, "Or I can go over there and work my sexual prowess on him."

"Ew, stop talking." Finn rewarded her with the smile that had let him get away with nearly everything he wanted when he was younger. However, just as quickly he frowned again and sipped his lemonade, thinking.

"You want something to eat?" she asked.

"Can I take a rain check tonight? I'm not super hungry."

"I'll keep it for you 'til later." Knowing him well, she suggested, "Why don't you go down and run by the beach?" The corners of his mouth lifted again.

"You handling me, old lady?"

"Yep, now do as I say and clear your head out. Po'ipū?"

"Yeah, that'll do as good as any."

"Okay." She placed a hand on his back, giving it a couple of gentle pats. "But be careful down there, will you? The weather's been strange today, churning up the wind in all different directions since late morning."

"You got it," he replied, kissing her temple.

47

Walking out the front door, Finn let the screen door snap back with a loud reverberating bang. He walked across the yard to the garage. He'd converted the room above it into an apartment when he was sixteen and took the steps two at a time. Entering the air-conditioned living room, he stripped off his shirt, changed into running shorts and re-banded his hair.

Within five minutes of making the decision, he was jogging the mile and a half toward Po'ipū beach. As he crossed the street on his final approach, Finn noticed a significant group of people gawking at a large black object. Intuition had him moving fast, and as he broke through the crowd, he saw they had surrounded a monk seal.

The group, fascinated by its find, had unknowingly cut off the animal's route to the water and was causing the teenage seal to bark and moan in great distress. No one had bothered to call in the sighting, so the volunteers weren't there to control the gawkers. Infuriated, Finn pushed through the crowd, past a sign directing people to abstain from the very behavior they indulged in.

"Back off," he barked. From the confident, forceful authority in his voice, everyone obeyed without question. "Move!" he yelled at two girls in bikinis when they didn't move fast enough. "She's scared, and you're making it worse."

Finn knelt, and without touching her, tried to ascertain if the animal was hurt or just sunbathing. He was considering her eyes and pulling out his cell phone for some help when he felt it, something strange pulling at him. Laughter filled the air, and his back seemed to warm. He'd been watching the eyes of the animal but felt compelled to turn.

The sun was setting behind her, making it difficult to see, but her entire being seemed to radiate light somehow. He raised a hand to shield his eyes, through his aviators, but there were too many people obstructing his vision to reveal her face. All he saw was golden hair and the impression of her body. Finn began to stand up just as the seal barked at him, causing a brief shift in his attention. When he looked back, she was gone. In fact, he wasn't entirely sure if she'd been there in the first place.

Chapter 5

Deidre Taylor had lived an intriguing life. A colorful, full, dramatic life. Born December 7, 1941, her mother Catherine labored and delivered Dee with only a neighbor to aid her and bear witness. While Japan mercilessly attacked Pearl Harbor and the evening closed in on the horrific images of the day, Catherine looked upon her little piece of immortality, sleeping peacefully in her arms. Little did she know that her husband had succumbed to a warm, watery grave under the USS *Arizona*.

For a time, all the Hawaiian Islands were on lockdown. Stranded, scared and in pain both physically and mentally, Catherine, along with everyone else, tried to make sense of the violence. However, immediately after the ban was lifted, Catherine and her new daughter moved to Kaua'i. They found a good life there through the uncertain years of World War II.

No stranger to tragedy, Dee would lose her own husband to a farming accident in a sugar cane field in Koloa, but not before the union gave her a perfect and cherubic son they named Matthew.

Only a year old when his father died, Matthew would feel that absence etched deep within him. He grew up headstrong and reckless, despite Dee's best efforts to restrain and prohibit the behaviors. When he moved from child to teenager, his habits became more toxic, experimenting with drinking and an extreme recklessness that endangered his life more than once. At sixteen, Matthew became a father himself. He looked at his infant son with dismay and fear, especially when the child's fifteen-year-old mother left for the mainland and never returned.

Now, as her grandson left to sort out his thoughts, Dee walked to the window to watch him, a deep furrow appearing between her brows as she frowned. Her bright blue eyes clouded as she closed them and remembered the visit when the boy became hers.

"Hello, Mrs. Deidre Taylor?"

"Yes, sir." Dee sighed deeply at the police officer standing in her doorway.

"Ah, ma'am, my name is Officer Marshall Kinney. I'm from the Kaua'i police department." He removed his hat.

"Hello, officer," she said sighing again. "My son, right?"

She leaned against the open door, shaking her head with frustration and disgust. When would the boy ever learn? After his wife left, she'd hoped he would step up and be the father Finn deserved. Instead, he turned to drinking and finally heroin. As the days progressed, so did his habit, usually supported through theft, many times from her own purse. Recently, she had begun trying to sweet-talk him into allowing her custody of the young toddler. Visits and phone calls from the police were becoming second nature.

"Yes, ma'am, I'm truly sorry to have to tell you this, but your son was found this morning at the base of Kipu Falls. H-he's passed on, ma'am."

"Passed on?" Dee asked, a greasy panic rising in

her gut. "Wait…what?"

"Yes ma'am, we think he drowned." The officer cleared his throat. "We finally had some of his, ah, friends come forward." He hesitated, looking into her face, then quickly averted his eyes. "It seems they were doing some partying on the rocks out there. He, ah, he jumped off and didn't resurface."

"Today?" she asked frantically, trying to calculate if he'd said anything about going there or if it was a mistake.

"Ah, no ma'am, I guess this was a couple of nights ago. We found your name in the system and…"

"Oh God!" she screamed out. "Where's Finn? My grandson, Finn, he's only a little boy and I…"

"Yes ma'am, he's safe. He's a little dehydrated but safe. Some neighbors called it in this morning. It seems they heard the boy crying and came over to find out what was going on. It's what prompted us to find your son, ma'am."

"Where's Finn now?"

"Social Services here on…"

"Just…just, don't do anything."

No longer able to spare a thought for her son, she only wanted to go to the best part of him. She ran to the table and grabbed her purse, hands shaking, as she searched for her house keys. The officer held her hand and said he would take her to the boy. Half an hour later, she held a wailing and frightened Finn in her arms and hadn't let go of him since. Though he also grew up headstrong and stubborn, he was also kind, loyal, and loving, not unlike like his grandfather.

Still looking out the window, her mind began to re-engage, and she shook her head at feeling so nostalgic.

Yes, in seventy-six years, Dee had seen some things and faced more than her fair share of loss, but her life had never honestly felt complete until blessed with Finn.

A sudden wave of vertigo washed over her, and she placed a hand on her stomach. It felt full, like a dozen tiny snakes wriggling, trying to gain purchase. The older woman turned and walked out to her garden to sit in her rocker. For when these moments happened, she tried to focus on them explicitly.

At times, Dee could see things, images, impressions really, that sometimes passed like clouds through her consciousness. Finn filled her mind, the wind and sea blowing in every direction as he tried to navigate to an unknown star. His life was about to be impacted. Would it be today? Tomorrow? She tried to focus. Would it be love? Harm? She didn't know, just that it would be significant and it was coming.

The warm wind and sunlight pulled the scent of the ocean through the troposphere like a reluctant toddler. Glenn Miller crooned about black magic when an even stranger energy stirred the air. The wind swirled stronger, lifting Dee's hat and floating her long, snow-white hair around her face.

Looking out toward the ocean, Dee gazed upon a giant funnel cloud that had connected with the water, creating a spinning spout. Inside the winding tube was a golden beam of light from the sun as it peeked through the clouds above. She squinted, as time and movement had a dream-like quality to it, then worried the palm of one hand with the thumb of her other. Looking over at her neighbors, she saw they were oblivious to the drama unfolding on the water. So, they couldn't see it, she thought.

A sense of foreboding propelled her to her room. Not knowing why, she was secure in the knowledge that was where she was supposed to go. Nearly falling, she steadied herself, took a deep breath, and moved more cautiously toward her closet. She felt a thrum in her head, as thoughts swirled around, similar to the water in the mighty spout.

She began to throw shoes, boxes, and clothes onto her bed until she could finally reach the cabinet deep within, withdrawing an ancient, metal-strapped wooden box. Feeling as nimble as a school girl, she crossed her legs and took a deep breath as she tried to open the lid.

Where before it never allowed entry, now it opened with reckless abandonment. Dee gasped while peering inside and saw a smooth, pale ivory hemisphere that glowed and pulsated. Not a crystal ball or perfectly rounded sphere like one would see in a cheap movie, but more like an orb halved, soft and glowing, with no apparent shell. The most ancient part of herself began to beat along with it.

Her body shivered with the knowledge she couldn't reach. Catherine had given the box to her almost fifty years prior and told her it extended down their genealogical line for hundreds of years. Dee herself had kept it more out of intrigue and nostalgia, just like her mother had.

Now she felt a whoosh of adrenaline, like oxygen permeating each cell of her body with energy and life. Her vision blurred, and when she removed her glasses, it crystallized into perfection. Dumbfounded, she noticed her hand still raised, was free of age or time, a feat that was rapidly ascending her arm, her lap, legs, and feet. Touching her face, she found the soft, smooth roundness of youth and a wheat-colored mane once again brushed the tops of her breasts.

Hesitating only slightly, she touched the surface of the orb and power exploded into her, causing her to spasm. A vibrant stream of energy connected her to the sphere. Paralyzed to speak, Dee closed her eyes in concentration. A misty form emerged in her mind. When she opened her eyes again, she beheld a woman.

Her hair fell around her like liquid gold, blowing gently across a gauzy thong that blinded her eyes. Her arms outstretched with what appeared to be luminescence, rather than skin. Robes blew in an unseen wind and knowledge seemed to emit from her, physically. Dee shook her head and had no idea how knowledge could be seen.

"I am Themis."

The name came from nowhere with a voice not her own. She cowered at the being taking the shape of extraordinary beauty and omnificence.

"Daughter of the goddess Demeter, it has begun. Two of the prophecy, sharing the same time and same space, endeavor to be joined."

"Prophecy?" Dee croaked hoarsely.

"Son of the mighty Poseidon and daughter of Apollo, for it begins with them. I may come to you now, with whom I have an affinity, mothers of those connected with new life and reluctant death. Our life, our death, our world."

"Our world?" Terrified, she didn't know what say or do. "I...I don't understand"—she looked around, gesticulating—"this. Who are you?"

"Builders of Troy must reunite to build the

foundation of our last stand."

"Last stand? Is it... What the hell is going on!" Dee shouted. The orb flashed in impatience, and the older woman cowered. "I..."

"Silence must prevail, for time grows short. Hold strong to what you know, what you see, what you dream. Beware for there are shadows among you, that will attempt to hinder your path. Our strength fades, and there must be a new beginning at each end."

"Each end?"

"Twelve in all, the descendants must unite, for Cronus grows stronger."

"Cronus? Who in the hell is..."

"The gods of the past will descend into Tartarus, and Cronus's power will grow unchecked. His power already sings in some who serve in your world. The implications have extended to your time, as well as mine." The image began to fade. *"My time grows short, so your question must now be asked."*

"O-okay." Dee searched for inspiration, but her mind went suddenly blank. She shook her head as if to clear it. "Ah, son of Poseidon, Apollo, that's mythology, right?" Dee looked helplessly at the beautiful being growing more translucent. "Wait, where's this prophecy?"

In a last effort, the bottom of the chest gleamed and Dee turned it over. The light settled onto a carving that hadn't been there before. She looked back up, but the lady was gone. A flood of heaviness and pain brought her up breathless, as arthritis once more seeped into her bones, her vision blurred, and hands once again threaded with age. Dee sat, cramped and uncomfortable. Her thoughts from before rushed in like a tsunami washing away what she had always known to be real.

Reaching a hand to her jackhammering heart and then her head, she wondered if she'd had some kind of stroke. Taking an internal inventory, she realized she felt incredible. In fact, better than she had in years—full of energy, optimism, and an innate curiosity about recent events. Taking a deep breath and with violently shaking hands, she turned the box over, which was once more sealed. Dee read aloud the words etched into the wood.

"Those that now rule will rue a day when those they command refuse to pray.
An old, most powerful foe will find a way, to escape the bonds of yesterday.
And with him will turn one once trusted, that gods persecuted and belittled and neglected. Mighty gods shackled and toiled, never to be heard, from Tartarus's grip deep in the abyss of the Underworld."

She continued to read, growing more and more uneasy until she finished, rigid with fear and tension.

"Holy shit," Dee said in a quavering voice.

She sat there blinking, with her mouth open for a full five minutes before shaking herself out of the fog. Reaching for the bed, Dee helped herself up on shaking legs, then raised a hand to her mouth, dragging it down her neck and onto her chest as if that could slow her heart's momentum. Only when she thought she could support her own weight did she take a step toward the door and then another, growing more centered. She walked into her small study and sat in the chair.

Mind racing with thoughts, she shook her head again to clear them. How could anyone have been prepared enough to know what questions to ask? If the chest was that important, why hadn't her mother told her? Had she even known? Thinking back, she tried to discern if her mother ever indicated they were capable of anything like this. Only a little fortune telling, and that was weird enough. So, strange in fact, that Finn didn't even know that side of her. Dee didn't know what was real. If there was some bizarre curse happening, wouldn't she have clues? She sat up straight. Bizarre curse thing? What the hell was happening, had she lost her mind? Reaching for her keyboard, she went to her search engine and typed in, *Greek Mythology.*

After researching for hours, Dee became frustrated with her inability to make sense of the internet, let alone the massive web of names, connections, and deities within Greek mythology. She pinched the bridge of her nose, exhaling forcefully through it, exhausted.

Finn called her name, and her head snapped up. She looked toward the hall, up at the wall clock, then out the window. The thick black of night was beginning to lighten. She called back and began to stack her papers and scribblings quickly. Dee only had the faintest thread of what she was looking at anymore and tried to widen her eyes and stretch her back, stiff from disuse, before Finn got there.

"Hey," he said, leaning against the doorjamb. "You're up late."

"Yeah," she said absentmindedly. "Are you just getting in?"

"Yeah, met some guys for a couple of drinks and some pool. I didn't know it had gotten so late." Sitting down in the chair across from her, he crossed an ankle over his knee and nodded toward the papers. "Whatcha working on?"

"Did you know there were a bunch of different gods, not just Zeus and Aphrodite and all that lot?" she blurted without preamble. He creased his brow and looked at her, tilting his chin a little.

"Gods? What, you mean like the Greek gods?"

"Yeah, Zeus had a father."

"Ah, yeah," he said very slowly. "If I remember right, his father had a father too. They cut off his pecker."

"What?" Dee's gaze snapped up, astonished. "They did what?" Laughing, Finn seemed to root around.

"Well, I don't remember all the names, but one dude's name was Uranus. You tend to remember things like that as an adolescent boy, in middle school." He grinned at her, and she studied him back, unsmiling, so he cleared his throat. "Anyway, so then that guy hated all his kids or something and sent them to rot in hell or something, which pissed off his wife, whoever she was."

"Why did he hate them?" His grandmother watched and listened intently.

"I don't really remember, but she got a big knife and asked her kid to cut off his dick. Maybe it was so she wouldn't have more kids or something. I don't know." Warming to the discussion, he interlaced his fingers over his abdomen. "Her son did it, and threw it into the ocean, making Aphrodite. That's why all the guys think she's hot, but thinking about it, I really can't see why that would do it."

"So the son's name was Cronus?" She smiled as Finn yawned.

"Was it?" he asked, furrowing his brow. "I think that guy freaked out on his kids too, thinking they'd do the same thing or something. They didn't cut off body parts, but they got rid of him somehow, and then it was all about Zeus."

He looked over at her in consternation, glasses perched on top of her nose, another pair on top of her head, brows furrowed.

"Why the sudden interest in Greek mythology, Dee?"

"Um." She decided at the last moment not to tell him what happened that night.

Dee didn't understand it herself and didn't want to worry him or have him think she was losing her mind. However, she did decide she would need help if she were to understand all the connections and relationships.

"Finn, I want to learn about this, but some of it's beyond confusing. Can you help me a little?"

"Sure, when I got time. I remember it being kind of cool. The gods were all horny little bastards, a lotta rape and pillaging going on. I think I just liked hot girls in togas. At least I did in college."

"College?"

"Yeah." He grinned. "The Sig Nu's had a Greek-themed party once, might've gotten a little outta hand."

"Yes," she said derisively. "Money well spent I'm sure."

"So, what group do you want to learn about?"

"I think the Cronus group and then the Zeus group."

"Okay." The man stood and pushed his chair into place. "Well, I can already tell you who the biggest badass was, and it sure as hell wasn't Zeus."

"No? Who was it?" She looked up and smiled at his grinning face.

"I gotta go with Poseidon. Earthquakes and tsunamis… Total badass."

"Right." Dee looked at her grandson incredulously and nodded her head. "Right."

Chapter 6

In the two weeks since Dee's revelation, Raven spent her time sunbathing by day and working on arrangements by night. She'd spent little time trying to get to know her island or its inhabitants. It was something Wyatt appeared to become more annoyed with her about and raised the topic ad nauseam.

"You look tan," he said, as they utilized the video phone on her computer. "I gotta come over there. I think I'm turning clear."

"It just takes two weeks of being a blob in the sun," she chortled.

"I think I could live with that. How many people have you met?"

"People?" she asked evasively.

"Yes, Rave, people. You know perfectly well what I'm talking about. Intelligent creatures that have fun, protruding playthings." She burst out laughing.

"I've met some people."

"You liar. You just said you've been at the beach and working on arrangements."

"Right, and I'm meeting with Jason in"—she looked at the clock on the stove—"about twenty minutes. He's here for a week, and we're going to brainstorm the future."

"Great."

"You like Jason."

"No, I've never liked Jason."

"Why? He's nice and good at what he does."

"I reserve judgment on whether he knows what he's doing or not. You should too, quite frankly. He's been on the job for exactly two seconds, he's weird, and likes you way too much."

"A terrible attribute to be sure."

"I mean he just smiles too much and touches you a lot. Just don't be alone with him for too long," he warned. Then backpedaled at her crestfallen face. "I mean, just, I don't know, go find a cool surfer dude named Kai or Breeze or something and hang out with him."

"You need to stop talking now."

"Okay, but promise me, for the next two nights, you go out somewhere and talk to someone different."

"Two nights straight?"

"Yep."

"Maybe." Evading, she switched to him. "Have you seen the girls?"

"No, I got offered that survival training gig and have been pretty preoccupied. Actually, it looks like I'm probably not going to be able to make it out there, either."

"What?"

"I know, I know. I'll let you know if it changes, but my first two groups will be coming through, and each are four-week courses."

"You were able to get off work for it?"

"Yeah. I didn't give them much choice though. They aren't exactly in the position to bargain right now. It might be time for a change anyway." He smiled at her. "Maybe it runs in the family."

"Well, maybe I should…" There was a knock on her door. "Oh Wy, I think Jason's here early."

"Shocker." She glared at him with irritation, so he responded earnestly, "Fine. Two nights though, okay, and call me later?"

"Okay." She blew him a kiss and closed the laptop, setting it down on the table. She smoothed down the short sundress covering her swimsuit and opened the door to her new manager.

"Jason," she said, smiling. "You made it."

"I made it." He grinned, and hugged her, then held her arms out from her sides and took her in. "Wow Raven, you look…amazing." Blushing, she pushed her hair back from her face. "I hope I look this good in a few days."

"I was just telling Wyatt, it's easy to get a tan when all you do is lay around. I probably need to start getting productive again. Ah, please," she advised, noticing he was still holding her hands and standing in an open doorway, "come on in."

The truth was she cared for Jason, just not the same way he cared for her. The problem was she hadn't been able to tell him she wasn't interested in him personally. However, needing a new manager, she resolved to promote him rather than disappoint him. Raven did understand that eventually, the conversation of a relationship beyond professional would have to happen.

"What a fantastic room," he observed, walking around the space.

The bungalow was large and airy, and with the windows opened, it almost looked like an outside covered patio. The white filmy drapes billowed in the wind, and the décor was all sand, seashells, and in colors of various shades of blues and greens. The ocean beckoned from the windows, and sunlight created thousands of diamonds on its surface.

"Is that plumeria?" he asked, breathing in through his nose.

"Yeah. I think it saturates the dirt around the bungalow here. Very Hawaiian. Here." Raven poured and handed him a glass of chardonnay before padding out to the deck. He dropped his briefcase on a chair, and followed her, sipping his wine. "So, have you been to the hotel yet?"

"No, that's the next stop." He stood and looked out at the lush foliage and beyond that, the crystal-clear blue of the ocean. "Wow. Are you ever going to want to leave here, when it's time?"

"I have no idea," she replied, laughing. "It really is paradise, right." Sipping her wine, she added, "Was your flight good?"

"Yeah, good… Long but uneventful."

They talked about the weather and news back home, as well as some of the things they wanted to accomplish in his short stay. After about thirty minutes, his stomach growled with complaint.

"Sorry, I waited to have dinner and thought maybe we'd go out. You can introduce me to Kaua'i." He looked over at her hopefully. Shit, she thought, he was just like Wyatt said.

"Sure." Improvising, she added, "There's a restaurant over on Po'ipū Beach." It was the only restaurant she'd had a meal at. "Po'ipū Lani's. It's close."

"Okay. I'll get settled in, then how 'bout I come pick you up? Or maybe just come with me."

"Oh no, I have to get cleaned up. I'll just walk over and meet you. You're at the main hotel, right?" When he nodded, she continued, "It's really close to that. In fact, it's about halfway between us."

"Yeah? Okay, so Pie-oop-boo?"

"No," Raven laughed, "Poy. Like toy but a P and poo. Po'ipū."

"Okay." Jason laughed too, "Po'ipū Lani's in forty-five minutes to an hour?"

"Sure, get settled in, and I'll see you over there."

He handed her his empty glass and kissed her cheek before leaving. Ugh, she thought, this is going to be so much work. Why couldn't everyone just do their own thing? Why did humans have such an insatiable need to coexist, she thought testily. Turning to her reflection in a mirror, she saw the old washed-out sundress, hair coming out of its braid, and no makeup. Fine, coexist it is.

Chapter 7

"Hey, Nate," Finn said into his cell phone, watching Jake throw a line to Dawson.

"Hey, I need you to come rescue me," Nate whispered. There was a noise and then the muffled sound of Nate's voice.

"Annie, I'm sorry, but I gotta meet Finn. It's about work; it's important." Noise again, then Nate was back. "Look, Finn, I understand you don't get what's happening but let's meet, and I'll explain it all again." Nate spoke loudly now. Finn knew he was officially under the bus to Nate's wife.

"Oh, yeah?" Finn said with a laugh. "So, not only are you asking me to do you a favor but I'm now a clueless idiot too."

"Uh-huh, uh-huh. Yeah, okay, I'll meet you at Lani's in an hour."

"You don't deserve that woman, you little cocksucker."

"Yes, I know, just calm down, and we'll figure it out."

The phone disconnected and Finn laughed at his pathetic friend. After finishing the day and a quick shower at home, he made his way into Po'ipū. He'd arrived early to make sure the seal hadn't returned. A green sea turtle, also endangered, had replaced the seal, but volunteers had efficiently placed stakes around him and were keeping a vigil against unwanted attention. The turtle glanced Finn's way but was content, so he decided to go to the restaurant and get started on a beer, rather than stay out on the beach to wait.

Inside was packed, mostly with tourists. The heady smell of suntan lotion and grilled food perfumed the air. He navigated his way to the end of the small bar and sat down on a barstool. When his beer arrived, he tilted his head back and took two thirst-quenching gulps, when he saw her and slowly lowered the bottle.

She was wearing a cerulean blue bohemian-style dress. Long, caramel-colored hair tousled over well-toned, tan shoulders. It looked like she'd just raked her hand through her hair, flipping it over her head. The soft blue of her dress vee'd over the crest of each breast, the material held together by a small threaded bow. Full, unpainted lips drained a glass containing some sort of clear liquid, with a lime wedge hooked on the rim. She nodded at the bartender for another, then glanced around like she was extremely uncomfortable to be there. Finally, her eyes locked with his and held, almost daring each other to look away. She did first, then pretended she'd never seen him.

Rather than approaching her, he resolved to just sit for a minute and enjoy the view, a hand running down his beard, sexy smile on his face. The waiter asked if she was waiting for a table, but he couldn't hear her response. Finn decided she was just trying to look busy when she whipped out her phone and began scanning its contents. He rose, grinning, willing to play the game, and walked to the barstool beside hers to sit down.

A warm wind blew into the open panels for windows, and he had a sense she knew it was him before even looking up. She took a deep breath and lifted crystal baby blue eyes to his. He looked back at her as she appeared startled. Finn was used to the attention his eyes seemed to attract. He used it to his advantage in all kinds of situations, this being one—keeping women off balance.

"Hey," he said quietly. "How ya doin'?" His voice resonated deeply in his chest, flustering her further.

"I-I don't know, but yeah, okay, I guess," she stuttered quietly, and flicked her eyes down, sipping her drink.

He drew his brows together. Not exactly the typical response he got, but he would go with it.

"What's your name?" he asked, as the bartender set down her drink. "Thanks, man," he said for her.

"Raven," she said quietly.

"Raven?" he repeated. "Great name. I'm Finn—Taylor."

"Finn?" She looked up now, confused. "Like a flipper?" Then seeming to realize how ridiculous that sounded, blushed furiously.

Okay, he thought with a smile, a little disappointed that maybe there wasn't a lot going on upstairs, but he'd known worse—hopefully.

"Or maybe even like a fin." He gestured at the bartender for another beer, then rested an elbow on the bar and ran his hand through his beard again, watching her.

"Right." She gave a nervous laugh. "Finn."

"So, ah," looking around the bar, he asked with a half laugh, "you aren't from Kaua'i, right?"

"Ah, no." She exhaled with a smile, then gulped her drink. "Seattle."

"Oh, Seattle. I've never been there. I hear it rains and it's cold."

"Sometimes, but ya know, not all the time."

"Right." She was white as a sheet, and he was beginning to worry that she'd actually dissolve into a puddle before his eyes. "So, you're on vacation then, with your family?"

"I, ah, no. I'm here for work and then a vacation."

"Oh, what do you do?"

"I, what?"

"Look, are you okay?" He stopped running his hand down his beard and tilted his head toward her. "You seem really nervous."

"No, I…shit." She dropped her bag on the floor and reached down to pick it up. Finn reached down to help, giving him the advantage of seeing deep cleavage and no bra.

Fuck me, he mouthed, then groaned and turned his head away.

"What?"

"Ah." Eyes wide, he shook his head a little. "Where d'ya work? What do you do?"

"Oh, I ah, I'm a musician."

"Really, like you got a band or something?" He was a little shocked that this woman could stand on a stage and be willing to have people watch her.

"Something like that, yeah. For the next couple of months, I'll be in Hawai'i."

"Oh, wow." Tilting his head, he tried to ascertain if she had a real job. "Where do you…"

"What do you do?" she asked at the same time.

"Me? Oh, I'm a marine biologist with SeaHunt Researchers. We have a privately funded program. The only one on Kaua'i. It's for research of the Hawaiian monk seal."

"Monk seal?"

The woman ran her eyes down his body. Uncharacteristically disconcerted, Finn regarded himself in the bar mirror checking for flaws. Hard, lean, broad chest, thick, shoulder-length hair, and short beard, all kissed generously by the sun. *I can't look that bad,* he thought to himself. He lifted the corner of his mouth in what was described to him as a purely sensual smile. Raven looked confused, as if trying to remember something. Her body jerked a little, in the same moment he realized, she was the apparition from the beach. Searching her face wildly, he tried to compare every expression and movement to his memory of that experience.

"Hey, was that..." He began, causing her to re-focus.

"Raven," Jason called, walking up to the two of them and causing both to jump. He quickly leaned in between them and kissed her cheek, trying to convey territory in what seemed like an intensely intimate conversation. "Sorry, I'm a little late, underestimated the walk."

She blinked at Finn, then looked up and smiled at Jason.

"Hi, um, don't worry about it. Jason, this is Finn Taylor." She gestured between the two men. "Finn, Jason Dell."

"Hello." Jason coolly extended a hand.

Finn didn't take his eyes off Raven as he extended a hand. With a look of supreme irritation, Jason squeezed overly hard, causing Finn to give him a warning look. Jason let go immediately, and Finn's eyes returned to Raven.

"Well, I think our table's ready darling," Jason said to the couple that wasn't listening to him. Reaching out a hand, he clasped her shoulder and gave a gentle squeeze. "Are you ready, sweetheart?"

Raven let the endearment go and nodded her head, but didn't move. Jason helped her to her feet, prompting Finn to stand too. As the newcomer led her away, Raven felt Finn's eyes watch her go but then he called out.

"Raven?" The couple turned, and he lifted his chin. "I'll see ya around then?"

Her eyes darted around the room as if searching for inspiration, before returning to his. She covered her bottom lip with her top and turned back to Jason.

"Okay," Jason nervously said after they'd ordered. "So that was weird, right?"

"What?" she asked, distracted.

Her mind raced to the images. It was a jolt to her nervous system when she realized he was the sun-bronzed god that knelt next to the seal. She actually conversed with him. Well, kind of. Finn seemed to realize it too. His eyes widened and searched her face, excited. She felt like the man bewitched her with those eyes. She had never seen anything like them before in real life—she remembered seeing them before she left Seattle, those eyes in her dreams, and it startled her.

"Hilo Hawai'i over there."

"I just saw him a while ago on the beach and forgot."

"Well," he said, abruptly changing the subject, "I know you wanted to be here instead of Oahu, but some things can happen over there next week." Gently leading her to a possible island hop, especially since Malibu Don Juan had discovered her. "Maybe this weekend we could go over there. Take in some culture," he suggested.

"Oh, well, I don't think I'm quite ready for that yet, Jason." She sipped her drink. "I genuinely want to take things slow and do it right. I need to, you know, decide on appearances and what kinds of performances and stuff."

"So, it sounds like you have some thoughts on that."

Their food arrived, giving her time to think. Looking wistfully out at the water, she began to fidget.

"I'm not"—she paused—"I'm not sure I want to do things the old way."

Jason had been looking out toward the water too, a satisfied smile on his face. She turned and watched Finn retreat into the darkness. She turned back to Jason and looked at him, confused. He simply stared back, an innocent expression on his face.

"What do you mean?" he asked, as if nothing had happened.

"I'm not really sure yet. I have some ideas, but I haven't fleshed it out all the way yet."

"Example?"

"Maybe go more acoustic, with original pieces, and soften the edges?"

Jason nodded his head, eyes cast downward as if trying to think how best to phrase his thoughts. When he looked up, she was studying him.

"Okay, I'm just going to say it. I think that's a terrible idea."

"Why?"

"Because you've built a following, Raven. You've cultivated fans for over the last decade. You're a successful brand."

"Great, now you sound like Donovan."

"Well, maybe on this one thing, he's right. Raven, at your age, you can't just call out redo. Only the Taylors of the world can transition like that successfully after they developed a following."

"So, you think I'm too old?" she said, starting strong then realizing she wasn't quite that brave and finished more quietly. "I'm not just starting out. I have a huge following. Don't you trust that they would follow me? I've sold out every arena for the past twelve years, Jason."

"No, I'm not saying that," he said, appearing to realize his mistake, and held her hand. "You're beautiful, vibrant, and so incredibly talented." He rubbed his thumb along her wrist. "What I mean is, Taylor created fame in country music, right, but created a niche with the tweens. As she developed, she was so smart and branched out the two, then grew as her fan base grew. So." He began to count on his fingers. "She had the tweens she started with, then the new ones that followed. On top of that, she had cross genres of country and pop, and she had youth and time."

"I think I have to change, too." Raven looked out toward the water again, feeling restrained. "I'm thirty-four years old, Jason, why would a tween want to listen to me? As I said, I have a following, and I have things to say. And I am willing to do cross-genre. That's exactly the kind of change I'm talking about. I'm not sure I can keep going unless something changes."

"Okay, well, there are things we can do. We can discard the songs you really hate, maybe blend in some new pieces of original work." He hesitated. "I'm not sure though. We'll have to listen and choose carefully. Maybe we should go back to your place, and you can play some things for me?"

Raven didn't play her unfinished music for anyone, and it irritated her that he didn't understand that or her need to expand. Suddenly, she wanted the night to be over and go back to the house or walk on the beach in solitude, anywhere now, without him.

"I'd rather not tonight. It's been a pretty long day." *Of doing nothing*, she thought sheepishly. "I think I'm going to head back, get some sleep, and maybe we can get some things started tomorrow."

"Sure. Why don't we go back to the hotel for a nightcap and then I'll drive you home?"

"No, thanks, I'm just gonna walk." Suddenly she just needed air. "Here, just put it on the expense card. I'll call you in the morning, okay?" She rose, and he quickly stood with her, looking surprised.

"All right. Hey, you okay? If you give me a second, I'll pay this and walk with you." He looked around for a nonexistent waiter. When she shook her head, he added, "Raven, have I offended you somehow?"

"No." she laughed it off. "Really, the air will do me good. I'll call you in the morning, okay?" She air-kissed his cheek and bounded down the stairs before anything could change her decision.

Once outside, she determined it best to walk the long way around to her bungalow, in case he tried to catch up with her. She'd only made it to Pane Road when the strap on one of her expensive leather sandals broke apart.

"Damn it," she muttered, pulling off the sandals and looking at the sharp, gravel-strewn sidewalk. "Oh, this is just great."

Angry and frustrated with her circumstances, both new and old, she gripped the sandal hard, wanting to throw it across the street, into the ocean. Raven looked back at the restaurant, expecting Jason to call out to her. Resolved, she took a deep breath and gingerly tried to sidestep the rocks, as tears threatened her eyes.

****

Finn had stayed at the restaurant only long enough to finish his beer, glancing over at the couple from time to time. He left feeling a little dazed and confused. Dazed that the woman actually existed in the flesh and confused about what he was supposed to do about it. She clearly had a significant other, a proprietary significant other.

He'd called Nate, telling him not to bother coming to the restaurant, opting instead to run a six-pack there to drink with Nate companionably on his back porch. When the man's wife joined them, sobbing that she was an awful mommy, Finn took his cue to abandon the mission and evening entirely.

He kick-started the motorcycle, made a U-turn, and drove back down the road toward home. He took in his surroundings as he turned onto Pane Road, when his headlight shone on what looked to be a drunk person, weaving across the street. As Finn moved closer, he thought it might be someone injured, then realized it was Raven and pulled to the side of the road. She turned around and literally groaned when she saw who it was.

"Yeah." He laughed, "I get that a lot."

"I'm sorry," she responded, blushing furiously. "I just, I just really had great intentions for tonight, and it didn't quite work out." She held up the broken sandal.

"Oh wow, that sucks." He swung his leg over the bike, without cutting the engine and stood in front of her. He glanced up and down the street. "Are ya close by? I can give you a lift."

"No thank you, I'm okay." She eyed the bike dubiously.

"Seriously, you're close enough that you're trying to walk, and I live close by, so you're probably not out of the way, promise." Grinning, he knew he was making progress and looked around again. "Where's your boyfriend?"

"My what?" she asked, nervously eyeing the bike again. He could see her weighing the option of a walk versus a ride home with a stranger that made her nervous. "Oh no, you mean Jason?"

"Yeah, Jason." He grinned more broadly when he heard, 'oh no.' "Why isn't he here helping you?"

"I told him to go home," she answered distractedly, and he grinned even broader, entirely liking the sound of that.

"His home isn't your home?" When there was no answer, he bent at the waist and tried to look up into her face. "Are you afraid of the bike or me?"

"What?" she asked snapping out of her internal debate.

"I said, are you nervous about riding the bike or me?" Knowing the pun was lost on her, he became thoroughly entertained.

"I'm not nervous about either," she retorted primly, realizing too late what he meant, and blushed again.

"Oh great, then hop on. I can show you a really cool vantage point that no one knows about. It'll be romantic."

"I-I, ah," she stuttered, and he tried to repress the smile at her tortured indecisiveness.

"Or, I can just take you home, and you can get back to your life."

"Okay, thank you." She licked her lips as she looked around nervously, then met his eyes. "I've just never ridden on a motorcycle before."

"Naaaaw, you're kidding, right?"

When she smirked and narrowed her eyes a little, he was relieved to see she had some fire after all. Grabbing his helmet, he secured it on her head. Covertly, he raised both eyebrows as she hiked her dress up on amazing thighs and climbed on the bike.

"So, where to?" he asked, chuckling when her arms instantly superglued themselves around his waist, and the sweet smell of her perfume wafted over him.

"I don't know how you say it, but it's Pee Road.'" she answered, blushing furiously.

"Don't worry." He laughed. "All the tourists call it that. It's pronounced '*pay-eh*.'"

"Oh." She laughed too. "Perfect. I knew I was saying it wrong."

After the initial fear broke loose, she seemed to relax and loosened her arms and their grip. The wind was warm on their faces, no wall or doors around them. It was exhilarating. He drove her a different way to prolong the ride, but she didn't seem to care. When they arrived at her bungalow, he helped her off the bike and gently reached under her chin to unstrap the helmet, his eyes never leaving hers. He forked his fingers through her silky hair, displacing the static electricity from the helmet, and looked at her mouth, prompting her to look at his.

"Well. Thank you." She bit her bottom lip. "Thanks for the ride. It wound up being kinda fun."

"No problem," he said, quietly looking at her lips again. "Sometime I'll take you over to the north side. It's a great ride. Hanalei and the falls are pretty amazing." He ran a hand through his own hair.

"Ah." She moved away nervously, awkwardly, and bit her lower lip again. "Yeah, maybe."

"At some point, I'm going to have to tell you to stop doing that."

"What?"

"Biting your lip. It's a pretty big turn on."

He looked at her lips again and then her eyes before smiling and sliding back onto the bike. He liked the way the comment sounded. He really liked looking at her but furrowed his brow in confusion as she paled. She was like a nervous little rabbit. If the woman never opened her mouth, you would only see this extraordinarily beautiful, well-put-together package. He didn't believe for a minute that she didn't have something more to offer. Maybe, he determined, he just needed to break down the barrier of nerves.

She walked back to the house quickly, and he focused on the sexy sway of her mighty fine ass under the thin fabric. She walked inside and he could see her through the frosted glass, reach over and flick a switch, causing the porch light to come on. She leaned back against the glass, and he chuckled, knowing she didn't understand that he could see her. God, who was this adorable woman?

****

Finn returned home and, seeing no lights on in the main house, took his stairs two at a time. Running through his nightly ablutions, he intentionally kept Raven from his thoughts. It wasn't until he was laying between the sheets, arms locked behind his head when he allowed her to drift into his mind.

His first thought was that the woman was an odd duck. Second, she was an odd, incredibly hot duck, and he was pleased she didn't belong to the asshole. Women fascinated him, every single one of them. They all had a story or a secret, and he loved figuring it out. Unwinding a woman, learning her story, then moving on. He knew it sounded callous, but he also knew what he was capable of, and monogamy wasn't it. Raven may have been intriguing because she was seemingly unattainable. Eventually, he slept.

Finn's research boat motored toward an island farther off their projected course. The weather was picking up, but he told the crew to push through. He barked orders to secure lines and equipment, as waves churned and white foam capped their peaks. The girls grabbed pails blowing across the deck, while Jake frantically tried to secure the lines whipping around in the wind.

What the hell was going on, Finn thought. This front had come in out of nowhere. Maybe there had been an earthquake. He looked down and in disbelief, realized he'd forgotten to turn on the navigating equipment. But how could that be?

Cold fear crawled up his spine as a massive wave

broke against the bow, causing Jake to bullet over the side of the boat and into the cold water. Finn screamed over the intercom for the girls to come help. When they didn't answer, he turned and saw they were gone too. One of Holly's flip-flops floated in the small pool of water collecting aft.

"Fuck me."

He ran to the back and saw the girls swimming toward each other without life jackets. Running to the bow, he saw Jake doing the same. Closer to the girls, Finn maneuvered the boat to retrieve them first, but by the time he'd arrived, they disappeared. Looking out toward the bow, he watched in horror as his male researcher disappeared beneath the cold blue surface too. Finn turned to run back to the cabin when he saw Raven steering the boat.

"Get to Jake!" he screamed, but she couldn't hear him. "Raven, Jake...Jake!" He pointed.

She turned and could see him gesture but didn't seem to know what he was saying. Alaula was on the bow now, barking loudly over the wind, her pup trying desperately not to fall off too. He ran down the hall as more water sluiced over the sides. The hallway lengthened, and he couldn't reach the bridge.

The water started to part, and Raven turned to look at it. Iron pillars began to poke through the surface of the water and Finn's back seemed to burn and tear and he cried out in pain. The trident tattooed along his spine stood before him in living color, but it was the length of several football fields and held in the massive hands of a man with Finn's eyes. Black liquid ropes bound themselves around his enormous biceps and strong wrists. Another thicker one coiled around his muscled waist and neck. He tried to lift the trident but failed. His unearthly eyes sparked at Finn, who felt the extreme heat all around him. He looked for the source and saw it was Raven. She was a ball of fire with wings unfurling, making a guttural scream.

Finn couldn't move, aware he was utterly powerless without the trident on his back. He looked back into the face of the great man. The man only had a moment to say two words before an enormous tsunami ran through him, blending to his shape, becoming the wave, then his outline turned to the ocean's spray. He looked back at Raven and the fire burst.

Finn's eyes flew open, and he expelled a gasp. Sitting up, he was shaking and covered in sweat. The aftershocks of the dream pulsated behind his eyes. What the hell was that? Breathing hard, he swung his legs to the side of the bed. Resting his elbows on his knees, he laid his head in his hands, as the two words seared into his mind. *Release me.*

Chapter 8

Raven lay in her bed the next morning, after a long night of restlessness, still mortified from the night before. Why couldn't she relax, and casually flirt with a good-looking man, who seemed interested in her. She could hear Wyatt advising her to have a little fun. Que would counsel a careless fling or do something reckless. She sat up realizing with surprise, she had, when she got on a stranger's motorcycle.

She jumped as her cell phone rang. She saw Que's screenshot face and smiled. Well, speak of the devil.

"Hey, Que," she said, laying back and putting an arm behind her head.

"It's me." Abby giggled.

"Well, Abby! How you doin' baby?" She glanced at the clock and did the math. "Aren't you supposed to be in school?"

"It's late start."

"Ahh, well, how're you feeling? Mama said you still weren't quite over that bug."

"I'm a little better, I wanna play basketball but Mama's bein' *rude*." She spoke the last three words loud enough for her mother to her hear. Raven had a stab of homesickness. She could hear Que scolding her daughter about being late for the bus. "Are you having fun there?"

"So far, so good. It's definitely warmer here than

there."

"I'm trying to get Mama to…" She heard Que's voice angrier now. "Damn, I gotta go get the bus."

"Don't swear," Raven softly chided.

"Love you, Auntie Raven. Here's Mama."

"Bye," Raven called out and heard mother and daughter exchange love and a muffled hug.

"Have a good day," Que said, then blew out a breath. "Whew, I tell you what."

"She feelin' better?"

"Oh well, you know, not as good as I'd like, but…"

"What did the doctor say?"

"He thinks it's asthma."

"Well, that's good news, to know I mean."

"Yeah, her inhaler doesn't work for shit though. We'll figure it out. Anyways," she said with a smile in her voice, "so how you doin' over there?"

"Good. I've got a tan."

"Ah, well, miracles do happen."

"Shut up, just cause your tan's permanent."

"Oh no, don't even get me started on that double-edged sword." She exhaled deeply. "Any hot new romances?"

"Well, Jason just got here."

"Girl, please." Que paused. "You've been there how many weeks? You're sittin' in that place all by yourself, aren't you?"

"No…"

"Rave?"

"I…"

"Rave?"

"Okay, fine, but don't tell Wyatt. He'll just get mad. I promised him last night that I'd go out two days in a row, so I'm doing that."

"Jason doesn't count."

Damn, Raven thought. Sometimes having a best friend sucked because they knew you too well.

"Fine." She paused for a long time, and of course, Que picked up on it.

"Unless…"

"Unless what?"

"Unless you saw yourself a hottie and were too shy to approach." When Raven remained silent, Que knew she'd hit money. "Oh my god. Come on, Raven. What's his name?"

"Finn," she said quietly and grinned to herself. "But it's nothing. It's—I don't know what it is."

"Finn?" Que started laughing. "Oh, that's perfect. That is so completely perfect."

"Yeah, I knew you'd like that."

"What's he do? He's a surfer, right?"

"No, he's a marine biologist."

"Oh thank God. The boy's got a brain. He's hot though, isn't he?" Raven remained silent, and Que lost her mind. "Oh my God, he's the mothership, isn't he? A brain, a bank account, and a mad, bad ass. Come on now, my life's so boring. Spill."

"It is not," Raven said, laughing.

"Okay, well, my sex life is boring. Come on tell me. Tell me. Tell me!"

"I've seen him twice, and when I say see, I mean just that. We've only exchanged a handful of words and both times I came across as a complete idiot."

"I'm sure you didn't."

"Oh no? I stutter and can't even talk. I bump into things, just…and I blush, it's just stupid." Que laughed a little too long to be polite. Raven smirked derisively.

"So, he just walked away then?" Que asked.

"What? No, he just…"

"That's right, no, he did not. What's he look like?"

"Oh God Que, he's so beautiful. His hair's long, and he puts it up in one of those bun things."

"That's kinda hot." Que burst out laughing again.

"Right? And its super blond and he has a beard and the most incredible eyes I've ever seen. They honestly don't look human. He's got muscles everywhere."

"So he's like one of those droids?"

"No, it's all real." Raven laughed. "I could feel his stomach muscles, and they were very genuine."

"What! You could feel his stomach muscles? Girl, what'cha doin' with his stomach?"

"I was riding on the back of his motorcycle, Que." She could hear the strangest noise and then her friend gasping for control to breathe. "Que! Are you okay?"

Her friend had swallowed wrong at Raven's proclamation and was trying to cough up the coffee that traveled down into her lungs and spurted out across her kitchen table. When Raven realized there was no emergency, she started laughing too.

"I know, I know, but it was so fun. It took forever for me to decide to get on it but when I did, it was so much fun."

"Well, I'll be damned." Que smiled, then asked with tenderness, "When do you see him again?"

"Oh, I don't know if I will. We made no plans at all. He says he lives close by, so maybe I'll run into him somewhere."

"Well, he also knows where you live now."

"Que, you don't understand. This guy is so cool

and amazing looking. He could have literally anyone he wanted."

"That may be Rave, but last night he wanted you on the back of his bike. Don't forget that you got the girl power too. I keep trying to tell you that. Not to mention your own rock star life and bank account. What did he think about hangin' with *the* Raven Hunter?"

"I don't think he knew who I was. I look a lot different from all that right now. It's been like walking around in a costume."

"Even better, that means he likes you for you."

Raven just smiled and shook her head. She'd believe that when she saw it.

****

"Hawai'i relies heavily on imports for their energy." Stuart King counted on his fingers. "Petroleum, coal, and electricity prices here are higher than anywhere else in the US. In fact, it's doubled in more than thirty-nine of the fifty states."

Finn's eyes ran down the man in his flawless suit and determined it was official. He hated him. He glanced over at Alan Sunderland, the head of the SeaHunt Researching Institute, who merely sipped his coffee and smiled. A second man, Brian something-or-other, stood and Finn felt he was watching a tag team, hitting their stride.

"That's what makes this region the best and biggest case study possible." Brian walked to the window. "You have sun, wind, and wave technology at your disposal."

"Gentlemen, no one wants to come to Hawai'i and see a bunch of massive equipment in the water," Nate responded. Finn looked at him briefly, then back at the man for his response.

"Correct, but that's not what we're talking about," Brian said, holding up a finger and clicking a remote with his other hand, causing the lights to lower slightly.

He clicked another button, and a chart appeared. Finn took his ankle off his knee and leaned forward in his chair as the man took out his laser pointer.

"Hawai'i is one of the pioneers of wind power. In fact, on Oahu, they housed the largest wind turbine in the world in 1987. The MOD-five B was a three-point two MW turbine."

"Of course, now we have the Vestas, with a rated capacity of eight megawatts," Stuart interjected. Finn thought the man was giving himself a hard on and laid his back on the chair again.

"You are also one of the leaders in solar panel technology." Stuart continued. "In fact, Kaua'i instituted the largest solar project in all of Hawai'i two years ago with fifty-nine thousand solar panels across sixty acres of land. In fact, in 2012 Hawai'i paid for itself in just four years' time and returned a profit of four times the cost over its…"

"I'm sure we could go into great depth of the advantages of alternative energy, Mr. King." Nate could feel the man working into a lecture rivaling a fevered pitch. "However, we're here to discuss the tidal turbines you want to install here on Kaua'i."

"Ah, yes." Stuart cleared his throat. "Sorry, but this is really exciting stuff when you think about the possibilities." Finn rolled his eyes and exhaled forcefully as the man continued. "We want you to be the pioneers in the US again, for tidal technology." He clicked the button, and the next picture came to life. Brian stood and walked to the screen.

"Now, what you have is a tube tower cantilevered from a base point." Brian indicated the long pipe extending from the sea floor to the surface of the water. "On top is the hub and access point. In the center"—he indicated two blade-like propellers, slowly spinning— "are the turbines, which are located underwater."

"And those turbines." Finn nodded at the photo. "Exactly how do you keep them from hurting the sea life we have around here?"

Alan narrowed his eyes slightly at Nate and then at Finn but turned to listen to the presenters.

"Now, I'm glad you asked me that, Mr. Taylor," Stuart responded. "I understand you're passionate about your little sea creatures, and who wouldn't be?" He turned toward the photo as Nate snaked out a suppressing hand on Finn's shoulder.

"Think about it," he murmured to his friend.

"You see, these turbines look like wind turbines, but they don't move nearly as fast." Stuart continued, not seeing the exchange or the effect of his words on the biologists.

"Seawater is almost eight hundred times denser than air," Brian interjected hesitantly. It was obvious Finn's anger hadn't escaped his notice.

"Yes," Stuart affirmed, "and this is important because it means the rate of speed is so much slower." He looked over at Sunderland and said, "I do have some environmental impact statements here."

He handed them to Brian, who in turn gave them to the men. Finn, exasperated, looked down quickly at the statement, then spun it onto the table.

"These statements are for Britain, Scotland, Ireland, and France. Last time I checked none of them had the climate of Hawai'i."

"As I said, you would be moving into newer territory, and you have had a lot of success with..."

"Look," Finn sneered, "my little sea creatures, as you so ineloquently called them, can't even count fourteen hundred animals. It's a species one hundred percent indigenous to the United States and these islands. Twenty percent of those 'creatures,'"—he threw his hands up in quotation marks—"are here because of research, restoration, and refuge outfits, the bulk of which are located on Oahu. Kaua'i counts one, and you're looking at it."

The suits merely looked at him, perplexed at what to say.

"I can appreciate the enthusiasm for making us your little trial and error case study, or however the hell you put it," Finn spoke with venom, looking from one man to the other and trying to contain his fury. "But my animals can't recover if your product fails them."

"Finn," Nate said quietly.

"Hawaiian monk seals are some of the most curious marine mammals you'll ever meet, and the noise of those things alone might attract them enough to wander over."

"Mr. Taylor," Sunderland warned. Finn looked at him and addressed the rest of his remarks to his boss.

"We've talked about this before, Mr. Sunderland. The seals are cut up in boat propellers all the time and when we get new pups"—his thoughts drifted to Kaimi—"they aren't going to be able to stay away."

"Mr. Taylor, could you please step out with Dr.

Bowman? Thank you." Without waiting for a response, Alan turned his attention back to the presenters.

"All right." Nate stood, advising, "Finn, let's go."

Finn eyed his boss angrily and then the presenters before rising and aggressively pushing open the door.

"God damn it!" Finn yelled when he got outside, walking across the gravel.

"I know," Nate said.

"Oh, really? Really, Nate? Because I sure as hell didn't hear you saying anything in there."

"What are you talking about? I sure as hell did. Besides, it's already been decided, Finn. I told you that. Sunderland was just showing us all of this as a courtesy." Looking out at the water, he said, "You know, I'm pissed too." Then glared back at his friend. "But I don't get the luxury of spewing out whatever feelings I have every second I have them. Being pissed isn't going to help and just might get you fired. That wouldn't help any of them or me, and it sure as hell would suck for you. You wanna move away from Dee and your life to live on Oahu, in some aquarium?"

Finn turned and stared daggers, knowing what Nate said was true. He shook his head, and Nate pressed his lips together in a hard line.

"Look, why don't you take off. They'll be coming out here soon, and I'm sure you've had enough for one day. Not to mention, Alan probably doesn't want to see you right now. If you want to come over for dinner, Annie's cooking steaks."

"Isn't that a man's job, grilling steaks." Finn attempted some humor by poking fun at his friend's manliness.

"Ah well, she's better at it than me," the older man

revealed without shame. He walked up the stairs and opened the door before glancing back with a smirk. "See ya tonight, then." When his friend nodded, he went back into the building.

Finn drove back into town and made a spur of the moment decision that had him continuing to the beach and Raven's street. He wanted to see if he could make her nervous or, failing that, blush again.

Knocking, he received a text at the same time, so he lifted his sunglasses to perch on his forehead. The door opened, and he looked up, smiling until he saw Jason standing on the other side.

He was wearing linen trousers and a white linen collared shirt, unbuttoned and untucked to fly open across his smooth chest. Having also toed off his shoes, he walked barefoot and laid a forearm against the open door. The breeze billowed open his shirt like something out of a Hawaiian vacation TV commercial, causing Finn to grin roguishly. The guy just made it too easy.

"Oh hey, Jim was it?" Finn said, successfully irritating the man.

"Jason," he corrected, clenching his jaw. "Is this a freak of nature or are you stalking Raven?"

"Stalking?" Finn ran his eyes condescendingly down Jason's outfit. "No, I was here last night, when I gave her a ride home." He delighted in the look of sheer disbelief that crossed the polished man's face.

"I see." Jason regrouped quickly. "Well, I can speak for both of us when I say that was nice of you to do. What can we help you with today, Mr. Taylor?"

"Oh, you… Nothing. But I was gonna ask Raven to take a ride."

The manager looked past Finn to the motorcycle

and quirked an eyebrow.

"I think you may be overstepping the mark here, Mr. Taylor. One, Raven and I have a pretty close relationship that's been progressing as of late. And two, I'm quite sure hell would freeze over before she'd get on that thing."

"Hmm, well apparently, you need some skates. Maybe you can't tell 'cause of that breezy get-up ya got going on there, but she was on the back of that bike last night." The side of his mouth slid into a smirk as Jason evaded his gaze. "Funny too, but she never mentioned you once in that whole time."

Jason's gaze snapped back to Finn's and, seeing the truth there, wisely didn't comment. He lifted his chin and breathed in.

"I can see that you like her, Mr…"

"It's Finn."

"Right—Finn. I can see you like her. I like her too." Jason smiled, genuinely trying to appease him. "I've been with her for nine years now. We've gone through a lot together, and she's had a legitimately rough time of it lately." He narrowed his eyes for emphasis.

Finn spread his feet apart a little, crossed his arms over his chest, and lowered his head, pretending he was listening intently to the asshole.

"She isn't the kind of woman that says no easily, therefore can be easily taken advantage of. Maybe you'd be willing to move on from her?"

"Really? So, you're implying that I'm after what, exactly? Sex?" Jason smirked at this.

"Well, I'm quite sure, we both know that's on your mind, but no, I actually meant her money."

"Money?" It was Finn's turn to frown in confusion. "What money?"

"I think we're done here, aren't we, Mr. Taylor?" Jason said, somewhat nervously, as if he said too much and wanted the conversation over. Finn took a step forward, making it impossible to shut the door.

"I don't know shit about any money, and as far as I can see, you might want something with her, but in nine years you've been unable to close the deal. So, consider my oar in the water, Mr. Crockett."

Turning, he walked off the porch to his bike and threw a leg over, whistling. He kicked the machine to life and noticed Jason still standing in the doorway, maybe trying to figure out who Crockett was. Finn slid on his sunglasses and yelled over the engine.

"If you could tell Raven I swung by, I'd sure appreciate it."

As he turned the bike and raced away, Finn smiled. Maybe the day wasn't a total loss.

Chapter 9

Jason stood in the doorway, angrily staring after Finn. *Oar in the water indeed*, he thought with disdain. He was the one who put in the time with Raven. He'd been the sounding board when her overbearing asshole of a husband micromanaged everything she did. He tried to mentor her, pick up the pieces, gently coax and prod her into the direction she should go. He made it abundantly clear that he was ready for something more. Yet last night, she'd allowed a stranger to bring her home rather than him. Jason closed the door and went back to the contracts on the table, indignantly.

He'd been struggling with the language of them. Seeing only a handful of contracts over the years, the new agent had never had to read through them entirely. It was overwhelming and boring as hell.

The warm wind caught his short dark hair, blowing it back. Dark chocolate eyes looked out toward the ocean. There was no way he would admit to Raven that he was having difficulty and risk her losing confidence in him. He couldn't go to Donovan. The man would eat him for dinner upon hearing she wanted to change things up. He picked up his coffee and sipped, breathing in the delicate but deep aroma.

Looking down, he frowned over the papers again, knowing he'd have to tread very lightly when it came to transitioning her style. The one thing he had in common with Donovan was a refusal to allow much change to occur. She became a wealthy woman on her ability to turn other people's work into pop sensations. Her originals were too earthy and simple. Her fans may or may not follow the change of direction and tone, and he wouldn't gamble any of their futures on it.

Jason threw the notepad down, distracted from Finn's recent visit. Raven was into him too, he knew it. Maybe she just needed to see a little more of the fun and reckless side of him too. One thing he was entirely sure of was that he sure as hell wasn't going to tell her Taylor sought her company.

By the time the singer returned to the bungalow, she was laden with bags, so Jason ran out to help her unburden the car.

"What's all this?"

"Oh, well, I thought I'd make some dinner," she replied, smiling at her purchases. "It's been a long time since I cooked." She considered him and resolved to be gracious. "You're welcome to stay if you want."

"I want. What're we having?"

"Vegetable lasagna."

"Sounds great. Do you have some wine I can open to breathe?"

Reaching into a bag, she produced a Malbec. She turned all the bags over, and vegetables rolled out onto the countertops. As she began to organize and clean them, Jason poured out the wine and turned on some music.

The scent of her homemade red sauce and spices filled the air by the time they sat down to eat, lending and air of domesticity to the evening.

"So, I went over the contracts today for a couple of

shows, but I wanted to ask what the publicist thought of doing some of the early morning programs here? Stir up some interest, throw a bone to the outlying areas?"

"Oh," she quavered, "actually, I didn't ask. I just thought they could call from Oahu or wherever and the interviews would be really brief, if at all."

"Okay, well, I think it would be best to continue to run things through the publicist. There's a reason we pay her the big bucks."

"All right," Raven said, feeling a little chastened. She probably should have thought about that for the flow of the brand, then stiffened at the direction of her thought.

"Now on to other things," he said, laying the papers to the side, sipping some wine. "What d'ya say we get out of the house tomorrow, go to the other side of the island, maybe Hanalei?"

"Oh, sure, I guess so."

"We can go swimming or hiking, just have some fun?"

"The Kilauea Lighthouse is over there, and some trails."

"Perfect." His cell phone rang and his brows furrowed. "Sorry, I'm going to have to take this."

She waved her hand in dismissal. How many times had Donovan said those exact same words during dinner, movies, even sex? Relinquished to second place by a hunk of metal and plastic. She stood and rinsed the dishes, before placing them in the dishwasher while listening to Jason's voice grow heated and more proprietary.

"I said no, Donovan." Her head jerked up and walked over toward the man pacing the floor. Why the hell was Jason talking to Donovan?

"I realize that you managed her career for fifteen years, but that job ended the minute your marriage did. Raven is my responsibility now, and I don't think that's the right project for her." He held the phone away from his ear, and she heard Donovan's booming and condescending voice bellow out.

"I don't give a sweet fuck what you think, you ridiculous, incompetent fool. She'd love this project. It's to her base. Your job is to manage. Try managing to tell your client she has an exciting opportunity for a worthwhile cause." Then there was silence.

"Hello?" Jason looked over at her sheepishly and admitted, "He hung up."

"What was that about?"

"He's putting together a charity project. A musical event to raise money for homelessness in Seattle."

"What?" she asked incredulously. "Homelessness in Seattle? Since when did he care about anything like that?"

"I think his new girl... I think she wanted to do something."

"His new...oh."

Jason walked over to her and put his hands on her shoulders, rubbing them up and down.

"I guess he's trying to activate her career and wants to surround her with some big names to draw the crowd."

"So I would be helping my husband's mistress get her start under the guise of helping the homeless."

"Essentially."

"When is it?"

"The first of August, but..."

"When does he need to know by?"

"A week, but Raven, I think we need to consider every angle here." Taking her hands, he continued, "Is the first solo project you want to do for your ex-husband?" He raised a hand and brushed back her hair. She unconsciously leaned back and away from the gesture, and he dropped his hand. "Isn't that a little counterproductive? And consider the image."

"That's what I was thinking about." She stepped away. "Don't you think he'd let it slip that I was too spiteful to help the homeless? All because of some tantrum I was having about a silly little thing like an affair?"

Jason took a deep breath and looked down, seeming to ponder the new information.

"I think we have a week. Let me just slow this down and consider all the options. I'll come up with a solution. Okay?"

She nodded but decided it would be near impossible not to agree to do it, and she was quite sure her ex-husband knew that.

"Come on, let's go for a walk."

"No, it's okay." She smiled. "I think I'm just going to take a bath, and then I'm for bed."

"Just a quick one." He walked to her and held out a hand. Not having a valid excuse to reject the offer, she reluctantly took it, and they headed for the cliffs near the bungalow.

"Raven, you're starting out so good, trying to get out from under him, let's not go backward now."

"I know, it's just… It feels like our lives are so intertwined and I'm not sure how to get out of it."

"Don't worry. I'll take care of it." He squeezed her

hand, effectively stopping them both, and stepped forward to kiss her, but she raised a hand to his chest.

"I appreciate that." She looked down, trying to muster up the courage. "All your help." She looked at him now. "But one thing I do know for sure is that I can't have a relationship with anyone in the business, ever again."

"So I'll quit." He grinned, but she didn't grin back.

"I don't think we should have that kind of relationship, Jason." Feeling horrible, embarrassed, and ungrateful, she stepped back from his astonished face.

"Oh."

"The business is just part of it. I just don't want anything like that for some time," she rushed on, trying to soften the blow.

"Okay, well, I'll back off and give you some time." She closed her eyes and decided not to press it anymore as he asked, "Are you ready to go back?"

"Yeah." He walked her home and at the door, gave her arm a gentle squeeze. "Thanks again for dinner. Get some sleep, and I'll see you tomorrow."

"Okay, see you tomorrow."

However, early the next morning, Jason called from his connecting flight in Honolulu. During the night, his father had suffered a massive stroke and was in an ICU in Seattle. Hearing his broken, exhausted voice caused her contrition at dismissing him. She reassured him that business would be put on hold as he took care of his family. They said their goodbyes, and he was gone.

****

As Jason arrived at the hospital, Donovan sat at his dining room table with his usual slice of dry toast and cup of coffee. At fifty-four, he could grudgingly admit he'd been more father to Raven than a husband. A master businessman with a keen ear, he remembered the day he heard her play at that art show, so many years ago. Her horrible, short, choppy hair, big, trusting eyes, and that incredible talent. The man knew instantly she would be a star and make him a lot of money.

Initially, the object was to manage her, but because of her trusting nature, he soon understood the benefits marriage would bring. He'd have more control over her money and projects, and it certainly didn't hurt having a beautiful, nubile bride to proclaim as his own. But Raven hated to play the games needed in the entertainment world. Her damned brother, also knowing the success she'd enjoy, usurped his authority in the beginning and protected her future assets. Donovan had almost walked away, but Raven unknowingly called his bluff, when she sided with her twin on the prenuptial agreement. Though he wouldn't make the money he initially thought, he would make millions.

The even younger one on his arm now was dumb as a stump, but he wasn't doing rocket science with her. Her longevity would be short-lived. However, Donovan was going to make more money off her naiveté. Now he just needed enough people that owed him favors on board. To his way of thinking, that included his ex-wife, in the form of one lucrative career.

He thought it was ridiculous that she refused his continued services for promotion and empowered her utterly benign assistant as her new manager. However, now the man had impacted him, and that was not to be borne, so he dialed her direct line.

"Raven?" There was a moment of silence. "Raven,

are you there?"

"Ah, Donovan, yes, I'm here."

"Oh, wonderful. Are you enjoying your time there in the tropics? I know you've always wanted to go."

"Ah, yes, it's been lovely, thank you. How have you been?"

"I've been fine, thank you for asking." Enough, he thought and began. "I'm not sure if you are aware, but I tried to send a proposal to your new manager but have been unable to reach him."

"Oh, right. Well, his father had a terrible stroke last night, and he's actually probably just landing back in Seattle now, as we speak."

"I see, how unfortunate."

"That his father's sick or he's unavailable?" Raven asked.

"Excuse me?"

"Um, I mean, yes, it is," she said quickly as if realizing she'd said her thoughts out loud.

"Well," Donovan replied, letting it go because it was, in fact, the latter rather than the former. "If you're operating without a manager, I'll just have to speak with you, won't I?"

"Jason did tell me a little about your project."

"Splendid. I know it doesn't sound much like me, but I gained some insight when I stepped back and reflected on our failed marriage. Of course, fault could be found on both sides, but I was walking along First Avenue and in a contemplative mood. There I saw the homeless problem firsthand. I decided that a little altruism may perhaps be in order."

"Oh," Raven responded, sounding like she didn't believe him. "I had heard that you were setting up a concert to debut Amanda."

"Yes, I know Dell took it that way, but I informed him that just because she's performing too does not make it her show. In fact, she'll be singing the least, as she isn't the true talent, of course."

"Oh?" Raven sounded unconvinced. "Naturally."

"Raven, we have most certainly had our differences, dear. Obviously, living together and being married were one of them. However, I've been a benevolent benefactor, who's provided you a pretty resounding platform over the years, don't you think?"

"I, um, yes, I suppose."

"I would take it as a personal favor if you would give your consent and play to this cause. What do you think?" He heard her deep sigh and knew she wouldn't refuse him.

"Yes, all right Donovan." A slow smile crossed his face

"Splendid, I'll send the contracts to Dell then, shall I?"

"Oh no, Donovan, I'll…"

"Fine, fine. All right, enjoy your quiet time there, Raven. I'm sure it's doing you a world of good. Goodbye."

Chapter 10

A week later the day began warm and just got hotter. Raven's thigh-length sundress clung to her damp skin as she stood in line for a shave ice. Ordering a peach and vanilla treat, she slid some money over in exchange for the massive orange and white ball of ice. Slinging her beach bag over her shoulder, she approached a large outdoor market. Vendors laid out their wares of flowers, garden whirligigs, and all kinds of tropical fruits and vegetables.

She had just taken an enormous bite out of her shave ice when she bumped hard into an older woman and nearly sent her flying. Clad in a deep purple and orange floral muumuu, the older woman wore a large floppy hat encircled with real sunflowers. She turned around with bright bluebell eyes and a broad smile on her tanned, wrinkled face.

"Oh no! Oh, I'm so, so sorry." Raven laid a hand on the woman's shoulder, steadying her. "I'm so clumsy."

The woman started to grin but her smile froze, and face paled when the young woman touched her, causing Raven even more alarm.

"Are you okay? Oh my God!" She looked around wildly until she spotted a bench. "Here, let's...let's sit down here."

The older woman nearly tripped before collecting

herself and patted Raven's hand as she escorted her to the bench. Raven brought out two bottles of water one-handed from her bag, handed one to Dee, then sat down to hover over her.

"No, no dear, I'm quite all right. Right as rain, in fact."

"Are you sure?" Raven asked suspiciously, looking for signs of impairment.

"Oh yes, my grandson will be coming along in a little while. Want to keep me company?"

Surprised at the request but realizing she had nothing else to do and had nearly flattened the poor woman, Raven nodded.

"Good. Now, what's your name, dear?"

"My…oh, um, it's Raven. Raven Hunter."

"Are you really?" Old eyes twinkled and danced. "What an incredible gift it is to meet you. But my goodness, I can barely recognize you."

"Yes." Raven laughed. "I've been getting that a lot." She ran a hand through her long hair. "I guess I just needed something different."

"I guess you did. Well, you look lovely. Everyone here calls me Dee."

"Dee," Raven confirmed and considered the woman. "Do you live here on the island, Dee?"

"Yep, but I was born on Oahu. December seventh, nineteen forty-one, actually."

"December seventh?" Raven looked amazed. "Your poor mother must have been terrified."

"Oh yes, she was. My father was in the Navy, and he was on the Arizona when it went down. So, she lost her husband and gained a daughter all in one day."

"That's terrible about your father. What did she

do?"

"Well, as soon as she was able, she moved us here to Kaua'i. She was originally from Kansas and a long line of wheat farmers, as it happens. But she got bored with the lot of them and married herself a good-looking Navy man. Then they found themselves on the islands when he got transferred here."

"Why didn't she go back home?" Raven asked, taking another bite of her treat. "I mean, after he died."

"Well, by that time, this was her home, and though she couldn't bear to live on Oahu anymore, she still wanted to be close to my father. He's still entombed over there, in that ship."

"She never remarried?" Raven hung her head at how strange that would be, to never have real closure, or what she perceived as real closure.

"No, I'm sorry to say she didn't, but I've been known to keep a person on their toes." Raven grinned at her.

"So she moved here with her little baby girl. And after all these years you never wanted to leave either?"

"Child, look at this place." Dee gestured wide with her arms, fingers outstretched as if encapsulating the entire island. "Now who in their right mind would ever want to leave this?"

"Well, you have me there." Raven looked around and laughed. "So you said you have a grandson. Does that mean your family is here too then?"

At this Dee's face fell and Raven felt uncomfortable knowing she hit a nerve. When she started to say never mind, the woman peered at her and seemed to decide something.

"Well, I was married to a sugarcane field hand.

One day, Arthur went to work, and got crushed under the harvester."

"Harvester?"

"It's a big machine that cuts down the cane, strips it and cuts it into sections. That was hard for me, but that beautiful man also gave me a beautiful son, Matthew." She looked down at her water bottle and sipped. "He struggled without his daddy to bring him up in the world and never really coped well with it. He was just a little tyke when it all happened, but it still affected him greatly."

"That's terrible, Dee. What happened to him? Your son."

"Well, he was sixteen when he and his girlfriend found themselves in a family way. They got married and had my grandson. Matthew's wife was so young, just fifteen at the time and so naïve. When she discovered herself in a delicate condition, she wasn't prepared to be a mother and left them both."

"She left her little baby?"

"Went on to the mainland and haven't heard a word from her since. Matthew. Well, Matthew wasn't prepared to take on a small child alone either. He overdosed on some drugs and drowned diving off the rocks at Kipu Falls, over there in Lihue. That was many years ago now."

"That is so awful." Horrified, Raven shook her head.

"Yes, yes it was. It was a horrible time but from those ashes came my grandson, who reminds me of my Arthur. He's a wonderful, loving, and kind man, that's been my greatest joy since the day he was born."

Raven beamed at her and marveled at the ability of

the older generation, to be so open and free with themselves. That Dee could bare her soul with a total stranger in a matter of minutes, was incredible. Maybe it was the simple frankness with which she shared her life, but Raven understood this woman was strong. She was a warrior who learned how to make her way in the world because she had to. Raven instantly liked her.

"Well, now that's enough of that. Tell me all about you." Dee reached for the younger woman's hand and patted it. "What are you doing here? Oh, sweetheart, quick slurp; it's melting." Raven giggled and took another bite, letting the sticky sweetness melt in her mouth.

"Well." Raven thought for a moment. She had never learned to share herself with anyone other than Wyatt, Que, and Abby, so simply said, "I've had some changes in my life too, and I'm trying to figure which direction to go now." She watched Dee, trying to gauge how much of the tabloid gossip had reached her, regarding Raven's marriage and personal life.

"It's terrible to have to live your life on display, isn't it?" Dee replied as if she could read her thoughts.

"Yes." Raven laughed, relieved. "Yes, it sure is."

"How old are you?"

"How old am I?" she said, taken aback.

"Oh, don't read into it. I'm seventy-six. If an old bag like me can say it, you surely can."

"Okay," Raven said, laughing. "Well, I'm thirty-four."

"Thirty-four. Well, that is just perfect, isn't it?"

"Perfect?"

"Perfect." Dee patted her hand again. "Because my grandson is thirty-six, and you should have an escort here on the island." The color drained from Raven's face.

"Oh, no ma'am, I couldn't. No, please don't…"

"And look at that timing." Dee smiled, looking up.

Oh my God, Raven thought, the guy was right behind her now, wasn't he? She turned, thinking, *what in the hell am I going to do*? Her jaw dropped open when standing in the sun, was Finn. He looked down at the two women in puzzlement like the combination wasn't possible.

"Hello dear."

Dee held out her arm so Finn could help her up. Raven stood too, dropping her water bottle off her lap. Still not speaking, she bent to retrieve it at the same time Finn did; their heads slammed together and Raven lost the rest of her shave ice. This seemed to delight Dee immensely. Cursing, Finn picked up the water bottle and handed it to Raven, who slapped her hand to her forehead, now in agony.

"Sorry. Thank you, Finn." He turned his gaze to his grandmother.

"Oh, you two already know each other?"

"Yeah, we met the other night."

"Really. Well, Finn, I was just saying to Raven that she needed an escort to show her around the island." His eyes shifted back to Raven, who flamed bright crimson.

"No, seriously, I hadn't gotten a chance to say"— she turned to the woman now—"but I've got a lot going on, and I'm sure Finn does too. I don't think…" She smiled nervously at them both. "In fact"—she looked at her watch—"I've got to get going now. It was so fascinating to get to know you, Dee." Her eyes shifted to him, and she nodded. "Finn."

"Raven." He nodded back and watched her walk away appreciatively. Dee noticed him look over the top of his sunglasses and she elbowed him.

"Come on Casanova, stop looking at her bum and help me get some groceries."

****

Appreciating Raven's assets, he watched as she turned to look at a stand filled with ripe mangoes, then followed Dee. Twenty minutes later, he slammed the car door closed on her sedan.

"You sure you don't want me to help you get everything home?"

"No, no. You're going to go meet all your friends over at the Bowman's cabin, aren't you?"

"Yeah, they'd love to see you though. What if I help you get this stuff put away, and we drive out together?" He glanced up and noticed Raven getting into her car.

"No, it's fine. I'm on the water guy now."

"The water guy?"

"The badass." He'd been watching Raven drive away, but at this, he dropped his eyes back down to his grandmother.

"Badass? Who the hell are you talkin' about old woman?"

"The water god."

"Water… Oh, Poseidon, you mean?"

"Poseidon, yes. You called him a badass, and I'm finally on him now. So, go have fun, and I'll see you later." He kissed her cheek.

"Okay, I'll come in and see you if your lights on, otherwise I'll see you tomorrow."

Closing the door, he tapped the top of the car, indicating she could go, then walked over to his bike. He watched the direction Raven left in and hooked on his helmet. It was time to take some action, and he wasn't afraid to be the one to do it.

Chapter 11

Raven had just brought in the last load of groceries and returned to the car to retrieve her purse when Finn pulled alongside it.

"Hey." When she only blinked at him, he grinned more broadly. "Come on. I wanna take you somewhere."

"Where?" she asked, irritated that her first response wasn't an automatic no.

"It's a surprise."

"I'm not going on that," she said nodding at the bike.

"Yes, you are," he replied coolly, taking off his sunglasses and treating her to the play of colors in his beautiful eyes. "Can't get there otherwise. Besides, you said you liked it."

"I... No, I didn't."

"Well, you looked like you did. What exactly are you afraid of? Me?"

"No."

"Prove it."

Moving forward, he turned and removed his helmet from its clip. Pulling her closer, he brushed back her hair and secured it firmly on her head. Finn didn't take his gaze off her flustered face, but once he clasped the hook closed, he allowed his fingers to linger at her throat. She looked at the blond hair straying wildly around his handsome face.

"Come on," he said with a devastatingly sexy smile. "Live a little."

The implied challenge prompted her to go. She climbed on, and he scooted back between her legs, causing her to wrap her arms around his waist.

The dregs of afternoon melted into the evening as they traveled over roads made of concrete, then gravel, and finally dirt. Finn pulled up onto a large grassy mound filled with cars next to a veteran's cemetery. He helped Raven off the bike and held her hand as they walked toward Nate's weekend home. A multitude of people began to move from the dilapidated cabin toward a small bluff to watch the sunset. A warm wind swirled her hair and dress.

"Where are we?" she asked, but before he answered, a tall, lanky man with a somewhat homely, but kind face greeted them. With him was a beautiful, petite Polynesian woman in a sundress, not unlike Raven's.

"Hey, bud." The two men clasped hands, and the woman kissed Finn's cheek before they both turned to Raven.

"Hi, I'm Annie. This is my husband, Nate. And this"—she gestured behind them—"is our very well-loved cabin."

Raven took in the tiny Hawaiian woman. Her long, straight, ebony hair, glittered in the sun, as her cherubic face broke into a welcoming smile.

"Hi, I'm Raven. And it's so beautiful; what a fantastic view."

"Thanks, we like it. The cabin's been in my family for generations. Nate and I have a house over by Po'ipū

Beach, if you've ever been there." Raven's gaze bounced off Finn's, then returned to Annie's.

"Yes, I've been there. It's terrific."

"Raven, you look so familiar. Have we met already?" Nate asked.

"No, I don't think so. I've only been on the island for a little over a month."

"Where'd you come from?"

"Seattle."

"Rain to sunshine. I guess I don't have to ask what prompted the move," Annie joked, smiling over at the men.

"It rains even more on the north side, Ann," Nate interjected.

"Actually, no, I didn't move. I'm just taking a break from working," Raven said.

"Well, that must be nice. What do you do?"

"I'm a musician."

"Oh, that's...that's," Annie broke off, widening her eyes. "Oh my God! Raven!" She stared at her, a little breathless. "Wow, oh my God, this is so cool. You look so different." She took a step forward, to Raven's chagrin, and ran fingers through her blonde mane. "Your hair. It's so beautiful." The men looked at each other baffled, trying to understand what was going on.

"Oh," Raven said, running a hand down the length of it, never quite understanding a fan's insatiable need to touch her. "Thanks. I decided to go back to my roots."

"Nate, you're not recognizing her," Annie said, noticing the men's confused faces. "Her hair was black before. Raven Hunter, the singer."

Finn's face froze in recognition. His eyes scanned

her face, her hair, her body, and then back to her face. She glanced nervously at him. She supposed she was a complete one-eighty from the seductress in the glossy magazines, television, and stage, he probably envisioned. His inability to articulate suddenly caused her an unexpected jolt of pleasure.

"Wow, what an honor," Nate said, shaking her hand. "We love your music. Some of which we'll be playing tonight, in fact." He pointed upward as if the music playing was hovering there. "I understand you can play any instrument. Is that right? It must have taken forever to learn how to do that." Nate looked over at his friend in wonder.

"Actually, fortunately, it came pretty easy," she said, quietly eyeing Finn too. "I mean, I guess I'm just lucky because it came naturally to me."

"Oh hey," Annie said, excited, "the sun's going down. Would you sing something on the bluff?" Nate jabbed her in the ribs, and she looked sheepish. "Oh, I'm sorry, you just said you were taking a break, didn't you? I'm sure that's the very last thing you want to do. Please just forget I said anything."

"No, I'd love to," she quickly replied, suddenly desperate to escape Finn's incredulous stare. "It's so beautiful here but maybe," she added looking around, "we could just not say who I am?"

"Sure, I totally get it. Nate, run and get the guitar." Annie frantically pushed her husband away before the singer could change her mind, then turned back to the couple, saying encouragingly, "Come on, follow me and I'll take you over."

As Annie walked ahead, Finn grabbed Raven's elbow.

"You're Raven Hunter?" Disbelief flooded over his features.

"Yeah, remember, we met a few days ago?" she teased.

"Why didn't you tell me you're that Raven Hunter?"

"I didn't know it was a thing."

"You didn't know it was a thing? You're famous."

"Well"—she snickered again at the reversal of awkwardness—"one part of me is, I guess."

They walked up to a small clearing. Many guests were already there, looking out toward the setting sun.

At first, people paid little attention to the woman with the guitar, allowing the music to flow over them. Raven wanted to keep it simple, so she played one of her original songs with a haunting melody. It slowly captivated her audience, then blended her vocals to a slow, seductive song. She sang about being stuck in silence and afraid to use her voice in the world. As the sun set and the melody built, her eyes closed and absorbed the music. Finn leaned against a tree, arms crossed over his chest, mesmerized. The shy, insecure girl was gone, replaced by a radiant woman, confident in her talent and ability. Her voice was much more beautiful in person than recorded and he felt the connection.

For the next half hour, she just played music and watched the people interact with one another.

"Wow." Nate walked over to Finn and handed him a beer. "Of course you're dating Raven Hunter."

"I didn't know I was," Finn said, drinking from his bottle. "And I'm not…really."

"Oh no? Pretty captivated over here."

"She's singing, Nate."

"Right."

"I met her a couple of weeks ago, and this is literally the third or fourth time I've even talked to her. I didn't know who she was until you guys figured it out."

"Well, now you know, and you looked pretty spellbound." Nate watched as someone walked up to her and requested a song. "I'm going to go rescue her."

Finn watched him help Raven up, make excuses to the person requesting a new song, and bring her over to a table with the keg underneath it. He stood close enough to hear what they were saying but decided to hang back.

"That was really cool of you to do," he said to her. "Believe me, we appreciated it. Made the night a little more perfect."

"My pleasure. Do you do this every night or just on weekends? I heard watching the sunset was almost mandatory in Hawai'i."

"For sure." He chuckled. "We usually have an informal thing every week or two. Playing"—he gestured to the guitar—"or just listening to music, have a few games, a few laughs."

"Sounds fantastic."

Finn watched her interact with Nate, not a nervous gesture in sight. So, it was him, and that made him smile with tenderness.

"We'd like to think so," Nate said in response. "So, you're on vacation then?"

"Well," she replied, "a working vacation, at any rate. I have a concert in a couple of months and am going through a re-branding of sorts."

"A what?"

"Precisely." She smiled.

Finn tried to focus on what they said next, but a gorgeous, dark-haired, woman suddenly approached, who'd been trying to get his attention for weeks. Anita, was it? Or maybe April?

"Finn, am I really so unapproachable, that you can't even say hello?"

She still wore her floral sarong and white bikini top from the day. Her nipples poked through the fabric thanks to the chill in the air. He glanced down at them and back up into her extremely naughty eyes, remembering an adventurous night the year before.

"I wouldn't say that," he countered. "More like you can scare the hell out of a man."

Her laugh tinkled through the night, and she rested her hand on his forearm, in an entirely female gesture. He looked up from her, already bored with the game and looked at Raven, who stared back looking uncomfortable.

"Hey, sorry Anita. I've just got to go see Nate for a sec."

"It's April," she said, face falling.

"Yeah."

He left her sputtering and walked over to his friends.

"What do you do?" she asked the older man.

"I work with Finn at SeaHunt." He gestured to Finn as he walked up. "Primarily researching."

"The Hawaiian monk seal?"

"Yep." Nate grinned. "It doesn't surprise me that's one of the first things you know about Finn," he stated, glancing at his friend. "The seals are his babies. I should have shown you when it was light out, but if you look straight across the bay here, you'd see our facility."

"So, you guys have been friends for a while?"

"Well, you could say that. We met, jeez, has it been ten years ago already?" He confirmed with Finn, who nodded. "Been a brother to me ever since."

"I can appreciate that. I have a twin brother myself."

"Really? I've heard that twins share a brain or sense each other's thoughts or something. Is that total bullshit or does it really happen?"

"No, it can happen with strong emotion. With Wyatt, if he's having a lot of pain or really happy, I can feel it sometimes. Not like I know what's happening or can read his mind or anything, just an impression. A kind of positive or negative impression. That's the best I can describe it."

Annie approached the trio and handed out beers before taking Nate to say goodbye to some guests.

"So, that was pretty amazing—different," Finn stated. "I guess I thought you did—more—I don't know." He gestured with his hands, searching for inspiration.

"Just more," she confirmed. "You can leave it at that. I'm trying to get out of my old way of doing things. I never really liked that style."

"Why'd you do it then?"

"Um, Donovan. That's my ex-husband," she clarified. "He was also my manager and always said elaborate productions were the best way to grab a broader audience. I always wanted to do my own songs." She saw Finn's blank face and clarified, "The songs and music I do, did, for Donovan were all written by other people."

He sipped his beer, deciding not to like Donovan.

"And you hated that, right?"

"Loathed it. I wrote a lot of songs, but he never wanted to use them; too simplistic for mainstream or something. And the industry is changing. He wanted me performing to my base, all the time."

"Why didn't you tell him to fuck off?"

She burst out laughing.

"I couldn't say that."

"Why not?"

"Because he's the manager, he knew what he was doing."

"You're the talent."

"Yeah, but a lot of people have talent. He created the magic."

"Magic?" he said derisively. "He tell you that?"

"It's true."

"It's bullshit."

"It's not bullshit. How many records have you sold?"

"None, but I know a manipulator when I hear one." A leaf fell onto her shoulder, and he brushed it aside, looking into her eyes. "And talent *is* the magic, that's why they call it talent."

"What about you?"

"What about me?"

"You work with those seals. Nate said they're like your babies. Why seals?"

"I've been interested in sea life since I was little. Dee always took me to the tide pools. Later it was snorkeling and diving. Absolutely nothing was hands off with her." His heart tripped, and his eyes lit up. "When you start spending time with them, you realize how intelligent they are. Not just the seals, but whales, dolphins, all of them."

"So why focus just on seals then?"

"I was maybe thirteen when I saw a seal and her pup get tangled up in a net, that was just lying there, left on the beach. They couldn't get free and had no control. I always think about how terrified they were, and I couldn't help them. They were too far gone when help finally arrived. I watched them when they closed their eyes and died."

"So you decided to help the other ones live?" Raven asked, touched.

"Something like that." He pressed his lips together and exhaled. "But it's a lot harder than it looks. There's a lot stacked against them, especially right now."

"Why right now?"

"We're fighting against a group that…" Suddenly he scanned her face and realized he could get a second date out of it, so backpedaled. "Actually, you should come out there. I can just show you what we do."

"Really?" Her face lit up. "I've never done anything like that before. That would be so cool."

"Well"—he smiled, amused to see her reaction— "unfortunately, I'm a little swamped for the next few days. I've had to deal with some fallout at work. So, maybe we could go Saturday. I don't suppose you have a diving certificate, do you?" Her face fell as she shook her head.

"Does that mean I can't do it?"

"No, it just means I'm going to give you a number. Then before Saturday, I want you to get a couple of classes in so you'll have some basics. We won't be down long or too deep, but long enough that we can't snorkel." Considering her, he challenged, "So, you up for some homework?"

"Sure, it'll be fun. So, where… Should I meet you somewhere?"

"Give me your phone." Perplexed, she handed it to him. He punched in his cell number, let it ring so he'd have hers, then gave it back.

"I'll pick you up around, like, ten. That work?"

"Sure."

They stayed another hour before saying goodbye to the dwindling group. Walking back to the bike, Raven gave an involuntary shudder. The day had been warm but with the sun down, and only a sundress on, the night had developed a chill. She clasped her hands together in front of her and brought her arms to her sides in search of heat. Finn caught the movement and ran back to the house to retrieve a jacket.

Raven closed her eyes and sighed in ecstasy, as the jacket engulfed her, a visual that caused Finn's groin to tighten. After he secured her helmet, she crawled on behind him, wrapping her arms around his waist. The evening was dark, sweet, and silent.

By the time they returned to her bungalow, there was a level of quiet intimacy between them. Finn switched off the engine and walked her to the door.

"That was fun," she said quietly, taking out her keys and removing the jacket to hand to him.

"I'm sorry, what was that?" he teased, leaning in closer and bending an ear. He took the jacket from her and threw it one of the Adirondack chairs.

"Yes, it was fun." She breathed out a laugh,

watching the progress of the jacket, and lowered her head. "Ah, thanks for taking me; you have really good friends."

"I have phenomenal friends," he countered and took a couple of steps closer.

"Yes." She laughed again nervously, biting her lip. "You do." She looked up and saw how close he was. "You're very lucky to have them."

"Yeah," he said, his gaze slowly pivoting between her eyes and lips. "I am."

As he moved a little closer, she moved a little back. He grinned and placed a hand on the door. When she looked at it and tried to move the other way, he placed his other hand on the door, boxing her in. Her eyes lifted again, darting between his gaze.

"I-I don't think this is a good idea."

"Really? 'Cause I think it's a perfect idea," he replied, moving closer.

"No, I just mean… I don't really do this."

"Do what," he murmured, just inches from her face, holding her gaze.

"I…"

"You…"

****

He lowered his mouth to hers, softly. Hesitantly, her lips parted, then she deepened the kiss, moving in closer to him. She could smell the campfire and sea on him. He hummed low in his throat as she pressed in. Slowly he lowered his hands to the small of her back, and she felt them ball into fists in her dress. In turn, her arms moved up his back and along his spine. Their bodies pressed closer together, complementing each other perfectly. Opening her mouth more with his, Finn invited their tongues to dance. He moved his hands from her throat, down her shoulders and sides until lightly brushing a thumb over a taut nipple, causing her to gasp and move away.

"Ah, okay, um, thank you…for…that."

"Thank you? For what?" he asked, with a breathless laugh. "Kissing you or…?"

She looked mortified and merely nodded, unable to speak. He raised his eyebrows.

"I'm not sure that's ever happened before, but you're welcome…Believe me, anytime."

"No, I've, ah, I've gotta go."

"Raven."

"It was a great night…really great night."

She withdrew her keys, fumbling to get the right one out. Finn calmly plucked them from her fingers, selected the right one, unlocked, then opened the door for her. Handing them back, he leaned in and grinned before raising a finger to touch her cheek. She blushed and retreated, quickly shutting the door.

She leaned back against the door, reached over, and flicked on the porch light. She stayed there until she heard the roar of his bike sound and disappear into the night.

Chapter 12

Dee scrolled through the pages of text, pictures, and symbols, read columns and graphs, tried to comprehend all the information and connections of the unfamiliar words spoken by the deities. She knew if she could only see the names Themis had said, she'd remember them.

Tonight, however, only one name caught her interest. The goddess called her the daughter of Demeter, and she wanted to understand that, to understand her. She learned Demeter wasn't as well-known as many of the other gods and goddesses. She was the middle daughter of the Titans, Cronus and Rhea, and known as the goddess of agriculture and harvest.

"Guess the mystery's over, how come I can grow shit," she mumbled to herself and smiled weakly, then used her finger to follow the line of text, as she read out loud.

"'The virgin daughter of Zeus and Demeter, Persephone, was desired by many but it was Hades that coveted her from first sight. He abducted her to the Underworld and fed her pomegranate seeds, thus forever connecting her to the dark lord and his domain.'"

"What an asshole." Dee had a righteous sense of indignation on the part of both Persephone and her mother.

"'Demeter, consumed with worry, searched frantically for her daughter, halting the seasons, causing all living things to discontinue growing. Zeus, understanding that extinction was inevitable, instructed Hades to release Demeter's daughter. Hades told the great king that Persephone was bound to him for eating the seeds of the pomegranate, nourishment from the Underworld.'"

"So, he roofied her. How rude." She leaned back, disgusted, sipped her tea, then leaned back in, reading to herself.

Zeus told Hades that the seeds only bound her for four months. She was to return to her mother, also for four months. For the remainder of her time, she would be allowed free choice. Eventually, Persephone grew to love Hades and spent most of her time with him. Demeter mourned her daughter when she was away. It was then she created autumn and winter when nature slowly dies. As she anticipated her daughter's return, life would begin again and grow abundant, creating spring and summer.

"That's right," she said aloud, then read on another screen, about Themis.

Her sister, Rhea, gave Themis to her son Zeus. Themis became his first wife and high counselor, even after they parted. Often credited with fathering the Moirai, in actuality, Zeus was only their protector and were birthed by Themis alone. She bore six children in all, three Moirai that brought death and three Horai that brought the seasons or life.

Themis said she shared a bond with Demeter. She understood it now because they both bore children that dealt with life and death. She looked up Themis and was startled to see a stone depiction of the woman that had floated in her bedroom.

"Life and death." She frowned. "Maybe because they lost their children to something evil."

She glanced up onto the wall where a picture of Matthew sat on the grass playing with Finn, in brief, happier days. She blinked and realized she lost someone she loved to evil too. Dee looked back at the computer screen, vision growing fuzzy with fatigue and tears. She saw a section labeled Demeter and Poseidon, so she quickly scanned the text.

The god of the sea desired Demeter and sought advantage, as she mourned the loss of her daughter. Evading his advances, she took the form of a horse to hide amongst his spirit animals. Discovering her, he took the form of a stallion and mounted her, giving her two children.

Dee sat back, disgusted again. What was it with these gods? Sex, rape, abduction, to say nothing of incest? Maybe the lot deserved some fiery hell. At the very least she knew some of the connections and surprised herself by yawning profoundly. Looking one more time at the website, she noticed a word that was becoming repetitive. It was also a word that Themis had used. Dee's finger hovered over the mouse to continue but then heard Finn's bike and didn't want him worrying over her light. She switched it off and watched darkness close in on the word *Moirai.*

Chapter 13

Finn knocked on Raven's door at five to ten on Saturday morning. She opened the door, then ran back toward her kitchen.

"Hi, sorry," she yelled. "My phone. Come in." She grabbed her cell off the counter. "Hello?" she answered breathlessly. "Jason—how's your father?"

Finn glanced over noncommittally. Her long golden hair was secure in a ponytail and cascaded through the back of a baseball cap. She wore a white tank top under a blue and white striped sweater and khaki shorts. She was packing something into a red and white cooler, her well-toned legs moving purposefully, as she cradled a cell phone to her ears.

He walked around her space, noting the décor and other items that made up her temporary life. The only thing he saw that seemed well lived at was the piano. There was a multitude of staff sheets and scratch pads containing music and lyrics scribbled all over their surfaces. A half-filled coffee cup sat on one side of the bench, while a half-filled glass of wine sat on the other. Her voice wafted back into his thoughts.

"Oh, that's at least good, right?"

He caught her watching him wander around the living room, and she quickly turned back to the cooler. Smiling, he walked to the patio where a hot breeze blew his board shorts and warm, buttery-yellow tee shirt, against his body. He continued to look out over the vista, anticipating the day, as Raven's call ended. Walking out to meet him, she explained the medical emergency and update that the man had graduated from ICU to the med-surge floor.

"That sucks but good he's doing better."

"Yeah, it is." She looked around. "So, I made sandwiches. I didn't know if we were stopping anywhere."

She looked at the cooler and then at him, as he approached. Her eyes seem to battle for what she wanted. Finn took her face in his hands and kissed her gently. Christ, he could get lost in her all day. He moved back and encircled her waist with his arms.

"So, hi."

"Hi." She breathed out a laugh and smile.

He leaned in to meet her lips again with his own. Her fragrance permeated his senses, and the softness of her lips caused him to want more. He ran his tongue seductively across the inside of her bottom lip, and she shivered. Raven placed a hand on the back of his neck and applied more pressure. The kiss became harder to control, and his body responded. He knew the instant she felt him hard against her because she tensed and pulled away, breathless.

"Why are you constantly moving away from me?" he asked her, exasperated, and hooked a hand on the back of his neck.

"'Cause you're confusing me."

"Well, that's a mutual thing, darlin'."

"Can't we just, you know, be like friends?"

"I'm feeling pretty friendly right now." She laughed before she could stop herself.

"I mean can we just take a step back."

"Yeah, well, ya got that down real well." He started toward her, but her next words stopped him.

"I just…please, I'm not ready."

Furrowing his brow, he took a deep breath and wondered if he'd just been reading her wrong the whole time. If she'd been hurt or scared, he didn't want to push her, so decided a day on the water would have to be enough, for now.

"Okay then," he said, quickly collecting the cooler and her beach bag. "Let's pack this up."

****

Relieved that Finn had taken a step back, she took a deep breath and followed, as he walked to the door. The truth was she didn't trust herself. It always felt like her choices and ideas were bad ones. Donovan had taken her virginity yet criticized her inexperience in bed. Often he would call her dull or lacking invention if he couldn't achieve orgasm. When she did try to take the initiative, he would make fun of her. To Raven, her public persona always felt like a lie. She could never understand how Donovan told her one thing in the bedroom but played up her sexuality to the public. In fact, almost being naked onstage in front of thousands of people had become easy. It was the one-on-one that was terrifying. She worried that the celebrity was what Finn thought he was getting. After the initial chemistry wore off and they faced each other in the bedroom, he would discover she had no seductive secrets at all, and she would be humiliated all over again.

They drove the twenty minutes to Nawiliwili Harbor to board Finn's twenty-nine foot Sunracer and were soon motoring slowly out of the harbor. She handed him one of the coffees she'd bought from a local stand, then gazed out upon the open water, beyond the levee.

"This is a pretty amazing research vessel."

"No." He chuckled. "This is mine. Our boat for SeaHunt is bigger and less aesthetically pleasing." He looked behind him for boat traffic and smiled at her look of serenity.

"Where are we going?"

"Over to Honopū Beach," he replied, setting the temple tip of his glasses in his teeth as he maneuvered the boat, making a few adjustments. "Have you heard of it?"

"No, is it famous? It seems like every famous tropical movie ever made was done here."

"Well, that's true," he confirmed, chuckling. "And this one won't disappoint either. Did you ever watch the king of all apes movie?"

"Of course."

"You know where they first get to the island and the girl runs up the beach, through the archway?"

"Yeah."

That's the beach we're going to. I thought we could move faster to get over there, have some lunch and stuff, then take it easy on the way home. Sound good?"

"Sure, that sounds great."

"You did bring a swimsuit, right?"

"Yeah, underneath."

"Okay, hold on," he advised as they cleared the harbor.

Sitting down on a bench seat, she held on tightly to her coffee as they sped across the water. While he drove, Raven watched him sitting on top of the backrest of his seat, his sunglasses shielding his eyes and the wind whipping his hair around audaciously. His tee shirt lay flat against his body, and his smile was boyish. He loved it, she decided, and looked back to the water, grinning herself.

As they approached Port Allen, Finn slowed the boat and pointed out the SeaHunt research facility, their vessel, and Nate's cabin from the water.

"Is there a reason the facility and boat aren't in the other harbor?" Raven asked.

"There isn't a real reason except for both Nate and I live on the south side and the seals really like Po'ipū Beach."

"When was the facility built?"

"We've been running for about seven years. Nate was on Oahu working as a biologist for the main operation when I first met him. Then he and I actively sought out funding, grants, donations, basically anything we could get to build a facility out here."

"If you didn't have it, would you have been able to live here?"

"No, I'd probably live primarily on Oahu. It would've sucked because Dee needs me here."

He picked up speed again, and they progressed around the beach line, talking about their home cities and how remarkably different each was from the other. He pointed out the PMRF, where the Navy did their missile testing. As they rounded the corner and approached the beach, Finn slowed the boat and cut the engine.

"Whew, a little fast but not a bad view."

Raven looked up at the profoundly corrugated

cliffs and valleys of the awe-inspiring Nā Pali coastline. It looked surreal and majestic, stealing her breath away at its sheer beauty and magnitude. Mouth open, she looked over at Finn and felt like she had the first moment that she saw him—overwhelmed.

"So, if you look over there," he said, seemingly oblivious to nature and pointing to a small beach before the larger one, "you'll see my favorite girl."

Smiling eagerly, Raven stood up and tried to see where he was pointing, not being able to mark the partially hidden seal. Finn grabbed her hand and pulled her in front of him, so she was in the same line of sight. He rested his chin on her shoulder and pointed straight out.

"Alaula."

"So, I'm assuming Ala …Alaloo is a seal?"

"*A-low-la.*" Finn chuckled. "And yes."

"Oh God," she exclaimed, finally seeing the pair. "Look at her little baby. How sweet!" She looked back at Finn, who was grinning proudly. "Okay, so Alaula, what does that mean?"

"It means 'light of early dawn.' She was born about six years ago at sunrise."

"Were you there?"

"I was. I named her."

"Aw." Raven melted a little. "And she had a baby?"

"A pup, yep, about a month ago. I named him too. Kaimi, the seeker."

"The seeker? Why that?"

"When he came out he just started looking around. He was trying to find his mom to nurse and couldn't." Finn laughed as if remembering. "He must have tried everything until he found the right thing to suck on."

"So it's not instinctive?"

"No, it is, it just took him a little while."

They remained as they were, except he had wrapped his arms around her waist and she instinctively leaned back against him.

"Can we go closer?" Raven asked.

"I'd rather not. Moms are protective of their pups and can get easily stressed out if they feel threatened. They also tend to get weaker as the weeks go on."

"Why?"

"Sorry, I'm used to researchers. When the mom has a pup, she doesn't feed again for anywhere between five and seven weeks. Everything is about her offspring and getting them strong and healthy. Only about twenty percent survive to reproductive age."

"Because they starve?"

"No, mostly people messing with them, but also fishing nets and equipment, waste runoff into the water and eating stuff they're not supposed to."

"What do you mean?"

"Like when they see a plastic grocery bag floating in the water, they think it's a jellyfish and try to eat it. So, basically man-made dangers."

"Like on the beach that day."

Raven turned her face back toward him, but he buried his face in her shoulder more and breathed in, causing her to become aware of their closeness

"Yeah."

She turned back to watch Kaimi nurse.

"It's because they're cute, right?" She stepped away and walked to the bow, sitting down on the forward cushions. Finn followed suit and put his hands behind his head, leaning back against the windshield. "Why people want to touch them, I mean."

"Probably, but moms don't like their babies to be touched, not unlike birds. Some will leave them behind if they're messed with too much. They want them to smell like they're supposed to." She looked over and watched his jaw clench.

"You love them."

"Probably," he divulged without looking at her but smiling with tenderness.

"So, you guys only help them out when they're distressed?"

"It depends. Most anything that's natural, we let happen. So, if they struggle with birth or something, we tend to leave them to it. But let's say they have a hook in their mouth or they need to be tagged, or medical care, then we'll help them with that." He looked out into the water. "We're pretty limited on what we can do here because we don't have a refuge or rehab place for them. We're primarily research."

"So what's happened with your work that they're being threatened more?"

Finn got up angrily and moved to the cooler for a beer. He popped the top and offered one to Raven first, who took it.

"See, the world's changing and everyone's looking for alternative ways to save money, create new energy, and try new things. Don't get me wrong that's a good thing, real good." He sat back down, facing her.

"But?"

"But we had this meeting the other day, and they want to put in these underwater tidal turbines, in an effort to provide more natural energy to the islands.

Which is all great, but they can't say how it'll affect sea life around here. My point is, maybe we put a little more time into researching possible harm to the animals and ecosystem in the islands before putting a lot of them in. But my boss feels he has enough information."

"Nate?" she asked, surprised.

"No. Technically he's my direct boss, but it's our boss, Alan Sunderland."

"How can these wave things harm the animals?"

"A lot of animals out here are incredibly curious. Those machines make noise, create movement. They have underwater moving parts—blades—that they can cut themselves on. The underlining point is, we don't have enough information to be confident in their safety. We need more research."

"But it's not just that, right?" she asked, sipping her beer.

He glanced at her and inhaled deeply.

"No, and it's not even just that people are curious. There are some sick sons of bitches that actively kill them."

"Why?" she asked, horrified.

"I don't know. Maybe the seals eat their catch, and the men live off what they capture. Or you might have a native that doesn't believe they belong here. Many feel they were brought by man and aren't indigenous. Who cares if they become extinct—it's nature's way." He sipped his beer again. "You've also got a lotta of rich people who don't like it when we cordon off the beaches. They think it's an eyesore." He took a deep breath. "Many people here love the sea life and want to protect them. They can be a great asset to us. But it's definitely a hot topic on the islands."

"Do you cordon the beaches off to keep people away?" she asked.

He leaned back, adjusting the pillow behind him, then stretched out his legs in front of him. He crossed them at the ankle, and then drank from his bottle again.

"Yeah, there's a group that got started here on Kaua'i, and when someone calls in a sighting, they set up barriers and man them until the seal goes back into the ocean to feed at night. There are around fourteen hundred monk seals left. A percentage of those are living because of what we do. Otherwise, they'd be dead too."

"So do I even ask how your meeting went with them? Are they moving forward?"

"Yeah. They are." He stared out at the mother and her pup, running a hand down his beard.

"I'm sorry, Finn." He closed his eyes and shook his head as if trying to clear it and the mood.

"So." He grinned at her. "Get certified?"

"I'll probably be able to after this."

"Good for you; you're going to love it. Wanna go swimming?"

"Here?"

"Sure. I won't tell if you won't."

He walked to the stern and kicked off his flip-flops, drained his beer, and took off his tee shirt, muscles flexing and contracting with the motion. Strong shoulders and an incredibly sexy chest caused a streak of lust to vibrate down Raven's middle. He threw the shirt on the nearest seat, then turned to see if she followed suit.

"Come on," he said, smiling, "It's okay, we aren't gonna stay long. It's hot."

She stood and turned her body away from him, unzipping her shorts. He sat down on the edge of the boat wall, watching her. His eyes looked hungry, and by the time she peeled off her own tee shirt, she could see his jaw clench and Adam's apple move in his throat.

Quickly standing, Finn gathered their gear and attached the BCD and regulators. He finished by hooking the small masks and consoles to the side of the packs. After checking the oxygen levels, he helped Raven into her gear before putting on his own.

"Ready?"

"As I'll ever be."

They jumped in, and Raven entered a new world. The bright aquamarine water danced around them like silk. She looked up and saw the sun overhead, shooting beams into the water, essentially lighting their way. Exotic fish of every size and color parted around them, and it wasn't long before two of Finn's favorite animals approached them.

He pointed to their back flippers where they were tagged, usually referred to by a series of letters and numbers. The seals, in turn, playfully zoomed around the bubbles the couple produced. Raven loved how graceful and beautiful they were underwater.

One seal approached her, coming so close she could see a fuzzy outline of herself reflected in his eyes. The animal's perfectly domed head and long whiskers surrounded a permanent smile. As another seal approached, they played roughly with one another, until moving off to scratch their backs on some rocks.

Occasionally, she'd watch Finn. His energy was not unlike that of the seals. The sea life seemed to congregate around him, and he looked euphoric. She imagined most of these kinds of dives were work-related, so the freedom of just interacting must be fun.

They splashed and swam for about an hour before returning to the boat. Once onboard, Finn grabbed two, gallon jugs of water and gave one to Raven. When she looked at him quizzically, he poured the contents over himself washing away a lot of the saltwater, so she followed suit. After cleaning and drying off, they sat in the warm sun, with the lunch Raven packed.

"So, going down there, is it hard not to work?"

"More like at work, it's hard not to play."

"It seemed like it. That one got so close. His whiskers were so cute."

"They are." He laughed. "Their whiskers are their radar. They're sensitive to vibration."

"That's how they find food?"

He nodded, taking a bite of his sandwich.

"Especially when it's close by and in the dark."

"How old were those guys?"

"About fifteen and seven."

"Wow, how long do they live?"

"Mm, about twenty-five, thirty years." Finn threw his paper towel onto his plate, then taking hers too, threw them in the trash. "So, you ask a lot of questions but don't talk much about yourself. Why is that?"

"I don't know. I guess I'm just private."

"How did you get started singing?"

"The streets."

"The streets?" His brows creased like he was trying to process the new information. "What were you doing on the streets?"

"Oh, it's a long story."

"We have a pretty long ride back." She only shrugged noncommittally, so he looked down, then out to the water. "Okay, so you wanna get outta here?"

"Sure."

They talked about Kaua'i and Dee. She asked him about his upbringing and college life. Their conversation was easy and effortless. So, when Finn tried again, several hours later, her guard was down, ever so slightly.

"So, you told Nate you have a brother, a twin."

"Yeah." Raven smiled. "Wyatt."

"Who else is missing you back home?"

"My best friend, Que."

"Que? Is that her real name?"

"No." Raven laughed, "Her name is Raquel, but she hates that. She's always just been, Que. She finally officially changed it."

"Hmm, Que."

"She has a seven-year-old daughter named Abigail, Abby."

"How did your folks come up with your name?"

Deciding they were once again moving into territory she didn't wish to enter, Raven opted to try and distract him.

"Um, I'm not sure. I never asked. Oh hey!" She pointed to a familiar beach. "Po'ipū, right?"

"Yep. Okay, come here." He moved away from the captain's chair with decision.

"Why?" she asked suspiciously.

"'Cause you're gonna steer."

"No."

"Yep."

"No!" she yelled in panic when Finn grabbed her

hand and pulled it to the wheel.

"Come on, it's easy." Moving her in front of him, he reached around and guided her hands, showing what instruments to watch for and what etiquette to use with other boats. "I'm going to get something, just go straight."

"Wait, what? Finn? You're gonna do what?"

Knuckles turning white, she gripped the wheel, afraid of a massive tsunami or freighter appearing out of thin air. He walked to a container and withdrew a bottle of wine. She smiled.

"If you steer the boat, I'll open that for you." She gave him a radiant smile and tried to bat her eyelashes.

"Chicken," he accused, switching places. She simply laughed. "See over there?" He pointed to a ridge, as he guided the boat into Keoneloa Bay. "The beach is Shipwreck Beach, and the Māhā'ulepū trail runs through here. If you're in the mood to hike, it's pretty cool."

"Is it a long hike?"

"It's about three or four miles, roundtrip. It's one of Dee's favorites."

Finn stopped the boat and dropped anchor in the bay, then walked back to her and took the glass of wine she offered.

"So what else about you?"

"What about me?" she sighed, slightly exasperated.

"Why didn't you let me know who you were?"

"I did." When he just looked at her, waiting, she admitted, "Sometimes it's nice to be just, unknown. You know—anonymous."

"I get it. That why you changed your looks?" She ran a hand nervously down her hair.

"I, um…"

"Don't get me wrong, you look a helluva lot better," he observed.

"Really?"

"All that other stuff seems over the top, now that I kinda know you."

"Yeah," she said, relieved. "I never liked it."

"Why'd you do it then?"

"Donovan said it's what sells."

"Right," he said, sipping his wine. "Donovan."

He looked out as the sun fell inches from the surface of the water and held out a hand. "Come here and look at this."

She walked over to him, and he took her wine, setting it on the floor with his. He sat down and opened his legs so she could sit down between them. Then wrapping an arm around her waist, he brought her back to recline against his chest. He handed her wine back to her, then took his. She wasn't sure if it was the wine, the sunset, or just content to be with him, but she released her guard and lived in the moment.

She began singing a song she'd written years ago, each note flowing into another, the way silk would sound if it were music. She was content.

A couple of hours later, they arrived back in the harbor. After cleaning out the boat and changing in the restroom, they drove back to the bungalow.

A warm wind picked up and carried the sound of the waves. Finn's gaze never left hers, as he moved to stand in front of her.

"Easy," he murmured, approaching her like a skittish colt, and cupping a hand around her neck. He drew her to him so that only their lips touched, then waited. The next move would have to be hers. Raven stepped closer and encircled her arms around his neck and drew him to her.

Chapter 14

Finn kissed her cheeks and eyelids, then hovered over her mouth before gently biting at it. He kissed her throat and collarbone, as her hand moved gingerly down his back. On a low groan, he hugged her more tightly to him and lightly fisted a hand in her hair.

She smelled the sea on him, as her lips parted and deepened the kiss, inviting his tongue to intertwine with hers. His body tensed when her hand smoothed over the curve of his ass. To him, it was as if the simple act had lain a hot wire on his central nervous system.

Slowly, he walked them backward toward her room. Reaching a wall, he stopped and pressed her against it, allowing his hands to move over her. Finn cupped a breast, then kneaded one erect nipple through the fabric of the tee shirt. As if impatient for more, he bent to take it into his mouth. Using his teeth, the sharp punch of pleasure caused her to go wet immediately. She moaned, placing hands on the sides of his face to keep him there and drew in several sharp breaths.

Raven's eyes glazed at the intense sensation and long liquid pulls of need. Mouth open, heart racing, her gasps made her light-headed. He stood and buried himself in another kiss, as they held hands on either side of her head, interlacing their fingers. She could feel herself slipping and had to stop this, or soon she wouldn't be able to. However, feeling his heartbeat throb wildly in his chest had her pausing. Raven's body sizzled with desire, and when his erection pressed hard against her, she wanted desperately to touch his flesh.

Opening her eyes, she glimpsed herself in the mirror, shocking her into realization. Panic set in like an icy wave as she felt her need and watched him all but feast on her body. She knew what came next. Humiliation.

"Wait."

"No." He expelled his breath and almost pleaded. "Please... God, come on Raven, don't say wait."

He laid his forehead on hers, breathing hard, and she almost obeyed from the simple need in his voice.

"No, I need you to wait a minute."

On an oath, he stepped back and looked at her with eyes so wild and vivid they almost glowed.

"I-I don't want this." She stepped to the side as he laughed sardonically.

"The hell you don't."

"Okay, well, I'm not acting on it."

He closed his eyes and jammed his hands into his pockets, slightly wincing as the fabric stretched hard against his erection, apparently painful in its captivity. He removed them again quickly.

"Why?" he asked with complete exasperation. Trying to move toward her, she backed away in fear, so he lowered his head with what looked like confusion and defeat.

"I'm sorry," she pleaded and tried to step toward him, but he held up his hands.

"No... Don't."

He turned around and walked over to the open patio door to look out at the darkness. He ran both hands through his hair, then left them locked behind his head and puffed out a breath. The soft waves in the distance lapped against the hard lava rocks, mimicking the couple themselves. Finn pressed his lips together in a hard line and turned around.

"Look, I have no idea what's going on. Sometimes, it's like you hate me, sometimes I think you like me."

"I do like you," she said quietly.

"Then what the fuck is this… Games?"

"This…I…this isn't for me." She gestured between them. "You don't want me."

He looked at her incredulously, then unconsciously glanced down at the large bulge in his pants, causing her to as well, and blush. He ran another hand through his hair and raised his head again, shaking it in disbelief, then looked back at her.

"The hell I don't."

"No, you want one part of me that I'm unwilling to give, so that makes you want it more."

"So, what then, are you playing some kind of fucking head game with me?" he snapped, angry now.

"No!" she exclaimed emphatically. "Of course not, I wouldn't do that. I'm just trying to tell you, it's a waste of time for you."

"My time." He shrugged. "How are you going to tell me what I want?"

Lowering her head, she leaned back against the wall, defeated. He walked to her and placed his hands on the wall, on each side of her head. He laid his lips on her forehead and spoke.

"You want this too. I know you do Raven."

"I…"

Finn released a hand, took her chin, and tilted her

face up to his.

"You can be nervous, but you can't be scared." He gently jerked her chin. "Look at me; am I really that scary?"

Raven nodded her head, then looked away at his irritated scowl.

"I'm just not very good at sex," she admitted, mortified.

"That cannot be possible," he insisted.

"It is," she yelled, embarrassed and angry. She pushed him away, hard, and walked to the patio door. "Look, I don't know how to do this." She shrugged her shoulders and lifted her arms in frustration. "Donovan was the only man I've ever been with, and he told me."

"Told you what?"

"That I'm terrible at this!" she yelled again. "It's why he left. He said I was boring. That I sucked at it. He had to go to Amanda because she knew what do to and I didn't." Her eyes flashed on his. "Is that a turn on for you, Finn?"

She couldn't believe the level of fury that bubbled up inside her or that she had just yelled at him. Baffled, she looked up and saw him grinning at her.

"How old is Don Juan?"

"What?"

"He's older than ya, right? A lot older?"

"So what?"

"So, Donovan's a dickhead. An old man fuckin' a young naïve girl, because she wouldn't know any better if he had a limp dick. For Christ's sake look at you Raven. Boring? Are you fucking kidding me? He didn't know what the hell he was doing." Finn smiled and strode over to her. "I promise you, I do."

She felt so stupid and her eyes stung with tears. He picked her up without another word and wrapped her legs around his waist before walking her back in the direction of her room.

"People think I'm something I'm not."

"Is that what you're worried about?" When she only nodded, he set her down gently next to the bed, then pressed his lips to her forehead. "I only know this Raven. I don't even know who the hell the other one is and quite frankly, I don't want to."

Untucking her shirt, he pulled it over her head, causing her hair to fall in silky waves, settling messily on her shoulders. His eyes darkened, and he shook his head a little, at the scraps of rose-colored lace and silk covering her. The final barrier.

"This one is definitely more than enough to keep me off balance. Okay?"

He kissed her softly again and moved his hands back to her face. She wanted to touch him but hesitated and dropped her hands, looking up dejectedly.

"I don't know what to do."

Finn smiled with tenderness and removed his tee shirt, reached for her hands, and placed them on his chest. The springy, golden curls whorled across the muscles and planes. As a look of supreme concentration crossed over his face, she shyly explored him. She tentatively kissed his chest, then ran her cheek over the soft hair. His fingers played lightly over her skin and slid through her own silky blonde mane.

He leveled his eyes with hers, and slowly but deftly unfastened her bra and let it fall to the floor. She swallowed audibly and was sure he could feel her heart beat frantically in her chest. Only then did he pull away and lower his gaze to her. Somewhere deep in his throat, he hummed. Looking so long and intensely at her, Raven looked anywhere but at him and finally, crossed her arms over her chest. Gently, he pulled her hands down and replaced them with his mouth for several moments before laying her on the bed.

"You are perfect, Raven." He kissed her collarbone. "Your body." He kissed her neck. "Your face." He kissed each of her eyelids, then looked down and grinned. "Your breasts." He kissed between them, then met her gaze. "It's all pretty incredible."

Relieved, she sat up, unfastened and removed his jeans. He seemed to rejoice in the release of restraint. Finn moved forward, causing her to lay back and close her eyes. She felt the exquisite pleasure of his mouth, drawing her nipple in, and the sensations of each new touch. He ran a tongue down to her navel and circled it.

Kneeling on the bed, between her legs, he gently moved them apart to fall open. His fingers deftly entered her, slowly moving in and out; her eyes closed and she purred deeply within her throat. When he removed his fingers and replaced them with his mouth, she quivered at the new, glorious sensation. There was a kind of pressure building inside her. Something so deep and immense, she whimpered.

"Finn, I-I need…"

"Shh, it's okay baby. I know what you need."

He spread open her folds and probed her with his tongue, concentrating on the tiny nodule center. When he sucked hard, Raven jerked, unaware the amount of sensation was possible as it built on itself like a fever. She screamed out, feeling as if her heart exploded and every cell of her body went rigid.

As the sensitivities peaked and burst within her, Finn opened her legs farther and entered her with one aggressive thrust. Her eyes flew open and a primal noise escaped her. His fullness caused even more friction, immediately creating a need to build within her again. His engorged cock rubbed hard and rough against her clit, and his hips pistoned against hers. Eyes opaque, she watched him, watching her, with dark, stormy eyes. Raven stretched around him, until her body once more built a delirious pressure and seemed to explode a moment before his. She felt him pulsate strong and deep within her, gaze still on hers, bodies tensed in frozen suspension.

Finn tried to keep his weight off her but seemed to lose his ability to support himself. He rolled to the side of her and left a hand on her stomach, groaning.

"Holy fuck," he said, breathing hard and staring at the ceiling. "Don't ever let anyone say that you aren't good at that."

She was breathing hard too and tried to wrap her brain around the possibility that she may have just experienced her first and second orgasm ever. Finally understanding what she'd been missing all those years with a selfish lover, she laughed.

"I didn't do anything. You did everything."

"Just…trust me," he said, running a hand down his heaving chest.

He closed his eyes, and she watched him, overwhelmed. As, if sensing it he held out an arm to her, "Come here, baby." She rolled over beside him and rested her head in the right angle of his neck.

Chapter 15

Finn woke the next morning with their limbs intertwined, her hand on his chest, his cheek on top of her head, and his arm numb. He didn't know what was more shocking—this position, the fact he'd slept over, or his cell phone bleating him awake.

Reaching over with one hand, he tried to silence it before it woke her. Victorious, she merely rolled to her other side, and he removed his arm from under her head, trying to shake the circulation back in. Scrolling down, he saw the message from Nate.

Go to Kukui'ula at ten instead. Gov trolling off lighthouse.

Annoyed, Finn just texted back one word.

Fine.

He rolled over, saw her smooth back, and his irritation vanished. Gathering Raven in by her waist, he spooned around her like a shield. He put his face into her hair, breathing in the faint scent of jasmine, mint, and the sea. Just wanting to touch her, his hand traveled up and down her body, feeling its soft, warm surfaces. It fell across a raised mark of some kind high on her hip. He began to look, but she whimpered and curled into herself, so he moved his hand and gathered her up again.

Raven realized she was in the ocean again, misty sea water with sunbeams piercing through its fluidity.

She saw Finn swimming over to a seal, away from her. Behind him, an object formed, an oily black snake-like object ribboning through the serenity. She swam toward Finn, to get a better look at what it was, when an unseen barrier between her and the vision arose. She tried yelling at him to listen to her and return. As the object closed in on him, she stood suddenly outside herself and watched as the darkness consumed first him and then her as well.

She woke, startled and confused at first, then comforted as Finn's strong arms encircled her, protecting her from the dream. Remembering the night before and the relaxed looseness of her own body, she grinned broadly, proud of herself. It didn't take long to understand that soon they would have to find their way out of bed, and into the sunlight. An awkward conversation was bound to ensue. Deciding it was best to slip out of bed while he still slept, she moved, and he spoke into her hair.

"Morning."

"Morning," she said shyly. "I should, ah, I should get going." She began to remove the covers when he strengthened his hold around her waist.

"Go where? You live here."

"Oh." She laughed, quietly mortified. "Right. Well, I'll make some coffee then."

"No, you will not."

"You don't drink coffee?"

"Of course I do"—he rolled her over and kissed her—"but I'm not done with you yet."

"No?" she said, astounded. He was already moving over her, parting her legs with his.

"No."

Sliding in, he closed his eyes, as she clamped around him. Slowly rotating his pelvis, he moved deep inside her, until they found a rhythm and pace that complemented the moment. She hesitantly kissed the side of his neck, and his eyes opened.

"Jesus, you're sweet."

They watched each other climax and continued to stare long after. Finally, Finn rolled off her, laying his head on the soft pillow.

Looking at the time, he noticed it was nine thirty and muttered a curse to his boss. He raised himself up on an elbow and allowed his eyes to run lustfully over her naked body, flush from their lovemaking.

"So, I got a text from Nate, a little while ago."

"I thought I heard something."

"Sorry, but he called us in a little early today."

Not being able to help himself, he took her nipple into his mouth and ran his tongue over it, sighing deeply with regret.

"I'm gonna have to go. Can I grab a quick shower?"

"Sure." Shirking the covers off and standing, she pulled a short, silk, periwinkle robe off a hook, and wrapped it around her body. "Do you want me to make you some coffee?"

He watched her, looking perplexed. Knowing she was beginning to show her insecurities again, Raven tried to brush them away and smile. Appearing to let it go, he kissed her forehead, before walking toward the bathroom.

"No, thanks. I'm on the bike. I'll get something there."

The shower turned on and grinning she ran to the

kitchen, started the coffee, and began making a quick breakfast for him. A knock on the door brought her up short. Tightening the belt on her robe, she went to answer it.

When she opened the door, Jason stood on the other side.

"Surprise." He leaned in to kiss her cheek until he saw what she was wearing and stepped into her personal space.

Raven knew the moment Finn rounded the corner. The movement seemed to draw the attention of her manager, who did a double take on her new lover. Jason's face dropped in astonishment. Raven turned and saw Finn had showered, slid on his jeans, leaving them unbuttoned, and only grabbed his shirt. She flushed at the sight of him bare-chested, with little droplets of his shower still covering his chest. Pressing her lips together, she wished they could return to the evening before and just start all over again. However, her brows drew together in confusion when she noticed Finn's jaw set and his muscles tensed. Confused, she looked back to Jason and realized his hand was still low on her back and standing very close to her. He had eyed her hungrily when she opened the door, seeming to understand she wore nothing under the short robe. Glancing quickly back to Finn, she determined he was rapidly reaching that conclusion too and grew nervous.

"Taylor, wasn't it?" Jason nodded his head toward Finn, crimson flushing over his neck and face, then shifted his eyes to Raven.

"Jason," Finn smugly countered. "What brings you here so early?"

"I could ask you the same thing, but I'm afraid I

don't really have a lot of time to hear the answer."

Jason gave Finn a tight smile, daring him to say more. When it looked like he might, Raven spoke up, walking back to the kitchen.

"You want some coffee, Jason?"

"Sure," he said, not taking his eyes off Finn. Finn in turn smiled and slowly put on his tee shirt. "Aren't you going to ask Finn too?"

"Oh, Finn's leaving," she said absently, causing her new lover to look over at her, confused. Jason's grin became broader, as if to say, *not that good, eh?*

"Unless you want me to put some in a mug for the road after all?" She glanced over in question. The two men, looked as if latched back on springs, so she quickly continued. "Aren't you meeting Nate?"

He looked relieved and once again smugly condescended to look at Jason as if communicating his superiority.

"Yeah."

"Okay, I'll walk you out." She said, handing some buttered toast to Finn, then some coffee to Jason. "Be right back."

Finn clenched his jaw again as Jason made a show of admiring her body in the loosely belted robe. He held her hand as they walked out onto the front porch.

"I thought he was in Seattle."

"He was supposed to be. I had just opened the door when you came out. Maybe his dad's even better. He must've known he was coming when he called last night and kept it a surprise."

"How nice."

"Finn, I know you don't like him, but he is my manager. I work with him."

He exhaled and looked through the window. She looked too and saw Jason unloading his briefcase.

"So, I'll see you later?" he asked, returning his eyes back to hers and brushing some hair back from her face.

"Yeah. When?" she asked contentedly.

"I'll call you after I know a little better." He leaned in and kissed her lightly on the lips and then her forehead. As he bounded down the steps, he turned and flung a hand out. "Aw shit, I forgot it's Sunday. Dee and I always have dinner."

"Oh, okay." Her face fell.

"You wanna come?"

"Yeah." She laughed in an exhale. "I'd like that. You sure Dee won't mind?"

"Mind? She'll be ecstatic."

Finn watched her bite her lip and smile, before turning and practically skipping back to the house. Her robe whirled with the motion and parted slightly at her breasts. As she took the couple steps to her door, her ass moved incredibly under the silk. She looked back at him and her hair had the look of a woman well bedded the night before, with the most beautiful sexy, sleepy face he thought he'd ever seen.

"Rave, do me a favor," he said while walking backward.

"What?" she asked hesitantly.

His eyes traveled up the length of her, creating a mental picture.

"Go get dressed, so I don't have to think about that asshole lookin' at you. I swear he makes me want to shoot him in the face with a whaling gun."

She bit her bottom lip again as if to stop herself

from laughing.

"Bye." She waved and disappeared back into the house.

Chapter 16

"I'll be right back," Raven called, as she ran into her room to change.

"Ahhhh." She exhaled deeply, two minutes later. "So hi, how's your dad doing? He must be better than you let on last night?"

"Yes, he is. how nice of you to ask. I guess you didn't receive any more of my calls yesterday."

Oh shit, Raven thought. She hadn't even looked after they left for the day. Jason took off his coat and stood at the window, jaw clenched.

"Is he okay, Jason?" she asked and lowered her head, chastened.

"What the hell's going on here, Raven? Isn't that the guy you just met? Now you're fucking him?"

"Shh, lower your voice." She winced, looking at her open windows.

"Yeah, you should be embarrassed. You should be ashamed of yourself. It's profoundly reckless. I mean, look at the guy." He gestured toward the door Finn had exited. "Let me enlighten you. He's a player. He sees dollar signs."

"Jason, it's not like that. He didn't even know who I was."

"Oh Christ, don't be so obtuse." He spat disgustedly. "Do you honestly believe that Raven? You're one of the most famous singers in the world. Do you honestly think he didn't know who you were?"

Well, it's not about money."

"Right, and I suppose his research funds itself."

The tiniest sliver of doubt eked in on a quiet whisper. *Finn would do anything for those seals.*

"Do you honestly think you're his type at all, that he's in it for you?" Jason continued. "Pull your head out of your ass."

Her eyes filled with tears as he confirmed all the insecurities she'd entertained and lent them credibility. Had it been too soon?

"I thought we had something starting between us." Jason gestured between them, looking at her pleadingly. She closed her eyes. "I know what you said before, but I also thought it was because everything was so new after Donovan. Do time and loyalty mean nothing to you? Look at me, damn it," he ordered when she kept her head down.

"Jason…" He held up a hand.

"Forget it," he all but spat, disgusted. "We have some things to decide, most of which I've already taken care of." He glared at her and noticing her eyes brimming with tears, softened. "Look, I understand you may be feeling unsure about everything that's happened, with the divorce, being alone for the first time, and getting older. But I've got a plan to get you through all of this." He brushed her hair back. "Nobody understands your circumstances or the solutions to those problems better than I do." He lifted her chin. "I'm going to take care of all of it, okay?"

"I just want to…"

"But you have got to get rid of this guy," he stated, effectively ignoring her and still holding her chin.

"He's completely wrong for you. He will hurt you, make no mistake about that. He's a total player and user. I promise he only got interested in you after I told him you had money."

Before she could question why Jason had brought up money with Finn in the first place, her cell phone rang. She connected the call as he walked to retrieve some papers.

"Hello?"

"Raven?" Wyatt's concerned voice sounded tinny on the line, indicating the miles between them. "You doing okay over there?"

Just hearing her brother's voice made her want to cry harder and tell him everything. However, to speak truly honestly with him while Jason was there was impossible, usurping Wyatt's ability to help in any discernible way. However, she also knew her brother and had to give him something.

"I'm fine." Looking over at Jason, who was busy setting out papers, she stepped outside. "It's just there's a lot of stuff to figure out, and not much time to get it done. I have no idea what I'm doing anymore Wy." Christ, she thought, had she ever.

"Remember, that's why you went there—to figure it all out, right?"

"It's just it's been busy. Jason just got back. His dad had a stroke, and he had to go back to Seattle. We've gotta figure out the whole Donovan thing. And then there's this…"

"Wait. Wait." Wyatt interrupted, "First, is his dad okay?"

"It looks good. He's out of the woods, so Jason came back."

"Good," her brother decided, then his voice became wary, "Now, what Donovan thing."

"I'm doing a weekend benefit for him and his mistress."

"You're what?"

"I know, I know. It's kind of a long story, but it's something I'm going to have to do, or I can see him smearing me in the press. So, I'll do it, then I can be done with him. Besides," she added softly, "it's for the homeless."

Wyatt sighed deeply. She could tell he had a lot of things he wanted to say but held back.

"You know, you've got time Rave, lots of time. You're not even halfway through. Everything doesn't need to be done in nanoseconds. Tell Jason to chill. It's important you do this for you this time, okay?"

"Okay."

"Really? 'Cause I feel it."

"Yes." She smiled at their code speak for, *I can tell you're upset.*

"Okay. I love you."

"I love you too, Wy."

When he disconnected, she continued to hold the phone to her ear, just wishing to absorb as much of his energy as possible before returning to Jason's papers.

"Okay," he called and gestured to a chair. "Sit down, and I'll see if I can't try and explain this all to you. First is Donovan's contract. I looked it over, and I think it will be fine," he said as if he'd never been against it.

"Were you able to negotiate my songs in?"

"You'll get three," he said almost shiftily. Raven looked at him trying to discern what she was reading in his voice. He quickly continued. "So, I need you to sign here and here, then initial here, here, and here."

"So what does this effectively say?" she asked, signing the papers.

"You'll do the two shows. You can't pull out without a penalty unless injured or ill, and even then, you'd need to reschedule." They spoke about ticket prices, venue costs, backup singers and getting the band members back. "They all know you're on the ground bleeding, so they want their pound of flesh too," Jason said. "I think we suck it up and just pay them because they know the sets and your style already."

"But we don't need all of that. Didn't we agree we're changing things up?"

"I thought you meant your makeup," he evaded and looked at her like she'd turned blue. "No Raven, we have a formula that works."

She stopped writing but still poised over the papers and looked up.

"When we talked, I told you I was hoping to go more organic. I've said that all along, Jason."

"Organic? What does that even mean?" He saw the look on her face and appeased her almost condescendingly. "I've done a lot of thinking on this, but you're right. We may need to make some changes. How about we compromise? You work on hair, makeup, costume, and maybe even some set decoration. Okay? All you. I won't say a word."

"But…"

"Okay, fine, we can even consider new backup singers and some choreography, but that's as far as I'm willing to go right now."

"Um," she said, shaking her head numbly.

Maybe she was just wrong. She did pay him to know this stuff. Donovan had indeed understood what he was doing. Raven felt as if she could no longer tell what was real or fake, right or wrong, or even up or down.

"So, what are we thinking about for timing? Jason asked, "If we have too many changes we're going to take longer to roll out the package, and we need to stay relevant." She frowned in irritation as if her talent was that of a young starlet, new to the industry. "We're going to need at least a month for new set designs and promotion, maybe two if we get new choreography."

They worked into the afternoon, making plans. By dinnertime, Jason had convinced her it was in her best interest to stay in his company for the evening. She'd said yes to dinner just as her cell phone rang. Looking at the caller ID, Raven saw Finn's number. Her stomach roiled with unease.

"Hi."

"Hey. How ya doin'?" he asked in a warm, resonant voice. "Good day?"

"Yeah, busy." She paused and looked at Jason, who was glaring at her. "In fact, so busy I think I won't be able to get away tonight for dinner." When she heard nothing but silence, she asked, "Finn?"

"Yeah."

"It's just Jason's here," she confirmed, "and I've got to get some stuff figured out before he goes back." She turned and took several steps away from her manager. "Plus, maybe we should think about things a little. We're moving pretty fast."

"Yeah, okay. I'll see ya around?"

"Finn?" She held the phone with two hands.

"Finn?"

When she heard nothing, she lowered her hand and looked out across the yard, thinking maybe Jason was right. He sure hadn't put up too much of a fight.

"All set?" he asked when she walked back in. "Okay. Well, let's go get something to eat and just have a good night then."

They ate dinner in the dining room of Jason's hotel and talked about his dad and the people they knew back home. He said he'd seen Que with Abby once and received a call from Donovan again.

"What did he say?"

"He's got Caprice Starr emceeing for you."

"Oh, how perfect." Raven raised her head, genuinely happy. "I haven't talked to Caprice in ages. It'll be great to see her again."

"He also signed Lanie Hart," Jason continued.

"Lanie Hart?" Raven stared at him. "She dots her I's with a heart and plays to teenagers, Jason."

"Your core group is teenagers and young adult too. At least it was, and you need to stay close to that group as we transition." When she started to protest, he boomed, "Damn it, Raven, this is why you pay me!" She jumped at the tone. "Stop fighting and second-guessing everything I say and trust me, for Christ sake!" He paused a few moments, looked around the crowded room collecting himself.

"Let's get out of here and walk on the beach. It's quieter out there." Without waiting for her reply, he signaled the waiter, and soon she was removing her shoes and stepping onto the soft, bleached sand.

"Sorry I yelled," Jason said, as they walked. "I want to do this right too, but I really do need you to trust me." When she didn't say anything, he gestured to some beach chairs, and they sat down. "It's peaceful here, isn't it?"

"Yeah, it's exactly what I needed."

He reached out and made small circles on her back. "That's good. Do you miss performing yet?"

"I guess…"

"But?"

"But I feel like every aspect of my life has been off balance since I signed my damned divorce papers and I hate it. I really want to incorporate more of me, and less of him, but I feel like no one's listening to me. I mean it is my show, right?"

"You want to play your music?"

"Yes."

"Okay," he said, standing up and reaching out a hand. "Let's go."

"Go?" she asked, confused.

"Back to your house. You can play me something, and we'll see."

"I don't like to play my unfinished stuff to people."

"Well, I'm not just people." She smiled cautiously but didn't say anything. "Raven, you're going to have to get over it and grow up if you want to be taken seriously."

"Okay, fine," she decided. "Let's go."

By the time they got back to her place, she was bubbling with excitement to prove herself. She unlocked the door, threw her purse and keys on the couch, and sat down at the piano. Jason walked over to her and gently helped pull off her cardigan.

That's what Finn saw. He took a step off the porch like someone had dealt him a physical blow. There was something in her voice when they talked earlier that confused him, and he knew it had something to do with Dell.

She began to play the piano. Jason sat next to her, his hand behind her on the bench. She'd started to perform a song, but her manager said something and gestured at her, which caused her to frown. She began playing a slow and haunted version of the newest, fast-paced pop song.

Finn watched Jason lean into her, not seeing that she was too absorbed in the music to notice it herself. It hurt him and that fact terrified him. So, turning, he walked back down the path. In his logical mind, he knew Dell was taking advantage of the situation and that Raven wasn't interested. However, he couldn't understand why she'd chosen an evening with the leech, instead of him. Jason Dell was never going to give her what she wanted, rather he would demand what he needed. The thought infuriated Finn. Frustrated and confused he swung his leg over his bike and drove back home.

It was several hours later, and Raven played her last song. She looked over at Jason, appreciatively and hugged him in thanks. In response, the man reached a hand to her face and pulled her close for a kiss. Quickly moving away, she stood up and walked away, placing the piano between them.

"Jason."

Smiling like he was tolerating a talkative child, he stood and collected his jacket, then walked to the door.

"Look, I know you're incredibly confused," he cooed, throwing an arm into the coat. "I want you to think about this, about us. I haven't hidden any of my feelings or intentions, Raven." He shook the jacket into place across his shoulders. "We have a lot of history, and we have a lot of future ahead of us. Get some sleep, and we'll talk in the morning."

Without waiting for a response, he left and once again she leaned back against her door. The only thing she knew was she wasn't going to be there in the morning when he came back.

Chapter 17

A man as ancient as time sat before a clock. The hands were replicas of Finn's trident. When the chime sounded, the trident slowly, painfully peeled apart, creating the strings of a harp. Dolphins in the sea raced against horses on land, sides sweaty and heaving. His grandmother leaned over her garden and came up holding a seed, as bright as the sun. Then there was Raven, heart pounding, eyes closed, as he loved her, the way he had the night before.

Finn woke in the middle of the night sweaty, confused, and angry. This woman had him off balance since the second he saw her, and he was sick of it. He remembered the dream he'd experienced, just after they met. It seemed to run parallel with the one that just woke him. Off center and out of control, and she seemed to be in the center of all of it. Brows furrowed he swung his legs off the bed and scrubbed a hand down his face. Deciding he wasn't going to wait until morning, he drove Dee's car to the bungalow. The front porch light came on, as he pounded on the door. When she opened it, he merely walked inside and paced like a caged lion.

"Finn?"

"Okay, so what is this?" he demanded, then stopped, and was instantly frustrated because he wanted to at least appear calm.

"What's wh—"

"I meet you, and you keep me at arm's length. Then it's no you're not interested. Then it's yes, then no. We have a pretty phenomenal time, then douchebag comes back, and suddenly I get the freeze again, and he's all over you. So, what in the hell is going on?"

"I—"

"I need you to be straight with me, Raven."

"I'm trying to…" Her eyes were sad as she bit her bottom lip.

"God damn it, stop looking at me like you're about to break!" he barked, causing her to flinch. "Shit!" he snapped, exasperated.

"Why are you here Finn?"

"What d'ya mean? I just told you. We fucked, and it was…"

"That's what it was, right?"

"What?"

"Fucking. You got what you wanted, and that was it." He just blinked at her incredulously.

"What in the hell are you talking about Raven? I invited you to dinner with Dee. You said no to me, then went out with whoever the hell that guy is to you."

"And that pissed you off, so you're done with me, right?"

He looked at her like she had entirely lost her mind. Turning, she walked back toward the kitchen, appearing furious with her life. He caught her by the arm, and she hit his chest. He reached out to stop her, and she hit him with the other hand. She continued to pound out her rage until he pressed her against the refrigerator.

"You don't know what the fuck you want, do

you?" he asked in realization.

"Get out!" she screamed.

"Do you?"

"Get out!"

"Really?" he growled, watching her hit him.

Her eyes, full of confusion and desire, kept shifting from his eyes to his lips. Each pass left her eyes growing wilder with...something. She leaned forward and kissed him once quickly, then kissed him again, hard. Kissing her back just as forcefully, he opened her robe to run his hands hungrily over her body.

As if scared, she pushed him away. Enraged, he slammed both his fists on either side of her head and just stared directly into her eyes, his own gaze firing back at her. A thousand words spoken between them, yet not one uttered.

She shifted her eyes back to his mouth, breathing hard. Raven leaned into him again, kissing and biting his bottom lip. He groaned and angrily stripped off her robe. She removed his tee shirt and unzipped his jeans. When they slid to the ground, she looked surprised to find only him and eagerly grabbed hold of his cock.

Finn picked her up and laid her on the table, bending her knees and entering her so forcefully a decorative bowl the color of cobalt fell off the table and shattered. She strained up to reach him and found him searching for her too, kissing each other greedily. His mouth left hers and fused to her breast, deliberately rough, as he moved in and out of her. Picking up speed and frenzy, he lifted her hips off the table. There was nothing tender, just primal until they climaxed together, each expelling their release in a scream.

For a few moments, neither of them moved or said

a word. Their chests heaved, rasping for breath and bodies slick with sweat. Slowly, Finn came to his senses first, as he realized in disbelief what had just happened. Never in his life had he lost control with a woman like that, and he felt shame.

Raven, stared at him as if surprised by her own aggressiveness. Breathing hard, they both looked down at their joined bodies, as he extricated himself from her. She sat up, watching him, as he bent to pick up her robe. Her face was flushed, and he could already see a bruise begin to mottle across her arm. Finn didn't know what to say as he handed her the robe, and silently dressed. He glanced at her once more in disbelief and heard her slide down the wall, to the floor and cry.

****

Raven smiled into the sunshine, holding her mama's hand, then Wyatt's, who was holding her daddy's, creating a perfect chain. Excitedly, they ordered everyone to march in unison. Right, left, right, left. The day was perfect because the sun was out and the small fair was in town. They petted the farm animals, jumped in the hay of the threshing bees, and watched the magicians and clowns. Her mother held her hand again, raising them high in the air, as they went down the roller coaster. She could smell the cotton candy and the tang of mustard on her hotdog.

Her father set Wyatt down, reached out, and spiraled her through the air, in a perfect circle, and onto his shoulders. The hot day turned into a warm dusk, with a slight breeze, as they drove home. After starting a fire, her dad brought out his guitar and let them stay up to sing around the campfire.

Raven asked if she could play the guitar too. So, he

moved it, allowing her access to his lap. Then replacing the guitar, he laid his hands on hers to guide her fingers. However, she simply began to play what he'd been playing. Astonished he watched her in great delight, as Wyatt and her mom sang. When she finished, she sat next to her mama, who pointed up at the sky.

"Look, baby, I brought down the moon just for you."

"Me too, Mama?" Wyatt asked.

"You too baby. Come here." Wyatt laid his head down on her lap, as did Raven and their dad began to sing again, smiling at his family.

"I sing to you a thousand words and a thousand feelings more. Of home and hearth and family, and sun and moon adored. And in my time remaining, to my cherished hearts, I sing. Grand love and peace and blessings I hope your life will bring."

She couldn't remember the rest of the song because she'd instantly fallen asleep in the trust that her world was secure.

Time passed, but not much. Raven emerged from a different sleep and saw red and blue lights straining to swirl through the closed window blinds. She heard strange, soft voices in the living room. Wyatt woke too and jumped from his bed into hers, wrapping protective arms around her. They trembled together, hearts pounding fiercely as if they shared the same beat. Something dark was coming, and she knew they should be afraid when the door cracked open, and the outline of a woman appeared.

"Mama?" Wyatt called, voice shaking.

The door opened wider, allowing more light and the crackling static and loud voices over radios.

"No honey, not Mama. Hello Wyatt, Raven."

An older woman turned on the children's nightlight to reveal soft, gray eyes, just like a dove's, with crinkles around them. Her voice was soothing as she held just a hint of a reassuring smile. Janie, their babysitter, stood behind her, face red, swollen, and tear-streaked.

"My name is Emily, and I need to talk to you both."

"Where's Mama and Daddy?" Wyatt asked quietly, and Raven began to cry. She already knew the answer.

"Yes, honey. Well, Mommy and Daddy were hurt very badly in a car accident." Emily's voice quavered just slightly when she locked eyes with Raven. "They both died in that accident. Do you know what that means—to die?"

"It means they won't come back," Raven squeaked.

"That's right, sweetheart. They won't be coming back." She looked around the room. "Now, we've been trying to figure out if you have a grandma or grandpa that we can call to come take care of you." When they didn't answer, she suggested, "Maybe an aunt or uncle?"

They shook their heads despondently. They had no one.

"Okay, well, we'll figure all that out, but right now I need for you both to collect some things, and we're going to take you somewhere very safe tonight."

"No!" both children said in unison, with quavering voices.

Raven clung tighter to Wyatt, feeling terror at possible separation. These people with their scary words and sounds would be the ones to do it. Raven began to sob.

"W-we c-can't go," Raven lamented. "W-what if they do c-come back?"

"Honey."

"No!"

Raven was adamant now and working herself into a wall of defiance. She screamed, cried, and kicked, causing Wyatt to do the same. A massive police officer strode over to her and towered. Her mouth dropped open when she saw the topography of large rope-like veins wind under the man's skin. He had an angry, disappointed face.

"Raven, Wyatt, this is what's best for you. It is happening. You need to do what you're told now and behave. What would your parents think about you carrying on this way? You need to trust that these people know better for you right now. So, collect your things and go with Ms. Meakan—now!" The lady looked at the officer, with an angry, stern face. However, when she turned back, she smiled serenely at them.

Raven felt black smoke encircle her wrists and tiny waist. She tried to pull them away, but they'd vanish and reappear. The black smoke hovered by her ear and stroked her cheek. It formed lips, and she heard the words saying, "You…Are…Now…Nothing."

She screamed and sat up on the cool white tiles of the kitchen floor, with the scent of wood smoke in the air. She raised a shaking hand to brush some hair away from her face and hooked it around her ear. What in God's name was happening to her?

Chapter 18

The next morning Raven woke early and opened the journal used by past guests of the bungalow. She was looking for something to do when a name stood out for a hiking trail.

"The Maha'ulepu Heritage Trail," she read aloud.

Remembering Finn's recommendation for the hike, she learned it was two miles long in each direction, beginning less than half a mile away.

Raven threw on some spandex, shoes, and threaded her hair into a ponytail before grabbing a water, scribbling a note to Jason, and running out the door. She felt like a naughty truant and grinned. Walking a little less than a mile, she approached Shipwreck Beach before hearing someone call out her name. Raven jumped and turned toward the speaker.

"Oh, Mrs. Taylor, I didn't see you there."

"What am I, an old lady? I told you, call me Dee. I'm sorry for sneaking up on you like that. I just saw you there and was about to take my own walk. Care to join me?"

"Ah."

She wasn't sure about joining Finn's grandmother because she knew thinking about, rather than hearing about him, was what she needed to do. However, Raven liked Dee, separate from Finn, and that was what prevailed.

"Sure, I'd love to. How far do you go?"

"Oh, as far as the wind takes me or until I have to pee." Dee leaned toward her and giggled, causing Raven to burst out laughing.

"Okay, show me the way, *sensai*."

They walked in silence for a short time as they climbed up the trail and onto the cliffs. Raven waited for her to start matchmaking when the older woman surprised her.

"Do you know anything about Greek mythology?"

"Greek mythology?" Raven furrowed her brow. "Wow. Well, not since I took it in high school or middle school. Why?"

"Well, it's kind of intrigued me lately, and I've been trying to learn more about it. There's so many connections and people though, it's pretty confusing."

"Oh, well, I'd probably be able to remember some. Strangely enough, when I took the class, I got a little obsessive about it myself. The stories are pretty fun."

"Right, that's what I say," Dee confirmed. "I know about the different generations, or at least I know some of the connections. What I don't understand or one of the things I don't understand, is their hell."

"Their hell?"

"Yeah, there's like levels or something, right? And Hades is the devil."

"Oh no, Hades wasn't the devil. He wasn't any worse or better than any other god." Having fun, Raven explained. "So, Hades just ruled over the Underworld and made sure no one left. He got a bad rap because people were as scared of death then, as they are now, I suppose. All that unknown."

"Aren't there levels in the hell or the underworld or

whatever?"

"Well, I think there were separate rivers or something down there and then once you're in you get judged by the Fates."

"Right," Dee said, excited. "Those are the Moirai, right?"

"Um, I can't quite remember. That could be right. The professor just called them the Fates. And the professor said their only weakness was dreams."

"Dreams?" Dee queried. "Why dreams?"

"I'm not exactly sure, but I remember the dreamers, maybe the possibilities from dreaming, were like catnip for the Fates. It was their one and only weakness." She looked over at Dee and smiled. "But to answer your question, the Tartarus is the level beneath everything. Where they sent the original Titans."

Dee's eyes sparkled like she had just confirmed something in her mind.

"Then there are levels above that, but I don't remember all the names. One was for like ordinary people, one was for people who wasted their life, and then there was the Elysium." Raven laughed. "The only way I remember that one is because of that beer that sounds like it. When it first came out, I instantly connected the two. "She looked back to see how Dee was doing. "Are you okay back there?"

"Oh yes, I'm doing great. It's all so fascinating. So, the Elysium…"

"Okay, well, the Elysium was kind of the rock star place where the people that served the gods or were righteous were sent. You got to decide to stay there or be reborn, but if you chose to be reborn, your memory was wiped clean. If you achieved the Elysium a certain amount of times, you went to a special island. I can't remember the name, but it was for the, like, one percenters of heroes or gods. Eternal paradise, like heaven. Oh wow, this is so incredibly beautiful!"

The red cliffs were like jagged pieces of stained glass. Looking down, she could see the rings of time layer them, as the waves pounded below, each spraying their mist high into the air.

"Yes." Dee smiled. "It's the most beautiful spot on earth." She looked down and exclaimed, "Oh no."

"What?"

"Someone lost a pair of glasses. Expensive, by the looks of them." She held up a pair of light, rimless trifocals distractedly. Raven just watched her in her floppy hat and distinct muumuu and smiled.

"Didn't you ever want to leave here, Dee?"

"How could I?" She encompassed her surroundings with her arms extended. "Like I told you before, I have it all. The sun, rain, flowers, sand, water, nourishment, and Finn."

"Yes… Finn." Raven continued to stare out to sea, not sure if she'd ever felt so confused or lonely.

Dee patted her hand like she understood the inner turmoil. Raven, feeling like she'd revealed too much, was relieved when the older woman didn't question her further.

"So, do you know about the individual gods too?"

"Oh, only the main ones, and then only some. Zeus ruled everyone. Hades, the Underworld. Aphrodite was the beauty. Um, let's see, Hera was marriage. Hermes was like the little messenger guy. Athena, wisdom. Dionysus, wine. Ares kicked ass. Artemis, hunting. I think there were some or one, that traded spots with

Dionysus. One was for the hearth, and the other was agriculture."

"Hestia and Demeter."

"Right, then there was Poseidon of the sea, and who am I missing?" She frowned as Dee's gaze bored into hers. The tension in the air seemed to ripple as she tried to remember. "Zeus, Hera, Hades, Hermes, Hestia." She counted on her fingers, "Poseidon, Demeter, Dionysus, Aphrodite, Ares, Athena, Artemis—and—oh, Apollo, her twin." Raven's medallion heated and she felt a little charge in her fingers, so unconsciously she shook them out.

"And what did Apollo do?"

"He was music," Raven said without hesitation.

"Music…like you?"

"Yeah, I guess so." She giggled. "Maybe he was my million times great-grandfather or something and…" She stopped. Dee stopped too, watching her.

"And what?"

"Oh, nothing." She laughed. "It's just I love music, and I have a twin too. Isn't that weird? Maybe we're long lost cousins."

****

Jason had been sitting at Raven's dining table for forty-five minutes, irritated. He'd arrived at ten to find the door unlocked and a note on the counter. The message said she was taking some time, but he thought she'd stepped out and would return quickly. Walking in, he set down his briefcase, before trying her cell phone. It had been turned off, and for a brief moment he wondered if she was with Finn but thought better of it. Their night had ended rather well, and she seemed more responsive than before. In fact, he'd blown it up in his mind so thoroughly that he envisioned her as a willing participant when he stroked himself the night before. He smiled just thinking about it, then heard a knock on the door.

"Have your hands full, do you?" he asked, thinking maybe she had groceries, but when he opened the door, his smile fell.

"What do you want, Finn?" He sneered, with no attempt at civility.

"Raven."

"Well, sorry to be the one to tell you that you can't have her."

He closed the door in Finn's face with satisfaction and walked back to the table. When the door snapped back open with a bang, he jumped in surprise and yelped, instantly irritated at himself for appearing weak.

"Where is she?"

"Out."

"Out where?"

"Look," Jason evaded, "as much as I'd like to play twenty questions with you, I…"

"It's one question. Where is she?"

"Why?"

"None of your fucking business, Dell."

"Okay, Finn." Jason held up his hands. "Let's have a truce."

"I'm not at war with you."

"Oh, the hell you aren't." He placed both palms on the table to support his weight.

"Look, I know you think you have an easy mark here with her, but I'm telling you to walk away, Finn," Jason said vehemently. "I know what you're trying to do, but Raven and I have history. We have a career together, and you're distracting her from her work."

"Yeah." Finn grinned. "It was a pretty incredible distraction at that." He crossed his arms. "Is that what's yanking your chain, that we fucked?"

Jason winced, then melted into a smile.

"The fact that you honestly think there's something there, beyond a troubled woman's rebound, is funny, yet also pitiful. That you think she's just going to walk away from everything that makes her who she is." He sipped from his coffee mug. "She's a star, she's loyal, and she likes her life or will once we define the parameters in this new normal we're in."

"New normal?"

"Her husband destroyed and humiliated her. And instead of hiding, we're going to re-enter the realm as a new and improved version."

"And you're going to be the one that decides that, huh?"

"I understand her and this business." He met Finn's eyes. "I'm the one that makes this thing work. I find the gigs, and I handle the money. I manage her. And despite what you may believe, she wasn't thinking about you last night when we were kissing."

Jason noticed Finn's temper flame—his hands balled into fists, and his jaw clenched. He grinned in the satisfaction that maybe, just maybe he was hitting a nerve.

"I doubt it."

"That's because you're an idiot. If there's anything I know about Raven, it's that her music is her entire life. It's everything she is. And if you don't understand that, then you'll never understand her." When Finn rolled his eyes, Jason smiled. "Finn, you've already lost, and you're too stupid to know it." He gestured toward the door with his head. "Now, I believe you know the way out."

Finn clenched and unclenched his jaw. He walked to the door and started to open the screen.

"Dell, ever notice how she just sends you home every night? Then maybe ask yourself one more important question. When you kissed her, did she actually kiss you back?"

Before Jason could answer, Finn walked out, letting the screen door slam.

****

The women hiked all the way to Kawailoa Bay, toed off their shoes, and sat down in the sand. Both looked out to the water, comfortable in her own thoughts. Finally, Raven broke the silence.

"So, Dee, what Greek god would you want to be?"

"Oh, I'm from Demeter, without a doubt."

"Why Demeter?" Raven asked smiling, missing the inference. "Because you go by Dee?"

"No, because I love everything living. I can grow anything. I'm good at it, and that can be a gift. And I love that boy to death. Persephone he ain't, but I love him as fiercely."

"Persephone? Oh yes, Hades' wife. That was pretty devious the way he stole her and wouldn't let her come back."

"Yep and her mama got so mad she stopped growing things."

"That's right—winter."

"Zeus made Hades give up his wife for a little while every year in repayment."

"Spring."

"When all new things grow again."

"Hmm." Raven smiled and closed her eyes. "That's pretty nice." She appeared to think for a moment then asked, "So, Finn's Persephone then? I guessed when I thought of a descendant, I just assumed they'd be the same sex, but I guess they don't have to be." Dee began to chuckle.

"You think Finn would come from Persephone?" She laughed harder, inciting Raven to laugh too. "Now come dear, let's think a little harder on that one."

Raven did for a second and seemed to realize her blunder.

"No, I guess you're right. He would have to be from Poseidon, wouldn't he? That was just dumb."

"Poseidon is probably a good choice. Moody, intelligent, and loves all the little sea things."

"Has he been that way all his life?"

"Ever since he was little. Always had that temper too, but I think it's because he likes to be in control of his surroundings and when he cares about something, he's passionate about taking care of it. When things don't make sense, it makes him nervous. He needs to figure out how to make it work in his life and control it."

"Hmm, well, I don't know him very well, but blanket control never did anyone any good."

"Ain't that the truth! Well now, what about you? I feel like I chatter away and I don't know very much about you at all. You said you have a twin. Is it a brother or a sister?"

"A brother. Wyatt. I have a sister too, but not by blood. Her name is Que, and she has a little girl named Abby. She's my god-daughter. That's my family back home."

"And you miss them?"

"I do, but I'm not quite ready to go home yet."

"Where's home?"

"Seattle. Washington."

"Oh, Seattle, where it's rainy."

"Yes." Raven laughed. It was always everyone's go to comment about her home city. "It can be rainy, but I heard somewhere that Kaua'i gets like the most rain on the face of the planet?"

"It can, up there on Wai'ale'ale. But Hawai'i, in general, only rains for about ten minutes at a time, and after the rain, the sun always follows."

"Well, I can't argue that. For us, it can last days."

"How did you begin to sing?"

"It was instruments first. It's one of my first memories I have with my mom and dad. Playing his guitar at a campfire, it just sorta came to me. Then in middle school, one of my friends had a violin, and I thought it was so cool. I asked her if I could try it and she laughed at me, saying it was incredibly difficult to learn. I picked it up, and, I don't know. It just came easily too."

"Is your brother musical too?"

"Wyatt?" Raven laughed. "Oh God no. He's a rugged man's man kind of guy. He hunts and fishes and stuff. He's a forest ranger and survival expert."

"A forest ranger."

Dee felt another piece of the puzzle drop into shape and tried to see how it looked in the big picture.

"Your parents must be so proud of all your success. Did you go to a special school for music?" Dee asked.

"No." Raven's vision darkened like shutters

levering closed. "My parents died when I was young. My brother and I were raised by foster parents that went on to adopt us."

"Oh, honey, I'm so sorry about your folks. How wonderful you found another family, even if it probably wasn't the one you wanted. So, your adopted parents kept you in music?"

"No, there wasn't a lot of extra time or money for things like that. Well," she said, glancing around in discomfort, then standing up. "We have a little trek ahead of us, do you want to head back?"

The older woman accepted the subject was effectively closed. After all, she understood the pain of losing someone you loved the most and decided to allow Raven her privacy.

"Absolutely. And Raven?" The young woman turned to look at her. "I'm so glad you recognize music as a gift. I want to hear you play sometime. Live and in person, I mean."

"I can sing you something right now if you sing it with me."

Dizzy with joy, Dee grabbed her hand, and they began to sing about dreamers imagining a world in peace.

****

By the time Raven returned home, the evening had settled into darkness. She and Dee spent the entire day talking about music and gardening. They spoke about Finn as a little boy and her time on Kaua'i. Raven connected with her in a way she might with her own mother or grandmother if she'd had one. The singer talked about her family, even giving their emergency contact numbers at the older woman's insistence, should something happen to her while on the island. And they talked about Greek mythology.

After parting ways, Raven walked home, fearful she would find someone on her porch. When she didn't, she sighed with relief and turned on her phone. Several messages were from Jason, and one was from Finn. She listened to Finn's first.

"I came by your place today. I thought maybe we should talk at some point. I hope you're out enjoying the island. Give me a call when you want."

Simple, direct and to the point, where every call from Jason seemed more and more frantic and angry. She texted him back.

I needed to do my own thing today and think some things through. Hope you can understand. Talk more tomorrow. Going to bed. Night.

Turning her phone off immediately, in case he called back, she decided not to respond to Finn at all. She hadn't the slightest idea what to say.

Chapter 19

Jason stayed almost a week longer before returning to Seattle to put the finishing touches on Donovan's benefit being held at the Tacoma arena. Raven drove him to the airport and turned her cheek as he moved to kiss her goodbye.

"See you in about a month?"

"Yeah." When he smiled at her, looking like he expected more, she simply said, "Have a safe flight, Jason. Give me a call when you land."

"I will. Let's finish up this recuperating and moping and get back to work."

He turned without even waiting for a response, picked up his suitcase, and walked into the airport. She stared after him, mouth slightly open, then turned to look straight out the front window with the same expression, feeling like a scolded child. She put her tongue in her cheek and narrowed her eyes, as a flicker of irritation sparked. Just a little spark, but it ignited.

On the drive home, she stopped for a latte and poppy seed muffin, but when she walked through her front door, her eyes fell on the piano. Dropping her breakfast and purse on the table to be forgotten, she sat down at it and began to play, compose, and sing.

Music had always been Raven, just as Raven had always been music. Her earliest memories included that campfire listening to her father play his guitar and mother singing in a perfect alto voice. When she asked to play, she instantly felt a connection and understood the instrument. It was almost as if they spoke to each other. Barely able to wrap her tiny hands around it, she mimicked what he'd been playing. When left to her own devices, Raven gained power from her music. She just couldn't explain it past that. It had been so long since she'd experienced any kind of power at all.

Now she performed without restraint, and it felt like she was breaking through a thick, sturdy barrier. She played the classics and then her own music, unaware of time or place. She continued to play that night and into the next day when he found her.

Finn walked up to the house and heard her playing the guitar. He stood at the screen door and knocked, but she didn't answer. Preparing to open the screen, he stopped when she began to sing. It was a beautiful, uplifting song about power and possibility. The next melody was haunting, about youth, pain, and distrust. Singing, crooning to people that no longer lived, she spoke of pain inflicted and love extinguished.

Sitting down and leaning back in the Adirondack chair on her porch, he just listened, running a hand over his beard. In the two hours he sat there, he learned more about her than the entire time he'd known her. Finn tried to process what it all meant. What part was story and what part was true until suddenly, it stopped. Looking in the window, he saw her walk toward her bedroom, and after ten minutes he chose to try again.

She opened the door wearing a salmon-colored sundress, her hair wet and loose from a shower. Freckles had popped out onto her peachy complexion, from her time in the sun, and her eyes looked crystal blue and clear. She was happy, he realized. Radiant in a way he hadn't seen her yet, almost making him sorry he'd interrupted.

"Finn, hi."

"Hi," he said, putting his hands into his jeans pockets. "Sounded good," he said, gesturing to the guitar, and smiled at the chaotic mess of papers and music she'd written. "Sounded fantastic actually."

"You listened?" Raven glowed. "Well, thanks. I've been working on some things, but it's time to stop for a while, so you came at a perfect time. Wanna get out of here?"

It was like they hadn't shared a bed, baggage, or time apart for the last week and it took him slightly aback. She'd never called or reached out in any way. Coming to her now was going to be his last attempt at contact. At least, that's what he had promised himself.

"Ah, sure. Where do you wanna go?"

"Surprise me. Are you on your bike?"

"Yeah."

"Perfect. Let's go."

Raven walked past him and climbed onto his bike. Watching, with his mouth slightly open in a half grin, he finally closed the door and walked to her. She balanced on it like a pro, and he genuinely laughed at how much she'd changed from the first time she saw it. She looked at him quizzically, as he shook his head and slid on sunglasses, possibly realizing the reason, as the corners of her mouth turned up too.

The bike sprang to life, and she snaked her arms around his torso, hugging him to her. When she laid her head on his back, he decided where to take her and moved onto the road, for the forty-minute drive.

When they arrived, a fence barred the road, reporting it was private property. Finn helped her off the bike, and winking, extended a hand to lead her over the barrier.

"Wait, can we go in here?"

Without saying a word, he just smiled, releasing her hand as they began hiking to the upper Ho'opi'i falls.

"So, how've you been?" he asked, pulling up a blade of long grass as they walked.

"I've been good, getting a lot of work done. You?" He looked out through the brush.

"Same. They set a date for beginning installation of the turbines." She stopped, causing him to halt. When she turned, he scanned her face, which showed genuine emotion for him.

"Oh Finn, I'm so sorry. There are no more ways to fight it?"

"No," he said, looking down.

They walked a little farther before finally turning the corner, and he watched her amazement as they approached the picturesque waterfall.

"Oh my God, this is so stunning," she said gazing upward.

"It's not even our best, but it's my favorite." The corners of his mouth turned up.

Finn grabbed some more of the grass he stood hip-deep in and began to shred it. Raven glanced over and watched him, as he turned to look up at the falls. After a moment, he threw the grass away, slid his hands into the pockets of his jeans, and lifted his eyes to hers. Caught staring, she quickly looked around.

"It's quiet. Doesn't anyone come here?"

"No, they do, just not many. It's hit and miss now that they've closed it."

"Why'd they close it?"

"Too many accidents. People go on vacation, feel invincible, and disregard nature. It happens a lot on the islands, unfortunately." He glanced around for inspiration. "I heard you went hiking with Dee."

"I did. It was so fun. She's the coolest lady."

"Yeah, she is." He decided it was time to cut the crap. "So, you've been a hard woman to get a hold of, Raven."

"Yeah, I guess."

"Jason?"

"Ah, he went back to Seattle."

"When?"

"Couple of days ago."

"But you didn't call."

"I was"—she smiled and looked up at the falls— "inspired."

"Inspired?" he said slowly. "By Jason?"

"No." She chuckled.

"By?" He stepped back onto the path a few feet away from her.

"I don't know, by being here, circumstances…"

"Circumstances?" He approached her, and she looked up at him.

"Yeah."

"So, I guess I thought something was going on with us. That first night we did pretty well together and hanging out, having fun." He felt like a clingy idiot, much like the girls he hustled out of his bed quickly.

"We did." She moved over to him, so they were a foot apart. "The second night had its moments too."

"Are you kidding?" He snorted.

"Well, it was exciting." She glanced at him and blushed. His laughter faded as he considered her, becoming more contemplative. "Jason said, you wanted money for your research, and I'm ashamed to say for a second I had doubt."

"And now?" he asked, jaw clenched at the insult.

"I know better." They exchanged smiles. "I just, I don't know, it all got kinda confusing."

"Confusing." He brushed the hair away from her face. "What about now?"

"Even more confusing."

She backed away from him. He exhaled hard and jammed his hands back into his pockets, looking toward the woods. When he glanced back again, she had toed off her tennis shoes and was pulling her sundress over her head. He raised his eyebrows. This was something he wasn't expecting. In fact, she was becoming more unpredictable as the weeks wore on. Looking around, he discovered there was no noise but for the water and birds. No people.

His gaze returned to her removing her bra, and his eyebrows went even higher. He scrubbed a hand over his face and beard because he knew how she'd feel. Finn toed off his own shoes and lifted off his tee shirt while approaching her. She removed her panties, and his gaze slid down her, scraping his teeth over his bottom lip. In a fluid movement, he relieved himself of the rest of his clothes as she had.

"So now, all of a sudden you're into skinny dipping?"

"I've thought about you," she quietly said and stepped into the water.

"I've thought about you too…a lot." He stepped in too.

Leaning over, Finn kissed her and enveloped her waist with his arms, lifting her up. She wrapped her legs around him, as he made his way farther into the cool water. They bobbed, as his hands moved over her ass and her arm held onto his neck. With one hand, he gently pulled her head back by her hair so that he could do his best on her throat and neck.

Breath coming short, Raven reached down between them, to find his cock, then impaled herself on it.

"Finn, this…" she began. "I've never …"

"Ah, Christ, Raven, you feel good," he said at the same time.

Hands on his shoulders, she supported herself, leaving him to love on her breasts, neck, and face, losing himself entirely. Raven kept her eyes on him, as she slowly rotated her hips around him. She closed her eyes and licked her lips, appearing lost in the sensations.

"I never… With you was the first time I ever had…" He watched her and slowed his progress, as he realized what she was trying to say.

"If you think that makes me think less of you, don't."

"I just didn't want you thinking that this wasn't …isn't…important, to me."

She didn't wait for him to answer and he couldn't concentrate on exploring those feelings in the present moment. As the dichotomy of cool water and their heat collided, she closed her eyes and opened her mouth. Making noises a man wanted to hear, her breathy gasps and small whimpers, complemented with an arched back, began pushing him to the edge. And just before he fell over, Raven looked directly into his eyes as they darkened and closed.

Chapter 20

Dressed in a long gown of creamy yellow chiffon, with a tight bodice and gathered scoop neckline, Raven felt like she was going to a prom. Her soft hair fell across her shoulders in waves as she pushed a diamond stud into her pierced earlobe.

Hearing a knock on the door, she spritzed herself with fragrance, then hurried to open it. Gone were the board shorts, sandals, and tee shirt. Finn stood before her in a charcoal suit, creamy ivory dress shirt, and knotted light charcoal tie.

"Wow!" He took in the length of her. "We're staying here." He kissed her cheek as she looked past him to see Nate and Annie.

"Too late," she whispered with regret. "You look incredible. I didn't think you even owned a suit."

"I don't. It's Nate's," he said with a sheepish grin. "Are you ready?"

"Yep, just let me grab my purse. Annie," she called. "You look so beautiful."

They arrived at the airport thirty minutes later and boarded the plane for the short flight to Oahu. The SeaHunt fundraising gala, thrown by their boss and his wife, entailed Nate giving a speech from the podium and both men selling their souls for donor funds.

Raven learned not only about the Hawaiian monk seal, but humpback whales, hawksbill turtles, and various birds scattered throughout the islands. Each was on the endangered species list and under the care of other branches of SeaHunt. Finn introduced her to the biologists specializing in the various animals and environments. She was fascinated to see what this group of people did and the passion and impact they had on the ocean and its inhabitants. Finn tried and failed to avoid his boss.

"Well Raven, it's wonderful to meet you." Alan extended his hand and smiled. "And don't you look breath-taking."

Finn explained how Sunderland became extremely angry when he learned a super star would be in their midst and they couldn't exploit it for more donors. Now he was all smiles and charm.

"It's a pleasure. Finn's told me about everything you do here. It's pretty incredible and very admirable."

"Thank you. We're proud of the work we do and the researchers that are out there every day in the trenches." He slapped a hand on Finn's shoulder while nodding to include Nate. "I don't suppose you'd be willing to perform a song for everyone? It would be a real treat." Finn moved away from his boss' grasp and placed a hand on the small of her back protectively.

"She's not here to perform Alan. She's here to enjoy the evening."

Sunderland's eyes went frosty. He apparently wasn't over his irritation toward Finn since the meeting with the turbine engineers. He opened his mouth to something but Raven, reading his displeasure, decided to interject.

"I'd be happy to."

"Wonderful, let's see…"

"Actually, Mr. Sunderland, how about we earn some money? Maybe set up an auction? I'd be happy to sing someone a song and offer a few signed programs."

The older man's excitement was apparent, as he condescendingly raised an eyebrow at Finn. He set a team in motion to make the rounds, as if the whole thing, was a furtive part of the original program.

"This is exciting and very appreciated, Ms. Hunter." He moved away to oversee the preparations.

"Mr. Sunderland," she called, and he turned. "I do have one request, however."

"Oh, yes, what can I do?" he asked walking back to her.

"I'll make it three songs, but the money raised goes to Finn and Nate's research exclusively, okay?"

Alan swirled his gaze toward the two men but didn't make eye contact. Nate, Annie, and Finn all looked dumbfounded and cast fervent glances at one another.

"Ah." Their boss glanced at the trio, who were smiling, and clenched his jaw. "Of course, Ms. Hunter, whatever you'd like. Let me just get the ball rolling here."

"Raven." As the man left, Finn held her elbow and led her away from the group. "You don't have to do this. Seriously, I can tell him right now you changed your mind, and we can get out of here."

"No." She smiled. "Come on, let's raise some money. Buy Alaula and Kaimi a beach ball to play with." Grinning confidently, she kissed his cheek.

When the auction was over, fifty-three thousand dollars, of the four-hundred-thousand grand total, had been raised by Raven's three songs. As she posed for pictures and signed autographs for the top bidders, she noticed Alan walk over to stand by Finn. She couldn't hear what he said but decided it couldn't be good when Sunderland left chuckling, and Finn simply clenched his fists.

****

After the gala, Finn spent the next two weeks divided between work, food, sleep, and Raven. He'd shown her most of the island, met most of his friends, and watched the sunsets. Many evenings she brought her guitar and played him her new songs or works in progress.

He took her on some research trips, to show her what they did in the field. However, some of Raven's favorite times were the ones they shared with Dee. The two women walked together, in the shared affection for one man. They also talked extensively about Dee's project and her insatiable desire for Raven's knowledge on the subject.

"What do you know about prophecies?" Dee asked, seizing yet another opportunity.

"Greek prophecies? Hmm, sorry, I don't know anything about them. Are there some interesting ones?"

"Well, Themis was a Titan…"

"That's the Cronus lot, right?" Raven asked to be sure.

"Yes. She handed down the ability to see and read prophecies to her sister, who also passed it down to Apollo."

Raven felt a tightening in her gut and placed a hand protectively on it; maybe she was just hungry?

"And what did they see?"

"Well, many different things, but I wondered if

there was ever one about Cronus overthrowing Zeus again. He had to be madder than an un-boiled potato."

"A what?" Raven giggled. "A potato?"

"Oh never mind, you know what I mean. He was probably pretty mad and wanted his revenge."

Still chuckling, Raven glanced over at Finn's grandmother, who today was wearing a lime green, yellow, and orange muumuu. Her floppy hat contained a combination of four limes, a lemon, and an orange on a bed of ti leaves and kukui nuts. When she first saw her, Raven had nearly bloodied her lip, biting down on it to keep from laughing.

She stopped laughing when she looked at Dee's profile. She took it so seriously, and Raven looked at her with apprehension. Some of Dee's queries were incredibly intense. In fact, Raven had the uneasy feeling that the older woman viewed them as real living and breathing people, at times. She decided to test the theory.

"Dee, Greek mythology is just that right, a myth? I mean, if you're asking in the stories did Cronus ever get out, I don't think he did. I mean I think Zeus maybe reassigned him to be like, the boss or head of part of the underworld. But he never came to power again." She glanced at Dee, then added, "In the stories I mean."

"The Elysium."

"Elysium?"

"He made him the boss of the Elysium I think."

"Really?" Raven was surprised. "Okay, but it would've been a kind of reward for being good or something, not causing an uprising."

"But what if he did cause an uprising and used the Fates?"

199

"The Fates?" Raven stopped walking and turned to her new friend. "Dee, Zeus was the Fates' father. They planned, like, all of time together or something. How would Cronus go around Zeus and get to the Fates, who were wholly controlled and committed to Zeus?"

"What if he had a helper?" Dee suggested after a minute of thinking.

"A helper?"

"Or dreams, maybe it was in the dreams," she exclaimed. "You said it was their weakness, right?"

Raven took a deep breath and determined the older woman was spending way too much time on the project.

"Hey," she said, trying to steer the conversation in a safer direction. "Fun fact for you. Do you know how Apollo got his lyre?"

"No. How?"

"From Hermes." Relieved to find she had the older woman's attention, she continued. "He was just newborn and very precocious. So, he went over to Apollo's place and stole a bunch of his cows. He then found a turtle and took out all its insides, using the shell and some cow guts to make the lyre." The older woman grinned broadly, delighted in the story.

"So, then Apollo was furious about the cattle and went to Zeus, who decided to punish Hermes. Well, the baby had already run back or poofed back to his crib. When they reached down to get him, Hermes pulled out the lyre and began to play. Apollo totally fell in love with the sound of music, and it became his most treasured possession. He felt so connected to the music that it became his power."

"What a great story," Dee said, laughing.

"Right?" Raven agreed. "Have you ever seen a lyre?"

"No. Well, maybe a picture. It's like a small harp, right?"

"Yep."

She pulled out her medallion necklace and showed it to Dee. The old woman's face literally glowed, and she ran her soft, wrinkled fingers over its surface.

"Oh my dear, it's so powerful, isn't it? So beautiful. Where did you get it?"

Powerful, Raven thought, what an odd word. Then she thought about it and realized that was precisely what it was. That strange, peculiar feeling she was growing accustomed to, crept in again.

"It was my mother's. She played the harp."

"Did she? I always wished I had learned to play an instrument."

"I could teach you. To play something, I mean."

"Would you? Oh, I would just love that. What about the ukulele?"

"Perfect, I don't have a lot of time left here, but I'm sure we can get some chords down, and you can build from there."

She continued down the trail and didn't see Dee's face fall.

Chapter 21

Jason walked briskly toward Fortner Talent and Publicity for his meeting with Donovan. He mumbled the speech he was hoping to give to the powerful and demanding man.

Most of the time he'd spent in Hawai'i he used to placate and reassure Raven. Yet, no matter what he told her he knew what he was going to allow and not allow. He'd try to negotiate a couple of songs, cover songs, sung and played her way. However, he wasn't going to mess with Donovan's temper or successful formula right out of the gate.

Not wanting to be outdone by the older man, Jason stepped into the reception area, wearing a designer navy wool suit. He had dropped a small fortune on it and a custom leather Italian briefcase.

Once allowed entry into the private sanctum, the men shook hands, sizing each other up, before Fortner gestured to a chair.

"Thank you for seeing me Donovan," Jason began. "I wanted…" Donovan held up a hand condescendingly.

"I haven't heard from you on the additions."

"Yes, I spoke with Raven, and I have the signed copies here, but she wanted me to stress …" Donovan looked down at some papers on his desk while extending a hand.

"Give them to me."

"Well, I wanted to discuss…"

"Give…them…to…me."

Jason reached into his briefcase and handed them across the desk. Donovan quickly flipped the pages, confirming everything was signed.

"All right, our business has now come to its conclusion," he informed the manager.

"Donovan, I came here to discuss the particulars and what we expect from you."

"What you expect from me?" Now Donovan did look up. "What you expect from …me?" Jason fidgeted in his chair. "Mr. Dell, I never approved of your presence. You were hired because Raven felt a nonsensical connection to you and that's all. Knowing the personal assistant position was a fairly inconsequential one, I allowed it to happen." His steely eyes bore into his prey. "However, make no mistake, you are not taken seriously at this level, not by anyone that knows this industry."

Jason felt the scathing remark, as hard as a physical blow. He tried to recover, so his voice wouldn't betray him.

"Be that as it may, Donovan, I am her agent now. I am in charge, and we need to discuss the negotiable portions of the contract. Raven wants to try some new things. Now, I won't let her deviate too much, but she's using the split from you as a reinvention of sorts, and we need to respect that."

Without looking, Donovan picked up the contract and pointed to the correct clause.

"Did you or did you not explain to your client that I am producing this show and that she has now agreed to do my show as I see fit? The time for negotiation is over. I'm paying her to be the Raven I created. Now, if on some ridiculous incompetence on your part, you choose not to read or disclose that to her before signing these papers, then that is your mess to clean up."

Jason licked his lip, heart racing as he realized he might have screwed up in monumental proportions.

"Ah," he said playing for time, "Ah, can we talk about the costumes?"

"Damn it, Dell. Her hair will be black. Her makeup will be appropriate. Her costumes will be elaborate to show off her body. Her music will be covers and done the specific way I've taught her to do it. That goes to her base, and it's what makes me money. I will consider one original song and one original piece, but if I decide to ax them, I will. That is as far as my charity will extend to you. Now"—he waved a hand, dismissing him—"fuck off."

Infuriated, humiliated and nauseous, Jason left the building and walked down Sixth Avenue. He had made a rookie mistake on his first major contract and assumed he would still be able to wriggle in a few creative control items, under the radar. Considering who he was dealing with, he realized the stupidity of that now. He would have to tell Raven.

Jason bought a latte and continued to walk down the street, trying to ascertain what the best course of action would be. He opted to wait out the month until she came home and he could talk to her in person. He sipped his latte, trying to forget that Donovan had essentially called him a pathetic joke.

Chapter 22

Finn smiled, watching the water sluice around the boat as they moved along the coastline toward Larsen's Beach. There was a possible sighting of a new monk seal, and it was also a diving day, to document findings.

"Holly," Nate called out. "We'll be there in about fifteen minutes. I want everyone geared up, okay?"

She gave a thumbs up and called to Jake and Dawson. When the cabin got crowded, she flattened herself against Finn, pushing her breasts hard to his chest. He glanced down at her as she let her hand linger on his ass as if trying to gain steady purchase. She gave him a dazzling smile.

"Sorry, tight fit." She looked at his lips then moved past him.

The play on words had him catching Nate's eye who merely shook his head and smiled. Finn rolled his eyes, but both men turned and watched her ass as she walked away.

Once anchored, Nate, Holly, and Finn donned wetsuits while Jake and Dawson motored toward the beach in a dinghy to see if they could find the reported new seal. Securing his last flipper, Finn lowered his goggles, placed the regulator in his mouth, and leaned back into the water. Holly followed him and finally Nate dove in last with the camera equipment.

They kicked down to the ocean's sandy floor and

watched a seal flipping rocks with its nose, trying to find food. Finn moved by it, to ascertain if it was their new seal but found it was one of their more playful favorites. He motioned for Nate to take pictures, as it played around two turtles.

The trio stayed for about thirty minutes tracking several seals, watching for anything amiss in their movements and functions. He also noted the environment and documented two safety areas that they'd need to address. Eventually, they decided to check in with the other two scientists.

"Was that Pepe?" Holly asked, breathing hard when they broke the surface of the water.

"Yeah," Finn said, laughing at the seal's playfulness. He could still feel them around his feet, calling out to stay and play.

"Did you see his bite? Tiger sharks have been in this area," Nate said.

"Yeah, it looked pretty well healed though," Finn remarked, swimming toward the boat.

Jake met them back onboard, where they removed all their gear. Nate asked the young protégé some questions as they piled into the dinghy and started for shore.

"So what d'ya got?" Nate yelled over the motor.

"Great news. There's a three-year-old in excellent condition."

"Is it the new one?" Finn asked.

"No, it's RWL-40. Dawson tried to get close to the other one that I'm pretty sure is our mystery guest."

"She didn't engage it though, right?"

"No, just observing, but from what we could see he's had a hard time of it. He's, it's, well, you'll just have to come see."

When they got to the beach, they found Dawson and followed her around a bend.

"Oh shit," Finn said, looking over at Nate.

"Holly, start documenting."

They approached carefully, not wanting to scare the animal. Nate flipped open his laptop, waiting for Finn, who took a deep breath and began dictating.

"I'd guess she's about nine feet long. Damn, gotta be close to seven hundred pounds." He stood back and scanned her. "She's not well. We're gonna have to get some samples."

"Shit," Jake murmured to Dawson. "I was afraid he was going to say that."

"She's been in the nets," Finn said and pointed to her neck. "Got some ligature marks." He slowly moved around the great behemoth, feeling her fear. "Had a couple of run-ins with some sharks before but they're healing nicely." He glanced over at Nate. "I think she's ingested something she wasn't supposed to."

"So, we gotta re-mark her?" Holly asked.

"I'm not sure she's ever been marked. I've certainly never seen her before." Nate yelled over to Finn, "She tagged at all?"

"No."

Tagging was Finn's least favorite thing to do, but it had to be done, to help the animal. Each person surrounded the seal, moving slowly. They had to place a restraining net on top of her, to obtain blood and blubber samples, to take back and examine for infection or parasites. Finn and Nate would also check pulse and breathing to find the best diagnosis and treatment plan. Surprisingly, the old seal didn't thrash for too long, seeming to understand and trust that he wouldn't harm her. They obtained everything they needed relatively quickly. Finally, they tagged her for tracking and identification, then left her alone again.

By the time the group was on its way home, a sense of celebration was in the air. The students were all aft, talking animatedly to one another. Nate approached Finn, steering the boat, not able to remove the broad grin from his face.

"Great day," Nate commented.

"Phenomenal day. The size of that girl! What would you guess for age?"

"Oh God, over twenty-five. She's a survivor."

Finn stretched behind the wheel. He couldn't wait to tell Dee and Raven. Nate watched him and seemed to read his thoughts.

"Ya gonna tell her?"

"Yeah, she's gonna go nuts."

"Getting laid by a good woman looks good on you, my friend," he said. When Finn's head snapped around, he raised his hands, laughing. "I'm just kidding."

"You're hilarious," Finn said, turning back to the water.

Nate rested his arms on the small workspace they had for charts. "I am. I also seem to remember getting a hell of a lot of shit from you when I met Annie."

"Well, you were pretty whipped."

"Yep, well, now you look just as stupid." Finn smiled just enough that only a friend would notice.

"Did she enjoy her research trip?"

"Yeah, she loved it." Finn added, "Oh, I forgot to mention, I was told RDL-35's all healed from the propeller. They're releasing him Tuesday."

"Ah, fantastic. You going?"

"Yeah, I think I'm gonna bring Rave too. She'd get a kick out of it."

"Sure, maybe I'll bring Annie then." Nate looked at his friend, hesitating only a little before saying, "So, this thing serious?"

"Of course not." Finn countered after a slight hesitation. "Damn, Nate, not everyone's like you. Some people just aren't built for greeting cards."

"Does she know that? She doesn't look like the type that has flings."

"Well, yeah." Finn's brow furrowed, a little unsure. "I think she does. She'll be leaving soon, so it doesn't really matter."

"Of course it matters, Finn. Jesus." Nate looked back out onto the water, thinking then changed the subject. "So, Annie wants another get-together tonight, why don't you bring her out to the cabin."

"Usual time?"

"Yeah." Nate took a deep breath. "So now we have to talk about something else."

"When are they putting them in?" Finn asked, resolved.

"They pushed up phase one, to September."

"Two months? Wow, they aren't wasting any time, are they?"

"Well, like I said, they already did all the research. Alan just wants it to happen."

"He's always been an impulsive bastard." Both men looked up when Dawson came onto the bridge.

"Alaula, two o'clock," she said. Finn maneuvered the boat to take a closer look. He idled and watched, as mother and child lay on the beach barking out to one another, then begin to play.

"I swear if they fuck up these animals, they're not gonna like me much." Finn spat.

"Don't worry brother. They won't be like me much either."

Chapter 23

That evening, when Raven and Finn arrived at the Bowman's cabin, the celebration was already underway. They took Raven's car, so she decided to wear a long coral peasant skirt and white eyelet blouse. Annie looped an arm in Raven's immediately and walked ahead of the men.

"Okay," Annie pretended to whisper. "I think you're going to need a cocktail and play on my team for volleyball."

"I'm not very athletically inclined." Raven giggled

"Oh bullshit, you run all over the stage in nine-inch heels. You could probably spike a ball over the net in them. Besides, Nate's terrible and I'm going to put him on the other team."

"You know I can hear you, right?" Nate retorted. "Never mind, I'm taking Finn then."

"You can't take Finn. He's the best player," Annie informed him without turning around.

Raven glanced back, and smiled at him in exaggerated admiration, causing him to shake his head. Games, music, drinking, and Hawaiian barbecue filled the evening, so by the time Nate hit a fork against a bottle, Raven felt slightly tipsy.

"Okay everyone." Nate raised his beer. "First, here's to our amazing friends and as always, thank you so much for coming. To the researchers of SeaHunt, great work on a pretty incredible day." Finn, Holly, Jake, and Dawson all raised a beer to him. "I also wanted to tell you that this isn't our regular little luau. Annie and I wanted to let you all know that come around Christmas, we'll be expecting another baby Bowman."

"*Hoopomaikai mai ia oukou hoaaloha maikai!*" Everyone yelled as excitement and cheers broke out.

"It just means 'bless you, good friends.'" Finn translated when she looked at him confusedly. Touched, she smiled warmly at the endearment, then laughed when Finn ran into the fray and twirled Annie.

"Why didn't you tell me, you asshole?" he exclaimed and clapped Nate on the back with enthusiasm.

Raven watched as the guests spoke animatedly to one another. They had all known each other for years. They knew each other's secrets and had intertwined their lives. It made her incredibly happy, then incredibly homesick for Wyatt, Que, and Abby. Her cell phone rang, and she groaned when she saw the caller. Walking to the perimeter of the party, she noticed a fifth of rum and grabbed it before connecting the call.

"Hello, Donovan."

"Raven, it sounds like I may have interrupted something." At another whoop of laughter, "Good God, where are you, a bar?" Donovan drawled.

"No, I'm at a luau. Is there something you need, Donovan?" she asked slowly, concentrating not to slur her words.

"We need to discuss your event."

"Can we do it later? Again, I'm at a party."

"No, we'll discuss it now. Jason is a complete moron and incapable of understanding how to negotiate a deal. I know you aren't much better at it, so I'm going to walk you through the particulars so that you may understand."

Resigned, she took a deep breath, then, realizing she was holding rum, took a considerable swill of it as he spoke.

"First off, he sent me your new headshot, and you look like a California cupcake." She took another pull off the rum. "Do you have no originality? Your look is edgy, that's your market, Raven. Your manager—and I use that term exceptionally loosely—is pulling you down an irresponsible and destructive path for your brand. You look absolutely ridiculous." She took another gulp, made a contorted face, and wiped her mouth with the back of her hand, trying not to giggle. "I'm sorry, is something amusing?"

"No. It's just that you called me a cupcake," she said, letting out a snort of laughter.

"If you want to look like a common beach tramp," his voice tightened, "do it on your own dime. We've spent hundreds of thousands of dollars promoting this and you. Do you understand me?" She automatically answered by nodding her head, then remembered he couldn't see her.

"Yes."

"You are now under contract to play the set I made for you, and as I told Jason, it's what your core wants to hear. More importantly, it's what I am paying for, do you understand?" When she said nothing, he said more loudly and sternly, "Do you understand me, Raven?"

"Yes," she said, quietly defeated.

"Amanda will follow your set and ..."

"Wait, what?" Her head buzzed. "Did you just say I'm opening for your girlfriend?"

"No, you are a professional, playing before another professional." She took three large swallows of rum, scrunched up her face, and exhaled through pursed lips.

"Just because she sang on a few sets with me does not make her a professional, Donovan. She's a glorified karaoke singer." Then realizing what she said, began to laugh.

"I know you are probably beginning to feel your irrelevance, Raven." The insult brought her up short, and tears stung her eyes, so she began to chug the rum.

"So, what, you just want to humiliate me again but this time on stage?"

"Look, Raven," Donovan said, sounding exasperated. "I have no idea what you've been doing to get by the last two months. It sounds like you've lost complete control of your faculties. You are washing out, and quite frankly, Amanda will become a huge draw as a result of this fundraiser."

She looked at the bottle and wondered if he could actually kill her with words. Shrugging, she gulped again, trying to gain courage.

"It's for the homeless though, right Donovan? This is all for those poor homeless people?"

"Do I need to remind you who handed you your life, Raven? Don't you understand that I can also take it all away? Would you like to see what I can really do?"

"No."

"Splendid. I will see you in ten days."

And without saying goodbye, he was gone. She sat down on a tree root sticking high up off the ground.

Dazed and numb, she remembered sitting on the floor of her condo in her fluffy socks and feeling the same exact way.

She looked at the bottle, then drank deeply before raising her head. Finn was through the trees a few feet away, listening intently to his friend Ray. His shirt was off, sunglasses perched on his forehead, arms crossed over his chest and one hand running through his beard. His strong oblique muscles vee'd down into his cornflower blue board shorts. He was hers or at least was for now. Her golden man.

"Oh, dude, check this." Ray became animated. "I just heard Texas traded Colt Stone."

"What? That's stupid."

"Right?"

"To who?"

"Seattle."

Raven stood and walked out of the trees toward the keg.

"They're trading the best tight end in the league to Sea…" Finn's voice stopped. "Hold up man, to be continued."

She weaved just a little and brought the three-quarters empty bottle toward her mouth but missed and poured it down her chest.

"Come on, Rave." Finn laughed. "Let's go for a walk."

"Aren't ya havin' any fun?"

"Sure, but getting fresh air is fun too."

She smiled at him, not quite realizing she stood in the fresh air and followed him to the beach. She held his hand as the sun began to set.

"So, what's going on?"

"What?"

He took the bottle from her, uncorked it, and drank a little. She reached for it too, but he held it at arm's length.

"You've had enough." Moving her in front of him, he placed a hand on her waist to support her better. "Now, what happened? Who was on the phone?"

"Oh, him."

"Him?"

"Donovan… He's such a dickhead," she slurred. Finn had just taken another shot, and this caused him to draw up short with a snort of laughter.

"Okay," he said, still chuckling. "And what did the dickhead want?"

"Well, he hates my hair and says I look like a terrible cupcake or something. Then he said when I do the concert, in a week, I have to do my old set, but I don't wanna. Oh, and his twelve-year-old karaoke mistress, well, I'll be opening for her."

He stopped laughing and let go of her as she staggered a little way ahead, then turned around to face him.

"What do you mean concert? Where, in Seattle?"

"Oh yeah, we stopped talking 'round then. We had sex though," she said, giving him a feline smile.

"Raven," he cautioned.

"We had such a great sex time." She stepped toward him, and he stepped back.

"A great sex time?" He grinned at her and brushed the hair back from her face. "God, woman, you're so wasted." She took another step toward him. "Seriously, you're really drunk and gonna make my life very hard." He paused, then added, "Literally and figuratively."

"I'm not a little drunk." She stood in front of him, eyes slightly unfocused but sparkling. "You're so pretty. Did I ever tell you I think you're pretty? Like a little golden man."

"Guys are not pretty. They're hot or sexy or something manly like that," he retorted as she began to unbutton her shirt. "Wait, Raven, there are rules here."

"We had sex in the water." She removed her blouse, and he scraped his teeth against his upper lip, staring at her black lacy bra. "And on my table."

"Stop." She took off her skirt, and he looked down at the matching panties and groaned. "I swear you got my libido confused with a twenty-year-old."

Raven grinned and decided she was winning. The sun had set in an afterglow of soft amber color, the peaceful tranquility juxtaposing the fire circulating through her blood. He looked helpless, scanning her body, as she removed her lingerie.

"Raven, there's rules," he said again with considerably less conviction. She walked up to him, grabbed a fistful of his hair.

"Fuck the rules, Finn," she whispered.

****

Surprise warred with lust inside him. Good guy? Bad guy? Fucking horny guy?

"Aw, shit," he gasped when she pulled the small tie on his board shorts and reached for him. Trying to pull away, he looked down the beach, but she was suddenly like a spider monkey, all over him and all at once. "What is it with you and the outdoors?" She pulled back and looked into his face through sexy lashes.

"Yep," she said breathlessly. "Very, very pretty."

"Okay, wait, damn it," he cried, as she placed his

hand on her breast, automatically causing him to squeeze.

"No." She pulled his shorts down, then pushed him onto the sand and straddled him. "Come on Finn, just have some fun with me."

He gave up trying to stop it and kissed her. Moving her off him, he laid her down on the soft sand, on top of their clothes. Feeling her body clamp down hard around him, he pulled back a little and watched her. Eyes closed, back arched, her magnificent breasts on display, she gyrated her hips on his. He could see the pressure building in her and felt it deep within him.

Overwhelmed with how beautiful she looked, he closed his eyes and listened as she made the little noises he'd grown to anticipate. Raven opened her unfocused eyes and hooked an arm around his neck, drawing him down to kiss her. When he opened his eyes again, she was staring into them.

"I love you, Finn."

Before he could say anything or process what he'd heard, an intense almost painful orgasm spread from his center and throughout his body. It was several minutes of clinging to each other and breathing hard before either could speak and even then, Raven just hummed. He reeled, trying to understand what the hell had just happened. He laid his cheek between her breasts and felt her heart beat fast as she stroked his hair.

By the time they got to his place, she was only sleepy. He carried her up the stairs, removed her clothes, and laid her in bed before climbing in himself. Putting an arm behind his head, he stared at the ceiling. She turned to him in sleep, and he automatically drew an arm around her, bringing her close. She wouldn't remember what she said that night, in the same way he'd never forget it. Not knowing where or if that fit in his life scared the hell out of him.

****

The blinding light was the first thing she recognized. Blinding sunlight and shocking pain, like someone was shanking her brain with a chard of glass over and over again. She opted to pull the covers up over her head and open her eyes in that cocoon first. Then, she exposed herself to a little more light until she could tolerate it without whimpering. Noticing Finn's sunglasses sitting on his nightstand, she grabbed at them greedily, before placing them gingerly on her face. The slight extra pressure caused her to whimper again. What had she done to herself?

Pulling the soft white duvet up over her breasts, she stared at the ceiling. Raven didn't know where Finn was and was quite sure she didn't want him to see her like this. Instead, she tried to piece together the night before. Volleyball, drinks, Nate announced his wife's pregnancy, which caused her to smile again despite herself, then more drinks. Then she got a phone call. Who had it been? Her face paled to paper white. Donovan. She was tipsy and talked to Donovan. What had she said? She couldn't remember. Then she was on the beach with Finn and…

"Oh my God. Oh my God!" She sat up and yelped again. "I did not," she announced to the room. "I…"

"Ah, yes… Yes, you did." Finn had been sitting in a chair. He folded the paper, stood up, and threw it on the table. He walked to the kitchen for the tray he'd prepared. "You were like a super sex freak on the beach," he said when he returned.

She paled even more if that was possible. Sitting down on the bed, he placed the tray between them. There was a large glass of water, some peppermint tea, a banana, some crackers, and some aspirin on it. She snatched the aspirin and uncapped the water.

"Shut up."

"Oh, shut up is it?" He gave her thigh, the closest thing to him, a gentle squeeze. "Now that I know you can bend around like that babe, it opens up a whole new world for us." He grinned more broadly when all she did was blanch, causing her to wonder what precisely she had said and done. Chuckling, he stood up and walked back to the kitchen table to retrieve his coffee. "Eat something. It'll make you feel better."

Dee called to him through the open window. Raven scrunched down into the bed. She was embarrassed his grandmother was there, and she was in Finn's bed. He padded to it and looked down at the foot of the stairs.

"Morning, Dee."

"Good morning, dear. I was just going to go to the market. Can I get you anything?"

"No, I don't think so." He turned to Raven and called, "Do you want anything different at the store?" She hissed at him to be quiet, and he gave her a perplexed look, before turning back to his grandmother. "I think we're good."

"Okay, well, tell Raven I want her to stay for dinner with us tonight."

"Okay, I will. Love you."

"Love you too, dear." And she was gone.

"So, can you stay for—" He turned toward her and got beaned with a pillow.

"Are you crazy? Oh my God," she squeaked.

He let the pillow drop, looking over at her with a strange expression on his face. She could see her reflection in the mirror next to him. Face pink, hair disheveled, his sunglasses on crooked, and one long, tanned leg was on top of the covers. She looked horrible, but he merely gave a slight shake of his head and smirked at her.

"What in the hell're you doin'?"

"Now your grandma knows I slept here last night, with you, in this bed." She pointed at the covers.

"So?"

"So! So! She's from a different generation, Finn. She's gonna think I'm a total slut."

"Well, there was last night. Ow!" She had thrown another pillow at him, and he roared with laughter. "She lived through the sixties, Raven." He walked toward the bed. "She's smoked pot, probably still does." He crawled over the blankets. "She wears flowers in her hair." He set her tray on the floor. "Have you checked out how she dresses? She was front and center of the sexual revolution in this country."

He took both her hands and held them over her head as he hovered above her. "Do you honestly think she cares if her thirty-six-year-old grandson, whom he loves, has sex with a thirty-four-year-old woman she respects, in his bed, at his house? Besides." He leaned down and kissed her. "We haven't had sex in this bed…yet." He widened his eyes devilishly at her.

"No, I will vomit on you." When he pulled down the covers to reveal her breasts and take a nipple into his mouth, she amended, "Okay, fine, but I'm leaving your sunglasses on."

Chapter 24

Dee made a dinner of poi, lomi-lomi salmon, rice, and pineapple. Asking the couple to set the table in the garden, she heard Raven gasp when she turned the corner into paradise. A warm wind blew through the ornamental grasses. The sun seemed to light from within the bright yellow flowers, gardenias, and orchids of every color, and the old banyan tree moved as if alive. Finn's grandmother watched as the impact of color and scent took Raven's breath away and to Dee, there was no higher compliment.

"Oh my God, Dee," Raven exclaimed and turned back to the woman, as she padded out the door. "This, this—I've never seen anything so incredible. How did you do all this?" Pleased, the older woman put an arm around Raven's waist and tilted her hand back and forth.

"Oh, a little of this, a little of that. You go on now. We'll have all night to admire my handiwork."

"Pretty cool, right?" Finn said, coming out to help her set the table. "The woman can literally grow anything."

"It's so incredibly beautiful. If this were my backyard, I'd never leave it."

"Yeah, she tried to teach me how to do this growing up, but I just wanted to go surfing and chase girls."

They sat enjoying their dinner, talking about Nate and Annie's announcement from the night before, leaving out Raven's drunken forays. Finn cleared the dishes and returned with a bottle of chardonnay. He seemed to read something in Raven's face, so he grabbed her a bottle of water, then handed a glass of wine to Dee. Afterward, he stepped down onto the grass and walked in worn, frayed jeans and bare feet around the garden.

"You still want to increase the size of this koi pond?" he asked, raising his voice to be heard.

"I think so, but let's wait until after summer." Dee looked around the garden restlessly, trying to figure out how best to broach the topic she most wanted to discuss. Finally, Raven gave her the perfect opening.

"Hmm," Raven said, closing her eyes and breathing in the scents. "I can see why you picked Demeter."

"Demeter?" Finn queried, stepping onto the deck.

"You know, Demeter from Greek mythology."

"Oh, wow, I forgot all about that." He sat down and turned his attention to his grandmother. "Sorry Dee, how's your project going?"

"Well, it's been pretty interesting...enlightening," Dee said.

"Enlightening, huh. How so?"

"It's how some people respond to the gods today. They pray to them."

"Yeah, I could see some people still believing in all that, especially maybe in Greece."

"Well, no, I meant here."

"Here?" He glanced over at her and looked alarmed at what she was sure was a flustered and anxious face. He leaned forward and took her hands. "Hey, you okay? What's going on with you?"

"Well." She gulped her wine, took a big deep breath, and decided to test the waters. "Something very—well, strange happened a few weeks ago."

Finn looked briefly over at Raven, with a concerned frown. He moved aside Dee's glass and put a forearm on the table, and an arm around her shoulders, peering at her.

"What're you talking about?"

"Oh," she said nervously, "you're going to think I'm so crazy, but I promise it's all real."

"Okay, Grandma, you're scaring me a little now."

Knowing that he only called her Grandma when he felt intense emotions, she tried to think about how to say things. Coming up with nothing, she decided to jump in with both feet.

"On April seventeenth I was out here working when the wind started acting funny," she blurted.

"Funny?" Finn looked intently into her eyes. Raven moved her head back and eyes cast downward as if making a calculation. "Funny how?"

"It slowed down, then sped up, then kind of swirled up."

"Swirled up?" he asked cautiously, eyes narrowed like she was a time bomb about to go off.

"Damn it, Finn. Sit back and drink some wine; you're making me nervous."

He did what she asked, and she continued to tell them about the strange water spout in the ocean and the golden beam of light. She explained how her own feet guided her to where she was supposed to go. Finn kept scrubbing a hand over his face, as Raven just gazed at the woman with apprehension.

"I-I was given something a very long time ago from my mother. It goes back in my family to I don't know when. I'm not sure anyone ever did, but I kept it because I knew I was supposed to and because it was a piece of her." She looked pleadingly at Finn, willing him to believe her. "It, like, called to me or something."

"Called to you?"

"I got the box out of where I had it and when I touched it, I felt like I was eighteen years old all over again. But then I didn't only feel that way, I-I looked it."

"Grandma, what in the hell are you talking about?" he asked in an almost melodic voice like she was crazy.

"I'm telling you, I looked down at my hands, and they were young. I sat cross-legged on the floor. My eyes were clear without my glasses. I was young again."

"You were dreaming." He stood up and reached down to her. "Come on, let's let you lie down awhile."

"Please just listen, okay? Let me tell you all of it."

"Finn," Raven said quietly, "come on, sit down." He did and let out a shaky breath.

"I took out the box and set it on my lap. I could never open it before. It's always been sealed shut but it just opened, and there was this kind of round thing inside. It was like part of a ball that looked like frosted glass, but it wasn't glass. It was like exposed electricity, only not electricity." She was disheartened because she couldn't articulate it well.

She chanced a look at Finn, who had his head in his hands, then at Raven, who had a hand on his back but just smiled back at her, sympathetically. Dee focused.

"The thing sparked. It had all the knowledge of the world, and when I touched the surface, a woman came out." Finn's head snapped up to look at her and narrowed his eyes again.

"A woman came out of a crystal ball? Is that what you're trying to tell me?"

"She was ghost-like and flowy, and her hair was long. She had a cloth around her eyes."

"Kinda like you this morning," Finn quipped, looking back at Raven and standing up.

"She said her name was Themis."

"Themis?" Raven spoke hoarsely. "The Titan lady…Themis?" Finn glared at her but looked back at Dee.

"Yes, yes." Dee sighed in relief. "Except I didn't know who she was then; it just felt like I should. Later, when I looked her up, I saw the exact same lady in a book. She scared me."

"You're fuckin' scaring me," Finn retorted.

"She called me the daughter of Demeter."

"So that's why…" Raven began, then seemed to realize she spoke out loud and leaned back in her seat.

Dee nodded slightly, knowing Raven now understood all her questions. Finn kept pacing the yard.

"She said something about a prophecy and that the two must unite because they share space together."

"Grandma, I…"

"The daughter of Apollo and the son of Poseidon." She yelled out in frustration, pointing to each of them, trying to make them see.

There was silence, except for the sound of birds. Raven's mouth fell open, as she stared incredulously at

Dee. Finn also stared at his grandmother with wide eyes, and he broke the stillness by sliding his hands into his pockets, then removing them again. Taking a deep cleansing breath and darting a look to Raven, he stepped forward and knelt beside Dee, taking her hands.

"Grandma, what're you saying? Do you honestly think you, me, and Raven are somehow connected to the Greek gods? Stories and people made up by other people? And somehow if Raven and I are together, we what, fulfill some kind of spell? Please, please tell me that you understand how incredibly crazy that sounds?" Dee lowered her head.

"Of course I know how crazy it sounds, Finn." She yelled at him, voice cracking. She stood, a sheen of sweat on her brow, and jerked her hands from his. "Sit down."

"Grand—"

"God damn it, I said sit down…now!"

He did, and Dee left the patio to go inside. She saw their reflection in the glass as her grandson mouthed, *what the fuck*. Raven just shook her head, gave a slight rise of her shoulder, and pressed her lips together in a worried line.

Dee returned holding a box, and the couple stared at it as if a duck had suddenly appeared in her arms. She held it tightly to her, then handed it to Finn upside down. He took it and jerked like he'd been shocked. He stretched his back and rolled his shoulders, sighing deeply.

"Read it," Dee demanded. Raven stood by Dee but leaned over to look at the intricately carved box, careful not to touch it, as Finn read.

"Those that now rule will rue a day when those

they command refuse to pray."

He looked over at Dee, who vibrated with anticipation. Raven gently rubbed circles on her back.

"An old, most powerful foe will find a way, to escape the bonds of yesterday.

"And with him will turn one once trusted, that gods persecuted and belittled and neglected. Mighty gods shackled and toiled, never to be heard, from Tartarus's grip deep in the abyss of the Underworld. There they will remain for as long as time rules until the last bead of their blood is collected and cooled. The demonic plagues that have yet to be seen, will devour all time and space, as the dark one will deem. The outcome we fear fate could yet reject if the children of tomorrow's lives intersect." Finn paused and looked up. "Grandma I…"

"Just read it," Dee commanded. So, he turned apprehensively and continued.

"And in their quest, three discoveries must be found, or the deities will face the Moirai and be cut to the underground. First, god and mortal alike a weakness to conquer, and only from that key may the children conjure. Second, something gods have naught to know, selfless-devotion and love-eternal the very hardest to sow. The final discovery for this quest to take place is when all children are in the same time and same space. Five arrows to join at the end of the day, surrounding heart's blood of great hope, it will lay, perhaps, even more, only Themis can say. Many eras have tried to face success and prevail, only to miss the connections and fail. The brothers may harness drops of their power to advise in this cause because it is written in Themis' divine law. For only then will the

threat be defeated, and to the Isle of Blest, the remaining gods be seated. And though their time of rule may end, full integration of immortal blood, this oracle will send. For even if one pure drop remains, ascending the steps, Olympians may again reign."

He stopped and set the box down as Dee opened her eyes to look at him, waiting. Raven trembled but remained silent.

"I can see this is very important to you," Finn began after several tense moments. "Believe me, I get it. Who wouldn't want to be part of something exciting and foreign and you know, god-like powers and royalty? But Grandma, I truly think this was an intensely realistic dream that lodged into your consciousness. Then when you started doing all this research, it got confused in your mind, you know?"

"Finn, I understand how crazy it sounds, I do. I knew nothing about Greek mythology or who any of these people were until she told them to me." Dee gestured to the box and took a deep breath. Suddenly she was exhausted.

"And now you think Poseidon... I'm assuming you think I'm some offshoot of Poseidon, right?"

"You have a trident on your back."

"Because I thought it was cool when I was twenty-years-old."

"And you've never felt anything strange that you can't explain?"

"And Raven," he continued, not willing it seemed, to entertain those thoughts. "Who I just met, is Apollo? You realize, Apollo was a dude, the boy half of the twins, right?"

"God of music."

"Jesus!" Finn barked out his frustration. He stood up so quickly, he knocked his chair over. "This is fucking ridiculous."

"Look," Raven said, trying to placate, "it's late. Everything is just confusing and out there. Maybe, let's just take a step back and let things calm down."

"What, are you actually giving credence to this bullshit?" he demanded, wheeling on her. Raven furrowed her brow at him, then looked at Dee.

"What I'm suggesting is we sleep on it, take some time to process what everyone has said, then talk tomorrow, okay?" Dee stood up and kissed the young woman on the cheek. She started back into the house, then turned to look at them.

"I don't want you to be scared, Finn. I was terrified at first. But now—I'm not scared at all anymore. This was real. As real as you and I are right now. I didn't dream it. I didn't want to be a part of it, and I'm not crazy." She turned and walked into the house.

"Well, that makes one of us," he muttered, looking over at Raven. "Come on. I'll take you home."

They arrived at her bungalow, and he switched off the motor. They hadn't spoken during the ride, and the silence was deafening. He walked her to the door, lacing his fingers with hers but when she opened the door, he remained where he was, causing her to turned around.

"Don't you want to come in?"

"Ah, no, I'm gonna call it a night. I have no idea what's going on with her, and I have to figure this out. It could be something serious."

"I think she's just confused, Finn. Between reality and some vivid dreams," she soothed.

"So, you're okay with this?" He looked at her incredulously. "An old woman just said you are related to a bunch of made up people. And now you have to go on a quest, to make sure they don't all die." He dropped her hands and walked to the stairs. "That's a hundred ways of incredibly fucked up shit."

"Of course I don't believe it." She walked over and stood behind him, wrapping her arms around his waist. "But she was getting upset, and everything needed to calm down. You know if you're tired enough or susceptible enough, you can believe just about anything. I can tell you. I've been having some crazy realistic dreams lately, where I wake up wondering if they're real."

"What kind of dreams?" He turned and looked at her, uneasy.

"Mostly trapped ones, some on the water, some having to do with my music and the concert, that kind of thing." She tilted her head at him, lost in thought, and placed a hand on his shoulder. "Hey, she's gonna be okay." Raven leaned in and kissed him. "Are you sure you don't want to stay?"

He shook his head, then wrapped both arms around her, kissing the top of her head. She felt so perfect he almost changed his mind. Squeezing her hand, he turned and walked down the sidewalk a little before turning around.

"Hey, Rave," he called, and she turned around smiling. "What day did you come here on the island?"

"April seventeenth." He frowned. "Yeah I know, weird, right? Night," she called and closed the door.

After he got home, Finn walked to the base of his stairs and put one foot on the tread, trying to decide if he should let it go or confront Dee. They'd always been able to talk and disappointing her was the one thing he couldn't bear. So, he opened the door and walked back to her bedroom. She was reading a book but set it down when she saw him leaning on the doorjamb.

"I know how it sounds, darlin'," she said before he could speak. "Don't you think I know how it sounds?"

"It sounds crazy, Grandma—it's wrong."

"And you're scared."

"Yeah, I'm scared about what it means for you. I think we should see someone."

"You mean me. I should see someone."

"Yes, damn it." Suddenly, he felt like a child. She patted her bed, so he removed his jacket and sat with his forearms on his knees. "Look." He turned to look at her. "I know you like Raven. I like her too—a lot. But I'm beginning to feel a ton of pressure from everyone right now. That I should be making decisions regarding her when I don't even know how I feel about it myself."

"Finn, anyone can see that you love her." He stood up and paced.

"Yeah, well, ya know what, that's just it." he retorted, looking at her. "I don't know what I feel, and everyone keeps telling me how I feel, and it's starting to piss me off. She doesn't stand up for herself, she changes her mind every two God damn seconds, she's not exactly forthcoming about her past, and I don't know where all that sits with me, okay?"

"Finn, come here," she coaxed. He sat back down and drew one leg under him, looking at her.

"Look, I know you want this for her and me. And this little story is, what, somehow going to do that?" he asked.

"I saw the woman standing right there." She pointed to the closet. "She was as real as you are sitting here. I wasn't hallucinating, I wasn't drinking, and no, I didn't have some kind of spell or attack. Something unmistakably happened." She looked by the closet then back at him. "You have known me your entire life, son. You are my entire life. Don't you think that if I thought something was wrong with my health or mental faculties, you'd be the first...the very first person I'd tell? If only for the simple matter of you not having to take on an invalid."

"Grandma."

"I just want you to think about this, right now. No more talking, just think. And when you're thinking, ask yourself, has anything strange been going on? Seeing things, dreams that seem very real? How did it feel when you read the prophecy? Feelings that are out of the ordinary." She leaned forward and placed both hands on his face. "Don't tell me anything about it, just answer the questions honestly to yourself. Without judgment and with an open mind. Will you do that for me?"

He closed his eyes, knowing he trusted her more than anyone else in his life, so he nodded. She kissed his forehead, and he stood to go.

"And Finn," she said, as he turned around, "sometimes not having the answer is also an answer." He blinked at her. "Good night, dear."

Lying in bed that night, hands interlaced on his abdomen, he reviewed the direction his life had turned. A few months ago, he was about as free as a person could be. He answered to no one, had reckless sex with different women whenever he wanted, and a career that he loved. All the rules he followed were of his making, and others followed them because he willed it. He slept sound, life made sense, and every day was a new sheet of paper. And he had a grandmother that wasn't certifiably crazy.

Now, he slept with one woman. An incredible, sexy, mind fuck of a woman, but one. His dreams filled with questions, darkness, and restlessness, which now seemed to have more credence, for some inexplicable reason. Something was happening to Dee that frightened him more than anything else, and his life felt like it was spinning entirely out of control. Now, in his career, he couldn't influence anyone or anything. They just wouldn't listen. He could barely hear the animals anymore, even Alaula, she…

He sat up. What in the hell… Hear the animals? What the fuck? He swung his legs out of bed and cradled his head in his hands. Christ, he was cracking up too. An unease came over him, and he found himself leaning over and pulling his phone from the charger. Tapping the screen, he found his photos. When they had left for Raven's, he walked to the buffet table, where his grandmother had left the box, and turned it over. He wanted to see if it was made in Japan or perhaps there was a reference he could find on some internet browser, to make Dee understand the craziness of it all. For some reason, at the last moment, he'd taken a photo.

However, as he sat up in bed and magnified the screen to read the script, a thick wave of vertigo washed over him. He set the phone down in his lap. His thumb had inadvertently swiped the screen to a photo of Raven and him on the beach. Their heads and bodies were pressed together in a selfie. He swiped again, and it was them at Nate's party before she got drunk. Swipe; she sat without reservation on his bike. Swipe; eating dinner together. Swipe; on the boat trying to find the seals. His eye caught something, and he rescanned, then magnified the shots. In each photo, she wore a disc on a chain, both of which appeared to be gold, around her neck. Had she always worn that? He hadn't noticed. He tried to zoom it in more, but the grainy photo wouldn't reveal what was on it. He set the phone down on his chest. When had she so completely taken over his thoughts, actions, time…just his life. Not only was she entrenched in his but Dee now had her in her sights. His grandmother wanted to settle him down because she read a poem on a box made in Asia. Irritated, he threw his phone back on the nightstand and eventually fell into a fitful sleep.

He was on Honopū Beach, walking through the arch, searching for Alaula and Kaimi, but he couldn't find them anywhere. She must have finished her nursing time and returned to the sea. He walked for what seemed like hours on the alternating rocky then sandy beach.

Eventually, he found the baby pup that now weighed a hundred and fifty pounds. Finn smiled at the growth, then heard a barking out in the water. Searching, he saw Alaula struggling with something and calling out for help. Strange blue-black bands circled the mother like a shark, then pulled her under the water's surface. Finn thought it was trash thrown into the ocean. Angry, yet bitterly afraid, he ran out into the water in an effort to save her but knew he'd be too late.

The last band laid itself over the mother's mouth, and nose then dragged her beneath the cold waves, now turning into ink itself. Finn heard Alaula calling for him to protect Kaimi from the blackness. He felt her panic and fear as she forcibly edged closer to the widening doom within the water's depths. He turned to sprint back and secure her pup's safety, as Kaimi called out for his mother. Finn was within ten feet of the animal when he saw the same bands snake across the beach for the pup. He lifted a hand as he ran.

"No!"

He sat bolt upright in the darkness, thinking he may still be in the dream and the dark, dank misery of it. He cursed his grandmother and Raven for putting the thoughts in his mind for dreams to fester.

Chapter 25

Monday morning, Finn woke surprisingly early after getting little sleep. He told Dee he'd probably be late that night and noticed the old wooden box was gone. Raven had already tried to call him, and he'd let it go straight to voicemail. Feeling itchy and restless, he punched the accelerator of his bike after he eased onto the highway. Only then did he start to feel more normal.

Holly was busy unloading her car when he arrived. She watched him park and dismount then turned back to her task. When she turned back around, he noticed her tank top was considerably lower, exposing more cleavage.

"Need some help?" he called and walked over to her, smiling.

"Yeah, thanks."

He reached in and grabbed the heavy box. When he turned, she hadn't stepped back and smiled up at him with that same hungry look she always did. He glanced down at her lips, then cleavage, prominently on display.

"So, where we going today?" she asked, turning and extending her body into the car to retrieve some scuba tanks.

"I'm thinking more along the coastline, here on the south side." Finn moved aside to let her walk ahead, so that he could admire her ass.

He grinned, feeling a little more like his old self,

when Raven's radiant face filled his mind, immediately triggering guilt. Trying to brush it aside, he set down the equipment on the dock, as the group began preparing the boat.

"Hey." Nate poked his head out the glass door of the building and called, "So, I think I'm going to have you go to…"

"Waimea," Finn shouted back. "Great choice."

"Waimea, why there?"

"Because we've been off the grid there for a while. I heard there were a few feral cats and a dog out there, so I wanna check it out before they get too near the seals."

"Okay." Nate paused, thinking. "Well, come on up to the office, and I can give you some stuff for there then."

"Finish gearing up," Finn ordered, looking back at the crew. "I'll be right back."

"So what are you going to do over there?" Nate asked when Finn walked into his office.

"I don't know, check about the animals, see if the nets are hung up there again. The park can get trashed pretty quickly."

"You okay?"

"Sure, why?"

"I don't know. Something seems off."

"Naw, just want to get to it. I gotta weird feeling we need to go over there, and it's been awhile."

"Okay, take off then. Let me know if you find anything."

****

All kinds of debris, nets, and plastic bottles, were strewn across the beach's surface. Frustrated with the carelessness, Finn returned to the boat in a caustic mood and discovered he'd missed two texts from Raven.

Hey, tried to call, everything ok?

Thinking about you, want to come over, get something to eat tonight?

He saw her face in his mind and wanted desperately to see it in the flesh, but knew he needed to step back a little and get some clarity.

They made it to Salt Pond and noticed a large crowd on the beach at the same time Nate's voice crackled over the radio.

"Yeah Nate," Finn said as he tried to get closer to the shore.

"Finn, I just got a call from Eddie Kameāloha, over at Salt Pond. He says they have a dead seal."

"Shit." Finn handled the throttle and maneuvered closer. "We're looking at something going on there right now and going in for a closer look. He say what happened?"

"Blunt force trauma. I'm on my way."

"God damn it!" Finn threw the CB. "God damn, sonofabitch!" His researchers watched as their boss strung a series of fantastic curses and threats together. "Take the fuckin' wheel," he barked at Jake. "And get me closer so I can get off. Then go figure your own shit out."

Jake got as close as he could, and Finn jumped off the bow into the hip-deep water, with Holly following his lead.

Making his way up the beach, he yelled at the sightseers and locals to get back. Hearing a seal barking, Finn thought maybe Nate had gotten some bad information. Encouraged, he yelled again for everyone to get back. As the last person moved, he saw her. Alaula, lay on her side, with her skull crushed and unseeing eyes for her pup.

"Oh God!" Finn screamed. "Oh no, no, no!" He raised his arms, locking his hands behind his head and paced a couple of steps back. "Oh God!"

He sank to his knees beside her. Holly began to cry, watching Finn's hands hover just over Alaula's once beautiful face, not quite touching her. Kaimi barked in pain, screaming at Finn.

What has happened to her? My mother? Please, I need your hands.

Finn just blinked at him in confusion then realized something was wrong. He ran over to the youngster and saw he'd been hurt badly too. Three long rake marks extended the length of his abdomen. Frantically searching his pockets, he realized he'd left his phone in his pocket when jumping into the water and turned to the crowd.

"Fuck. Phone, phone, someone give me a God damn phone."

Reaching Nate, he explained what had happened, and was able to set in motion the process of getting Kaimi and the remains his mother to the refuge center on Oahu.

****

Finn squatted down helplessly on the balls of his feet, looking down at Alaula's blood in the sand. Nate could hear the tourists talking about the pictures they got and the van rolling across gravel, taking her away. He knew there were no words of comfort he could offer his friend.

"I've got to stay and puzzle some of this out," he informed Holly, eyes slightly haunted. He handed her his car keys. "I'll go back with Jake and Dawson on the boat. Can you bring Finn home?"

"Sure. What're they going to do with her?" Holly asked, face red and puffy.

"Well, we'll do an investigation; this isn't the first time this has happened, and unfortunately, it won't be the last." Nate eyed Finn. The sun was bright in the sky, maligning the dark hue cast over him, as Finn looked down where the mother had lain. "Alaula was his first primary. He watched her birth and watched her give birth, so this one's pretty hard."

"Yeah." Holly followed his gaze. "I'll bring him back." A couple of men stepped out of a sedan and started walking toward the beach. "Who are they?" she asked, nodding her head at them and Nate looked over.

"That's the DLNR—Department of Land and Natural Resources. They're going to work with NOAA on the investigation. It's lucky they happened to be on the island—we were going to have a meeting." He looked at Finn again and nodded at her. "Okay, go ahead and get out of here."

****

Finn rode the way back to his place in silence, looking at the blood of both mother and pup on his clothes, mixed with sand and dirt. Understanding his need for quiet, Holly just concentrated on the road.

"Come on," she said, after they arrived back at his place, "let's go have a drink."

They went upstairs and into his living room. Finn walked to his cupboard, pulling down some whiskey. He poured three fingers for each of them, quickly drank his, then poured another, before handing one to her. Cradling the second drink in his hand, he sat down on the couch.

"I'm so sorry Finn. I know how I'm feeling right now and that's nothing to how you must feel." She leaned down and looked up into his face.

"Thanks, Hol, and thanks for driving."

"Of course." She leaned over and kissed his cheek. Then thinking better of it, she slid off the couch and knelt between his legs. She placed her hands on his thighs and rubbed them up and down.

Finn looked at her with such sadness and ran a finger down the side of her cheek. She saw the moment he realized she wasn't Raven. Draining his glass and grimacing at the spirit, he took Holly by the shoulder and moved her back so he could stand and move around her. He patted her on the top of her head once.

"Thanks again, take the day, get cleaned up." He walked toward the counter, to pour another drink. "I'm gonna grab a shower. I'll see ya tomorrow, Hol."

She watched him walk away and sighed with frustration. She knew he'd been seeing Raven, but also knew his reputation from before. He was hurting; so was she. Okay, maybe she didn't care as much as he did, but she was sad about the way the seal died. She'd been waiting for Finn to make a move for so long and felt now, she could be the right person, at the right time. Maybe she could cheer them both up.

Finding and retrieving one of his tank undershirts from a drawer, she removed her shirt and bra, before slipping it over her head. She stripped off her pants and stood in front of a mirror to see the effect. The tank was big, so the sides of her breasts were exposed. And what man didn't like a girl in a thong? If anything, she'd be able to take his pain away for a short while. As the shower water still rained down, she was trying to decide if she should join him, when there was a knock on the door.

Holly almost let it go but knew Finn would be out soon. She wanted to get rid of whoever it was, so as not to take his attention away, now that she finally had it. Opening the door, distracted with the anticipation of what was coming, she looked straight into the concerned eyes of Raven. The singer's eyes scanned Holly, clad only in his undershirt and thong.

"Oh," Holly's voice quavered, surprised. "Raven, hi?" When the woman didn't say anything, Holly lowered her voice, "Finn's just finishing up a shower."

No sooner had she said it when the bathroom door opened and Finn walked out with a towel wrapped low around his hips, followed by a cloud of steam. He reached across the table to grab something, then turned and saw both women staring at him. When he saw Raven, he began to smile in relief but then noticed Holly in her state of undress and furrowed his brows in confusion. Realization seemed to dawn on him, and his eyes snapped back to Raven's.

"Raven…" She turned and fled. "Raven!" he yelled, but when he reached the porch, she had closed her car door, turned over the engine, and backed out with tires screeching.

"Fuck. Fuck! God damn it!" He walked back into his apartment and looked exasperated at Holly. "What the fuck're you doing?" he demanded.

"I-I thought we were heading in this direction," she stammered, watching him walk back in, securing his towel better.

"Christ, how in the hell did I give you that impression?"

"Ah, you've flirted with me, and we've had a connection for months, and just now you touched my hair and…" She trailed off, realizing how absurd it sounded.

"Flirting? Really? Are you kidding me? You haven't noticed that I'm with someone right now?' He glared at her. "This day's a clusterfuck nightmare!" He released his breath forcefully, "I've been nice to you and yeah we might have flirted a little but have I ever acted on it? I touched your head because it was incredibly cool of you to drive me home and drink with me when I was feeling shitty." He raised a hand to the back of his head and gestured at her with the other emphatically. "You came on to me, and I got up and left so that you wouldn't get the wrong impression. How does that say, let's move on to fucking?"

"Wow, okay, whatever." Closing the door, she peeled off his undershirt. Glimpsing bare breasts, he quickly turned around with his hands on his hips and stayed that way until she was dressed and back at the door. "Sorry Finn, I didn't mean to cause any trouble."

As she walked out, Finn sat down on his bed, cradling his head in his hands, trying to decide what to do next. Should he run over there when Raven was strung out and hurt? Somehow try to convince her that she didn't see what she thought she saw? He laughed out loud. That's what every guy says when caught with a near-naked woman in his room. He resolved to let her cool down and go to her that night, to try and explain. At that moment, he didn't have the capacity for anybody's emotions besides his own.

Chapter 26

Raven sobbed in her car, and by the time she arrived at her house, her head had begun to throb. Unlocking the front door, she threw her keys violently against the wall and gave one loud, guttural scream. How the hell did this happen to her—again?

The phone rang and thinking it was Finn, almost decided to let it go until she saw it was from Que. That's who she needed. She needed her best friend.

"Que," she said, her voice quavering, "you're just the person I needed to—" There was a primitive howl from the other end. "Que! Que!" Greasy licks of panic crawled through Raven. "Que, what's wrong, are you hurt? Are you in trouble?" When there was no answer, she screamed as loud as she could into the phone, "Que!" It was enough, and she heard her best friend try to draw in a breath that didn't seem to come. "That's right, that's right, come on sweetie. Take a, take a deep breath and tell me."

"A-Abby collapsed." Her best friend hiccupped.

"What? She— Where is she?"

"At the game. Sh-she just kind of went down hard."

Raven raised a hand to her mouth so her friend wouldn't hear her cry out. Silent tears stung her eyes and overflowed.

"Where is she, Que?"

"It's her heart, Raven. She has something wrong with her heart. She died twice. Oh God," Que howled.

"What do you mean? Que is she..." Raven couldn't speak the words.

"No, they brought her back." Que hiccuped again. "But they think she needs surgery. Rave ..."

Raven's heart sank at the tortured defeat she'd heard in her friend's voice.

"Tell me where you are." She wrote down the name of the hospital on a piece of paper. "Okay, I'm coming, Que. Okay, I'm coming home right now. Let me get to the airport, and I'll call you from there."

They hung up, and Raven ran over to the wall where she threw her keys, grabbed her purse, and fled, forgetting both the piece of paper with the hospital name or to lock her front door.

****

She landed at SeaTac airport six hours later in a plane she had chartered. A car was waiting to take her straight to the hospital, where she found Que. Raven thought she looked almost unrecognizable, as they immediately fused together, sobbing.

"What's happening? Can I see her?" Raven pleaded in a whisper.

Que nodded, and they walked into the room. Raven swallowed hard, determined not to show fear as she approached the fragile, tiny girl. Connected to a hideous amount of tubes and machines, Abby opened tired eyes, and looked at her godmother. She tried to speak but struggled through the oxygen mask she wore.

"Shh, shh, baby, don't talk right now." Raven held her hand and watched as Abby squeezed out tears from panicked eyes. "Hey now," Raven cooed. "Shh, it's gonna be all right, baby, you're gonna be just fine."

Abby nodded as a petite, dark-haired woman with very large, distinct, sage-green eyes entered the room. She wore a long white coat and a stethoscope draped around her neck.

"Oh hello," she said, smiling, showing deep dimples in a face dotted with light freckles. "You're not Que."

"No, I…"

"Here I am," Que announced, standing up from a chair by Abby's bed. "Sorry, this is my sister, Raven." As she said it, Wyatt sprinted into the room. "And this," Que said as he wrapped an arm protectively around her, "is my brother Wyatt."

Raven was relieved that Que decided to make them family, in case the hospital wanted to deny them access. The doctor blinked at each of them, and Raven could see the wheels turning. Blonde-haired, blue-eyed girl. Large, dark-hair, dark-eyed, mountain man, and lovely African American queen. *Sure*, she seemed to reconcile, *a true American family*. Lilly grinned at Que and the twins, winked, then extended a hand to each.

"Hello, I'm Dr. Lilly Morgan, and I'll be taking care of this lovely young lady today."

"Dr. Morgan, can you explain to them what you told me?"

"Sure." The doctor turned to the twins and started explaining the trouble. "Okay, well, so Miss Abigail was working her heart pretty hard at her basketball game. And that really sucks when you have a heart condition that you don't know about." She looked at her audience, then back at Abby and winked. The little girl looked relieved to see her.

"Abby has a condition called Obstructive Hypertrophic Cardiomyopathy," she said, pronouncing each word carefully and distinctly. "It's a mouthful, I know. Now, HCM is rare in children this age, but it does happen." She peered at a monitor, adjusted Abby's IV, then walked to a whiteboard on the wall. She drew a rough, lopsided heart, with a cross extending out from the center of it.

"So, what it means is, Abby has a thickening in her actual heart muscle. It's the thickening in this part," Lilly highlighted the center line running vertically down the middle of the drawing. "That causes a reduction in blood flow to here." She highlighted the left ventricle. "It means the heart must work really, really hard to get the blood back out."

"You said you were looking at some tests," Que asked, hopeful.

"Right, well, we looked at her echocardiogram, which essentially shows the thickening of blood flow I've just described. The results we were waiting for, Que, indicate that her scarring is in fact, significant. It's over twenty-five percent. It just increases her chance of more cardiac events."

"What causes this?" Wyatt asked, one arm crossed over his rib cage, the index finger of the other pressed against his lips, studying the drawing.

"She was probably born with it." Lilly looked at Que and shook her head. "No one's fault; it's just we aren't perfect as a species. In some cases, it's the luck of the draw as to which conditions we get. Usually, this condition doesn't present until after puberty, but some genetic stamps can come out differently." The doctor looked at the concerned mother. "In fact, Que, I'm recommending we do some tests on you as well, just because it does have a high genetic implication."

"Lilly said most of the time there aren't any symptoms, except Abby had the shortness of breath," Que said, eyes filling again.

"Yes, but what did I say about that?" When the mother didn't answer, Lilly looked at the twins. "Abby had shortness of breath, and Que took her to the doctor for that," she said, leaning back to look at the girl's mother. "This is so rare in children this age, that most doctors wouldn't think of it. Treatment relating to asthma or allergies would've been the logical first step." Lilly looked back to consider her drawing before continuing. "The thing is, her thickening and scarring are quite extensive. She went into cardiac arrest twice, and it was a little dicey." Wyatt put an arm around both the women in his life and winked at the third.

"She's pretty tough though."

"Yes," Lilly agreed, "she's very tough. And to keep her that way, I want to take her in and remove a portion of the septum and implant an ICD, which stands for implantable cardioverter defibrillator. In this case, I think we'll have better success with that, rather than just with medication or even an alcohol ablation."

"Alcohol ablation?" Raven queried.

"Yes. Simply put, we put her into a tiny, controlled heart attack, killing the heart muscle responsible for the thickening, reducing its size, but…"

"We aren't doing that," Que said, looking at her daughter's panic-stricken face.

"No," confirmed Lilly, winking at Abby, "we are not doing that."

"Can I still play basketball?" Abby asked in a high

muffled voice, causing the room at large to smile.

"You know, Miss Abigail," Lilly said, reaching for her hand, "I have a son that is exactly your age, and he loves football as much as you love basketball. I know he'd ask me the very same thing. And I'm going to tell you what I'd tell him, and that is we simply have to wait and see." Since the immediate answer wasn't a resounding yes, Abby's face fell, so Lilly squeezed her hand again.

"I won't say never, but I can't say yes either. There are so many things that must happen before we can decide on that. There's also a lot of time it takes to heal things up correctly, so the simple answer is we just don't know yet. Okay?"

The doctor noticed Abby's teddy bear next to her. She picked it up and tickled the little girl's nose with it before laying it softly in her lap and brushing a hand over her head. A great commotion began down the hall from Abby's room, and soon a small entourage walked past by the window. Wyatt's head whipped around.

"Was that Derek Watson?"

"Yep, QB1 in the flesh." Lilly grinned. "A lot of the players and celebrities make the children's hospital their charity."

"Do you see them a lot?" Abby asked through her mask.

"Well, some more than others. But we love that they donate so much of their time and money to give back. So," Lilly said, taking a deep breath.

"What happens during surgery?" Raven asked.

Lilly eyed the singer. The woman looked like she needed more reassurance. Glancing back at Abby, the little girl wore the same expression. Lilly decided to speak so the little girl would understand it too.

"Abby'll get some giggle juice to knock her out and make her sleep. I'll make a little cut right here," she said, revealing Abby's sternum. "It'll be about this long." She measured seven inches between her fingers. "We go right through here." She indicated where the aortic valve would be. Lilly looked over to make sure the three adults were grasping the planned procedure too. "She'll be placed on a heart and lung machine." She looked down at the little girl. "I know that sounds scary, but it actually helps because we need your heart to not move. You've got a bunch of love bouncing around in there, and we need it to stay super still, so there are no mistakes.

"The machine takes over for the organs to protect the body while we work." she clarified, looking over to the adults. "Then, we'll place a thingy called an ICD just below here." She touched Abby's collarbone. "And then we connect it to her heart." She leaned down and looked into Abby's eyes. "Then we're going to turn everything on to make sure it works, and you'll be good as new. Easy-peasy."

"How long will all this take?" Wyatt asked.

"In a perfect world, she'll be going back in about two hours for pre-op. I'm anticipating the surgery to be about four hours. She'll be in ICU about one to two days after that. Then we'll move her to the floor for about another three to five days." She looked back at Abby. "You are a young, beautiful, healthy and strong little girl. We're gonna do right by ya." Abby smiled, and Lilly winked.

"Okay then." She looked back at the room. "Now I'm gonna go have a steak dinner and some cocktails.

I'll be back after that." They laughed, as she chuckled out the door.

****

True to her word, six hours later, Dr. Morgan came out to the waiting room in her institutional green hospital scrubs, searching for the trio. They flocked around her, as she told them how well Abby had done and that the surgery was a huge success. Afterward, each was allowed to see Abby, just long enough to see she was okay.

Que stayed but insisted the twins leave and get some rest. They arrived at Raven's condo, where Wyatt immediately toed off his shoes and shed his jacket in the hallway. He padded over to the sofa and flopped down face first.

"I'm not sure I can move," he announced.

Raven walked over and smacked him on the butt, then fell onto the couch beside him.

"She looked good though, right? I think she had some good color."

He rolled onto his side and groaned as he sat up. Putting elbows on his knees, he vigorously ran fingers through his hair and scalp for circulation, exhaling deeply.

"Yeah, the little shit looked good." He glanced over at his sister. "In fact, you look worse than she does." He narrowed his eyes. "So, what's going on with you? And don't tell me nothing."

"What?" she said, not meeting his eye, then stood and walked to the kitchen.

"What?" He mimicked in a falsetto. "Is it just this or are things not okay in paradise?"

When she didn't answer Wyatt stood up and

walked to her. Taking her by the shoulders, he looked directly into her eyes and saw the truth there. As the tears formed and overflowed, he cradled his sister's head to his chest, as she cried. When the worst was over, he held her on either side of her face and tilted it up to his.

"Now tell me what the hell's goin' on."

So, she did. She told him about meeting Finn and Dee, about Jason coming over and the two men sparring with each other. About Finn's first kiss, the seals, his work, then the strain between them and that last morning. The only thing she left out was Dee's theory.

"He'd just been acting a little off, not taking my phone calls, and then his friend Nate called me about Alaula." She looked at her brother. "That seal and her baby were like family to him. I-I just wanted to help him, talk to him. Then," she howled again, "a naked woman answered the door."

"Naked? I thought you said…she was completely naked? Didn't you say he looked surprised?"

"With what she was wearing, it wasn't a stretch to think that she'd be naked soon or had been shortly before." She moved away from him. "And if he was surprised, it was because he didn't expect to see me, though somehow I missed the bit when he dissolved our relationship."

"I just don't get it, Wy." She flopped back down on the sofa. "How did I read this so wrong? I thought he was going where I was. If you saw him, you'd know exactly how stupid that was."

"Why?"

"He's like a model, and he's just…"

"Raven, you're a successful, intelligent, gifted

254

woman. And even if it's coming from your brother, you're hot, you've always been hot. So, don't tell me you aren't worthy of this guy, or you'll seriously piss me off."

"How come I meet these guys and just get it so wrong?"

"Because you're trusting and for some unfathomable reason, you don't yet understand that you don't have to take their shit." He sat down. "As for this thing, emotions were high everywhere, and people always make stupid decisions when that happens, right?"

"I guess."

"I'm not saying he didn't fuck up. Maybe he did, but I can tell you that sometimes things aren't always as they seem. If there's an explanation for what happened, you both deserve to hear it. Ya know what I mean?" She nodded absently. "There's too much going on right now. Everyone needs to stop and take a collective breath." He inclined her head up. "Now go take a hot shower and get some sleep. We'll want to go to the hospital early."

"I should've stayed for Que's sake."

"There was no place to stay, and she was right. Better to sleep well here and come in early than sleep shitty and not hear anything new anyway."

****

Finn walked up the path to the bungalow that evening but saw the lights were out. Turning, he noticed her car wasn't in the driveway either. It didn't matter; he would wait as long as he needed. Yet when he stepped onto the porch and noticed the door ajar, he became worried, opened it, and called out.

"Raven?" Receiving no answer, he yelled louder, "Rave?"

When this still elicited no response, he checked each room, then ended with the backyard, but there was nothing. Walking back through the kitchen, he passed by the pad of paper on which she'd written the hospital name. He decided to call her and reached for the cell phone in his back pocket, then cursed remembering it had been ruined when he had gone to Alaula. Noticing the cordless phone by the sofa, he dialed her number, but it went straight to voicemail. Rubbing the phone on his forehead, where a monumental headache brewed, he desperately wanted to start this day over. He decided that she was probably trying to cool off. He'd give her the time and space she needed.

****

However, a week later, when she still hadn't called or taken his call, he was determined to go to her again. This time, seeing a foreign car in the driveway, he jumped off his bike and ran into the house.

"Rave?"

Jason turned around and smiled at Finn. "She's not here, and she's not coming back." The manager apprized him.

"Where is she?" Finn demanded.

"Ah, back home where she belongs, getting ready for her show."

"Oh yeah, her show," Finn said in disgust. "Fuckin' show must go on, right?"

"That's right." Jason looked around the room and started collecting papers and tapping them evenly on the table. "Glad to see you're finally on board." He paused and tried to inject a little warmth into his look of triumph. "I know you've enjoyed your time here with Raven, but whatever you think you had going on, it was only ever a summer romance. I tried to tell you that."

"What're we, at camp?"

"If you like." Jason smiled sarcastically. "Honestly, she's back home with her brother, Que, and Abby. She's happy." He stepped forward. "I don't know what happened in the last couple of days she was here, but she's made it very plain to me that she'd like to forget all about it. Can you respect that?"

Finn just stood toe to toe with him, wanting desperately to punch him. He looked down and saw the pad of paper with two words written in Raven's neat handwriting: *Children's Hospital.*

"So, if you'll excuse me," Jason continued, "I'd like to finish packing up her stuff so that I can get the hell off this godforsaken island. Nice to see you, Finn, thanks for stopping by, and have a great life."

He extended a hand, which Finn ignored and walked out.

Chapter 27

"Raven, we'll be fine," Que said, scrunching up her hair and looking at her friend in the mirror. After her first trip home since Abby's admission, Que was headed back to the hospital and Raven was leaving for her performance.

Wyatt stepped out of the bedroom in a crisp white-collared shirt and jacket over nice jeans.

"Well?" he asked, "I'm sexy and…" he gestured at the women to finish it for him.

"We know it?" Que answered as a question. He pointed to her and Raven smiled, then turned to collect the rest of her things.

"Let us just take you, then you can arrive at the hospital in style, and I can run in quick and see Ab," Raven whined.

"Fine." Que sighed and grabbed her purse.

****

Dr. Morgan approached the hospital holding the hands of two small children. Que rolled down the window of the limo and called out to the trio. The children's faces lit up like neon signs when they saw the car.

"What's all this?" Lilly asked, then remembered. "Oh, is it tonight?"

"Yeah, I just wanted to see Abby again," Raven said. "Being in rehearsal all day, I haven't gotten a chance to, and I need to get her request." She opened the door, and the kids sprinted over to the car, mother forgotten.

"Ah well." Lilly gestured at the kids' retreating. "My sitter just dropped the kids off unexpectantly, so my hour of rounds just went into an exhaustive sprint. I was going to check on Abby first anyway, so let's go on up."

"Is this your car?" the little boy asked Wyatt.

"Oh, I'm sorry, these are my kids," Lilly said. "My son Travis is seven, and Chelsea's six."

"Wow, a year apart. You were busy," Raven noted. "Right?"

"You're cool, right?" Wyatt asked, peering at each kid. Travis straightened, looking at the big, handsome man in the fancy car.

"Yes, sir."

"Me too, me too," sang Chelsea.

"Well, cool kids deserve a ride in a cool car." He looked over at Lilly's tired face." "Ask your mama if she can find something to do for fifteen minutes."

"Really?" Travis glowed with hope and turned to his mother. "Please Mom, can we go?"

"Please Mommy!" Chelsea said immediately after him.

Lilly looked back at Wyatt helplessly, who nodded his head and winked at her. She also looked at Que.

"I was going to stay with him anyways," she remarked. "So I can bring 'em up when we get back, and they can play with Abby; she'd love it."

"See, everything's arranged," Raven sang and grabbed Lilly's hand, who yelled over her shoulder to be good. The door, however, was already closed and the car, rolling off the curb.

"Your kids are pretty adorable. They both have your eyes," Raven said as they rode the elevator.

"Yes." Lilly smiled. "And my freckles but the rest, especially Travis, is all their dad."

"Oh, what's your husband's name?"

"It was Dave, David. He passed away three years ago." The elevator pinged open, and they walked in.

"Oh wow, I'm so sorry Lilly. Can I ask how?"

"Stage four pancreatic cancer. We started all the treatments but just caught it too late. Dave died about ten months after diagnosis. The kids were just three and four."

"So young."

"Yeah, it's harder now 'cause I'm not sure if they have a real memory of him left or if it's just my stories. He was a pretty fantastic guy. So, I got to be the domestic goddess of my home for about two years before everything went to hell."

"How are all of you now?" The elevator pinged and they got out on Abby's floor.

"Oh, you know, we muddle through. Travis especially has a hard time. He's at the age when a boy really needs his dad. But I don't like them to wallow in misery too much. So, we turn lemons into lemonade or whatever ridiculous adage they use these days, as often as we can."

When Raven looked down at the floor, Lilly stopped and laid a hand on her shoulder. "Thank you for asking, seriously. We have good days and bad ones, and the only thing I truly know is life is short. There's absolutely no time to waste on regret or living in the past too long."

Raven nodded, knowing full well the pain Lilly's children faced. Having such a well-adjusted mom would help. The doctor grabbed Abby's chart from the nurse's station and nodded for Raven to go in first.

****

"I want it a little heavier in color. The costume is turning her orange. She needs some more makeup. Damn it, Raven," Donovan yelled, and she jumped. "You know what tanning does with the makeup and costumes. How could you be so careless?"

Raven was getting ready with Caprice Starr, the Hollywood siren, that had come to lend her support to the cause by emceeing the event. She hadn't noticed her ex-husband's entrance, and after three months, that was likely the only welcome she'd receive from him. Behind him followed a pretty brunette in stilettos, her old backup singer, and his mistress. She gave Raven a self-conscious grin, who smiled back despite herself. A stagehand approached.

"Raven, your costumes are in one. And here's the final set list." He handed it to her, and she read it over. Jerking her head up, she noticed her ex's retreating back. He was still barking out orders and instilling fear of his wrath upon everyone.

"Donovan?" she called but ignoring her, he kept walking. "Donovan!" she yelled more forcefully and his shoulders hunched, red-faced and fuming.

"Do not shout at me again."

"Sorry." She held up the papers. "You said I could have three originals and I only see one on the set sheet."

"I only ever agreed to consider one. Now we don't have time for any. Perhaps tomorrow I'll consider a vocal piece. It will not be an instrumental."

"But Donovan…"

"One." He held up a finger in her face, then turned and bumped into Jason, and closed his eyes with frustration.

"You said we'd have three." She looked at Jason pleadingly.

"I know, I know," he agreed, "but we'll do tonight his way to placate him, and then we'll do our thing tomorrow." He looked at a guy with a clipboard. "Oh Mike, hold up." Turning to Raven, he cooed, "Go get on your first costume. I gotta talk to him."

Caprice gave her cascade of strawberry blonde hair and freshly made up face a glance, before watching Raven in the mirror. The seductress lowered her eyes and seemed to make a decision.

"You know honey, at some point you're going to have to take a stand."

"I keep hoping he'll see my point in all this." Raven looked at her, and the corners of her mouth turned slightly up.

"Oh come on." Caprice laughed. "You don't genuinely believe that?" She stood and smoothed her hands down the emerald green silk gown she wore over her insanely lush curves. "He's Donovan Fortner. Everyone knows who and what he is. I'm not sure I've ever heard what Raven Hunter stands for." And with a final glance in the mirror, Caprice laid a hand on her shoulder and walked toward the stage.

Raven walked into her dressing room and eyed some of her old costumes and skyscraping high-heeled shoes that always pinched her feet. The first costume, marked with a large red one, was an electric blue micro-mini dress, with feathers, fringe, and rhinestone chains hanging from the bottom to mid-thigh. Trying to zip it up, she felt like it cut off her circulation. She gained some weight on her ultra-thin frame. Jason walked in and seeing her only half dressed, never looked her in the eyes. He clearly opted to covet her barely covered naked breasts.

"Jason, can you try and zip this?"

"Happy to help." She turned around, exposing her bare back to him. He walked over and bunched the material together so she could pull the dress up and be zipped in. He leaned forward and kissed her shoulder before she could evade. "Wyatt's outside, should I have him seated?"

"No," she countered eagerly. When her brother was at a show, he always watched from the wings, staying with her until she had to step on stage. He walked in a second later and simply gawked at her.

"What?" She touched her back-combed hair, shellacked with hairspray. "Good?" She watched him furrow his brows. "Bad?" When he still said nothing, she said, "Damn it Wy."

"No, it's just…"

"What?"

"You look exactly the same as you did before you left."

"Okay Rave, we're a go." Jason checked his watch, while she simply stared at her brother, his words still vibrating in the air. "Earth to Raven, I said let's go."

"Watch from the wings?" she pleaded, and he nodded.

Wyatt's eyes shifted to all the clothes, makeup, curling irons, hairspray, and shoes, then sighed, before turning to follow her. They walked into the large, brightly lit, reception area, and watched as people ran around in confused chaos.

They parted ways, at the stairs—Raven to her mark and Wyatt to his place in the wings. As he approached the area, Donovan raised a hand to stop him.

"Wyatt, this section is restricted."

"Not to me," Wyatt said, brushing past the man. Donovan strode around him and put a hand on his shoulder squeezing hard.

"You will not test me on this. I assure you, you will lose."

"Take your fuckin' hands off me, Fortner, you piece of dog shit." Wyatt growled deeply, his eyes darkened, and his face reddened. Immediately Donovan snatched his hand away as if bitten. Wyatt, six inches taller and thirty pounds of solid muscle more than the older man, stepped toward him, precipitating an immediate retreat backward by the older man. "If you honestly think you have any power over me whatsoever, Fortner, you are pathetically mistaken. I don't have to tolerate you anymore. I'm standing in the wings, where my sister asked me to stand. If you even think of trying to put me out, I will end you." His face was inches from Donovan's. "Now fuck off somewhere and twitch."

The older man stepped back, eyes unblinking and jaw clenched. Wyatt knew the older man understood he would not win this verbal battle any more than he'd win a physical one. Fortner looked as if trying to ascertain if anyone had witnessed the exchange. With a final steely look at Wyatt, he slithered off, quietly cursing his once-brother-in-law. The announcer's voice boomed across the loud-speakers.

"And now the moment you've all been waiting for. She's been away too long! The one. The only. Raaaaven Huuunter!" The music cued, and the lights came up, spotlighting Raven's return.

Chapter 28

"Wine?" Wyatt asked, sounding exhausted, as they walked into her condo.

"Vodka," Raven replied.

He laughed, nodding his head in approval, and moved over to the wet bar. He gave each a heavy pour and handed a glass to his sister. She spent the entire hour, traveling in the limo, attempting to brush out the backcombing in her hair and wipe off several layers of makeup from her face. Donovan said he wanted her to leave the stadium in character for pictures and autographs. Not obliged to do so by contract, she decided to be amicable, trying to make the decision to let her play her songs the next evening easier.

"Did you talk to Abby?" Wyatt asked, clinking his glass to hers.

"No. I wanted to do it here, where I could actually hear her."

"Well, maybe give it 'til tomorrow. When I talked to Que, she was talking about putting her to bed."

There was a knock on the door, and Wyatt lifted his eyes in question. She wrinkled her brow and shook her head at him to indicate she wasn't expecting anyone. He walked over and opened the heavy door. Standing on the other side, soaking wet, was Finn. His worried face turned into an angry sneer when he saw the strange, good-looking man answer her door.

"Who the fuck're you?" Finn demanded vehemently.

"What?" Wyatt's usual calm demeanor flared a little, and he shot back, "Who am I? Who the fuck're you?"

Raven's eyes widened when she heard Finn's voice and rushed over to calm the sudden spike in testosterone.

"Finn, what're doing here?" Seeing both their faces, she stepped between them and slapped a hand on each chest, taut for battle. "Ah, Wyatt, this is Finn Taylor. Finn, my twin brother Wyatt." Sneering with what looked like unsuppressed jealousy, Finn stepped toward the other man, then stopped short.

"There it is," Wyatt said patronizingly. "Yep, *brother*." He pronounced it distinctly and with sarcasm. "Now that gives me the right to ask again, who the fuck're you?" Raven closed her eyes at the ridiculousness of the male ego.

"This is Finn. I told you, I met him on Kaua'i."

"Never heard of him," Wyatt said, waving a hand with dismissal, then padded back to the living room. She rolled her eyes.

"What're you doing here?" she asked helplessly.

"What am I doing here?" Finn moved closer to her. "What the hell're you doin' here Raven?' He took in her appearance, "And what the hell're you wearing?" Finn's eyes scanned her face, hair, body, then face again, appearing to look for anything he recognized. Shaking his head a little, he focused on her eyes. "You just disappeared. Just left your door unlocked and disappeared without a word?"

"I told Jason when he went back to…"

"Oh yes, right, you told Jason."

"Yeah, Jason. You know, her manager?" Wyatt yelled out. "Tall, good-lookin', rich."

"What, are ya, fuckin' him?" Finn spat at Wyatt.

"No, but…"

"Stop it!" Raven yelled. "Stop. Come here."

She grabbed Finn's hand and dragged him to her room. As the door slammed shut, Wyatt grinned. Well, this was getting interesting, he thought, enjoying himself. He leaned back on the couch, propped his feet up on the coffee table, sipped his drink and smiled, as he eavesdropped.

****

"Look, I'm sorry about the way I left," Raven said. "It was incredibly complicated." She followed Finn with her eyes, as he paced her bedroom like a huge cat. "My best friend Que—her daughter, Abby, had a heart attack playing basketball; she's only seven. And she…"

When she paused, he stopped pacing and looked at her, as if he knew what was coming.

"Wait, how in the hell can you come here and lecture me about anything?"

"I tried to tell you, but you left and wouldn't let me explain. Then I go to your house and your door's unlocked. I tried calling; you wouldn't answer. Nothing happened with Holly."

"Right. Okay, Finn. It sure as hell didn't look like nothing. Or are you going to say now it didn't mean anything?" She glared at him.

He clenched both his fists, then jerked them down once, as he grunted out frustration.

"I came out to grab my toothbrush. She drove me home. I didn't even think she was still there, let alone half dressed. I saw her at the same time you saw each other."

They were silent for a moment, each visibly depleted, so he asked quietly, "Is she okay? Your friend?"

"She's seven and had to have open heart surgery, but yeah, she's okay. She gets to go home after a couple more days." He nodded then looked around the room and sat down on her bed, placing his head in his hands.

"Why didn't you call me back?"

"Well, I called Jason. Everything was so crazy, and I just assumed."

"I asked him, and he wouldn't tell me shit. Apparently, I'm not part of the inner circle when it comes to your personal life."

"I'm sorry Finn. He shouldn't have said that." Remembering the vodka in her hand, she sipped it. Finn took it from her and drained it. "I didn't know we were there anymore, or if we ever were," she retorted.

"Where exactly?" He glared at her. "I go over to your house, and you're not there. Your doors are unlocked, and the door's open but you're gone. For Christ sake, we're fuckin' each other, don't you think a little communication is good, before falling off the face of the earth? So maybe, I don't know, have to worry that something horrific has happened to you?"

"Can you not call it that?" Raven said.

"What?"

"Fucking!"

"Oh, we aren't fuckin'?"

"No… I… No, just don't call it that."

"What would you like me to call it Raven?"

"Making love," she said quietly, "or having sex."

"Making love, Christ."

He laughed derisively and threw up his hands, appearing to want to hurt her in any way he could. He yanked opened the bedroom door and stomped to the refrigerator and yanked open the door. Grabbing a beer, he popped the cap and drank deeply. The fact that the raging man knew there would be one in there seemed to impress Wyatt. He shifted to watch the show. Raven narrowed her eyes at him.

"What're you, sixteen?" Finn replied scathingly, and suddenly she felt a glorious rage bubbling in her blood.

"No, I'm thirty-four. I stopped being a frat girl a long time ago."

"Frat girl." Finn laughed. "I'm fairly certain you were never a frat girl."

She looked over at Wyatt, who looked like he'd jump in at any moment. She simply narrowed her eyes again, indicating she wouldn't tolerate his interference.

"No, you're right," she yelled at him. "Never was a frat girl, never got to be that free. I'm tired of your bullshit, Finn. My whole life, I've been someone else's possession, and I have no interest in being yours now. Go home. We're done here."

He stared at her throughout the outburst and could obviously see the fat tears forming in her eyes and cast his eyes down.

"Raven…" He set his beer down and reached out to touch her face, but she evaded, and ran out of the condo, slamming the door.

****

Finn felt utterly dejected and frustrated. He locked his fingers behind his head and exhaled, puffing out his cheeks. Wyatt stood up and walked to the kitchen.

"I'm Wyatt," he announced, extending a hand. Finn automatically extended his own hand, distracted. "Finn, right? Nice to meet ya."

"You too." Finn looked at the man smiling at him. "Brother, huh? Where you from?"

"Oh, I'm from here too. I'm a U.S. Forest Ranger up on Mount Baker-Snoqualmie, but I also do some survival training and just finished a stint when Abby got sick. It's why I wasn't able to get over to the island to see Rave. It's, ah, been pretty emotional around here lately."

"Forest Ranger." Finn crossed his arms over his chest, not rising to the bait. "I'm not sure I would've pegged ya for that."

"Funny hats, khaki shorts, and clipboards?" Wyatt laughed. "Yeah, I know the perception." Finn's smile didn't reach his eyes.

"No, it's just that I've just never actually met a forest ranger before."

"Well, I've decided not to hold that against you, so it's all good. You're a marine biologist, right?" Finn's eyes snapped up, widening, then accusing. "Okay, she might have said something about you," Wyatt admitted sheepishly.

"Yeah?"

"Always worked on Kaua'i?"

"Yeah, for the most part. I was born there."

"And you work with some kind of seal, right?"

"Hawaiian monk seal. Are we done with the pleasantries yet?"

"Hey, look, man," Wyatt said, facing him. "I don't know what this whole badass thing you've got going on here is, but I can tell you, if you want any future with my sister, you'd better lose it."

"Or what?"

"Or she'll dump ya. Actually, I'm pretty sure that she just did," Wyatt stated as Finn shifted uncomfortably, "Yeah, weren't expecting that, were you?"

"Cut the shit."

"She's on a different level, man. Things happened to her you can't even comprehend. And the people that love her would never let another asshole come into her life."

"What things?" When her brother just stood there, Finn grew more aggressive, "What God damn things? Why the fuck're ya tauntin' me, man?"

"Look." Wyatt's eyes sobered and bored directly into Finn's. "I don't know you. I don't know what my sister feels about you, but I can tell you that you've been a regular ball of sunshine since you walked in here." Finn lowered his eyes, afraid her brother would see his panic. "If your *intentions*,"—he held up his fingers in quotation marks—"for lack of a better term, if they're good, I'm on your side, all the way." Finn took a deep breath and stepped back. "But if they're not, you'll get nothing from me, man. In fact, I'll actively work against you."

"I don't know." Finn exhaled deeply and looked hesitantly at the man, unsure of himself, and admitted, "Okay, yeah, I care about her." He scraped his teeth over his bottom lip.

"Well, hell, son, why didn't you say so?" He moved to the refrigerator for a six pack and handed a beer to Finn.

"But that's it." Finn took the beer, opened it, and took a long swig, "I don't do...this."

"Yeah, me neither." Wyatt nodded his head. He was quiet for a few moments, then seemed to make a decision and said, "Okay, so, I'm pretty sure she's never said this to you, but my sister and I are damaged goods. Our folks died when we were eight. Had a pretty good life up until that point." Finn sat and looked into his beer. He wasn't sure he was ready to hear this but couldn't stop himself either.

"How'd they die?"

"Drunk driver."

"Wrong place, wrong time?"

"No just an asshole that didn't give a shit about anything or anyone made a choice and destroyed our life." He sipped again.

"What happened to the guy?"

"Involuntary manslaughter. Sentenced twenty years, served sixteen, with time off for good behavior." Wyatt's jaw clenched. "We didn't have anyone to go to, no family or friends, so we went into the foster system, and were adopted by a family in Missouri." Finn looked over at Wyatt, suspect. "Yeah, it was pretty bad." He sipped his beer again and took in a deep breath. "You said you like Raven, right?" It was an unexpected question, so Finn locked gazes with her brother and gave a nod of his head.

"Yeah."

"Do you like her, like maybe love her, or are you just trying to...wait, how did you so ineloquently put it, fuck her?" Finn winced.

"Dude I...I don't even know how to respond to that."

"Our adopted father repeatedly beat Raven and me." Finn jerked in his seat as Wyatt eyed him carefully. "It was pretty brutal from the time she was eight to 'bout sixteen when we ran away. We came to Seattle on a bus in the middle of the night and slept on the streets for a few weeks before we found jobs and an apartment with our friend Que. Her daughter is the little girl that just had surgery. After that, we never looked back." Wyatt seemed to be looking back into the past.

Finn closed his eyes and exhaled deeply, trying to absorb the new information.

"Did you ever report it?" When Wyatt shook his head no, Finn demanded, "Why the hell not?"

"I'm not sure. Probably young and dumb. Thought he'd find us or they'd somehow make us go back. The Colonel, well, he was a mean sonofabitch, especially when he drank, but that wasn't always the precursor. Broke more bones of mine then I could probably count. We always went to different hospitals and clinics. If I didn't comply or if he thought I'd say something, he hurt her and vice versa. It's a different life than most people experience and I don't expect you to understand it." Finn was on fire with rage, so stood up to pace.

"Where's this guy now?"

"Dead. Lung cancer." Wyatt was at peace with the knowledge. "Raven had to grow up fast—we both did. She never got to be a kid or free, like she said. She just had this talent, this one place she could retreat into, even if it was just inside her head." He sipped his beer again. "She never dated much but when she did, they were users that expected her to change for them and she did. She would change her entire world and identity, just to be accepted. Married the last dickhead. When he realized he wasn't good enough for her, he picked her apart, and she let him do it. Donovan took most of what she had because she wouldn't stand up for herself."

Finn looked around the cold, sterile condo that she had shared with her husband and the massive wedding photo over the fireplace. Raven, with jet-black hair, her ethereal skin, covered in heavy makeup, wearing an elaborate wedding dress. Standing next to her was an attractive older man with a condescending smile, commanding the photo. Finn couldn't take his eyes off the incredibly foreign-looking woman, trying to reconcile her to the one he was resisting to love.

"Where's he now?" Finn asked, gesturing to the groom.

"Donovan?" Wyatt laughed. "Well, he contracted her for two shows; one was tonight, and one's tomorrow. She's upset because he made her wear all that shit again. One of the nastiest assholes you've ever met. She thought she was going to be able to do some of her new stuff. That's what Jason promised, but it was all bullshit, and he screwed her. Made her play the opening act to his mistress."

"Jason allowed that too?"

"Wouldn't surprise me—he's a douche. She's as loyal as they come though. And when Que and I told her to chuck him, she wouldn't listen." Wyatt sipped his beer, then set it down. "Look, I don't just offer this shit up. Between the two of us, you could probably count on a single hand who knows about our life. Not even the asshole she married. You could fuck us a hundred different ways by going to the press."

"You don't have to worry about that."

"Figured." When Finn didn't respond, Wyatt

continued. "She's had counseling, and she knows what happened to her when she was young wasn't her fault. She just doesn't always see her own worth." Finn saw the dejection and what looked like guilt on the man's face.

"I'm doing myself no favors by telling you this," he admitted, as if reading his mind. "She's going to be livid, beyond livid, for exposing some pretty honed-in secrets."

"You don't have to tell her."

"Yes, I do." He held Finn's gaze. "We've always been straight with each other. It's what we've got. I'm telling you because if you like her, and want something more than sex with her, you have a right to know."

"Look, I don't know what I think. I'm not looking for anything."

"Oh, well, if that's true, then you've just gained some insight that may make you treat her better."

"I've got my own issues, man. Believe me, she doesn't want to take that on any more than I do."

"If she likes you, don't be too sure of that." Wyatt paused and glanced out the window toward the moonlight on the water. "Finn, she's a phenomenal person that's been trying her whole life to figure out who she is. The only thing that's becoming crystal clear to her is that she doesn't want to be this." He gestured around the room. "She's literally on the verge of figuring it all out, man. She just doesn't know it yet." Wyatt drained his beer and stood up.

"Well, right now she's going to go to Que's, probably to wash off all that crap. Then when she thinks you're gone, she'll come back, 'cause she won't want me to be alone." Giving a small laugh and shaking his head, he looked at his watch. "So I'm guessing maybe in a couple two or three hours."

He extended a hand to Finn, who shook it. "If I were you I'd crash. It's been a long night. Let her sleep and talk in the morning."

"So, what—I should just wait?"

"You didn't come all this way for nothing, right?" When Finn nodded, Wyatt gestured to the couch. "Well, I guess you have your answer. See ya."

After the man left, Finn grabbed another beer and settled in for the storm to come.

*****

Raven walked into her condo around two the next morning to find Finn asleep on the couch. She sighed and quietly closed the door, palming her keys, so they didn't make any noise. Standing at the coffee table, she watched him dream. His arms crossed over his chest, ankles propped up on the couch armrest. Donovan would've gone ballistic at the desecration of it all. It just made her smile.

She remembered seeing Finn for the first time and thinking he was the type of guy she could never have. Then they became lovers—she frowned—correction, fuck buddies. Disgusted at her ignorance and naiveté, she walked to the window and looked out at the city. By the time he woke that morning, she was gone again.

Chapter 29

The day started with a visit to the hospital. Raven lay next to the little girl on her bed, reading to her. Abby played with the gold medallion on its chain around her neck, as Wyatt and Que played cards on a small table.

Abby dropped the medallion as the story wrapped up and went back to securing a small woven bracelet of yellow, black, and gold threads around Raven's thin wrist.

"I still can't believe that you made this yourself, baby." Raven kissed Abby's forehead, hugging her gently. "It's so beautiful."

"Are you wearing a wig?" Abby asked with the verbal freedom of a seven-year-old.

"No, I can't stand those things," Raven remarked distractedly.

"How did you get your hair so black?"

"It's called a rinse. You run it through your hair, and it colors it, but only for a while. My hair will keep getting lighter as it fades out again."

"Oh," Abby said, a little sadly. "I like it way better yellow."

"Me too," said Wyatt.

"Me three," said Que. "Oh, gin, ha-ha."

"Aw, shit," Wyatt said.

"I know you ain't using that foul mouth in front of

my baby."

"Sorry kid," he muttered.

"It's okay, Uncle Wyatt." Abby giggled. "Mama says a lot worse."

"Oh, *hell* no, little girl." Que went over and rained kisses on her daughter's face. "You're lucky I can't tickle you yet." Abby looked up at her with tired eyes.

"I love you, Mama." Que's eyes filled, eliciting tears in Raven's as well. She looked over at Wyatt, who nodded his head that it was time to go.

"Okay, miss Abby, me and Uncle Wy are going to go so I can do one more of these things."

"Auntie Rave, will you sing me a song?" Abby asked, a little breathless.

"Sure baby, which one?"

"Um." She sat, thinking, and saw the book they'd been reading. "I want the snowman one."

"The snowman one?" Raven giggled and sang about building one, as Abby laughed. She hugged her closely, trying to imagine Donovan's reaction to this request and burst out laughing. "Well, I'm not entirely sure they'll let me sing that one. What's your back-up?"

"How about the rainbow one?"

"You've got a deal."

****

Raven arrived at the Tacoma Dome and added Abby's song to the setlist. Her hair and makeup artist, Barb, immediately washed and saturated the black rinse into her hair before creating the shellacked helmet that was her trademark. Sitting in her periwinkle silk robe, Raven closed her eyes as Barb applied smoldering smoke to her eyes.

That's how Finn saw her, in the robe she'd worn

the night after they first had sex, slowly having the rest of her identity stripped away. Next to her, he recognized Caprice, also half dressed. The actress lifted her eyes to his and smiled seductively, before glancing at Raven, to see if she had noticed his presence. He smiled back in spite of himself, understanding in the back of his mind, that somehow she was on his side. Seeming to sense someone, Raven opened her eyes and connected with his, sighing in resignation.

"All done, Miss Raven," Barb said with a flourish. "I'll tell Nicole you're ready for wardrobe." The artist looked at her watch as Raven watched Finn through the mirror. "Oh shit, we're late again."

"Yeah," Raven said distractedly. "Okay. Thanks, Barb, I'll get going." The woman turned to go, and Raven called out, "Barb, can you also have Simon talk to Donovan about the prompter again?"

"Sure." Barb's eyes darted to the good-looking blond, then swiveled them back to her boss. "I'll send Nicole back in two."

"Ah, there you are, lovie." Caprice sighed and stood when her own handler came in with her gown. She flung off her robe and stood naked, prompting Finn's eyes to nearly fall out of his head at the exposed voluptuous body parts of the actress. Once zipped in, she turned to Raven, exchanging grins because both women knew the effect she had on the male population. "Break a leg, honey," Caprice said and winked first at Raven and then at Finn, before gliding her way out of the room.

"Oh you too," she called.

Standing, Raven walked over to a rack of sequined costumes, unbelted her own robe, and threw it on a chair. Finn's eyes flew open a second time, as she stood clad in a tiny push up bra and thong in the center of her dressing room, filled with three other people. Nicole, her handler, selected the costume and began helping her in it when Jason ran up to her.

"You're late," he hissed. "Come on." He glanced over at Finn, still staring at Raven half-naked, and did a double take. "What the hell are you doing here?" He looked back at Raven in accusation.

Nicole, held the costume up over her chest, as Raven removed her bra. Finn's body seemed to vibrate with fury at Jason's proximity to her, who had no shame in watching the display. The costume was skin tight with a padded bustier to amplify her already well-endowed form. She glanced at Finn, who looked at her with outright disgust on his face, and lowered her head while taking a deep breath for the dress to be zipped up. Jason grabbed her by the elbow and dragged her out of the room without a word to Finn.

"A little nuts, right?" Finn turned in horror, but Wyatt just shrugged. "Now ya know why she went off to Hawai'i. Come on." He jerked his head toward an area just offstage, where they would watch the show.

At her cue, she took her spot and posed behind an enormous white screen that would silhouette her every curve. The curtain rose, and she began her set. Finn watched, thinking she looked like a stripper, just missing her pole. He tried to remember what he used to think when he'd see a picture or video of her performing. A sexy, beautiful provocateur, looking like she was having the time of her life.

He clenched his jaw because he could now see she was miserable. The carefree raw version of herself on

Kaua'i was the real Raven. This before him was senseless exploitation, as she moved from young, upbeat pop and sappy ballads, utilizing her voice, guitar, and piano talent.

At the break, she prepared to end the set with Abby's song, which Wyatt would record for her. She didn't see her guitar, and the intermission dancers came out, giving her nine minutes to get hydrated, towel off, and change. Confused, she came offstage looking for Donovan, but couldn't find him anywhere. So, she approached Jason, who happened to be standing close to her brother and Finn, without realizing it.

"Jason, we were supposed to do Abby's song."

"Yeah, Donovan said we're running over, so he cut it. Grab some water." Without another word of explanation, he walked to one of the assistants with a clipboard, thus avoiding confrontation, again.

"Come on Ms. Hunter. We need to get you changed." A stagehand gently guided her to her dressing room. Her brother followed, visibly upset in his sister's wake. The stagehand brought her into the changing room as her brother turned his back for modesty and began to rage.

"What did he say?"

"He said we're running late and I can't do it," she called out in a shaky voice, that close to tears.

The attendant helped her into the red sequin dress Raven hated most, with matching six-inch stiletto heels. She'd be lucky not to fall over, she thought.

"That's bullshit, Raven," Wyatt yelled, when she told him he could turn back around. She hooked a long red ruby earring into her lobe. "Abby's looking forward to this. You have to do the song."

"What am I supposed to do Wyatt?" she screamed. "The set's over. I'll tell the guys to move one of the songs in the next set, and I can dedicate that to her."

Her eyes shifted to Finn, who leaned against the doorjamb, arms crossed over his chest and listened with a quiet intensity at the sheer chaos of her life.

"I'm going to find that dickhead," Wyatt said and left.

"No, wait, Wy—"

She turned as the assistant left and looked at Finn, who just continued to stare at her in the mirror.

"What the fuck are you doin'?" he asked quietly.

"What?"

"Dressed like that."

She looked at herself in the mirror and saw an utterly foreign woman looking back at her. Her glossy-black hair, teased, high at the crown. Black kohl caused her eyes to unnaturally form cat eyes, with high slanting wings at the corners. Bright red lipstick stained her lips, and all the highlight and contouring changed the structure of her face completely. Her dress caused her breasts to swell over the top of the costume, threatening to spill out with one misstep.

"Singing shit you don't want to, not singing shit you promised." He continued. "Allowing them to dress you up like a..." He gestured up and down her body with revulsion.

"Like a what, Finn?"

"Like a whore," he retorted brusquely.

"A whore?" she asked disbelievingly.

"You look ridiculous. Tell these guys to go fuck themselves and change." When she stood there, mouth open, sputtering like a fish, he continued, "You can't do this shit anymore. This isn't you. You know it isn't. Come on." He motioned, waving his hand like an impatient parent. "Let's go. I'll tell 'em." She stood where she was, and he turned, irritated. "Raven, I'll take care of it, come on."

"I don't need you to take care of it."

"Someone has to."

An assistant came in, glancing nervously between the two people in obvious turmoil.

"Ms. Hunter, you're on in two."

"Piss off," Finn growled, and the woman scampered away. "Come on." He held out a hand.

"I'm not going anywhere with you, Finn. In fact, go home." She moved to walk past him, and he grabbed her arm.

"I'm not letting you go out there, looking like that, playing this ridiculous game with them." Wyatt walked up, red-faced, from one confrontation to another. She jerked her arm from Finn's grasp.

"Do you honestly think you're any different than any other man in my life? Go back home, Finn. I don't want you here."

Then she turned her head so he wouldn't see her eyes sparkle and fill. Finn stood where he was, as if she'd slapped him. Wyatt looked at him briefly, before he tried to catch up with his sister.

****

Finn slammed open the heavy metal doors without saying a word to the beefy security guard that escorted him out. He flipped up the collar of his jacket and leaned into the dark rainy night, thinking about what had just occurred.

The assistant, seeing trouble, had run to get Jason

and stood just behind Finn with the security guard, smirking.

"I want him out of here," Jason announced to the guard, who immediately jerked a thumb at Finn to start walking. Jason delivered a parting shot. "Don't worry, I'll take good care of her."

Finn didn't give a moment's hesitation. He just balled up a fist and let fly, hitting Jason dead in the face with great force. Turning, he left the arena without a word, striding past the startled security guard.

****

Raven made it through the program and was set to play Abby's song, essentially ending the show. She'd take a short break for the last costume change, then do the encores. All she wanted was to be done, so she could go home and curl up in a ball. She became numb with disbelief when the dancers returned before she could play the little girl's request. Donovan yelled at her to get off stage and shoved Amanda out to get her. When Raven stepped behind the curtain, Donovan started in.

"Jesus, Raven, what the hell has happened to you? Have you lost all sense of professionalism?" He spat and pointed to her dressing room. "Get into your room and change. Now!"

Jason walked up, head back and blood all over his suit, but she barely registered it.

"I was supposed to get to play my song," she said, aware that she sounded like a little girl pleading about fairness. Wyatt walked over to her but took one look at her face and backed off.

"I told your ridiculous excuse of a manager that the show was running late."

"And it was just my songs that got cut?"

"Raven, I don't know how you can be so obtuse about this. You wanted to play a children's theme song at this venue, for Christ sake. You also wanted to sing that alternative ballad that isn't any good and won't sell. You have no concept of what it takes in this business, which makes you an incredible idiot since you've been doing this for fifteen years. Just do what I told you to do and stop thinking you have some kind of brain or knack for this."

"Now Donovan," Jason said in a wet, nasally voice, "we tried to negotiate those songs and just because you don't like the one she picked doesn't mean…"

"Oh, shut up, Dell. You've negotiated nothing. In fact, you've allowed this," Donovan spat, gesturing to Raven, "to happen." Jason turned to Raven.

"Okay, Rave, why don't we just finish the show? You only have the encores left anyway, and then we'll go back to the drawing board and write something that can complement your brand."

Caprice stood to the side and quietly watched as Raven's eyes never left Donovan's. A stagehand ran up to them pleading she get changed for her cue. Donovan turned his back on her and began to walk away.

"You…suck," Raven said quietly but loud enough for him to hear.

"What?" he asked, completely shell-shocked. "What did you say to me?"

"You're a ridiculous, small, insignificant man. What the hell has happened to you, Donovan?"

"What are…"

"How did you become so weak?"

"Me! How dare you speak…"

"I used to think you were so handsome…accomplished…intelligent." She scanned his face. "I used to think you had my best interests at heart because after all, you were my husband, right?" She looked at Amanda onstage with pity. "I thought we did things your way because you truly knew better."

"I do know better. I made you. And lest you forget, we do have a binding contract. Now shut your mouth and get your fat ass on that stage."

She glanced over and saw Caprice beaming at her and nodding encouragement, so she stepped out of her painful heels.

"You're an ugly man. A user." She stated it with such pity, it caused him to turn dusky. "You're old and sadistic. A man that builds your life off other people's work and talent because you have none. You build your confidence off cheating and belittling."

"Raven, I think…" Jason began, but she rounded on him.

"You aren't any better than he is. You're a spineless, selfish man and I've let entirely too many spineless, selfish, and cruel men dictate my life to me."

"Ms. Hunter?" The stagehand quietly interjected and looked between all the parties involved, before hesitantly offering, "Should we change?"

"Yes." Raven grinned. "Yes, I'm definitely going to change." Turning, she looked at her brother, who seemed to be radiating pride and grinned. "I'll be out in two," she said, and he nodded.

True to her word, hair in a messy bun, dressed in yoga pants and a sweatshirt, she walked out of the dressing room and grabbed Wyatt's outstretched hand.

When Donovan saw her, he looked positively apoplectic.

"Are you fucking crazy? We have a damn contract, Raven. I will sue you! You have forty thousand fans out there." He grabbed her arm forcefully and jerked her around, and Wyatt moved closer.

However, Raven pushed him back and slapped the older man's face with all the force she could muster, leaving a handprint. Then she slid on dark sunglasses.

"You know what you're doing Donovan. I'm sure you have options on another brand." She nodded her head toward the television broadcasting Amanda's performance. "You'll figure something out." She looked with disgust over his shoulder at Jason, and without saying another word walked out the large double doors and fans that waited outside.

Chapter 30

Raven arrived home and opened the car door to get out. Wyatt began to follow, but she stopped him.

"Wy, I need to go in by myself. Can you crash with Que tonight?"

"Is that a good idea?"

"Yeah, I just…" she stopped and communicated with her eyes.

"Okay," he acquiesced, "I'll be over there." She hugged him, breathing in his aftershave and sweat. "Promise you call me in the morning?"

She nodded, and he kissed her forehead before she turned and got out of the car into the brisk night air.

That night, Raven took a long hot shower, shampooing her hair several times to get as much of the rinse out as possible. Afterward, she sat on the water-warmed tile, not crying but drained. It was one thing to stand up for herself for the first time in her life and say all the things she wanted to say. It was quite another to blow up her professional life, with no guidance, and expose herself to lawsuits. However, what was also rapidly crystallizing in her mind, was performing would be done her way and her way only in the future. The dilemma was how to do it. In many ways, Raven felt she was back to square one again, but now every nerve ending was raw.

Her thoughts turned to Finn, and the revulsion

etched on his face. The harsh words and disappointment. He'd be on his way back to Kaua'i now, to Dee or maybe to his pretty little researcher, Holly. His life would no longer include her and she, in turn, would have to rediscover herself. In a daze, Raven stumbled into bed and thankfully slipped into the oblivion of sleep without dreams.

By mid-morning she sat in Abby's hospital room, awaiting the papers that would discharge the little girl home. She regaled the group with the events that transpired the night before and her role in them.

"Oh my God girl, I cannot believe you did that," Que exclaimed. "You really slapped him?"

"Yep," Wyatt confirmed. "Then slid on sunglasses like a famous waif of the 1960s and walked out. It was beyond brilliant."

"You didn't!" Que doubled over, laughing so hard, she passed gas, causing everyone to laugh and cry uncontrollably.

"Well, I'm fairly certain I'll be getting sued," Raven calmed down and commented, "but it's okay. I'm done with all of it."

"Done performing too?" Lilly asked, pen still poised over Abby's discharge papers.

"I don't know." She evaded. "Maybe I'll give it up and start teaching piano lessons."

"Well, I was truly proud of you," Wyatt championed. "I thought you were really brave. It was incredible to watch and something I'll never forget."

Wyatt went over and gave her a one-armed squeeze.

"And what about your mothership?" Que asked. "Where's your man at?"

Raven's face fell because she knew he wasn't "hers," anymore. In fact, she wasn't sure if he ever had been.

"I'm sure he went home." Raven's glassy eyes connected with Que's. "I'm going to try very hard not to regret anything that happened over there. For the most part, it was a fantastic, beautiful three-month holiday."

Wanting desperately to change the subject, she nodded at Abby, who was coloring in a book.

"So, Dr. Morgan, does this beautiful little princess get to go home?"

"Well, I think it's time unless you can't bear to live without me, Miss Abigail?"

"No, I'm ready."

"Ouch. For sure?" Abby only giggled and nodded. "Okay then, I'll finish these up, and you'll be outta here."

They brought the patient back to a warm homecoming, resplendent in balloons and crepe paper. Abby chose the activities of the night—cards, movies, and dinner. By the time the clock struck eight, the little girl was fast asleep. Wyatt made the long trek up Snoqualmie Pass for home and Raven went back to her condo, to determine what came next.

She made herself some tea and started a bath. When the lavender bath bomb hit the water, she watched it fizz and spin as it disintegrated. After lighting some scented candles, she gave an orgasmic groan, as she sank deep into the hot, sudsy water. She ran her hands over her stomach, breasts, and hips as if collecting inventory until her fingers ran over the small scar on her hip. Closing her eyes, stinging sharply from tears, she transported back to the night she received it.

They'd been placed in foster care with a retired military family in Bethany, Missouri. The couple had a son, Kevin, one year older than the twins, but were unable to have any more children. Hazel, their new mother, bore the brunt of that failing. When she pleaded with her husband, retired Colonel Jonathan Knapp, to adopt a little girl, he scoffed at raising another person's "brat." Upon hearing they could earn an extra fifteen hundred dollars per month for the twins, he changed his mind.

They had passed the requirements of a foster family. The Colonel, as everyone called him, didn't like the revolving social workers showing up without notice or care and eventually adopted the Hunter children, yet never gave them his last name.

Life for the family was always strict. The Colonel's taste for whiskey increased, as years and regret sank in. When the boys began competing for grades and sports, Knapp made it known that his son came first. If Kevin didn't perform better than Wyatt, his father rained taunting and ridicule down on him. The rules of his house were non-negotiable. Any infractions resulted in strict discipline and corporal punishment.

It started as a cuff on the ear to Raven for not setting the table fast enough, an open-palm slap on the face for Wyatt for talking back, a kick in Kevin's back for sloppy painting. They could hear Hazel's cries and scary grunts at night in their darkened room. Meals revoked for bad grades, friends not allowed in the home for any reason, and nothing short of perfection tolerated—even then, it was left to the discretion of the Colonel as to whether or not it was perfect enough.

So, when the Hunter children arrived, bearing the

scars of grief over their parents' death, the Knapps made little accommodation. Raven had horrible nightmares, resulting in bed-wetting and the ire and insults of her new father. When she got older, the accidents became less frequent. Raven tried to change the bed herself quietly or with Wyatt before the Colonel could see. On one such night, she tripped on a blanket and fell headlong into the wall, causing him to get up. He hadn't been asleep but watching TV, drinking whiskey, and smoking a cigarette. This disruption and its cause infuriated him.

"What in the hell're you doin' out here?" he demanded.

"I, um, well I..."

Wyatt got out of bed and peeked out the doorway into the hall, as Hazel and Kevin followed suit. He grabbed Raven's arm hard enough to make her yelp and the sheets to shift, wafting the unmistakable smell of urine.

"God damn it, did you piss your bed again?" He looked down the hall at the family. "You believe this shit, Hazel? She pissed her sheets like a damn baby again. What the hell I gotta do to make you learn, little baby?" He pulled her by the hair and shoved her down on the floor, wiping her nose into the blanket, like a dog. "Now get that shit to the laundry."

Trying to ball it up tightly so she wouldn't trip again, Raven took the laundry down to the washing machine. When she returned, Hazel had brought her fresh sheets.

"No, damn it." Knapp stomped over to the fireplace and grabbed some newspapers, as if it were obvious, and threw them at Raven. "You act like a* *damn dog. You can sleep like a dog."*

Crying silently, she returned to her room, and Wyatt helped her with the newspaper.

"When he goes to sleep, you can come over with me," he whispered.

"Like hell, she will." The man spat, hearing the exchange and causing Raven to cry louder. He walked over to her and slapped her hard. "Now if you wanna blubber, I can really give you something to blubber about."

"Johnathan," Hazel began softly.

"What!" he roared. "If you were doing your damn job I wouldn't have to." She tried to speak but just closed her mouth. He turned back to Raven, standing in her underwear, trying hard but failing to stop the tears. "Okay then, let's see if we can't teach you not to piss your pants."

He spun the little girl around and thinking she was going to get a spanking, Raven clenched her bottom and tried to evade. Instead, the Colonel pulled down the side elastic band of her underwear and stubbed his cigarette out on her upper hip. She screamed, and Wyatt threw himself at the man, in only the way a nine-year-old boy could. Knapp yanked him by the arm and twisted it while throwing him against the wall. There was a loud grinding crack, then sharp snap, as Wyatt also screamed out in pain. Kevin ran back to his room and muffled his cries with a pillow, while Hazel closed her eyes as he passed her, throwing a shoulder into hers, muttering.

Appearing not to know which child to go to first, the older woman simply left and returned with a useless bag of frozen peas. Raven clutched her brother and sobbed, as Hazel placed the peas on his arm, causing him to cry out more.

"Oh shh," Hazel whispered quickly. "Shh, it's gonna to be okay. Come on now Wyatt. You need to simmer down. He's gonna hear you."

The smell of her own burnt skin made Raven's stomach recoil. She watched her adoptive mother's brows draw together in sympathy, and carefully avoided her burn. Hazel brushed Raven's hair back and kissed her temple before turning back to the boy, removing the peas and peering at the swelling.

"Okay now. Now hold on, Wyatt, I think we might need to go to the hospital for this one." She searched for inspiration. "Okay, so we'll tell 'em you guys went outside, and we hadn't yet noticed the frost. Your feet just came clear out from under you, and your arm landed on the stone border. Okay? Wyatt, now you tell it to me back honey." She gave a quick side-long glance to Raven, as he did. "Okay then, let's get our clothes on now, and we'll get goin'."

"She ain't goin' nowhere," the Colonel snarled from the doorway, and everyone jumped. He walked over, addressing all but never taking his eyes off Wyatt. "She'll stay here and clean up this disgustin' mess. You go if you're that big a pussy, but if you even think about tryin' to make me look bad or make this somethin' other than it was,"— he sneered at Raven—"I will hurt her…bad. You understand what I'm tellin' you, boy?" Wyatt nodded nervously.

Raven stared at the small light brown circle as if it belonged to someone else in a different life. She dried off and put on her fluffy white comfort robe while walking out to the kitchen. She steeped some more tea, then cuddled up on the couch and stared out the window. They had endured that treatment for eight long years. He never burned her physically again, but mentally the Colonel let her know she was only a girl, who was insubstantial and incapable. Wyatt bore the brunt of his adoptive father's ire for his sister, as well as himself, whenever possible. The chamomile and lavender of the tea hovered thickly around her head. She sipped and thought back to that last day.

They were sixteen. Wyatt came home one night, elated to tell everyone he'd made the varsity basketball team. Kevin had to remain on JV and was irritated, knowing the shame he'd receive from his father. He gave his adoptive brother a hard shove. Wyatt, off balance, bumped into Hazel, who had been carrying a hot casserole to the dining room table. It flew out of her hands and onto the wall but not before some fell and seared into Raven's shoulder. Before she could stifle it, she screeched in pain.

"What the fuck're you doin'!" Knapp stood up, knocking his chair to the ground. "Are you stupid?" Raven emitted a small cry before she could help herself, eliciting a glare from the cruel man. "Shut up! Mother…" He nodded at his wife to take care of her, then turned back to Wyatt, who clearly seethed with rage.

"Kevin pushed me into her," Wyatt retorted in an uncharacteristic act of defiance. Then raised his arms as the man advanced on him and grabbed him by the hair.

"What did you say?"

"I said, Kevin's pissed, 'cause I made it, and he didn't. He pushed me into her. You should be mad at

him." He raised his arms again, as the Colonel bore down on him and dove off the cliff. "Deal with it."

"Who in the hell do you think you're talkin' to boy?" He whispered in a deadly drawl. "Deal with it!" He slammed Wyatt's head into the sheetrock. The plaster dented and Raven screamed. "That what you said to me boy, deal with it?" Knapp picked him up and shoved him into the wall again, knocking his breath out.

Dazed, Wyatt slid down the wall onto the floor. He had no ability to defend himself as the Colonel inflicted a series of hard kicks to the ribs.

"How d'ya like how I'm dealin' with it, you little piece of shit?"

Forgetting her pain, Raven ran to her brother, crying, and flung her arms around him, as she got kicked in the head. Kevin, though also used to beatings, opened his mouth to try and calm the situation. He met the back of his father's hand, hell-bent on regaining control of his family.

Wyatt sat up in pain and regarded Hazel, whose eyes were cast downward, then back at the Colonel.

"You ever touch my sister or me again, I swear I'll kill you myself."

Knapp just laughed and grabbed a knife off the table, as if picking up a baseball. He placed the sole of his boot flat on Wyatt's painful chest.

"I got every right to discipline you any way I want." He held the knife loosely but menacingly in his hand. "You wanna play with me son? I will fuckin' slice her." He pointed the knife at Raven. "And then you." He pointed it back at Wyatt. "Do I make myself clear?"

Without waiting for an answer, he removed his boot and turned to his wife. "Call me when my supper's *ready and you got this damn mess picked up." He walked back to his study, muttering. Reaching for the door, he turned and yelled to his wife. "Oh, and no dinner for these three little fuckwits. They can starve for all I give a shit."*

After a few moments, Kevin reached a hand down to help Wyatt up.

"Don't fucking touch me."

Leaning on each other, the twins went to their shared room and Raven helped him remove his shirt. She gently probed the area.

"Does it feel like anything's broken?" she asked in a frantic tone.

"Hell if I know, just hurts."

"Okay, well, maybe should you lay down?"

"Maybe we should get the hell outta here," he wheezed. "It's time, isn't it?"

"We can't," she admonished in a whisper. Her eyes darted around the room in case their abuser was in the hall. "We don't have enough money yet," she whispered, acknowledging the paltry amount they'd been able to squirrel away.

"We have the fake IDs, and we could get jobs."

"What about school?"

"We'll have to figure it out when we get to the new place. But that motherfucker's crazy, and he's only getting worse."

She saw him glance at the scar above her eyebrow from when the bastard had backhanded her, cutting her open with his ring.

"We gotta be done here, Raven. We've been dealing with this shit too long. He's gonna kill someone someday, and it won't be Kevin or Hazel first. I can't

stay here another night." Not being with her brother would never have occurred to Raven, so she just hung her head. Breathing hard, he lifted her chin with one hand while holding his ribs with the other and considered her eyes. That's all it took.

"What do we need to do?" she asked.

"You get as much food and water packed into the backpacks. I'll get as much as I can from their wallets. What else?"

"Blankets, clothes?"

"Yeah, okay. We won't be able to take a lot. We'll wear as many clothes as we can and fit the rest into a garbage sack. Not too heavy though. We don't want people to notice us too much. Then we'll just figure out where to go after we find out how much money we have."

When he rifled through Hazel's purse, he realized the gods must have been smiling down on them. She'd recently been to the bank and two hundred and fifty dollars sat neatly tucked in a teller's envelope. As the Knapps slept, Wyatt entered the lion's den and grabbed the Colonel's wallet off his dresser, before retreating back to their room without a sound.

"How are you going to put that back?" Raven whispered.

"We won't need to. We'll be gone."

She watched her brother peel out two hundred and thirty-seven dollars from the money clip and throw the rest of it on the ground. Collecting all they could, they escaped out their bedroom window and ran down the street, toward the bus station. Thirty minutes later, they were searching for the earliest bus leaving Bethany and bought two one-way tickets to Seattle. By the time the

Colonel woke that morning, the twins were passing through Clear Lake, Iowa. Fifty-seven hours after that, Wyatt saw the lights of their new city and woke his sister.

Immediately, they met Que, another runaway, who helped them get jobs and find shelter. Eventually, they all found a place to live together, received their GEDs, and utilized every benefit they qualified for, including counseling for the horrors they suffered at their adoptive father's hand and parents' tragedy.

The trio became family and it was their second Christmas together when Wyatt gave her that first guitar, thus beginning her career.

Raven thought of her brother's sweet and handsome face and how he had affected her life. The one person, her person, in the world. He gave her wings to begin this life, even though he would be horrified to know she thought of it that way.

Now looking out of her million-dollar condo at the gray skies of Seattle, tears ran as silently down her face, as the rain slid down the glass windowpanes. She thought of the Colonel, wondering what imprint he left on her? Fear? Helplessness? She didn't know. And what about Donovan? Dependence? Isolation? Her mind drifted. What about Finn?

She turned toward the room and peered down at the coffee table, where the morning paper headlines were, *Raven Hunter Collapses at Concert*. It was accompanied by a very unflattering photo, looking like she had overdosed. Donovan's handiwork, no doubt. She shook her head. All that counseling, she thought, all that preparation to overcome her early existence, and look where she was now.

Chapter 31

Back in his car after being thrown out of the concert, Finn flexed and balled his fists, working out the knuckles that connected with the manager's face. The sickening crack of Jason's nose breaking gave him immense satisfaction and caused him to grin malevolently. He sat back and closed his eyes. Images and memories of the horrible things he said and the pain on Raven's face at hearing them, flooded in. It was plain to see she was miserable and hadn't slept in days. Probably thinking about a little girl laying somewhere in a hospital, and he just added to that pain.

Glancing down on the passenger seat, he eyed his cell phone, laying in wanton accusation. He retrieved it and stared at the screen for a full minute before connecting the call and lifting the phone to his ear. It went directly to voicemail, which wasn't a huge surprise.

"Hi there, you've reached Raven. I'm busy lying on the beach and drinking cold beer. When I get back, I'll call you. Bye." Finn smiled at the message she'd recorded for her island stay. The fact she hadn't erased it yet kept the smile in place until he spoke.

"Raven." He paused, looking out into the night. "I'm…I'm sorry. Really sorry I hurt you. Can I just… I wanna talk to you. There's a lot of things you don't know. What you saw that day. And I just want a chance to explain."

Not able to think of anything else to say, he disconnected and drove back to his hotel.

By the time he lay down, sleep had decided to elude him. So, he listened to the jets arrive and depart from the airport nearby and waited for morning to come. Every time he closed his eyes, he saw Raven in that ridiculous outfit, her face and hair so foreign, making him angry all over again. Her full allowance to be a prop, miserable and unhappy. What was worse was she didn't seem to see it, just blindly trust the empty promises of life in a fishbowl. He could never live that way. In captivity.

Now all he wanted was to return to his life, but when he tried to envision that, he drew a blank. He could see her in his bed, mid-orgasm; arms wrapped around him as they rode his bike down the highway or deep in the water, swimming in his life force.

****

Finn's plane began its descent into Kaua'i. He hadn't slept for twenty-seven hours and could barely register a clear thought. Walking through the small airport lobby, happy people, relieved to be on vacation were everywhere. He envied their careless freedom.

Dee, dressed in a muumuu with oranges on it, also wore a matching hat. She welcomed him with an enthusiastic hug and smile, yet driving home, remained quiet and unassuming as she turned to study him.

"Ah, yeah, we're done, Grandma," he confirmed, glancing at her.

"What happened?" she asked, sounding dejected.

"I'm not sure. It was all so fake. She just looked so

fake. I tried to tell her she didn't want all that but she didn't listen." He put one arm on the wheel, and ran his other hand down it, almost like he was cold.

"Why do you think she doesn't want it?"

"Dee, come on." He looked over at her blank face. "Seriously? You're seriously asking that?" When she said nothing, he stated, "She looked like a total prostitute."

"Please tell me you didn't say that to her," she chided.

"Well, somebody had to."

"Finn Taylor, what the hell's wrong with you?"

"What?"

"Don't you see what her life is like?"

"Yeah, I got a great snapshot of it in the last two days. You should see where she lives. You could perform surgery in there. She strips down damn near naked in a room full of people to change, and her ex stands there, screaming at her the whole time."

"Yes, she told me a little about that ex-husband of hers. He sounds like an overbearing asshole. That other character that you told me about too—was he there, what's his name?"

"Jason? Yeah, I broke his nose." Finn grinned thinking about it.

"Well, I'll at least give you points for that." She looked out the window. "It seems to me, Finn, she has enough people telling her what to do and very few people asking her what she wants to do."

"I tried."

"Did you?" She cast a steely gaze on him. "Did you really try or did you just give up?"

"I just hate that she won't stand up for herself," he

evaded. "They treat her like shit, and she just takes it."

"What about her parents? Oh." She lowered her head remembering. "That's right, they passed on, didn't they? But she has a brother, right?" When he nodded, she said, "Well, I wonder what he thinks?"

"I didn't ask." He thought about Wyatt. "I thought he was an asshole too at first, but he turned out to be a pretty decent guy. I did look over at him a few times, and he looked pissed too, but I think he just wants her to stand up for herself. I don't know. Maybe he just tries to let her do it at her own glacial pace."

"Maybe you should too."

"No, I'm done. There's entirely too much baggage there, and it's certainly not the life I want for myself." Shooting a glance in her direction, he saw her crestfallen face. "Oh, come on, Dee. My life's pretty simple here, don't ya think? I wake up in paradise and play in the water all day." Dee opened her mouth to speak again but closed it, causing him to take a closer look. "Oh hell, is it that thing again? The Greek thing? I'm so done hearing about that too, old woman. Please do not make me have to institutionalize you."

"Maybe I'll have to put you in the looney bin instead," she retorted. "You're ten kinds of stupid."

"Thanks." Sobering, he asked about Alaula. "They hear anything?"

"No, nothing yet," she responded.

"Did you talk to Nate?"

"Only a little, but he was pretty busy, and I didn't want to intrude. It was Annie I spoke with, and only right after you left, so something might have changed since then."

"Okay, I'll call him when I get home."

"Finn…"

"Grandma, I'm sorry, but it's over."

She merely looked out the window and shook her head.

Chapter 32

Two days after the concert, Raven woke still dazed, not quite believing the events that had transpired in such a short amount of time. Rising from the fluffy, buttery yellow, comforter, she padded to the bathroom. Bending the magnifying side of her vanity mirror, she inspected her red-rimmed, darkly haunted eyes and stained hair that now looked the color of mud.

How did one go about changing their life, when everything inside them screamed for the safe status quo? She stared at her foreign image and felt like everything was always just outside of her reach.

Deliberately dressing, because she'd remain in pajamas all day if she didn't, Raven performed the morning ablutions of everyday life. Upon approaching the kitchen, she discovered she was ready for breakfast. Sitting at the dining room table was a yellow legal-sized pad of paper. She eyed it dubiously, as she made coffee and toast, then approached it warily as she sat at the table. It wasn't until her fingers took hold of the pen that a measure of peace came to her and she began to write. Two and a half hours later, her cell phone rang, jolting her back from her thoughts.

Noting the caller, she groaned, closed her eyes, and connected the call.

"Hello, Jason."

"Hello!" A wet nasally voice came across the ether.

"Hello...are you fucking kidding me, Raven! What the hell happened to you? Have you lost your God damn mind? Do you understand the shit storm we're in?"

"I do understand the situation I've put myself in, yes."

"No, no," he squawked, like a petulant child, "it's not just you, Raven. It's my life too."

"Jason, you don't need to worry about it anymore; you're no longer my manager or part of my life." The silence down the line was deafening, and she almost thought he'd disconnected the call.

"What are you talking about now?"

"I'm letting you go."

"You're letting me go? Oh, is that right?"

"Yes, that's right."

"We have a contract together Raven, something you don't seem to quite grasp as of late. I can assure you Donovan gets it, as do I."

"Sure, so sue me." Raven walked to the window and looked across the buildings to the water and listened to the stunned silence. "Or you can cut your losses and get out now, with a possible business still intact."

"What are you talking about, I—"

"You're a personal assistant that I should never have promoted to manager. You didn't listen to your client, not professionally or personally, and continued to cross the line. You didn't read the contract or work to your client's best interests or wishes." Her gaze dropped to her notes to check if she was on target for the bullet points of the phone call with Jason. Her finger traveled over the next line. "That doesn't make it entirely your fault because I didn't read it all either. I was naïve enough to trust you. I can tell you, however, that this will go one of two ways. You can sue me, and I will make sure every artist and celebrity I know hears of your gross misconduct and incompetence."

"What gross misconduct? Did you see what your fucking boyfriend did to my face?" She couldn't help it. The giggle came on so fast she had to pull the phone away from her face. Quickly composing herself, she continued, "Or you can walk away now, and I'll announce that our split was a mutually satisfying decision and we wish only the best for one another. Which one would you like it to be, Jason?"

"I have nothing to prove here…"

"If that's true, then go with option A." The silence was once more deafening, then she heard his deep sigh.

"You know I never wanted this to happen, Raven. I cared a great deal for you."

"I know what you expected, Jason. For me to fall in line, so you could continue where Donovan left off. If you want to keep doing this, that's your prerogative. Quite frankly, I think you should find a different profession, but I don't have to stand in your way if you choose to continue this."

"Fine, we'll dissolve our partnership, and I would appreciate your support."

"Okay, let's meet next week, maybe Wednesday or Thursday, for some lunch, and get all the papers signed?"

After finalizing the arrangement and meeting, Raven disconnected the call, let out a whoosh of breath and stood in the center of her condo, raised a fist and squealed with excitement because she had power.

****

That night she went to Que's for dinner and stupidly grinned as she watched Abby play a board game with her friends, including her new one, Travis Morgan.

"You got this Rave, and it's gonna turn out perfect," Que said.

"Jason was one thing Que; Donovan's going to be a completely different animal."

"How do you know, is all I'm sayin'."

Que split a look between Raven and Lilly. The three of them had begun an unlikely bond in the new roots of friendship. Lilly was reluctant at first, citing conflict of interest, but quickly acquiesced.

"Jason's a pushover that had no idea what he was doing."

"Then why did you hire him?" Lilly asked.

"Because," Raven said sarcastically, "I didn't know that at the time, ob-vee." She rolled her eyes at herself and laughed. "I don't know if it would've mattered if I did. He said what I needed to hear, to think he could do it." Raven thought about it for a moment and sipped her wine. "He didn't know if I was really going to sabotage him. I could almost hear him thinking on the other side, going, 'Okay, she already went crazy, is she also insane enough to screw me over?'" She shook her head. "Suddenly, he had no idea what the hell I was going to do and that hadn't happened before."

"So you bluffed," Que stated, taking a sip from her glass.

"Maybe. I'm still not sure."

Lilly's cell rang, and she jumped up to answer it. Que watched her walk away.

"It must be nice knowing that when your phone

rings, the person on the other side is desperate to talk to you."

"Que, you're getting drunk. They're calling because someone died, and they need a heart, or there's an emergency. I think she has incredibly mixed feelings about hearing it ring."

"Wyatt asked her out."

"What!" Raven exclaimed in a whisper, eyes widening. "Our Wyatt? He asked her out? Did she go? Why am I just hearing about this?"

"Yes, once, but I think that's it."

"Why, does she have a problem with my brother?"

"No, I don't think…"

"Hey, Lil." Raven ran a hand down the back of her head, as her new friend reappeared.

"Yes, Wyatt and I went out. Yes, we had a lot of fun. In fact, we laughed our asses off, it was great, we're friends, okay?" When they blinked innocently at her, she continued quickly. "Really, I appreciate the energy, ladies, but my primary concern is my kiddos. And everything else is second." Raven shrugged and raised a glass.

"Okay, well, welcome to the family." Then she exchanged a meaningful look with Que and Lilly groaned.

"Anyway," Lilly said, exasperated, "what did I miss about Donovan?"

"I have a meeting with him a week from tomorrow, so I gotta figure it all out by then."

"Well, you da OG now and I think you can take his boney-ass," Que quipped.

****

Over the next week, Raven prepared for the

meeting with her ex-husband by speaking with her lawyers and accountant. She knew the best thing to do would be to stroke his ego but decided she didn't want to do what was best for him. When she walked into the posh restaurant for lunch, she was ready.

Donovan had already arrived and sipped a bourbon, neat. He nodded at Raven but inconsiderately remained seated as the concierge helped seat her.

"Madam, may I bring you something to drink?"

"Just water, with lemon. Thank you so much."

He handed her a menu, which she immediately laid on the table, then lifted her eyes to her ex-husband. The old Raven would apologize, bargain, whine, and cajole. Deciding she wanted to set the new tone, she started from a position of equality and remained silent, which appeared to infuriate him.

"Well?" he sneered.

"Well?" Raven agreed, smiling.

"Well, what do you have to say about your hideous display?"

"To you? I don't believe I need to say anything." Locking her eyes with his, she clarified, "I'm sorry Donovan, was there something confusing about what happened that night?" He stared at her, as if she had tentacles.

"You broke a contract and disappointed your base, to say nothing of assaulting me."

"Well, let's discuss that," she said almost cheerily. His brow furrowed like he hadn't heard her correctly. "First, I had fulfilled the contract, save the encores. I never committed to any number and obviously chose none." She sipped her water, hoping she looked relaxed. "I understand I trusted someone that didn't have my best interests at heart, a common theme among the professional men of my life." His gaze scurried away from hers. "I believe I made myself crystal clear on what I wanted to happen, regarding my set."

"You were supposed to sing a song with Amanda, during the encore, to introduce her."

"I never agreed to sing a song with Amanda, and that was certainly not covered in my contract. Nor would I ever have done so. What was it you said all those years ago?" She pretended to think. "Oh yes, I don't feel her talent extends that far and I don't need that kind of exposure with her."

"I see, so your jealousy, rather than professionalism prevailed, is that it?"

"No." Raven suddenly felt a kind of pity for the man. "Amanda is a gorgeous, naïve young woman. Exactly your type." Donovan clenched his jaw. "However, she doesn't have it and furthermore you know she'll be a flash in the pan. Then what, Donovan? Drop her for the next one? I just wanted the songs promised to me."

"I told you before why those songs wouldn't work. I've been doing this for a long—"

"A long time, yes, I know," she said, sounding completely exhausted. "A really, really…really, long time, Donovan." When he started to sputter, she sliced through him by raising a condescending hand. "I have spoken with my lawyers. Legally, I fulfilled my contract with you. From what I understand, my portion of ticket sales for those two nights was"—she looked at her paperwork—"one point two-three-nine million. Deducting your twenty percent and Jason's ten, minus crew, lights, sound, hospitality, transportation, venue, and my donation, my take was around six-hundred and fifty k, am I correct?"

Donovan blinked like an owl at the odd, foreign woman sitting before him. Nothing could have prepared him for her confidence or demeanor.

"Raven, I don't think…" She held up a hand again A sizeable purple vein protruded from his forehead.

"Here's what I'm willing to do. I will donate an additional two-hundred and fifty thousand dollars to the charity, for any inconvenience not performing encores created. Which again was at my discretion. You could've been SOL."

"All right, I've had about as much as I can handle here. If you honestly think I'm going to allow you to sit there and speak to me in this fashion, we can get our lawyers involved, for physical assault. Not to mention that there seems to be some serious concerns about your mental capacity. I'm sure your fans would be horrified to hear you're unstable."

"Sure." Raven leaned back, smiling. "I'm all in, let's go. I was trying to give you a great deal. In court, you'll lose. You won't get one dime, and I'll go after damages."

"Damages for what?"

"Well, first your recollection of the events is skewed."

"Skewed?"

"Yes. If you remember you grabbed my arm first—in front of dozens of people I might add—so I was protecting myself." His mouth dropped open, and she continued, "Secondly, somehow it slipped from one of your people that I had some kind of a breakdown. There's a clause in your contract that states if I'm ill or don't have the capacity to perform, I wasn't obligated to honor the contract at all."

"It stipulates you'd reschedule."

"I can't reschedule if I'm mentally unbalanced and if I had a breakdown, I could certainly keep that up in court. I guess the papers getting that information was just your misfortune."

"What in the hell are you talking about?"

"See Donovan. You aren't the only one with connections. I have them too. All those lowly little people that have watched you walk on me, and them, for over a decade. You aren't as well respected as you think. Every one of them has assured me they'd have no problem standing up for me in a courtroom to give their insights into our relationship."

"Are you now suggesting that I somehow mistreated you?" Shocked, he sat back in his chair.

"I know that you don't understand it, but yes, you did. All I want, Donovan, is to be done with you and with this ridiculous farce. I want to record my own music, my own way. I want every connection to you, over. And I'm quite sure you're rapidly coming to that same conclusion, aren't you?" He became introspective, eyeing her as he sipped his drink. He seemed to be gauging her resolve, then concluded.

"Your terms are?"

Outwardly she smiled; inwardly she was at a rave party.

"To be free and clear of the concert and you. In actuality, I don't owe you a dime, or at least it's a point arguable in court." She sipped her water. "However, I'm willing to part with the only thing you seem to respond to and give you the extra two-hundred and fifty

k. I can appreciate the hardship and struggle the homeless go through every day, more than you know. We've already solved everything else in the divorce. You'll be leaving with a tidy profit for your charity and time with me, which I know is so very important to you."

"I should. I made you."

"You promoted me, Donovan, and any influence you had on me is being rectified, at the moment. It's my talent, my gift, that made me, not you."

"What a blissfully, ignorant sentiment."

"Well, I'm taking a little pity on you because I understand that I'm speaking with a blissfully ignorant man." She extended a hand. "What do you say? Shall we end this thing finally and be done with one another?"

For an awful moment, she thought he was going to say, game on but she saw something in his eyes and realized he too was tired. He held out his hand, and she shook it, then left without eating. Three weeks later, all her legal ties to Donovan, Jason, and her old life were signed and submitted. Raven was officially free.

Chapter 33

Finn woke the morning after he'd arrived back home feeling hungover. Retrieving the newspaper, he sat at his kitchen table, eating a bagel, and unfolded it to read. The front page had a small thumbnail of Raven, with *Singer Collapses* splashed under it. Worried, he scanned the article.

Singer Raven Hunter, 34, collapsed during her closeout performance at the Tacoma Dome in Washington State yesterday. Official sources say the singer's collapse was due to dehydration and exhaustion, but insiders suggest the singer's condition was a possible breakdown. Whether physical or cognitive, they were unwilling to say. Neither the singer nor her manager could be reached for comment.

He glanced at the photo. She was in the red outfit and only had one set left to perform when he'd left, so the collapse, or whatever it was, happened just after he'd gone. Concerned, he tried to call her again, but the phone went straight to voicemail, which had changed.

"You've reached Raven, please leave a message, and I'll return it as soon as possible." She sounded tired but otherwise okay. Choosing not to leave a message, Finn exhaled profoundly and tipped the rest of his bagel into the trash.

****

"Hey Finn," Jake called, a little wary when his boss

316

arrived. Finn glanced over and took off his helmet.

"Oh, hey Jake, what d'ya got."

"Dawson and I were wondering if we could take a trip to the south side, while you and Dr. Bowman work with the cops."

"Are they here?"

"No, Dr. Bowman said in about an hour, but wasn't sure if you were going to stay for it."

"Yeah, okay, take off." When Jake turned to go, Finn asked, "You said you and Dawson. Where's Holly?"

"Ah, I guess she transferred or something."

"Okay, thanks. Go ahead," he said, relieved.

The deep, fragrant aroma of good coffee filled the office. As Finn stepped into the conference room, he noticed a confectioner's feast lay spread across the table. Nate looked up from where he was sitting, with a welcoming smile.

"Annie?" Finn queried.

"Yep."

"God bless that woman."

"Right?" Nate agreed. "So, how'd it go?"

"Didn't."

"What happened?"

"I don't wanna get into it. I heard we're talking to some cops. Do they know anything?" His friend looked at him for a moment, then poured him a mug of coffee. "Really man, I do not want to get into this."

Nate simply selected the best maple bar, placed it on a napkin with seahorses on it and slid it over to Finn, then raised his eyebrows. When the younger man still said nothing, Nate lost his patience.

"Just tell me what happened."

"Nothing, really." Exasperated, Finn blew out a heavy breath.

"Well, why did she leave?"

"Her friend's kid had a heart attack or something."

When Nate frowned at him, Finn lowered his eyes.

"She came over to talk to me about Alaula. Did you tell her about that?" Nate confirmed it with a nod. "Holly drove me home. We were both a little freaked out. I had blood and shit all over me. She tried to make a play, and I thought I evaded. I brushed her off and told her I was gonna take a shower." Nate watched him and sipped some of his coffee. "I intended that to mean, I'm taking a fucking shower, go home."

"How did she take it?"

"You're taking a shower. Okay, I'm gonna get naked and wait for you in bed." He explained how Raven came over and saw both him and Holly in their state of undress.

"Aw, shit. Were you able to tell her?"

"I got a towel on Nate. How the hell's she gonna sit there and listen to me make excuses? She wasn't gonna listen."

He explained how he'd tried to call, but she'd never pick up. He told him about discovering she went back home and her friend's kid in the hospital. Then going to her condo, meeting Wyatt, and the fight that ensued.

"So she walked out pissed, and when I woke up, she was still gone."

"So, you never saw her?"

"No, her brother brought me backstage at her show. But by the time we got there, things were almost ready to go. Nate, I didn't even recognize her, man. She looked like a fuckin' stripper." When he noticed his friend's eyebrows shoot up, he clarified, "Not in a good way." Sitting down, he sprawled his legs out in front of him.

"All of these people were yelling at her, telling her what she was supposed to do, say, play, dress. It was bullshit, man." Angry again, he stood up and began to pace. Nate followed him with his eyes, quiet, until he sat back down. "She looked miserable, and she didn't say a God damn word...nothing." He raised his hands to interlock behind his head. "I don't know. She was damn near crying because they wouldn't let her play a song she promised the sick little girl in the hospital, and I don't know, I just lost it."

"Kicked some ass?"

"No." He sat down, dejected. "I yelled at her."

"At her?"

"Yeah, at her," Finn said defensively. "I just thought if she could see herself. See them. She'd like, snap out of it and tell them all to go to hell." He leaned an elbow on the table and ran a hand down his jawline absently. "It went wrong. I fucked it up."

"How?"

"I told her she looked like a whore."

"A whore?"

"I know, I know, I fucked up, Jesus!"

"Well, come on now, Finn. This isn't insurmountable. It's a lot of confusion, misperception, and emotion, maybe. I know. I live every day with a lady in the first trimester of pregnancy. Try waiting and call her again, in a couple of days."

"No, I'm just gonna..."

"Hello?" Two men walked into the reception area.

"Hey," Nate said, "are you the guys from the DLNR?"

"Yes sir, I'm Dennis Mathison, Department of Land and Natural Resources, and this is Henry Kauffman from the National Oceanic and Atmospheric Administration. Are you Dr. Nathan Bowman?"

"Yeah, I'm Nate, and this is my head biologist, Finn Taylor."

After shaking hands, Nate gestured them to chairs. After distributing refreshments, they all sat down and began the discussion.

"So, I wish we were meeting under better circumstances gentlemen. We are here to give you our findings on RCW-429," Henry began, causing Finn to close his eyes at Alaula's official name.

"She was killed by blunt force trauma to the skull, a pretty vicious attack. Struck multiple times and with great force," Dennis intoned.

"Was it quick?" Nate asked for Finn's sake.

"No." Dennis hesitated. "Unfortunately, Dr. Bowman, she did suffer. There was massive internal bleeding. Prior to the second strike, she sustained a deep laceration on her underbelly. We're pretty sure her pup was attacked with the same knife. We found no traces of disease there so…"

"No," Finn said quietly, "she was really healthy. So was Kaimi when they returned, after weaning."

"Kaimi?" Henry looked blank for a second, then with understanding asked, "the pup?" Finn nodded, and he continued. "Locals noticed her alive and well at fifteen hundred hours and was found, as you know, at sixteen twenty-five."

"Any leads?" Finn asked impotently.

"No, we think it's the same person or persons that killed RCW-125 last year and the other one a couple of years back. Exact same MO. We don't think they live on the island but haven't ruled out anything." When his audience only nodded solemnly, Henry looked down at the table, then tried to contribute. "We want to catch these guys too, and eventually they'll make a mistake. We do have one person saying that they may have seen a man in the area but her memory is a little fuzzy and she's trying to work with a sketch artist we brought over. The best possible lead we've had on this guy so far."

"And you know how many in this community are invested," Dennis interjected. "They're mad as hell. We have the posters up and the ticker and hotline numbers going."

"Yeah, I think they'll be having a rally to try and raise reward money," Nate supplied.

"Which will, of course, be matched by ours. I think we might have a chance at catching this guy," Henry said.

It wasn't the news Finn wanted to hear but was the report he had expected. After a little more discussion, they walked the gentlemen to their car.

"I understand you guys have been fighting for a rehab facility here, is that right?" Dennis asked before getting in the car.

"Yeah, for some years now. We get so many of the seals on these beaches, and it takes a long time to get here from Oahu," Nate confirmed.

"What about your benefactor?"

"Ah, no, he's too interested in putting in turbines to waste his time with rehab. Why help 'em when you can place enough hazards to kill 'em." Finn snorted.

"Ah, yeah." Nate laid a hand on Finn's shoulder. "It's been a rough few weeks around here. We've been slowly collecting the money. We'll get there."

"Well, I can tell you that we, along with HWF are considering expansion out here with the Marine Mammal Center." Nate looked over at Finn.

"Seriously? You guys would be willing to consider that?"

"It's being seriously discussed. Let's set up some meetings to look at your numbers, and what it would take to set up out here because we agree, there seems to be need."

They parted company with Nate saying all the right things about becoming more diligent and working with the community and possibilities, but Finn's heart wasn't in it. All he felt was exposed.

Chapter 34

Filling yellow pad after yellow pad of notes, music, lyrics, and dates, Raven made plans. Lots and lots of plans. Thinking of the new direction she wanted to take her life and what she wanted from it was exhilarating. Then solving the puzzle and creating the steps to achieve it, brought her a sense of completion. She only hired people with her vision in mind. Every new decision caused her to feel more independent and free. It wasn't until she put her condo on the market that her family determined it was time to intervene.

"This seems pretty drastic, Rave. You're going awfully fast for a pretty lucrative place here," her brother stated.

"I can't live here anymore. There are too many memories. It feels more like a jail cell than a home."

"But what about all this stuff?" Que asked, looking around at the high-end furnishings.

"I'll sell it, maybe on one of those sites on the internet."

"Very funny."

"It's never felt like mine, anyway. I'll sell it and throw whatever I want into storage until I find something different." Facing Que, she asked, "Ya still willing to room with me again? At least we don't have to share a bed anymore."

"I don't know why you don't just stay with me?"

Wyatt questioned.

"Because it's in the middle of nowhere."

"It's peaceful."

"It's forsaken," Raven quipped. "I want to be a little closer to civilization."

"Where are you playing at tonight, again?" Que asked, changing the topic.

"A little place in Bellingham. Why? Are you coming?" Raven asked, hopeful.

"I thought I might. Lilly asked Ab to go spend the night."

"Perfect!"

"I can't believe no one's recognized you yet."

"No one knows me blonde. It was the same in Hawai'i. Pseudo name, completely different material, small gigs. It just works out perfectly, almost like starting over."

"At least you get a pure read off people and if they like it," Wyatt contributed. "That's gotta feel good."

After they made their plans for meeting and travel, Que left to get ready and Wyatt decided to take a nap. Raven sat at her table looking at her master list of action items.

~~Talk to lawyer re. legalities~~
~~Talk to CPA~~
~~Fire Jason~~
~~Fire Donovan~~
~~Cancel tour dates~~
~~Sell Condo~~
~~Figure out living situation~~
~~Arrange new/old music and lyrics~~
~~Plan new show~~
~~Hire new agent with my vision~~

~~Speak to publicist~~
~~Rehearse~~
~~Arrange new tour dates~~
~~Promotion tour~~
Finn

With the promotional dates set and everything prepared, there was nothing more to occupy her mind. Allowing him to flood into her consciousness, and try to make sense of what occurred, she thought she could possibly release him.

Her mind drifted to that last day and the call she'd received from Nate about Alaula. All Raven could think about was getting to him, wanting desperately to console and mourn with him. Then arriving at his door to see the pretty young blonde in his clothes and her underwear. And the look of shock on his face at seeing them both together. Maybe he had been honest with her. As beautiful as she thought him to be, he never gave her cause to question his loyalty to her, until then.

Her thoughts also traveled to Dee and her ridiculous notions of the prophecy. It still sat so uneasily within her. It was almost like the angel and devil sitting on the shoulders of her dreams warring with good and bad fortune. Light and misery, poetry and discord. Those dreams which were so realistic, she felt she could touch them, enter them—or had they done the devouring. Her medallion, always a relatively harmless, sentimental object, had turned into a virtual living being. Heating, vibrating and pulsating against her skin at times. It was something she could no longer explain away.

Her unease was almost palpable. What was the catalyst to all this? She walked to her living room window.

"She thinks I'm Apollo," Raven said out loud, then laughed at the fact she was lending any credence at all to it. However, now that the thoughts were there, they rooted.

The music, something to do with the music. It was as if there was something immediately behind her vision but just beyond her grasp, just unable to see. She glanced at her watch, she had hours before Que would be back and Wyatt would wake. With decision, she walked to her laptop on the table and typed in *Apollo, Greek Mythology*, and began to read.

Apollo, god of music, sun, light, oracles, archery, plague, medicine, poetry, and knowledge. Born to Zeus and Leto; twin brother of Artemis, goddess of hunting, moon, archery, forests, and hills.

"So how does Apollo connect with Poseidon? Aren't they both men?" She scanned for the connection and almost shut down the computer to laugh at herself. That was when she saw it and ran a finger over the text.

Poseidon and Apollo lost favor with mighty Zeus over Hera's plan to overthrow her husband. They were stripped of their status and sent to Troy. Laomedon, the mighty king of Troy, charged them with building the walls and foundation of the city.

"So, they built a foundation and what, suddenly they're spawning children together?"

She read that Apollo was bisexual.

"So what, the man still couldn't have babies or was he asexual somehow? Can gods do that?"

And what about Poseidon? She didn't think he was bisexual. She sat back, frustrated, looking at the pictures of the two gods.

"So, obviously, Apollo slept with someone, who slept with someone until finally what, I'm supposed to have come along, with my twin."

She lifted her eyes from the book and wondered if all of them were twins, the ancestors of the music god. Grabbing her pad of paper, she flipped to a clean page and drew two columns, labeling one side Raven, the other Apollo. She tried to denote similar characteristics.

"Music, song, poetry, yes. Oracles, healing, plague and disease, no." Her finger followed along the text as she read. "His sacred animal was a raven and his object a lyre." A lyre?

Raven looked down at her medallion, really seeing the lyre embossed on it, then glanced back at the page and the depiction of one there. She blinked. They were exactly the same. Scared, she realized she was talking to herself, so closed her laptop with a firm snap.

She was genuinely losing it. The words Finn said to Dee, about her desperately wanting the information she uncovered to be true, streamed through Raven's mind. Now, she was doing the exact same thing. Even if in some bizarre, crazy, freak of the universe it was true, why her, why now, why Finn? And now that their relationship wasn't happening—she laughed out loud.

"It didn't happen, and the world didn't fall apart. Raven, you're an idiot."

****

A perfect snowy white swan floated in a pristine lake, with its surface reflecting the sky above it. A dolphin swam around the swan in circles, ripples streaming out from the center of the duo.

"But how can a dolphin enter a lake?" Raven asked aloud, breaking the serenity.

"The swan showed it the way."

The most beautiful man she'd ever seen stepped out from the forest. His hair was as white as the swan's feathers, curling to kiss the tops of his shoulders. He held a bow as if he had been recently hunting. He wore hunting clothes but sandals on his feet. She curiously moved to touch him, but he was behind glass.

"But there's no stream."

"There's a waterfall." He gestured and turned his head. The movement caused a lock of hair to slide across his forehead. At the same moment, a lock fell into her own eyes. They both brushed them aside with the same gesture. A gentle breeze lifted the air, causing it to shimmer with the seductive scent of hyacinth.

Turning, she beheld a magnificent waterfall cascading over a steep and rocky cliff. The spray danced around her in suspended droplets. The roar of it was deafening, and its color was like Finn's eyes. She looked down at the swan and playful dolphin, then back at the man, who seemed endlessly fascinated by her.

"Is Finn the dolphin?" she queried.

"He is the great rock of the cliff."

"Am I the swan?"

"No, you are the waterfall."

She woke startled and looked around her dark room for the man, but the residue of the dream was already scurrying from her mind and into the ether. It was early the next morning, the successful performance of the night behind her. She lay awake, trying to decipher the vignette and had a sudden urge to touch Finn. Instead of repressing them, as she was growing used to doing, she let the feelings come. Raven could almost feel his hands on her, the mesmerizing way he kissed, looking at her with those intense eyes.

From the beginning, he had been truthful with her. She didn't know how she knew that, but she understood that it was truth. His words didn't always sit well, and some were painful, but they were real. He didn't tell her he loved her because maybe he didn't feel that, but she knew without a doubt he cared for her. Her pride told her he cared a great deal.

The night of the concert now six weeks prior, he had told her the truth. The truth that she couldn't even admit to herself, but he knew it, knew her, and had said it. He didn't handle her with kid gloves but rather as a woman who could be capable. Besides Wyatt, no other man had done that. Raven knew she loved him, had known a long time, and wondered if she was yet strong enough to face him and let go. For her own sanity, she needed to find out. So, picking up her cell, she entered the digits and heard a sleepy voice.

"Hello?"

"Hi, Dee? It's Raven."

Chapter 35

As six weeks closed in on Finn, he went to rallies to stop the construction of the turbines, but initial installation ensued two months after Alaula's death. He began a renewed campaign to raise funds for the rehabilitation facility, propelled by the promise of matched funds. On the day Kaimi returned to the sea, Finn was there to see it, though the day was bittersweet. Feeling a growing detachment with the animals he researched, he experienced fleeting thoughts about change, yet quickly dismissed them. What else could he possibly do? He surfed, drank, rode his bike, hung out with Dee and his friends, even tried dating once, but upon bringing the woman to her door, couldn't make himself go in behind her.

It was a Saturday night, and Finn opted to stay in for the evening. His grandmother was playing Bingo with friends, and he was restless in the house. He passed by her study, paused, then doubled back, sipping on a beer. She'd left the light on, and the illumination highlighted a single piece of paper on her desk, like a beacon. She'd typed out notes, essential facts she deemed worthy. Sighing, he sat down and leaned back in her office chair, taking another pull from his beer, while absently reading her scribbling.

Poseidon, god of the sea, earthquakes, storms, and horses. Symbol, the trident.

He sighed again and then, if only for a moment, admitted to feeling life within that mark on his back. Reluctantly, he thought about it and the date Raven had come to town. The strange experience when he first saw her. Then recognizing that maybe the communication he had with Kaimi and Alaula was special. He left the idea to continue to float and kept reading.

Finn and Poseidon similarities.

Animals—dolphins, fish, seals anything sea life.

Water—tsunami, funnel cloud (Raven's first day). I think she has reactions to her medallion (cliffs)

Personality— angers quickly, possessive, moody, smart, loyal

Trident

Poseidon and Apollo—they were the builders of Troy

Shaken, Finn threw the paper back onto the desk. It was all so stupid. He was an intelligent man. Intelligent men did not believe mythical gods existed because if they did, only then could one imagine they had surviving offspring. He sighed and stood, cursing Dee for ever bringing it up in the first place. He moved to turn out a light when a name caught his eye. Raven had used it, so had Dee. He looked at what she'd written on the paper.

Demeter mourned the loss of her daughter, Persephone, and hid in a herd of Poseidon's stallions. When he came to her, overcome with her grief, they coupled, and she bore two of his children.

So technically and mechanically speaking she could be Demeter, his Dee if one were so inclined to believe it. He looked at her note below the line.

What do the Moirai have to do with the prophecy?

Dreams?
Three sisters/fates/Moirai, they doomed the gods?
Why?
Who else is involved?
Finn's tattoo means something!

He brought a hand to his neck and touched the place where the ink had permanently settled into his skin. The trident had been in every dream. He'd been helpless without it. It had split into a lyre. He couldn't protect Alaula, each dream so vivid and real. Raven turning into fire when his researchers drowned. No control, just unanswered questions. Misery and Discord— Misery and Discord? Why did those two words scream in his head? Suffuse themselves in his dreams. He shook his head a little in disbelief, then reached up and turned out the light.

****

"Hey, you all done down there?" It was a couple of days later when Nate walked down the ramp and onto the dock after the team had left for the night.

"Yeah, just," Finn said, stepping onto the small pier.

"Wanna get a beer?"

"Sure. I think I heard people talking about meeting up at the Crab Shack. You wanna go there?"

"Naw, let's do this one solo."

"Great, why don't I like the sound of that?"

"No, it's good, really."

They cleaned up and went to a small outdoor pub and ordered whiskeys. Sipping companionably, with the fresh scent of the water wafting over them, Finn waited for Nate to begin.

"So, we just got some new funding."

"Yeah? How much?" Finn's hopeful smile finally reached his eyes.

"Wait for it…one point eight-five"—he watched Finn—"million. All designated for the monks."

The air seemed to leave the open-air bar they sat in. Nate just smiled and sipped his beer, watching his friend's reaction.

"What?" Finn was incredulous, with an expression almost akin to fear etched on his face. "Are you shittin' me?"

"Nope." Nate began to laugh and shake his head. "Already in the bank."

"Ho…ly…shit." Finn scrubbed a hand down his face and over his beard, then began to laugh. "Oh my God. One point eight million dollars? Million?"

"I know."

"Oh my God. Nate." His eyes darted around in disbelief as realization sank in. "Do you know what this means?"

"It means we've got it. All of it."

"Shit… Who's the donor?" It was everything Finn could do to contain his excitement. He wanted to scream.

"Anonymous, but Sunderland's pretty sure it's that outfit in California. They floated a number like that after NOAA got involved and wanted it kept quiet."

"We'll have to try and reach out to them."

"I already asked. I'll do everything I can to make that happen."

"Oh man. Sunderland, we can be done with him." Finn sat back in his chair and picked up his whiskey glass again, then let the amber liquid glide down his throat. "We can do it now, can't we Nate?" He looked over at his friend, whose eyes glistened and whose grin could light the sun. "Shit." Finn had tears in his own eyes. "We can really do this now. We need to celebrate."

"Cabin?" they both said in unison.

"Absolutely," Finn affirmed.

"Okay, I'll tell Annie. Bring Dee too. She'll love it."

"Around six?"

"I'll have Annie call everyone."

****

For the first time since Raven left, Dee noticed that Finn appeared to enjoy his friends. Discussions about the project and possible ways to increase awareness and include the community in its construction were exhausted. She smiled as he talked to Annie about her pregnancy and flew their son, Tanner, over his head like an airplane.

It was only later, with the celebration in full swing, that she saw him sitting alone on a dune, in relative quiet, overlooking the sea. He stared at a place on the beach, with a faraway smile. Dee's heart broke a little, and she approached him.

"May I join you?"

He turned in surprise and looked up at her.

"Absolutely. You want me to get ya a chair?"

"No, no." She patted his leg after she sat down. "What're you doing over here by yourself?"

"Just my new favorite pastime, basking in newfound happiness." She looked at the colors of the sun going to sleep, then back to her grandson. The amber gold shimmered on his face and hair.

"It's nice to see you happy Finn. Been a while."

"Yeah, sorry 'bout that." He smiled at her and swung an arm over her shoulders.

"Why don't you call her?"

"God," he said exasperated and removed his arm again. "Why don't you mind your own business."

"Because you are my business honey, don't you know that?"

"I'm sorry," he said, abashed.

"Why are you being so headstrong here?"

"Dee." He exhaled. "I could never live in that kind of environment. It's insanity. Besides," he said, looking back down onto the beach. "She made it crystal clear that we're done."

"And that really chaps your ass, doesn't it?"

"What?"

"That she decided. That it wasn't up to you? Did you ever think that maybe the lesson was hers to learn, Finn, not yours? Do you know what she did after you left?" she queried, looking out at the amber hues.

"Yeah, she collapsed, a.k.a. went into hiding so her handlers could figure out what to do with her next."

"You're an idiot." He looked at her patiently.

"Okay, so let's summarize. I'm an ungrateful idiot, a control freak, and a selfish, headstrong asshole? I'm sure there's a home I can put you in somewhere, old woman."

"I might just admit myself." She chuckled. "So I don't have to watch this nefarious scene play out."

"Oooh, nefarious is it?" he chuckled.

"She told both those assholes to shove it and walked out."

"What?" He stopped laughing. "What're you…"

"I'm telling you, our little Raven flew the coop."

Her voice cracked on the last word.

"Dee?"

"Apparently, something about not getting to do what she really wanted to do and then when they demanded she go back onstage, she said no and left, then fired both of them."

"Both?"

"Both," she affirmed. His mouth fell slightly open as he cast his brilliant gaze outward, glowing with pride. "As I said, maybe the control was hers to learn."

"Well, I'll be damned." He laughed, then sobered. "Good for her." He ran soft golden sand through his fingers. "How did you find out about all this? Her cell changed."

"Oh, I spoke with her brother," she said, deciding on the spot to fib but happy to hear he'd at least tried the old one.

"Wyatt? How do you know Wyatt?"

"Raven gave me his cell number a long time ago, and I wanted to know how she was."

"Well, thanks for that. I'm sure she'll think I put you up to it."

"No she won't. I only talked to him, and just said I missed her. He said I shouldn't have to miss her long."

"Did he say why?" He looked at her quickly.

"Yes."

"Well?

"Well, what?"

"Well, are you gonna tell me?"

"Oh, you're interested? Okay, well, she's giving a concert on Oahu, Friday, at the amphitheater."

"She doing a concert here?"

"Well, on Oahu, remember, I just said at the…"

"Smart ass. How come I haven't heard about it? A show of that magnitude, you'd think it would be everywhere."

"It has been everywhere, Finn. You clicked off, but the rest of the civilized world kept spinning."

"Smart ass," he repeated, rolling his eyes.

"Besides it's not that kind of show."

"What kind of show is it?"

"I guess you'll have to escort me to find out."

"No."

"But, I want you to come with me."

"No."

"Finn…"

"No, she wanted it over and damn it, it needs to be over."

"Maybe things were said and regretted on both sides."

"Did Wyatt say that?"

"No."

"Then come on." He stood, then helped her up. "Let's go home."

****

The ground trembled beneath his feet. He saw no one but heard a voice that felt like it could be everywhere, all at once. Approaching the woods, he turned a corner and saw an ancient man, his hair and beard snow white. So brilliant and bright were his eyes, Finn could barely connect with them. He sat on a protruding root of a toppled banyan tree, as a king might sit upon a throne.

"My pride has resulted in this fate," the man said quietly, without preamble.

"Who are you?"

He ignored Finn's question.

"Eternity elsewhere, never fully formed within my mind, for I was once immune."

"So, what? You're the ghost of Christmas past, telling me I'm going to wind up in a hot oven somewhere regretting my life." Finn looked around and saw horses in a field and pointed at them. "Yours?"

"My power, my control was second to only one, my brother, but still we did not know."

"What the hell is this?"

When Finn still received no answer, he turned away disgusted, and the man turned into a rage of blue fire that shook the earth once more, then split.

"Perhaps the question isn't who I am, for I am you, an answer for which you know not." He actually sparked with anger. "Who am I? I am pride, greed, wrath, regret, fear, and now"—there was a pause— "apparently, stone."

Finn turned, and the man was indeed stone, with a live silky-black, raven sitting on his shoulder. It circled him once and flew away.

Chapter 36

Raven sat in her periwinkle robe, watching Abby spin around in a chair, chattering away about her surfing lesson that morning. Her corkscrew curls blossomed from her head in every direction, swept away from her face by a silky white hairband. She glittered under the lights in her gunmetal dress, as she climbed down from the chair and clicked across the floor in tiny-heeled shoes.

"Can I get my makeup done too Rave?" Abby pleaded.

"Well, you'll just have to ask Miss Barb here if she has time, and then ask your mom if it's okay."

"Okay, I'll be back." Abby giggled, forgetting the hierarchy, and ran off to find Que.

"There." Barb ended with a flourish. "I think you're all set. You look perfect." The stylist turned her boss around, and Raven gazed in the brightly illuminated mirror. She saw a soft, flawless face reflected back at her, with enormous curlers in her hair.

"Oh Barb, it's perfect."

"Well, it sure is a helluva lot better than before," Barb reassured, then handed her the water bottle poised precariously on the corner of the counter. "I'll just be a second and then we'll get you going on your hair." As Barb walked out of the room, Abby dragged Que in.

"Mama says it's okay."

"Well, I think I said you also needed to ask Barb, Ab," Raven chided. "She'll be back in a minute, and we'll ask if she can squeeze you in."

"You look pretty," Abby observed, and her mother quickly agreed. Raven beamed, but before she could respond, her stylist reemerged and smiled at the room.

"So, soft and romantic, right?"

"Absolutely." Raven looked in the mirror at Que and asked, "Did anyone show up?"

"Girl, the hill is filled," Que said, indicating the slope behind the theater seats and in front of the stadium seats.

"Here we are." The women looked over at Wyatt resplendent in a dark suit, carrying three glasses of wine and one glass of sparkling apple cider. He handed one to each of his ladies before raising his own. "Okay, to my brilliant, beautiful, and talented sister, embarking onto bigger and better things. And to my other sister, who had to go where no mother should ever have to and showed us what real strength is all about. And finally, to my lovely little lady, who is the light of my life and the coolest, bravest girlie I know." Hearts melting, all the girls simultaneously kissed him on the cheek and clinked glasses, as Abby reached out her hands to him, to be picked up.

"You really are the sweetest man on the planet," Que said misty-eyed. "Too bad we're the only ones that know it."

"Well, I wanted to say something sweet before telling Raven that she looks like a bobblehead of toilet paper rolls." She tilted her head and smirked in sisterly tolerance as Barb chuckled and began to dress her hair.

****

Twenty minutes later, Raven stood in a gossamer blue and white ombré dress that floated around her ankles. The silky material connected to a delicate chain that went over one shoulder. Centered on the fabric was her gold medallion necklace. Barb had swept up one side of her loose golden waves and secured it with fresh yellow plumeria, tipped in pinks and corals.

Behind the scenes, her new agent, Elizabeth, and stage manager, Barry, were quietly running the show. Backstage there was a level of high expectation yet still relative calm. Wyatt seemed to know intuitively he was no longer needed for reassurance and sat out front with Que and Abby.

Backstage, Raven stood in the wings, face tilted up to the sky, nervously preparing herself. It felt like the very first time she performed before a live audience. After her introduction, she walked out, waving and smiling with genuine confidence to the microphone. Raising a hand to shield her eyes from the lights and looking out at the crowd, she saw indeed each chair and patch of grass filled. Her mouth curved into a smile at the standing ovation.

"Aww, you're sweet. Thank you so much." When they continued to applaud, she opened her arms as if to embrace the collective and responded by saying, "And I haven't even done anything yet."

The crowd laughed and continued to applaud. She lowered her hands and her eyes connected with Dee in the front row. The older woman beamed at her and waved, and Raven waved back with excitement. She saw Nate and Annie seated next to Dee, as well as many of the friends she'd made while on Kaua'i. However, the one person she did not see was Finn. Her eyes scanned as far as the lights allowed and her heart sank. She thought he would come if only to support this new choice she'd made. Biting her bottom lip to suppress emotion, she continued.

"So, again, thank you so much for coming out tonight. As you can see, we're doing things a little differently. I'm trying some new music, and new songs. I hope you enjoy them as much as I have, preparing them for you."

She walked to the white baby grand piano and began to play her music and songs, her way. At first, the audience was confused, but when they realized what was happening and that the concert marked a significant change, they responded. As she played some of her more meaningful pieces, she'd introduce them and give a quick explanation for their origin. Her songs poured out of her, and she crested on the tops of them, delighting in the response of the audience.

At the break, she'd requested solitude as Polynesian dancers swayed and performed to her music. Sitting in her chair, she closed her eyes, listening to the quiet and felt peace. By the end of the concert, she was ready to celebrate with her family and friends. So, sitting on a stool, she set up the final song.

"Many of you might have noticed, I've changed my show drastically. In my early twenties, just starting out, there's wasn't a lot of experiences to draw from, so you draw from others. You trust others because you don't always trust yourself.

"As I've grown older, I've drawn my own conclusions on life, and for years, I've been writing them down. What you've heard tonight is the accumulation of a lifetime of experiences, seen through my filters. I've been extremely fortunate to come from gifted, talented people. A strong line of women and men who tried to leave their mark on the world.

"So, with that in mind, this last song is a little different. Out there somewhere I have a twin brother." She gestured toward the audience, skimming over Wyatt, in case he didn't want the attention. "And after our parents died, we had to rely quite heavily on one another over the years. But our parents were musical, and there's one song I remembered my father used to sing."

She locked eyes with Wyatt, who looked surprised.

"My brother just fell out of his chair. Right now, he's looking at me and thinking, *what*." Raven laughed with the audience and continued. "Anyway, my father sang this, and for some reason, it has carried me through the good, the bad, and very ugly times." She looked into the glossy lights at the eager faces looking back at her in anticipation. Que and Wyatt beamed at her choice to risk vulnerability, knowing what it meant to her.

"So, this last song is just slightly borrowed from my father. In fact, I only knew one verse of one song. I chose to make it the chorus and write the rest myself. So, this is for…Well, my apologies, but it's for me, and it's entitled, 'I Sing.'" She took a deep breath and began.

This journey I have made, and the lessons I have learned.

I walked with you my brother, our parents' voices strongly heard.

For when we walked together, your strength to me you'd bring.

But I must travel on today and with my own voice, sing.

I sing to you a thousand words and a thousand feelings more.

Of home and hearth and family, and sun and moon adored.

And in my time remaining, to my cherished hearts, I sing.

Great love and peace and blessings, I hope your life will bring.

Wyatt bowed his head and listened, smiling at her words and tribute to himself and their parents. He lifted his head and nodded at her, and she smiled back.

There was a reason, the thieves could steal my will.

My barriers were broken, and the scars refused to heal.

Until I found my power and struck the mighty blow.

To those that would seek me harm, now they reap what I did sow.

I sing to you a thousand words, and a thousand feelings more.

Of home and hearth and family, and sun and moon adored.

And in my time remaining, to my cherished hearts, I sing.

Great love and peace and blessings, I hope your life will bring.

Her eyes traveled over the audience as she sang the chorus. However, her attention was strongly pulled in one direction and finally settled on Finn, as it had the first time she saw him. He was standing alone to the side, leaning against a pillar, looking every bit as beautiful as he did the first moment she saw him. The strangest expression was on his face, and she shifted her body slightly to sing his verse to him.

Once I had a moment, just a precious point in time.

Like music over water, that I was yours and you were mine.

And now that we have parted, and our hearts no longer true.

You place in my forever, for forever I'll love you.

As she finished the last chorus and the vibrations from the guitar strings ended, the crowd roared to its feet, applauding. Raven closed her eyes and paused, allowing in the approval. Flashing a brilliant smile, she stood and took her bow. Looking back to the pillar, Raven saw that Finn was gone. Again, as if taking a page from their first encounter, she wondered if he was ever really there. She bowed again and waved while walking offstage.

Elated with the triumph, Raven passed behind the curtain to thunderous applause from her crew. She blushed and clapped for them as well. Wyatt came running in and swooped her up into a dizzying spin, as Que and Abby joined them. Raven hugged each in turn, as champagne was popped and poured. Nate and Annie approached, and Raven rubbed her baby bump, before finally seeing Dee.

"Dee!" She ran to her and rubbed a cheek against the older woman's papery cheek. "I'm so glad you came. Did you like it?"

"It was all so wonderful." Dee patted her hand. "Just perfect. I'll never forget it, not ever. You look so beautiful. And the way you blended everything together was just wonderful dear, pure perfection."

Tonight, Dee's trademark floppy hat contained

sizeable pink hibiscus flowers woven into the band and she held it at her side. Her long, wavy, silver hair was down and loose on her shoulders. Raven wondered how she'd missed this beautiful aspect of her friend and held the older woman's hands out, admiring her white eyelet dress.

"Wow, look at you—you're breathtaking." Dee's cheeks bloomed into a blush, and she held Raven's hand. The younger woman chanced a glance, hoping she'd see Finn, but Dee answered the question she wouldn't ask.

"I'm so sorry honey, he went back. He's…" She waved a hand in frustration and dismissal. "It took a lot just to get him to come."

"Oh. Oh… No, I completely understand," Raven said, trying hard to steady her voice. "It was really nice to see him. In fact, I wasn't entirely sure it was him." She bit her bottom lip, to keep the tears at bay. "Just tell him I'm honored he came, okay?"

"Yes, I will. Now let's get you some champagne."

****

Finn watched her glide onto the stage, looking happy, so damn happy and so incredibly beautiful. He exhaled a breath he didn't know he'd been holding. Watching her perform made him think of that first barbecue at Nate and Annie's. Raven singing, as the sun set, was probably the moment he fell in love with her. He knew it was true, but still, he didn't stay with her. He couldn't believe the performance. It was everything she said she wanted and the fact that her life had shifted so dramatically from the woman he'd last faced, shocked him.

When she reached the last song, he understood how

much it cost her to open so much of herself to another person, let alone an entire amphitheater of people. The verse she'd written for her brother and parents had been touching. The verse she sang to him, confusing. He didn't know if she was talking about their past or that her feelings still included him.

Finn wanted desperately to tell her he was proud of her but some unforeseen element wouldn't allow it. So, when the crowd stood, he'd decided it was the perfect time to make his exit. He saw what he'd come to see and he was incapable of the required small talk and pleasantries. The alternative would be hurt and disappointment, from his past actions. Neither seemed appealing. So, he texted Dee and went in search of a drink, then bed. He approached the cabana and ordered whiskey. After paying and taking a sip, he turned and ran right into Wyatt.

"Sorry man," Raven's brother began, then did a double take. "Hey, what's good, brother?" He held out a hand, and Finn clasped it.

"You look good."

"Thanks, you too," Wyatt said, then nodded to the reception area. "She had a good night, didn't she?"

"Yeah, fantastic." There was a long agonizing pause, so Wyatt turned to the bartender and showed credentials.

"I need three champagnes." Turning to Finn, he asked, "You wanna come back?"

"Ah." He looked around. "Nah, I'm good."

"She'd love to see ya, man."

"Yeah, it's been awhile, right?"

"Yeah." Wyatt rocked back on his heels. "Lot's happened since then." When the blond man only nodded, he continued, "If her song was any indication, I think she misses you." Finn looked up quickly, searching Wyatt's face, confused. "What? You don't think that song was about you?"

"I thought… I mean, I didn't…"

"You really are an idiot." The bartender handed three flutes to Wyatt, who continued to look at the other man. Finally, he turned and grabbed them, starting to walk away. "Are you coming or not?"

"No." Finn sulked; he was getting real tired of being called an idiot.

"Fine, whatever, but you're making a mistake, and what's worse is, you know you are." He turned to leave and almost disappeared behind the curtain.

"Wait," Finn called, and Wyatt turned back around, grinning.

****

Raven enjoyed the after party. She watched friends of her past collide with those of her present, enjoying one another. Dee had attached herself to Abby and listened tirelessly as the girl chatted away about everything from her next birthday party to her surgery. She admired the girl's sparkling dress and long spiraling curls. In turn, Abby tried on the older woman's hat and giggled at the flowers.

"Abby, are you being good?" Raven asked as she approached.

"Look at me Raven, can I show Mama?"

"Who do you need to ask?"

"Dee, can I?"

"Of course, dear," Dee said, then chuckled as the little girl scampered away.

Raven's gaze followed her too but knew the smile

didn't quite reach her eyes. She looked at Dee watching her, waiting.

"How is he, Dee?" Raven asked, giving up the pretense.

"He's been okay. Work's been keeping him busy, but he's been doing well. Got a big donation and it looks like they're going to get their rehab facility." Raven's entire face lit up.

"Oh Dee, that's fantastic. Nate didn't say anything. They must be so excited."

"They are," Dee confirmed. "He's excited and proud of you too."

Raven nodded and looked over at Que, breathtaking in a fit and flare silver dress that matched her daughter's. Two Polynesian men in Hawaiian shirts flanked her and she had one eye trained on her daughter as she twirled. Without reason, Abby ran back to the women, efficiently ending their discussion. The party continued for a couple of hours until one by one, the guests said good night for a final time.

Raven's group returned to the hotel so Que could put Abby to bed. Wyatt walked on the beach with his sister, as the moon glowed bright, illuminating the sandy beach.

"Why are you smiling?" she asked, looping her fingers around the straps of her shoes to carry them.

"Why not?"

"What did you do?"

"What do you mean?"

"You have that look."

"What look?" He stopped and looked at her with all innocence.

"That look that you've done something you're not

supposed to. Was it the hula girl?"

"No." He looked at her in mock offense. "Seriously, is that what you think of me?" When she only stared at him wearily, he confessed, "I'm just gonna say she was a phenomenal kisser and had healthy coconuts."

"Not enough time to close the deal?"

"Right," he said, grinning, then swung an arm over her shoulders and tapped his temple to hers. "I was proud of you tonight."

"It was good, wasn't it?"

"Yeah. I didn't remember that song until you sang it. I think the melody was close to the way he did it."

"I thought so too but wasn't sure, so thanks for confirming it."

"Did you see Taylor?"

"Yeah, Dee said he left."

"Left where?"

"I don't know. I assume home. I didn't ask Dee. Did you talk to him?"

"No, I didn't see him until you looked over there." He evaded. When she remained quiet, he glanced at her, then looked ahead. "Oh hey." He pointed to a little hut. "Can I buy you a drink?"

"Ah, ye-ah."

"Mai Tai it is. Just chill."

He walked over to the hut, and she sat down on the silky sand, smiling serenely when she heard him order the drinks extra strong. Leaning back, she extended her arms behind her to support her weight and tilted her head back, feeling the warm wind on her face. She could hear him clink the glasses together.

"You ordered them extra strong, and now you're

going to spill them everywhere?" she asked, chuckling and bending her head back farther to look at him upside down, but it wasn't her brother.

"Finn."

Chapter 37

Raven scrambled up and turned to see Wyatt's retreating back. He had obviously stayed only long enough to make sure she was okay with the turn of events.

"How are you?" Finn asked.

"I'm…good. How have you been?"

"Ah." He looked at the beverages. "Well, not great." He set the drinks down, which promptly spilled, unnoticed, and stood again.

"No?"

"I…" He lowered his head and took in a deep breath before looking at her again. "I haven't handled anything right here, have I?" She breathed out a short laugh.

"Neither have I."

"What happened in Seattle? Dee told me some stuff but…"

"After you left, I…well, I was pretty hurt. What you said really hurt me."

"I know. I'm sorry Raven." She shook her head.

"But you also confirmed what I'd been feeling for a long time. So, I walked out."

He looked down the surf and back at her, beaming.

"Please tell me you flipped off Dell. My life would be seriously complete."

"You fractured his nose."

"All the better."

"No, I didn't, but I fired him and slapped Donovan."

"You did not."

"I did, I really did." She looked down the beach, laughing freely. "Afterward, I went home, and for two weeks I didn't leave. Not because I was depressed or anything, but because I wrote down pages and pages of things. Things I wanted to do, songs and music I wanted to write. I sold my condo and car for a great deal. Settled everything with Jason and Donovan. Well, basically got rid of everything in my old life that I didn't want anymore."

"Where are you living now?"

"With Que and Abby," she answered, laughing. "It's been a lot of fun."

"How's the kid doing?"

"Oh, she's so great." Raven's face lit up. "If you're staying, I'd love for you to meet them."

"I already did, when I came looking for you."

"Why did you come looking for me, Finn?" He slid his hands into the pockets of his jeans as they began to walk along the beach.

"When I came back nothing was the same. Alaula was gone and Kaimi…"

"Is he okay?" She panicked and put a hand on his arm. "I never got to tell you how devastated I was and am for you about Alaula. She meant so much to you. I'm so sorry Finn. Do they know what happened to her?"

"Thanks. She, ah, she was clubbed to death by someone. They have leads, but they haven't found the guy yet. Kaimi's great. We released him a couple of weeks ago." She beamed at his words, and he stopped. "Nothing happened with Holly, Raven. I swear I didn't even know she was still there."

"I know."

Relief washed over his face, then he gazed out toward the water before looking back at her.

"I'm a sonofabitch. I always thought being in control of your life meant that somehow, you could control what comes in and out of it. When you're like that, you don't always appreciate other people's right to free will. In the span of three months, I lost control of literally every aspect of my life."

"So you freaked out?"

"So I freaked out, yeah, big time." he agreed, with a laugh. "I pushed you out and pretended it was because of your issues, people pushing at me, and Dee thinking we're part of some weird Greek curse thing."

"I think we are." He flicked his gaze to hers and held it.

"So do I."

"You do?" she asked incredulously. "You do not?"

"Yes, damn it."

She started to laugh and couldn't stop. Soon he was laughing too. As she wiped a tear from her eye and held her side, he stopped and just watched her.

"God, you are so damn beautiful. You overwhelm me. You scare the absolute shit outta me."

"You don't scare me, not anymore." She quirked a smile and stepped toward him.

"Your show was pretty special." He took a step toward her.

"Were you there for the whole thing?" She moved again, standing inches away.

"Did you mean what you said in that song?" he asked, withdrawing a hand from his pocket, and reaching out to brush the hair back from her face.

"Yes… I love you, Finn."

"I love you too, Raven."

Closing his eyes, he placed his forehead on hers. After a moment, she lifted her lips to his and kissed him softly. He leaned into it and increased pressure, letting his hands move up and down her back. They pulled apart a little breathless, and he whispered against her mouth.

"Are you gonna marry me?"

"Yes," she answered, smiling.

"Yes?"

When she only nodded, he lifted her under her arms and held her suspended in the air for several seconds, before setting her back on earth and into his arms.

****

The sun rose, shooting streams of sunlight through the open patio door. They spent the night talking and making love. Raven told him about some of the things she'd transformed in her life and how she'd done it. Finn told her about the Rehabilitation Center donation and what they were going to be able to do with it. Somewhere around four in the morning, they fell asleep in each other's arms, only to wake to a pounding at their door.

Finn stood up, pulling on his jeans, zipping but not bothering to button them. He padded to the door to find Abby on the threshold when he opened it. The sight of the muscular, bare-chested man took her by surprise enough to look at the door again and make sure she had the right room.

"You lookin' for Raven, kid?" When she only nodded, he gestured toward the bed, just as Raven called out to her, hastily throwing on Finn's tee shirt. Abby moved past the man warily, then hopped on the bed and began jumping on it.

"Guess what?"

"Be careful now. What?" Raven jostled from side to side with each hop.

"Mama said we're going to go see the seals you helped save."

"Abby." Raven jerked her down, and Finn tilted his head in confusion. Abby had the good sense to look abashed.

"You guys helped some seals here, where at?" He looked quizzically at Raven.

"Yeah, there was a baby who lost his mama and Raven wanted to help. So, she just gave away a lot of money and Mama was like, '*What*, are you crazy girl,' and Raven was like, 'You don't know what you're talkin' about,' and Mama was like…"

"Abigail…" Que appeared at the open door Finn still held, listening to most of the conversation but letting her daughter speak so Finn could know the truth. Knowledge bloomed across his face.

"How much did you get for your condo, Raven?"

"Finn…"

"Raven…"

"Wait… Finn, it's just that I didn't want any of that money. I wanted my own money. I was going to give it to a charity, and then I thought, hey, there are some researchers I know that could possibly benefit."

"Get lost, kid," Finn said, keeping his eyes on

Raven.

"Come on Ab," Que called on a laugh to her daughter, who instantly began whining about just coming into the room.

"Finn, it's my money, I can spend it any way I want to." Slowly, he crawled over the bed and pulled down the blankets. "What're you doing?"

"I'm about to make love to my fiancée, and then I'm going to take you home."

Epilogue

They flew back to Kaua'i, and from the moment they landed, the island snapped with electricity. Finn had a constant buzzing in his head as if swarms of bees engulfed him and hot current coursed through his blood. As he drove home, he held Raven's hand and could tell she felt it too.

Upon arrival, Dee quickly moved to retrieve the box, seemingly confident in the knowledge that soon they'd have answers. When she returned, she set it on the table, then ran off once more for pen and paper.

The couple, suddenly tentative and nervous, looked at the object with wary new eyes. It was an ordinary box, except for a top, ornately carved with an agglomeration of symbols, some discernible, others not. Fire chased a dove, an owl seemingly perched on a shield, a full cornucopia, thunderbolt, lyre, and symbols for man and woman.

"Why are there two tridents?" Raven asked, indicating the two objects coming out of either side of the shield. Finn, at a loss, just shrugged.

Dee set her papers down, went over to the box and laid her hand on it. Looking up as if to say something, her body seemed to go rigid. Once again, the lines on her face filled and age spots on her hands and arms began to soften and fade. Her loose and sagging skin tightened, as spider veins scurried away one by one.

Her beautiful silver hair turned to golden wheat, thickened and became luminescent. Her eyes became clear and the blue iris's saturated deeper. Brightness illuminated her skin and her lips colored and plumped. When Dee turned to look at them, she appeared twenty-years-old. Awed and slightly terrified the couple could only stare at her.

Finn's mouth dropped open; whatever he'd been thinking, it wasn't this. And if what he witnessed was real, it meant that everything else she said was true. He couldn't take his eyes off his grandmother, finally accepting she'd been right.

"Dee?" Raven's hand drew to her mouth, and she looked over at Finn, who was now white as a sheet.

The woman tried to lift the chest, but it had become too heavy. She turned to her grandson, almost phosphorescent.

"I can't move the damn thing. Finn, help me." Apprehensively, he walked over, followed by Raven. When he tried to pick it up, it still wouldn't budge. Dee tried to push alongside him but to no avail.

"Maybe if all three of us…" Raven said, and touched one handle, while Finn still held the other. The moment both hands fell upon the box, the medallion around Raven's neck began to heat.

"Ow." Raven leaned forward to release the disc from her skin and rubbed underneath it. She looked down, trying to ascertain what happened. "It's hot. I think it burned me." Wincing, she drew in a sharp breath, so Dee unfastened it for her. The medallion fell onto the chest and instantly turned into liquid gold.

"Oh, Jesus Christ!" Finn exclaimed, jumping back and automatically throwing both arms out to shield the women. They watched in disbelief as the metal formed and reformed, moving along the surface of the box.

A groove began to etch itself into the chest, made by unseen hands. The gold settled into the groove on top of the chest and took shape of an odd-looking arrowhead. It hardened then cooled. Raven vee'd her thumb and forefinger across her chest where the necklace had been, leaving the faintest hint of a small lyre burned into her flesh. Her mouth was open, and she was breathless.

The box seemed to tremor and the lid burst opened; each person jumped and leaned away from it. Inside a sphere glowed in diffused light. A mist started to rise and eventually formed into a woman. Themis stood erect with the blindfold of impartiality firmly affixed to her eyes. She turned her head in the direction of the trio and spoke in a distinct yet monotone voice.

"Daughter of Demeter, you have created sanctuary for your mother and begun the process we've long sought."

Dee gave a weak smile but didn't speak and looked over at Finn and Raven, who both stared wide-eyed at the vision. She understood they hadn't honestly believed all of it until just that moment and felt some vindication. Themis turned to Raven and spoke in a liquid, melodic voice.

"Daughter of Apollo. Your own power from within, you have tirelessly sought. The selfless love of another, each has now been caught. The medallion you possessed has been the sacred key. The master musician left it for you to see. Its ore once lay in his golden lyre, and now its safe return after generations of tears. The sun god acquiesces his endowment comes

from music and lyric, rather than his gift deriving power from his own hand and lip. Your father may now lay on the heavenly mound, in the Elysium and heart of the underground."

Trembling, Raven was terrified and squeezed Finn's arm, rigid with suppressed adrenaline. The mist of the sphere blossomed into the room. Raven gasped as the young man of her dream appeared.

Atop his head of long, soft, white curls sat a crown of laurel. Apollo's intense blue eyes connected with Raven's and he smiled serenely, trying to take in all of her at once. Then beaming with pride, he touched his head and heart, rose fingers to his ruby lips and extended them out toward her and smiled again, brilliantly. He lifted his lyre made of gold, reclined his head back, and closed his eyes. He appeared to stroke the cords once and his entire body exploded into glorious beads of light. They floated in frozen suspension for a moment, then sucked into a vortex and disappeared. The sphere went hazy, and Themis addressed Finn.

"Son of Poseidon. Control and pride are the most difficult to tame. Relinquishment of each, mastery sustained. Devotion at another's behest has locked your key into this great chest. Your skill with the sea's beasts is set free, together with your lover's song, so may it ever be. Poseidon's overbearance vanquished and for always it will remain. The first of three unyielding brothers whose character has now changed. Your father may lay on the heavenly mound, in the Elysium and heart of the underground."

The orb pulsed and a massive wave curled. Prongs of the great trident appeared, causing Finn's back to fire and throb. He flinched, and Raven squeezed his hand. A massive being, half man, half sea creature, rose, enveloping the entire room. His voice resonated power as he formed into the man of Finn's dreams. He turned slowly to first look at Raven and bowed deeply, then to Finn and addressed him.

"My son, I am one of three brothers that rule our kingdom, our universe. We may join our power for a brief moment in time to offer you guidance, so you must ask the questions you seek swiftly, then you must listen."

Finn stared wildly at the man, an older version of himself, and looked at Raven for help.

"Who?" She prompted.

"Ah, o-okay, um, so how do we find these other people?"

"Your woman has recently met the next to follow."

Poseidon gestured to Raven and Finn looked at her accusatorially. She just shook her head and blinked, so Finn turned back.

"Um, h-how long do we have?"

"Before the Immaculate Conjunction, the quest must reach its end."

"Conjunction?" He looked at Raven again and then Dee, who was scribbling frantically on a piece of paper.

"We'll figure it out," she said quickly.

"Can we get help from you somehow?" Finn said.

"I will now reside in the Elysium, until the last day."

"So what happens if we don't figure it all out by then?"

"Myself, my brothers and my sisters will dwell in damnation of the Tartarus. Cronus has power to

unleash evil upon mankind. The last plagues upon the earth and heavens. Affecting my time and yours, the likes of which our worlds have never known."

"What kind of evil? P-plagues? Can anyone else help us?" Finn asked in rapid fire succession. Poseidon began to fade. "Wait, why's all this happening? How did it happen?"

"We were betrayed by one of our own, who, in turn, was tricked into this fate by father." Poseidon grew breathless, eager to reveal as much as he could. *"You will need their gift for the final test, my son. Beware of Lyssa and Phthous—Cronus controls them. Success lies in the keys and the Oneiroi."*

The last three words were a whisper. Poseidon's colors deepened and intensified. Finn considered the face of the great man, whose eyes matched his own. Then, like in his dream, an enormous tsunami ran through him, blending to his shape, becoming the wave, and his outline turned to the ocean's spray and was gone. Themis appeared a final time.

"Now to the future outside of one another. Ares, the warrior, and Hera, the mother. For it is they that must complete their turn in this quest. All gods' sanctuary to the Isle of Blest."

An intense buzzing and tension of foreboding filled the room, as the fog settled and the chest slammed shut, sealing with finality. A spark of light sped across the lines of the lyre, trident, and cornucopia. Each symbol glowed, before the light disappeared into the thunderbolt, leaving the trio in stunned silence.

Dee felt her age return and with it, the discomforts of time. She massaged her hands, looking dazed. After several minutes, Finn spoke.

"O-okay." Trying to break the silence, he said very slowly, "So, how do we go about finding ten perfect strangers, and tell them they're the descendants of the mythical Greek gods? And oh, by the way, you need to fall in love with a certain specific person. But we don't know who, how or where. Just that you have to so you can save said gods from the pits of a fiery hell and some pretty horrible, evil things that some asshole's gonna let loose on the world?" He looked at them. "I mean, where do we even start?"

"Um." Raven thought, looking at her medallion, now melted into the chest and didn't even think, just said, "SOL."

Dee laughed and hugged her tightly.

"Is this seriously our life now?" He looked incredulously at the two women. "This shit doesn't happen." He looked at Dee. "Grandma, I'm so sorry."

"Well," Dee said in a shaky voice, then looked at her piece of paper, "now there's three of us, and they already gave us a clue."

"What clue?"

"He said you'd already met the next one." Dee looked hopefully at Raven.

"Ah, okay, well if I'm supposedly of Apollo…"

"Supposedly?" Finn laughed.

"Okay, if I'm a descendant of Apollo and he's a twin, wouldn't it go without saying Wyatt would be the other?" She thought for a moment, then laughed. "Only God knows how I'll explain this to him though."

"She said Ares and Hera," Dee remarked.

"And it would seem each could be either a man or a woman," Raven acknowledged.

"Apollo and Raven, music, Poseidon and Finn, the

sea. It would go on then that an Ares and Hera descendant would maybe have their traits as well, somehow." Dee looked between the two as if looking for confirmation. "Or maybe in the same field or something. So, we'll have to look those two up and see?"

"Well, I can't remember too much about Hera and what she's the goddess of, except that she was Zeus' wife. But Ares was like anger or something, right?" Finn looked at Raven.

"No, it's not an emotion, it was like a battle or fighting." She pressed a hand to her temple, adrenaline pumping like a steam engine through her blood as she tried to calm down enough to think. "War." She smiled, relieved. "He was the god of war."

"Well, that doesn't sound like a good thing at all, now does it?" Dee bit her bottom lip, "And it sure doesn't sound like that sweet brother of yours neither."

"No, it doesn't," Raven confirmed. "And Hera was the goddess of marriage, but that sure doesn't sound like him either."

"Plus, the vapor chick said you've just met the next one."

He looked at her perplexed when Raven laughed at his description of Themis. She decided not to correct him that it was actually Poseidon that made the statement.

"That, to me," he continued, "means someone you've known, less than thirty-four years, that's not Wyatt. Maybe someone more apparent," Finn suggested, then added, "although, I guess Wyatt could be the Hera lady since you're from the Apollo dude. Maybe we're missing something, and it has to do with your parents. Dee's right—we'll have to look them up, along with those other names he said."

"Well, I guess it just depends on how long...Oh God...wait, of course," Raven's head snapped up, looking from Dee to Finn. "Oh my God, I think I know who it is."

A word about the author...

Jeny Heckman loves romance. She especially loves romance with a paranormal and historical twist. Educated as an artist, sales clerk, model, TV extra, draftsman, jewelry maker, nursing student, charity fundraiser, hospice volunteer, photographer, mother, and wife, she felt her calling lay elsewhere. While taking care of an ailing loved one, she was inspired to write her first novel entitled, The Catch, about a female Alaskan crab fisherman, and self-publish it.

Deciding she loved writing but wanting to try something different, she pitched an idea to a New York Publishing house, who told her to run with it. The Sea Archer is the first book of that seven-part endeavor.

When not ignoring her family and friends by writing, you will find her time exclusively on them and photography. Jeny lives in Washington state, with her husband, of over twenty-five years.

https://jenyheckman.com/

Thank you for purchasing
this publication of The Wild Rose Press, Inc.

For questions or more information
contact us at
info@thewildrosepress.com.

The Wild Rose Press, Inc.
www.thewildrosepress.com

To visit with authors of
The Wild Rose Press, Inc.
join our yahoo loop at
http://groups.yahoo.com/group/thewildrosepress/